Strangers in the Night

by
Jay Wright
and
E.M. Jeanmougin

Dedication

To Delaney, our first fan

Acknowledgments

We'd like to thank all the people who helped support us by reading this book and offering suggestions and edits.

Delaney, Deb, and Peter, thank you for loving these characters as much as we do.

Taylor and Cory, thank you for convincing us that this was a story worth sharing with others.

Terry, thanks for pointing the way and giving us the resources we needed to make this book as good as we could.

To the Fellowship, thanks for being as excited as we were about making this really happen.

Special thanks to our amazing artist Claudia Caranfa for bringing our cover to life, and to our editor Pauline Nolet for fixing our mistakes.

Prologue

It was well before sunrise when Ella Black came sauntering down the New York street, the short hem of her blue skirt swaying with each long-legged step, stiletto heels echoing in the semi-silence of 3 a.m. in the city. Finding herself at a crossroads with no particular destination in mind, she went to the right.

This street was like the one she'd just been on, narrow and tattered, the buildings on either side short and dark, their windows showing no signs of life. Just like all the other houses in this area, except for one key detail. Halfway down, illuminated in the yellow circle of a streetlight, was a young man, very tall and very thin, leaning against the light post, cell phone in hand. He was focused on the screen, a mess of red-tinted curls falling across his face. When he heard her heels, he looked up, shaking them back. Ella noticed he was younger than his height suggested, maybe seventeen or eighteen, more pretty than he was handsome.

His eyes were bright green. When they met her blue ones, he smiled, softly and shyly, and looked quickly back at his phone.

Oh, she couldn't quite resist that, could she?

Walking over, Ella was very aware of her short blue skirt and her tall white heels, knowing exactly how they made her legs look endless. From her tiny purse, she pulled a metal cigarette case and put one between her luscious, full lips. The boy looked up, one eyebrow slightly raised.

"Hey, mister," she purred. "Got a light?"

"I, uh…" The boy stood up straighter, patting down the pockets of his jeans and leather jacket. "Uh, no, I don't. Sorry."

"Oh, here's mine," Ella said, pulling a thin black lighter from her purse. She looked into those green eyes with a coy smile. "Light it for me?"

He leaned forward, just as she expected him to. Humans were so easy, and this one was just her type.

The flame flashed to life between them, and she kept her eyes on his as the end of her cigarette caught in a short blaze. The flame guttered out, but neither of them moved away, his gaze unwavering on hers.

Perfect. Just perfect.

As he passed the lighter back, Ella captured his hand in her own. "Why don't you come with me?" It was not so much a question as it was a command, and she was pleased when the boy nodded, easy as could be.

Taking his hand, Ella tugged him out of the circle of light. Dark buildings surrounded them, looming in the murky secondhand glow of the city's latent light.

The boy's hand was warm, his fingers calloused and strong, his pulse beating steadily against her wrist. And his scent! Filtered through the cigarette smoke, it was strange and bright, like sunlight shining through a windowpane on a summer morning. It was an unusual scent, but not entirely unlike those she was used to.

What would he taste like?

She couldn't wait.

A narrow alley sat tightly between a dark-windowed office building and a laundromat. Ella pulled the boy towards it, feeling his pulse pick up slightly. The alley was barely wide enough to allow for two people, and it smelled stale and stagnant, hardly romantic. She shoved the boy against the rough brick wall, grinning wickedly sharp, and put her body flush against his. She heard the skip of his heart in his rib cage.

"Um," said the boy, his hands floating uselessly at his sides, too shy to touch her.

Oh, it was just delightful.

"Why don't you kiss me?" she whispered, their eyes meeting again. It must have been the light hitting them because now the boy's eyes looked different, less green and lighter, almost shining in the dark.

"Okay."

Ella smiled at him. She leaned further in, her full lips parted over elongated canines and—

The silver stake slid easily between her ribs, right under her perfect left breast. Ella hissed and tried to pull away, but it was too late, the boy—*the Hunter*—was too fast. The stake pierced her heart and there was the most intense and all-consuming pain.

And then there was nothing except a shower of dust.

Chapter One

—

Along Came a Spider

Jasper Craig withdrew his weapon, smearing the congealed blood and vampire dust on the thigh of his jeans with a sigh. At least the vampires didn't leave a body behind to deal with afterward, though he'd be scraping the dust from his boots for a week.

He slid the silver stake neatly back into its holster and reached for his cell phone.

A gentle twist deep in his gut warned him he was not alone.

A tortured cry, louder and angrier than any natural beast, rose above the sounds of distant traffic. He drew his matte black .45 Glock, darting his gaze along the rooftops as he jogged towards the end of the narrow alley.

Movement flickered overhead and he fired without question, silencer whistling.

The vampiress, Ella Black, was known for her tendency to hunt alone, but tonight was obviously the exception. He could *feel* the others. Not one or two, but many, and coming in fast.

Goddamn fucking vampires.

Something sprang across the gap above him, a featureless shadow in the night. He turned the muzzle upward and fired again, catching a glimpse of the demon twisting in midair, plummeting to the pavement and bursting into an ashy cloud on impact.

Jasper didn't wait for the others.

He cut through another alley. The empty parking lot behind it was painted with faded yellow lines. Its old light posts were dark. A corroded chain-link fence stood on the opposing side.

He was almost to it when a figure stepped from the shadows in front of him, barring his way. Others emerged from his left and right, racing towards him in fanged blurs with glittering red eyes.

Jasper got off a single shot, landing it in the forehead of the vampire at the head of the pack, dusting him before he even had time to scream, but by then two others were upon him, more coming from behind. He blocked the onslaught of swinging fists and biting fangs, swearing as one of them wrested the pistol from his grasp and sent it skittering on the asphalt.

Sharp canines broke against his fist. He drew the hidden short sword from under his jacket, catching two on the upswing as he unsheathed the silver blade. One screeched and staggered away with his hands clasped to his face. The other stumbled with a smoking gash slashed across his chest. Jasper drove the sword into the vampire's spine as he tried to turn and flee, and the creature dissipated around the blade just in time for two pairs of hands to seize Jasper around the shoulders and force him down onto his back.

His head cracked against the pavement. Stars burst at the corners of his eyes. He brought his feet quickly up, catching one of them in the chest with both feet, bending his knees and then quickly straightening them to throw the lunging vampire back.

Sharp fangs grazed his throat. He saw the white flash of a brow and brought his head forward as hard as he could. His forehead collided with the vampire's hard enough to pop his own ears. Or maybe that was the demon's skull cracking. Either way, the vampire's hold loosened.

Jasper wrestled his wrist free and slammed his fist into the other's jaw, scrambling to find his footing as he pulled away.

He was almost back to his feet when something slammed into him from behind. Just like that, he was back on the concrete again, now with a hissing, spitting demon latched onto his back.

He braced to feel fangs pierce his throat.

The CRACK of a gunshot split the night, echoing and reverberating in a nauseating cacophony. The weight on his back alleviated, motes of vampire dust raining down, filling his lungs, choking him.

Skull still ringing with the impact of the pavement, vision blurry and a little woozy, he rolled over and pushed himself up.

The image before him swam in and out of focus. The vampires stood in a loose circle, but not around him. At the heart of the ring, barely visible through the encroaching shadows, was the very definition of a tall, dark, handsome stranger, revolver held still extended in one hand.

Jasper groggily grasped for his own gun. Where the fuck had it gotten to?

"You shouldn't be here, werespider," hissed one of the vampires. "This doesn't concern you."

"Kind've seems like it does," replied the newcomer. He was taller than the others, bronze-skinned, and dressed in a long black leather jacket. The bright red sheen of his eyes combined with the urgent kick in Jasper's gut immediately dispelled any notion that he might be anything other than a demon, but the way the vampires were pacing nervously around him made it obvious he was not a member of their pack.

Werespider, the vampire had said.

But that couldn't be right. He would have known if something as rare as a werespider was lurking around Brooklyn.

No time to wonder about it now.

Jasper wrenched his attention away, scanning the ground until his eye caught the dull glint of his pistol. He was inching toward it when a blond vampire jabbed a finger in his direction, halting his advance before it even began. "This *thing* murdered Tyler's mate." He gestured to a darker-haired vampire, who crouched some distance away, with his hands clasped to his steaming face, small mewls of pain escaping him as the silver continued to sizzle. "It is our right to kill him."

"You don't got any fuckin' rights in *my* territory, jackass." The werespider had a sort of Old New York accent that was best kept entombed in *film noir* gangster movies, sneering and haughty. "So round up yer goons and y'know... fuck off. I'll give you, I dunno, about... three seconds?"

The blond's fangs bared, fists tight knots at his sides. "Your territory ends back *there*, you goddamn relic. Walk away."

"Whelp." The demon clicked his tongue against the roof of his mouth and thumbed back the hammer of his revolver, the dry snap loud and clear. "That was more than three."

The vampires lunged at him from all sides. Seeing an opportunity, Jasper raced for his own gun and snatched it from the wet asphalt even as another ear-shattering CRACK cut short a vampiric screech.

Over in the corner of the lot, Tyler lowered his hands, revealing a long, bloodless and slowly healing gash that ran from his forehead all the way down to his chin, bisecting his nose and lips. Considering the plight of his pack, it would only be natural for him to be looking towards them, but he was not. He was looking at Jasper. In the next moment, he was running towards him.

Jasper aimed and fired twice. Both bullets found homes in the demon's body but hit neither his heart nor head, and he just kept barreling on through the pain, roaring anguish and fury.

The vampire grabbed at his wrists, bearing down with his fangs, and Jasper was forced to wrestle him to the ground, his eyes shining white with the effort. The demon's long, hard nails bit into his flesh, blood bubbling up around his fingertips. Jasper held him determinedly down and struggled to turn the pistol toward his head.

Behind him, the sounds of screeching and shouting grew exponentially. Somewhere amid their cries, a softly mocking voice goaded them on. Underneath him, Tyler thrashed and screamed, his insults indistinguishable through the hissing and spitting. The vampire's fangs sank into his forearm and just as quickly released with a harsh gagging sound. For a split second, the demon lost his grip, and that was all the time Jasper needed.

He wrenched the muzzle against the vampire's temple and squeezed the trigger.

Thick, black blood fanned in a spray across the pavement, speckling Jasper's chin and cheeks. The solid body he'd been struggling with gave way, the remains of the vampire's face holding their shape for the blink of an eye and then crumbling into nothing but ash and dust.

Jasper knelt for a moment, catching his breath.

The screeching behind him transformed into panicked screaming.

Swearing, every inch of him now throbbing with scrapes and cuts and bruises, Jasper stood and lifted the gun as he turned.

Then lowered it.

Only one vampire was left, and he was on the ground, with a hand held out in front of him, face turned away. His mouth was ringed in his own thick, dark blood, one of his eyes swollen completely shut. Below the other, his cheekbone was split. Neither wounds were healing with traditional vampire swiftness, probably because his body was focused on trying to heal his arm. The lower half was splintered nearly in half with white shards of bone driven jaggedly up through puckered flesh. It bent at an odd, sickly angle, wobbling. "Please don't. I'll leave. I'll never come back. I'm sorry. I'm so, so sorry."

The werespider stood beside the injured vampire, with a revolver aimed loosely at his tear-streaked face. The red popped out of his irises just long enough for him to roll his eyes. He made a little can-you-believe-this-guy gesture with the gun, then slipped the revolver back into the holster and grabbed the vampire by his uninjured wrist and by the back of his shirt.

A small panicked sob escaped the other demon as he was hauled to his feet. He kept his face turned away, head down, broken arm cradled against his chest, shaking but not daring to move.

The werespider gave him a hard shove. "Alright already. Go."

"*Thank you.* I won't come back. I—"

"Yeah, yeah, yeah. I get it. Gods, will you get the fuck outta here? You're ridiculous."

The vampire woozily nodded, swallowed hard, and then, staggering and limping, made for the nearest crossroads as quickly as he could.

The werespider didn't even watch him leave. He was too busy patting down the pockets of his long coat, looking for something.

"You're just letting him go?" Jasper said, indignant.

"He won't be back." Producing a pack of cigarettes from his pocket, the werespider took one out and lit it, the fire glowing in his dark eyes and flickering his sharp-cheeked profile into brief view. He gestured with the open package to the gun still in Jasper's hand. "You're not gonna be a problem, right? Because if you shoot me right now, I'm gonna be pissed. And, honestly, a little hurt."

Jasper scoffed. The bullets in his gun were all silver, perfect for fighting vampires, but useless against a werespider who could obviously move fast enough to avoid a clear headshot. Without the aided poison of gold, he wouldn't be able to kill him. Better to play nice.

For now.

"Why would I shoot you?" Jasper lowered the weapon but wasn't able to bring himself to holster it. "You just saved my ass."

"Well." The werespider raised an eyebrow and blew an impressive cloud of smoke. "Ass like that's gotta be saved."

Jasper blinked, heat rising in his cheeks. "What?"

The demon drew closer. The light found him clearer here. Under its glow, the long raven locks of his hair tumbled and cascaded in waves like waterfalls just past his lithe shoulders. His almond-shaped eyes were the color of liquid chocolate, set in a flawless bronze palette of smooth, clear skin and accentuated by sharp, high cheekbones and fierce, delicate features, symmetrically aligned in a face too beautiful to belong to a human. His steps had a catlike prowess. Easy. Measured. Pointed. "Let me buy you a drink. My favorite spot ain't too far off."

"Uh, I don't think so, man." Offending him didn't feel smart, but neither did following him to a second location, where he might or might not inject him with a venom that would liquefy his internal organs in mere minutes.

"So you're just gonna stand here and wait for the cops to show, then?"

As if on cue, the sounds of sirens grew in the distance, screaming towards them. The demon's revolver must have woken damn near everyone in the borough. "C'mon." The demon grinned around the filter of his cigarette. His voice was different than it had been before, still heavy in Brooklynese, but softer, lighter. "It'll be fun."

Jasper hesitated only a beat. Then red and blue lights flashed in his peripherals, and running became the only option.

Chapter Two

—

Strangers in the Night

The demon was fast and Jasper had to sprint full out to even keep him in his sights. More than once, he thought about turning aside, maybe even just stopping and making a call back to the agency. Yet he found himself running on.

A werespider.

He could hardly believe it.

Up ahead, the demon reined to a halt under a striped overhang, and Jasper stopped beside him, trying to soften his labored breathing before it could become too obvious. The neon sign above the door glowed eerily in the thin fog, bleeding red into the night. The sign read *Rascal's*. The glowing R was beset with pointy devil's horns, and the long snakelike tail on the *s* ended in a triangular point, the sort an uninspired cartoon artist might use in their depiction of Satan.

Typical.

"You're pretty quick," commented the werespider, holding the door open and leaning in towards him with a fascinated smile, all straight white teeth and soft brown lips. Demons had no right being so good looking. "I've never met a demon with eyes that *glow white* before. You got territory around here or...?"

"I'm not a demon," mumbled Jasper, putting as much space as possible between them as he dipped into the seedy little bar. The place was a low-lit dive, complete with ragged pool tables and an out-of-date jukebox, the yellow-orange glass light fixtures hanging over each booth giving the sparse room a sad sort of ambience. The stale stench of beer hit him as soon as he stepped inside, and he wrinkled his nose.

This was bad. He shouldn't be here (and with a werespider, no less), but he wasn't sure how to get out of it without arousing the other's suspicions. Outing himself as a Hunter would be as good as signing his own death warrant, and explaining how he had let a rare, dangerous werespider slip away right out from underneath his nose would be beyond humiliating. If he had to play along for now, so be it.

"Course you are." The werespider hopped onto a raggedy red barstool and rapped his knuckles against the stained and scratched counter.

It was near closing and the place was practically empty. The bartender was a young tatted-up blonde woman, light complected and dressed in a strappy black camisole with the bar's logo plastered over the front. She was already on her way towards him. "Hey, Chris. Let me guess, tequila?"

"She knows me so well." The demon grinned. "Nikki, I want you to meet my friend. This is, uhhh..." He paused, considering. "Sorry, handsome, I think I missed your name."

"It's Jasper," said Jasper, and immediately wondered why he hadn't made a different name up. His head still ached and he felt vague. Scattered. The twinkling lights behind the bar hurt his eyes, and the crackle of music from the ancient speakers overhead throbbed in the back of his skull, making Sublime sound anything but.

"You look a little dazed," said the demon.

The woman poured two shots, filling them all the way to the rim.

The demon knocked back the first and offered the second to Jasper, who turned it away. With a shrug, the demon drank it as well. "Does your kind get concussions? Cuz your pupils are huge."

A... concussion? He'd had them before, but usually they didn't linger like this. Like his glowing white eyes and ability to sense demons, that was just part of the way he was. He felt delicately along the back of his head, flinching a little at the sting. "I'm fine. What did you say your name was? Chris?"

"Uh..." A third shot was already halfway to the demon's lips. He glanced at the bartender, who offered him the bottle with a roll of her eyes and walked to the other end to check on another of the patrons. The demon spun back towards Jasper. "Sure. Chris. Christopher Redd." He made as if to shake.

Jasper looked at the proffered hand, with its smooth lifeline-free palms and printless tips, an oblong of dark blood still smeared on the heel, then squinted at the werespider suspiciously. "That's not really your name, is it?"

Chris shrugged. "Doesn't matter." He slid the two empty glasses together and balanced the third between them, making a small pyramid. "Anyway, you didn't answer my question."

"Which one?" Jasper felt like he'd done nothing *but* answer questions.

"Do you have territory around here?" It was a little more pointed now, an undercurrent in his tone.

"You mean do I *live* around here?" Jasper grasped for a lie. "Sort of."

"I was just curious," said Chris. "I mean, what a person does on his or her own turf is his or her own business, but you were killing vampires on mine, so I think I gotta ask...?"

Alarm cut through the ache in his skull. He told himself not to look directly at the EXIT sign in the corner. "I was hired." This part wasn't completely untrue. "Private sector." But that part was.

The werespider leaned on the bar, casually sipping directly from the clear bottle.

Too casually?

Jasper blinked the thought away. "You sure ask a lot of questions."

"You sure avoid answering a lot of them." Chris took another sip. "Do you wanna play a game?"

"Uh... I really think I ought to be heading out."

"It won't take long," said the demon. "Humor me."

Jasper frowned. How long did he need to stay to assure himself that the werespider wouldn't tail him back to the agency? It already felt like an unbearable amount of time. "What sort of game?"

"*Quid pro quo.* Y'know, sorta like *Silence of the Lambs*? I ask a question. You ask a question. I ask a question. Back and forth until one of us is too drunk."

"One of us meaning... you?" This was the *last* thing Jasper wanted to do, but he could see the benefit. It wasn't every day one ran across a werespider, after all, and they usually weren't so friendly-sharey. "Alright. Fine. Who goes first?"

"Hmm... Well, I'm a little ahead. So, let's say you."

"Okay. Why did you help me back there?"

"I didn't help you. You helped me. Ella and her pack of cronies were a godsdamned blight. Killin' every night, runnin' a-fuckin'-muck. I didn't need them drawing the attention of every Hunter in the city, especially not when I live right next door." He unstacked his makeshift pyramid and filled the glasses one after another with surprising precision. "Besides, I was curious."

"About what?"

"Nope. See, it's *my* turn now."

"Alright, *fine*. What's your question?"

The werespider slid a shot glass in front of him, grinning. "Can I buy you a drink?"

Jasper slid it back, forcibly enough to slosh the tequila onto the back of his hand. "*No.*"

"I guess that makes it your turn."

Jasper simmered. Something about the demon set him on edge in more than the usual way. "So, what are you expecting me to believe here?" Even to his own ears, Jasper's forced casualness sounded more forced than casual. "That you're a... good werespider?"

The werespider was midway to taking another shot of tequila but drew it away from his lips at the last second, sparing himself the minor tragedy of coughing it up in the sudden burst of laughter that erupted from him. He had the sort of laugh that could fill a whole room, loud and pleasant and a great deal less nasal than his heavy accent might have entailed.

"Good? Nah, man. Nah." He composed himself long enough to throw back the shot and clap the empty glass down on the counter. "I'mma great werespider. Best in Brooklyn. New York. Whole state, even." He laughed again, but Jasper wasn't sure why. Maybe he was just drunk.

"That doesn't really answer my question." Though by now he was certain he knew the answer.

"Maybe you shoulda worded it better," said the demon. "My turn. What're you?"

"I'm a mercenary." This lie had already been established and it wasn't really what the werespider was asking. He *knew* what the werespider was asking. Just as he knew he was (and always had been) different. Most demons just didn't notice nearly as quickly as this one had. The thing was, he didn't know *why* he was different, and even if he did, he considered the whole matter very private.

"No-no," slurred the werespider. "I mean, like, what's with the eyes? And your scent. You smell weird. I mean, there's definitely human in there, but what's the rest of it?"

Jasper's blood boiled. He bit back a string of nasty retorts, all of them involving the demon's own disgusting heritage, and instead replied in a cold, biting tone, "Maybe you should have worded your question better."

The werespider blinked, swaying a little on his barstool. Slowly, a crooked grin spread across his face. "Oh, I like you. You're fun." With that and no other forewarning, he slid off the stool, landing in an educated, well-practiced stagger and almost taking a waitress down with him.

The woman threw him an angry, venomous glare. "Chris, you're drunk. Go home."

"Pfhhtt... you," said Chris, but she was already walking away, her fists bunched angrily at her sides as she shouted for the manager.

Chris wheeled back around to Jasper, grinning his big, stupid, too-handsome grin. "Alright, man, I gotta go home and pass out 'fore I fall down." As if this had been his own idea. "You want me to wait for you to, uh... call a taxi or somethin'? Notta great neighborhood t'be walkin' alone in the dark, if ya know what I mean."

"I think I'll be fine."

"Or I could walk you home." He slid closer, head tilted, coy expression reminding Jasper suddenly and powerfully of the vampiress he'd slain just an hour earlier. "Unless you'd rather stay the rest of the night at my place."

Jasper was up and off the stool so quickly he actually *did* knock it over. "No, I don't think so, man. It's basically morning now anyway, and I got a pretty bad headache."

"Alright." Chris shrugged. "Suit yourself. Guess I'll see you around, then."

"Oh yeah, for sure," replied Jasper. He made a mental note to avoid this place at all costs.

He followed Chris out to the street.

The werespider loitered near the adjacent alley, struggling to find first his cigarettes and then his lighter, then dropping the lighter almost as soon as he removed it from his jacket. Then he dropped the cigarettes.

Jasper watched this, thinking with growing wonder that this dipshit had killed nearly half a dozen vampires, presumably for no better reason than that they'd been wandering at the edge of his territory.

Chris finally got the cigarette lit. He glanced Jasper's way and threw him a crooked mock salute. That was probably meant to pass as a goodbye, and he supposed he should offer one of his own, but felt silly waving at him like he were just an ordinary person.

Jasper went left.

The werespider, shrugging his jacket further up on his shoulders and turning his collar against the wind, went right.

Chapter Three

—

St. James Academy

The sun was coming up by the time Jasper made it back to the agency, the dawn's light turning the buildings gold. The city was waking up, although it never really slept. Businesspeople in suits walked past schoolkids with too heavy backpacks; homeless people held cardboard signs asking for change as dog walkers with a dozen leashes in each hand maneuvered their beasts down sidewalks and towards parks; and taxis honked their horns at anyone who walked in their path, which was almost everyone. Jasper slipped between them all, just another cog in the machine, liking the rhythm of the city, easily finding his place among the steel and concrete. He hadn't been born to New York, but he couldn't think of ever finding another place that felt so much like home.

St. James Academy was a large building, nearly an entire city block wide, and stretched sixty-seven stories into the sky. Despite its size, it was well hidden, covered in protective wards and disillusionment spells, making it look, to the untrained eye, like a cluster of smaller, less impressive office buildings. Jasper saw through the glamor easily to the actual building underneath. Dark glass reflected the city back at him, runes and marks etched into the metal supports that ran between the panes. The doors were likewise covered in runes, made of silver and double wide, stretching twelve feet above him. They looked like it would take a cluster of bodybuilders to force them open, but with just a simple push they opened for him, leading him into a large lobby.

Polished dark wood made up the floor; the walls that were not windows were a fresh, clean white, devoid of art or embellishments other than the large St. James crest behind the long, low white desk on the far side of the room. The crest was elaborate, showing an angel wielding twin swords, face covered by a sharp metal visor, with flames licking at its feet, the sun piercing down through smoke. Runes were strewn throughout, speaking of power and justice and victory, the entire thing crafted of many metals, iron and gold, silver and bronze, dusted through with precious gems. Jasper waved briefly to the pair of guards manning the front desk and signed in on one of the sleek silver computers at either end of the desk.

After checking in, Jasper took the elevator up to the twenty-second floor, where the dormitories were located. He knew his adoptive father, who was also his captain, would be looking for an update on his mission, but he was tired. He was fairly used to staying out late—hunting demons sort of called for it—but all the fighting had worn him out, and he still had a headache from talking to that infuriating werespider. He'd crash for a few solid hours and then find Charlie.

Jasper walked down the hall, slipping around other Hunters who were milling about in different stages of their day. Some were just waking, still in pajamas or casual clothes, the younger ones on their way to class. Some, like Jasper, were returning from a hunt, dressed in their traditional hunting gear of black leather. He unlocked the door to his single and went inside, shrugging off his jacket and hanging it on the back of his desk chair.

His room wasn't large, but it didn't need to be; it had everything he needed. A built-in bookcase covered most of the left side of the room. On it was most of his possessions: dozens of schoolbooks on various demons and the best ways to slay them, even more novels shoved into the spaces the schoolbooks didn't fill. On the top shelf he kept a short row of ratty-looking paperbacks, their spines so creased that the titles were illegible, but Jasper knew the name of every one by heart. Those had been his mother's, and her name, Amelia Craig, was still written in her faded cursive on the inside of each cover.

The bottom shelves held something of equally great value: his father's records. Not Charlie's things but David's, a man he'd never met but could almost imagine he knew by listening to those old rock albums, tapping his toes to a beat his father had known well. There were other records too, and an admirable collection of CDs stacked next to a stereo. Jasper hit play, and the first notes to "Waiting" by Tom Petty and the Heartbreakers sang out.

His small closet was filled with jeans and T-shirts as well as two identical outfits of Hunter's gear—sturdy black clothes made of leather, reinforced Kevlar, and thick, heavy-duty canvas—and a dresser held favorite weapons in lieu of clothes. A desk was next to the bookshelves, underneath a window that looked out on the building across the street, and though there was a laptop set up on top of it, he rarely found much use for the thing.

Jasper unhooked his weapons and set them in a small pile on his desk, turned the volume on his stereo down low, and sat on his double bed, leaning to undo the laces on his boots and pulling them off before flopping down on the rumpled bedspread. He sighed softly to himself, running his hands through his hair, mussing it up into an even bigger mess. He felt grimy from sweat and vampire dust but was too tired to do anything about that right now. Throwing an arm over his eyes to block out the ever-rising sun, Jasper fell asleep.

#

An insistent knocking pulled Jasper from his slumber though he did try his best to ignore it. Letting one eye slide open, he glanced at the clock on his nightstand; it was afternoon. He'd slept for nearly five hours and felt like he could sleep five more. With a reluctant groan, Jasper pulled himself out of bed and opened the door.

"Hey, Dad," he said, his voice raspy with sleep.

Charles Gosson stood on the other side of the door, looking clean and orderly in a dark gray suit and red tie. His brown-black hair was short and styled simply, the fluorescent lights catching the gray that had started to take over, making the hairs shine. Jasper was taller than him by several inches though this was a relatively new development—just over a year and a half ago, Jasper had shot up half a foot, making him taller than his adoptive father and most other adults he knew. But where Jasper was thin, covered in lean muscle, Charlie was stout, wide in the shoulders, chest, and hips. He'd grown softer than he had been when he was active in the field but was still strong. Dark hair dusted the back of his wide hands, and he looked at Jasper with steel-gray eyes from behind thin-rimmed glasses.

They looked nothing alike.

"Hello, Jasper. Happy hunting?"

"Oh, peachy keen," Jasper replied, stepping back and opening the door wider for Charlie to come in. "What's up?"

"I called your phone, but you didn't answer."

Jasper shrugged. The soft chirping of the ringer was hardly enough to wake him.

Charlie's answering frown was very slight. "Ready for a debriefing?"

"Can I at least take a shower first?"

"Of course," Charlie said. "My office, half an hour?"

"Be there in twenty."

#

Jasper showered quickly in the shared bathroom on his floor and went back to his room to get dressed in a pair of jeans and a T-shirt basically indistinguishable from what he'd been wearing the night before. For a few minutes he struggled to do something with his hair, but, as usual, his hair was going to do whatever it was going to do, and he gave up. Still feeling half asleep, he took the elevator up to his father's floor, walking past the empty classrooms to knock on his door. Maybe he'd be lucky and Charlie would have a pot of coffee on.

It had been exactly twenty minutes.

Jasper opened the door without waiting for an answer and found Charlie seated behind his desk. The office was smaller than the one he had in his apartment, sadly lacking the large windows that overlooked the city. What it lacked in windows it made up for in books—two of the four walls were dominated by filled bookshelves. Most of them were history books, recounting hundreds of unique events in the Underworld's past. Some of them, Jasper knew, had been written by Charlie himself. His father had a passion for history and was often researching obscure events and creatures. A low table ran across another wall; a sad-looking plant and a picture of Charlie and Jasper from five years ago sat next to an unfortunately empty coffee machine.

"Alright," Jasper said, dropping into the leather armchair in front of Charlie's desk. The arms of the chair were worn down and soft, canvas showing through the dark leather. "So the female vampire, that whole deal went off without a hitch. She walked right into it, practically begged to be staked. The only problem was her pack. It's way bigger than we thought it was. And they were *pissed*."

"You seem to have handled it quite well."

Jasper ran his finger across the arm of the chair, drawing an imaginary circle on the fabric. He almost didn't want to mention it. "Well... I had a little help."

Charlie raised an eyebrow, curious.

"It sounds crazy, but this werespider helped me."

"A werespider?"

"Yeah." He knew how stupid it sounded. "How did we not know there's a fucking werespider in Brooklyn?"

"Oh, we knew."

Surprise and annoyance reared up together at this news. "And you didn't think to let me in on that little secret?"

"St. James has never considered him a priority. Apart from the odd victim, he doesn't do much. We haven't even turned up one of those for almost two years. I figured he had moved on. Or died. But you say he helped you? Why?"

Jasper remembered the echo of the demon's revolvers, the burning red of his eyes, the way his laugh filled the bar. "He said they were in his territory, causing trouble. Acted like I was the one who helped him out." *And then he asked me out,* Jasper thought but did not say. "He said his name was Chris. Christopher Redd?"

Charlie stood up from his desk and went to the short row of wooden filing cabinets against the wall. "He's used that alias a lot in the past," he said, opening a drawer and flipping past several folders before finding the one he was looking for.

"That's not his name?"

"You'd be hard-pressed to find a werespider with a name like that." Charlie returned to his desk to look through the folder, his glasses perched on the end of his nose. "His name, I believe, is Crimson Apocalypse."

Jasper laughed out loud. Charlie did not laugh with him. "You're kidding, right? What the hell kind of name is that? What is he, some sort of death-metal, end-of-the-world cult guy?"

"Werespiders often have... a flair for the dramatic. And this one's certainly no exception. I can't believe you found him."

Jasper started to point out that the werespider was the one who found him, not the other way around, but just shook his head instead. "Alright, so what's the deal? You wanna take him down? I saw him fight—he's good. I mean, he seems like a bit of an idiot, but I think it's mostly a front. We'll probably need a team. Did you have anyone in mind?" Jasper snapped his fingers. "You know who's good? The Neilson brothers—I know elementals are more their style, but—"

"Actually, Jasper, I was thinking of something else. Something a little subtler than a team of Hunters, guns blazing. This werespider, he's very old. And a demon doesn't get to be that old without some help. He's been in New York for hundreds of years. I bet he knows every demonic haunt and safe house in the city."

Jasper frowned. "You want to try to catch him?" Killing demons was much easier than capturing them.

"Well, they did catch him. In the late seventies. Let's see..." Charlie flipped open the case file. "They had him in the holding cells in '75. But he and his cellmate escaped. It was a vampire. No name."

"Bullshit. No one gets out of here; the place is a fortress."

Charlie spread his hands before him as if displaying the evidence. The werespider was free in Brooklyn, not held in the basement at St. James. Jasper's frown deepened.

Charlie traced a finger down the text, reading over his glasses. "A different team managed to take out his pack in '84—a strange bunch: a female werespider, a werewolf, and a human warlock—but he eluded us again."

"Alright," Jasper said, "then what?"

"Then nothing. They expected him to retaliate, to fight back. Instead, he more or less disappeared. At least that's what it looks like. He was actually kind of my pet project when we first moved here. I did all sorts of research, but it doesn't amount to much. Most of the old computer files are corrupted. All the information I have I got from hard copy—paper records, books." Charlie handed the folder over to Jasper. "Everyone told me it was a waste of time."

Jasper opened the folder and flipped through it. There wasn't much. A few brief mission summaries that Charlie had already covered, and a handful of copied photos. Jasper looked at one that showed a group of people and demons, easily finding the werespider he'd met the night before in the middle of the small crowd. His arm was around the shoulders of a shorter, bespectacled man, and the photo had been captured while both were mid-laugh. The werespider's partner was wearing a dark green flight jacket and had a tattoo of a snake's head on the side of his neck. Neither was looking at the camera, both seeming far more interested in one another. The pair was dwarfed by a massive woman in plate armor, who had an equally massive ax slung over one shoulder. Her other hand rested between the nubby horns of a satyr, while a robed figure wearing a skull mask floated in the background, opalescent blue eyes creating a flare on the lens. There were several other people, most of them seemingly human, some of them decidedly not. The most bizarre was a snakelike woman with her long body coiled underneath her torso to prop her upright, the tip of her tail lying over the werespider's boots.

Jasper turned the photo over, looking for any more information, but there wasn't so much as a date, and it didn't appear to be connected to any sort of text. The Hunter flipped the folder closed and drummed his fingers thoughtfully on the cover.

"What are you thinking, Charlie?"

His father placed his elbows on his desk, bringing his hands together as if in prayer. He rested his steepled fingers beneath his chin and looked at Jasper. For a long moment, he said nothing. And then he lowered his hands. "He liked you."

Jasper scoffed.

"He didn't kill you. He engaged contact. At the very *least* he's interested in you. And we're interested in him. I'm thinking that if we could get close to him, we could find out what he's been up to. Learn his connections. Find his haunts. It would be an easy segue into the city's underbelly. The only known werespider in New York has to have some interesting information, don't you think, Jasper?"

"Sure," he allowed, sitting back in the chair, his arms folded over his chest.

"I want you to go undercover, so to speak. Get close to him, find out what he knows."

"Are you nuts? It's a miracle he didn't figure out I was a Hunter *last night*. He'd kill me in a second if I went poking around."

Charlie smiled. Jasper had seen that look before. "I happen to have a few ideas about that."

#

The werespider's territory wasn't spectacularly large, centralized to Huntsman Avenue and spilling into the surrounding blocks. In the past days, he might have pushed into the sections left vacant by the vampires, but as far as Charlie had been able to tell, it was just the werespider by himself—no pack to speak of.

Jasper spent the day packing and repacking his one bag, reading old manuals that barely held his focus, and shooting questions and answers back and forth with Charlie to make certain he had his story straight. More than likely, the whole thing would turn out to be a bust, so he didn't know why he felt so nervous. He hated to admit to himself that his real anxiety was rooted in the idea that everything would go off without a hitch.

The sun was riding low on the horizon when Jasper exited the agency, gun at his side, backpack slung over his shoulder. The city smog caught the glowing beams of light as they faded to the west, painting the sky in hues of pink and purple with darting wisps of golden-orange shot along the undersides and edges in an exquisite hemming.

Jasper walked in the opposite direction with the fading light on his shoulders.

By the time he reached Gravesend on the outskirts of Brooklyn, it was full dark. Huntsman Avenue featured a handful of low-end restaurants and sleazy bars, their flashing signs promising "cheap beer" and "great food." He passed most of them and was beginning to think maybe he was out a little early for the werespider (it was only now just after eight) when his stomach curled strangely.

It was not the same feeling he got near a vampire or a werewolf; the sensation was deeper and heavier with a fullness he associated with something very big or very strong.

Jasper stopped under the striped overhang of Rascal's and peeked through the grime-covered front window.

The restaurant looked even gloomier than he remembered. Kitschy and outmoded, obviously on the brink of financial ruin.

Crimson was practically right where he'd been the night before, sitting at the bar with a small pyramid of shot glasses stacked in front of him, as if he'd never left. His elbow rested on the counter, and he was turned slightly on the stool to face a twentysomething man whose long golden hair was held back from his face by a black bandana that sported white skulls and crossbones.

Jasper readjusted his jacket to make sure it concealed the firearm, and stepped through the swinging glass door.

He was so focused on getting across the room and intercepting the werespider before he could do something unspeakable to the oblivious human that he almost ran headlong into the tall, bulky man who stepped into his path to stop him. "Sorry, kid, it's twenty-one and over after eight. Nothing personal."

"Wha...? Oh, uh..."

He hadn't had any trouble here the other night, and it hadn't occurred to him that this might be a problem. He pretended to check his wallet. "Well, shit. I left my ID at home."

The man shrugged with a good-natured smile. "We're open until two. Should give you plenty of time to run on home and grab it."

"That's not really necessary, is it? I was just in here the other night and—"

"Hey! Tony! Let him alone. He's with me." Crimson waved him over like they were old friends.

Tony looked surprised, glancing at Jasper up and down. Then he grinned knowingly and shot Crimson a glance. "I thought Nigel was 'with you.'"

"Who the fuck is Nigel?"

The blond man beside him angrily cleared his throat. The demon arched an eyebrow. "Ew, that's not really your name, is it?"

Nigel snatched his drink off the counter. "Fuck you, Chris. Seriously."

"Yeah, you wish." Crimson laughed as the other man slid down from the stool and stalked toward the door. His shoulder jostled hard against Jasper's as he passed. He paused only long enough to give Jasper an exasperated glare.

"He's all yours, man. Good luck."

"Nigel, wait—you can't take alcohol out of the—goddammit, man!" Tony chased him out the door to retrieve the stein he'd carried out with him.

Crimson didn't seem sorry to see either of them go. He smiled at Jasper, easy and friendly as could be. "Couldn't resist my charms, eh?"

"It's not exactly like that," replied Jasper. He adjusted the strap of his backpack. "I'm not... like that."

"Guess I shouldn't have pissed off Nigel, then," replied the werespider, spinning back to the bar and standing on the footrest to lean over the counter and grab a bottle. The bartender, Nikki, watched him with a bemused expression, one hand on her hip, pierced eyebrow raised.

"Anyone ever tell you that you drink like a fish?"

"If a fish drank like me, it'd drown," said Crimson. "Is he for real still just standing there? *Jasper*, c'mon, work with me here. If we're gonna pretend to be civil, I can't be the only one trying."

Jasper really *was* just standing there, partially because he was beginning to reconsider his options, and partially because he was still trying to understand what had just transpired. He remembered that he needed the demon to like him and forced a smile. "I'm not pretending to be civil." He took a seat at the bar and set his backpack on the floor at his heel. "I *was* actually looking for you."

"No shit?" Crimson sounded unimpressed. "Here I thought an underage, nondrinker like yourself just happened to have wandered into my favorite bar, all by coincidence. It's such a hotbed of activity." He sarcastically swept a hand to indicate the nearly empty room. At the other end of the bar, the only other patron, a drunken old man, fell from his stool and hit the hardwood floor with a *thud*.

Nikki swore and ran to check on him.

With her departure, the werespider's manner changed—his back straightened, his eyes flickered with a dangerous glint, and his brows drew down. "So what's up?"

"I have a favor to ask."

"Well, you'd better be careful about that." The grin showed through the scowl fleetingly, like the flicker of a strobe. "You don't know what I might ask in return."

Jasper's stomach fluttered. The back of his neck felt hot and he hoped his blush didn't show in his face. Flirtation wasn't uncommon in demons, but Jasper didn't usually have to put up with their leering longer than it took to draw his gun. He cleared his throat and pitched the story he and Charlie had come up with. "My last client burned me, and that vampire you let get away has my number. I'm running into hits left and right, and I've got no place to go. So I was thinking maybe since you were so nice before…"

Crimson took the lead, hook, line, and sinker. A look of surprise registered on his face. "You're kidding, right?"

"I just need a place to crash for, like… a few days. Maybe, like, a week…"

"Nikki, could I get a shot of something stronger, please?" Crimson called down the length of the bar. Jasper opened his mouth to speak, but the werespider held a hand up to him. "Just… lemme have a shot, okay?"

The pair of them sat in silence as Nikki, a cordless phone wedged between her ear and shoulder, dug one-handed beneath the counter. She poured a green splash of absinthe into a tumbler and made a shooing gesture before pointing impatiently to the man on the floor and then to the phone in her hand.

Crimson tossed the shot back, clapped the glass down, and spun towards him. "You know what you're suggesting is pretty fucking weird, right? Did one of those vamps latch onto your brain and just suck the common fuckin' sense right outta it? You don't *know* me. I could be a serial killer. *Fuck*, Jasper, I *am* a serial killer."

Jasper looked at Nikki, fully expecting her to be staring at them, but she hadn't reacted to the werespider's voice. She was crouched by the old man, trying to bring him around with a none-too-gentle smack on his cheek.

"And," continued Crimson, as if nothing of interest were going on, "even if I weren't, I don't know *you*. You could be—" He paused, cocking his head to the side. "*In fact*, you're *also* a serial killer. Hell, you could be a Hunter for all I know. So why the fuck would you think that (a) living with me was a good idea or that (b) I would even let you?"

"You invited me back to your place the other night."

"Yeah, but not to *live* there. Don't you have somewhere else you can go?"

Jasper had a very complicated answer lined up in store for this question, but he changed his mind at the last second. "Alright, if you're too scared of me, I'll just try somewhere else." He started to get up.

The demon caught him by the collar of his shirt, dragging him back into the seat.

"Alright, don't be fuckin' obnoxious about it." He drummed his fingers on the bar, pensive. "I guess you could be useful to have around. For a while." The drumming stopped. "But I'm warning you, if this is all some sort of, I dunno, insanely elaborate trap, you'd better back out now."

"It's not a trap," Jasper assured him. Crimson was dead on the money, but Jasper couldn't tell if this was because he'd done something to give himself away to the werespider, or if the demon was simply paranoid. "I just need a place to stay."

"Well, you would say that," replied Crimson. "One way or the other." He paused. Sighed. Kneaded his temples with his long fingers. "Alright, you can stay, just for a few days. Until you sort your shit out or whatever."

Jasper smiled a smile that was as relieved as he genuinely felt. "Thanks, Chris. I really appreciate it. Do you live around here or, uh…" A horrifying thought occurred. "You don't… live in the bar, do you?"

"Only when I'm awake," said the werespider. "And it's not Chris, by the way. No sire in their right mind would name their fledgling 'Chris.'"

Werespiders were a rarity, hardly ever seen, seldom taken alive. Jasper knew the basics of them—their fatal allergy to gold, their ability to change shapes into large spiderlike creatures, the hypnotic thrall in their eyes, and their highly effective pheromones, which drew humans to them like pigs to slaughter. He didn't know their sires named them when they were reborn.

The demon offered him his hand. "It's Crimson. Crimson Apocalypse."

"Jasper Craig." Jasper gave his hand a firm shake. He started to let go, but Crimson's fingers tightened, sharp focus cutting through his woozy gaze. He pulled him an inch closer. His voice was dangerously low.

"Y'know, most people react when I say that name. Can't help but notice you didn't."

"Do they usually react by laughing in your face?" Jasper laughed, hoping it sounded less nervous than it really was. When the demon didn't return his smile, he cleared his throat. "Look, man, everything I own is in a bag on the floor right beside us. I have no place to live. Your name could be Jack the Ripper for all I care."

Crimson's grip tightened just slightly.

He looked a thousand years old.

He looked nineteen.

He let go, spinning back to face the counter and pouring himself another shot. "Mm-hm... Okay. Whatever ya say, man."

Chapter Four

—

Welcome to "Paradise"

The bar was open until two a.m.

Crimson made no effort to leave, even when the owners flipped on all the lights and started shooing stragglers away. More people had come and gone than Jasper expected, with the bar filling up and becoming noisy from eleven until after one.

An eclectic mix of people wandered in and out, college students and grizzled old men, young professionals and women with lines around their eyes and too much makeup, girls with tattoos on every exposed piece of skin and boys with piercings. They were all human, not a demon among them except for Crimson. Many seemed to recognize the werespider's human persona, catching him with friendly slaps to the back and calling him by his false name. Crimson was as deceptively friendly as he had been with Jasper the night they met. He wafted from group to group, finding free drinks wherever he went, hustling games of pool and poker, and smoking despite the many prohibitory signs suggesting he shouldn't. Trying to keep up with him was impossible, and the constant sound of raised voices was giving Jasper a headache, so he settled at the bar to observe instead.

"Hey, kid, you sure you don't want something to drink?" asked Nikki, mixing and pouring a complicated round even as she spoke. "I can put you on Chris's tab."

Jasper glanced across the room to where Crimson was thoroughly distracted by a game of quarters. Then back at Nikki. "No, thanks. But, uh, how long have you two known each other? You seem pretty close."

"Me and Chris?" Her demeanor changed on a dime, suddenly nervous. She grabbed a rag from a bucket of sanitizer and began needlessly wiping the bar in front of Jasper. "I dunno. We go way back. He's like a fixture around here, y'know? Helps look after the place, makes sure no one causes too much of a fuss."

"Like a bouncer?"

Nikki giggled. "No. Not exactly. But yeah, sort of, I guess."

She didn't seem hypnotized or bewitched. Apart from being a little tired, her eyes were as clear and blue as a sparkling day. But if the werespider frequented this place, she surely would have noticed something off about him.

A familiar, then. And by that virtue, not worth inquiring further. The werespider obviously had some bargain with her or had her so tightly wrapped around his little finger that she didn't care if he killed her patrons. Familiars were no better than the monsters they served. "I'll just have another water."

When the crowd started to thin out, Crimson settled back at the bar, but Nikki continued to bring him drinks long after last call.

It wasn't until the far-off rumble of thunder threatened rain that he dragged himself off the barstool and headed for the door, barking for Jasper to come with him, even though the Hunter was already right at his heel.

Storm clouds rolled overhead, the first drops of rain already breaking loose. Crimson assured him it wasn't far but didn't seem to be in any great hurry as they walked side by side past ruined buildings and run-down storefronts with blacked-out windows. A faded green sign posted crookedly at the intersection of a dead-end street read "Huntsman Avenue." From there, the lackluster state of the buildings only grew sadder.

They finally stopped in front of an old Victorian house, now little more than a beaten-down shack, slumping on its cracked and sinking foundation. It was set further back from the road than its neighbors, the overgrown hedges out front half-masking its ivy-covered facade from view. Most windows were broken and boarded over by pieces of weather-beaten scrap lumber. The wide yard and wraparound porch were completely overtaken by ivy and weeds, sloping as if it might collapse if you so much as thought about walking on it. Vines twisted and snared around the spikes of the wrought-iron fence that lined the property, leaves ruffling eerily in the rising wind.

The old gate looked like it might not have moved in decades, but when Crimson lifted the latch, it swung inward with only a low creak of protest. The path beyond was cobbled in stepping-stones. Nature had dug her way underneath the flat pieces of rock and forced them out of alignment, so the walkway weaved and jutted drunkenly to the crumbling porch.

With the wind howling and the rain gathering strength, Jasper sheltered under the terrace and waited impatiently for Crimson to find his keys in one of the many pockets of his long coat. He got the door unlocked and both of them inside just as the storm clouds cracked open and started pouring down sheets of heavy rain.

Flashes of lightning shined through the slats on the boarded windows, illuminating the interior in brief bursts of static blue-gray that were followed closely by booming rumbles of thunder. In the flashing light, the inside of the house looked like something out of a gothic horror story—wallpaper peeling in narrow sheets, floorboards cracked and rotting, old paintings hanging crookedly or fallen entirely from the walls.

Jasper flipped on the screen of his phone and shined it around to get a better look. The foyer was dominated by a large stairway. He jumped a little when, halfway up, the shine caught the sleeve of Crimson's jacket—Jasper hadn't felt him move past him nor heard him start up the steps, and this eerie behavior combined with the practically nonexistent lighting made him suddenly more aware of the weight of the gun holstered on his hip.

"You'd better come upstairs," said the werespider, his voice heavy with reluctance. "There's no electricity down here, and the rain will get in if it keeps up." Behind him, the steps stretched up to a darkened landing on the second floor.

Well. Now that he was standing alone in the nest of a very dangerous demon and admitted killer, he really wished he wasn't, but he followed the spider up the stairs, listening to them creak and squeak and expecting to fall through the bottom of them every step of the way. A hallway off the stairs was swallowed in darkness, as was the next flight that the werespider turned up, disappearing up to the third floor. The hallway to the right of the landing was marginally brighter and hemmed with cardboard boxes and crates whose contents were overspilling with papers and books and all different manner of useless trinkets. Crimson weaved through the cluttered maze, making barely a sound. Gold-tasseled runners, frayed and stained and faded to a murky pink, lined the warped hardwood floor. The walls, decorated every few feet by burned-out sconces, groaned forlornly. It was impossible to guess what color they had once been.

Crimson came to a halt.

At first, Jasper thought he must have gotten turned around, because the hallway ended in a wall and not a very impressive one at that. Then the werespider reached out and opened it, and Jasper felt stupid, wondering how he couldn't have seen the door that was so clearly there all along.

"Magic?" asked Jasper, surprised that he hadn't noticed a glamor.

"It's an old druidic warding charm."

"I've never met a demon who could do magic," offered Jasper, meaning it as a compliment.

"Well, you still haven't." Crimson reached into the room and gave a drawstring overhead a brisk tug. The lights popped on, revealing another stairwell. These steps were in a better state of repair, almost new but for slight wear and tear.

Jasper followed Crimson up the stairwell, into the attic. He looked around and breathed a sigh of relief.

The room was entirely different from the rest of the house in the sense that it actually looked habitable. The ceiling was high and arched with globe-like glass light fixtures attached to the exposed wooden rafters. To the right of the stairwell, a long counter divided a quadrant of the room into a small kitchenette, complete with cabinets, table, dishwasher, and refrigerator. In front of him, two beds rested on a low platform underneath a large curtained window, and in front of that, a leather couch, two armchairs, and a coffee table were clustered on a carpeted section of the floor around two televisions, one broadcasting a black-and-white security feed of the property, the other dark.

Crimson shrugged off his jacket and tossed it on the hook at the top of the stairwell. "It's not really much."

"No, it's, uh… nice. Just not what I was expecting." Jasper wondered if it would be rude to ask him what, exactly, a werespider needed a *kitchen* for. He tried for a more tactful question instead.

"Have you lived here long?"

"You could say that."

"And it's… just you, right?" He couldn't help but notice there were two beds.

"Not anymore," replied Crimson, but his levity was belied by the look he gave him—all piercing, dark eyes and heavy brows. "But if you're asking if there's a pack involved, the answer is no." He kicked off his boots and pushed them under the bed closest to the window, then unlaced the holsters on his hips and strung the straps through the headboard so that the ivory butt of one revolver hung in easy reach. "It's just me."

It was highly unusual for a demon to live all on his own. Charlie had said most of his old pack had been killed during a raid, but that had been almost twenty years ago, and Jasper would have expected that he'd have been accepted into a new pack by now. "Isn't that dangerous?"

Crimson threw himself down on the bed with a yawn. "Now who's the one asking a lot of questions?"

"Just wondering if I have to, like, sleep on the couch or if the bed is cool."

"Are you sure you wouldn't rather share this one?"

God, this guy was persistent. And impossible to gauge. "No, thank you."

Crimson lifted one shoulder. "Suit yourself. That mattress is awful though."

"I'm sure it'll be fine." Jasper set his backpack at the foot of the second bed. The demon made him extremely self-conscious of every move he made. He was relieved to learn he wouldn't be thrown in with a whole pack of them. It was bad enough having to keep up the charade with just one. He looked around again. The only doors were the one at the bottom of the stairs, and what was obviously a closet, one door hanging open to show the dresser inside, overstuffed with clothes. "Do you have, like, a bathroom or…?"

"It's on the third level, down the hall. I was gonna put one in here." Usually, this phrase was followed by an explanation, but this time it wasn't. "I think it all still works and everything. I know the shower does."

"Alright," said Jasper.

"Just don't touch any of the sconces."

"Alright," said Jasper again, then, "Wait, why?"

"Just… like… don't touch them," repeated Crimson. "In fact, try not to touch much of anything." Then, grabbing the edge of the comforter, he rolled himself into the blanket and dragged the pillow underneath his head. "Hit the lights on the way out, would ya?"

Jasper took his bag with him to the bathroom, shining his phone up along the wall as he went. As far as he could tell, there was nothing strange about any of the sconces other than them being ugly and gothic, like something from a cheesy horror movie. The werespider was probably just fucking with him, trying to keep him off-kilter. Goddamned demons.

The fluorescent lights on the bathroom ceiling buzzed and flickered when he flipped the switch, revealing a gray tile floor that he desperately hoped wasn't originally white. An old claw-foot tub, showerhead attached, took up the majority of the space. Its deep red shower curtain didn't match anything in the bathroom. Well, unless some very suspicious stains near the sink and on the floor counted.

A soft creak drew his attention down the hall behind him.

He froze, half in, half out of the doorway, carefully watching the darkness. Listening. Every instinct, inborn and trained, told him he needed to get the hell out of this place. The werespider was *acting* friendly, but Jasper was pretty sure it was just an act. He was old, he was bored, and he was toying with him. The moment the game ceased to entertain him…

There was another creak.

Closer?

Jasper dipped to his backpack and drew out a stronger flashlight.

He darted the beam back and forth between the cardboard-box pillars. A BOOM of thunder rattled through the house, making the bathroom light flicker. He saw—honest to God *saw*—the demon watching him from the shadows, until he steadied his hand and realized it was only an old worn shirt hanging out of the edge of one of the boxes.

He steadied his breath. Some demons played very elaborately with their prey, but this one couldn't even be bothered to mop his bathroom or keep track of his keys. He probably wasn't patiently awaiting an opportunity to act out a scene from *Psycho*.

Unless…

That was just exactly what he wanted him to think.

Shut up, shut up. Jasper stepped into the bathroom very quickly, closing the door immediately behind him. He threw the lock—flimsy in the beaten frame—and took several steps back until he was almost touching the other wall.

Waited.

Waited.

Not a creak. Not a stir.

The lights flickered twice more, always with the rumble of nearby thunder. Cautiously, Jasper washed his face in the sink, the water warm and the basin clean, and brushed his teeth. The toilet was less clean, obviously unused for a long time, the water having left a rust-colored ring where it rested, but the flush worked. Within the wall, the pipes screamed their protest at having to work.

Gripping the heavy flashlight with a white-knuckled hand, Jasper slipped back into the hallway, eyes darting through the many shadows, expecting something at every move. He reached the attic unharmed and went up the short flight of stairs.

Crimson was right where he had left him, asleep in bed.

Chapter Five

—

The Crystal Ballroom

The first night Jasper didn't sleep at all. He couldn't even entertain the idea with the demon so nearby. Crimson, it seemed, was not so bothered.

While the demon slept, Jasper took the opportunity to poke around the upstairs apartment, careful not to make a sound. Along with a sizeable collection of liquor bottles and cigarette packs, Crimson also had a large movie collection, mostly DVDs but some VHS tapes, and more titles than Jasper hoped to recognize. They didn't seem to be organized in any recognizable way, simply shoved in any available space. The books were disappointing, a few stuck wherever they would fit, less than a dozen overall. He picked up a faded copy of *Don Quixote* and started to look through it, but it was so old and so well-read that he was half-afraid it would fall apart in his hands, and he put it back.

It was impossible to describe the style of the decor because nothing appeared to match anything else. The couch was an overstuffed black leather affair from the '80s, pockmarked with cigarette burns and duct-taped to keep the stuffing in. The armchairs to either side were considerably older. One was an ugly paisley thing, green and fuchsia, definitely a relic. The other was brown leather, with a pull lever to recline. It reminded him of one Charlie had when Jasper was barely five.

A glass-top coffee table, covered in empty bottles, Marlboro packages, and general junk, rested between the couch and the TV, while the series of mismatched throw rugs and runners carpeting the hardwood floor in pathways could have spanned from the Victorian era to the early 2000s. A black suit of armor, posed upright with a lance in its grip, stood half-hidden behind a fallen tasseled midnight-blue drape, giving Jasper a slight start as it was revealed. Hidden behind the drape and suit of armor was a badly chipped baby grand piano, alongside a dresser wedged against an unused brick fireplace, the mantel above cluttered with more junk. Jasper carefully rehung the drape, watching Crimson from the corner of his eye as he did so.

Weapons were everywhere, scattered about in the open, on shelves and tables and stashed away in closets and cupboards, which were empty of all foods except a large canister of coffee grinds and a few long-forgotten cans of fruit salad. Mostly the weapons were knives, ranging in size and material, but there were others too, guns and throwing stars, brass knuckles, and even a quiver and bow stuck in the top of the closet. What he assumed to be swords were wrapped in cloth and leaning against the inside wall of the closet. Jasper left them there, not wanting to risk waking the spider with the sound.

A heavy wooden behemoth of a trunk sat at the foot of the werespider's bed. Or perhaps *chest* would have been a better word. It looked like something you'd find in the hold of a sunken pirate ship, but it was plastered with travel stickers, the oldest dated 1890. Jasper tried the latch and felt a sharp sting like a needle. He bit his tongue to suppress a yelp and jerked his hand away. A small bead of blood clotted as quickly as it bloomed.

Christ, he hoped it wasn't poisonous or something.

Overall he couldn't find anything useful in the upstairs apartment, but the house was large, especially by New York standards, three stories plus the attic room, and from his brief journey through the house, Jasper knew it was stuffed full with potentially interesting crap. He glanced at the werespider still asleep in his bed. He'd barely moved the entire night, his revolvers still within easy reach. Jasper grabbed a heavy flashlight from his backpack and headed down to the next floor.

The gloom of the third-floor hallway was thick, broken only by the cracked bathroom door. The beam of his flashlight broke through, bringing the dusty piles of boxes and broken furniture into sharp contrast. Besides the bathroom, three other rooms were on this floor, the doors closed. Jasper went to the room closest to the attic and tried the door, finding it locked. Picking locks always took him forever, and kicking the door down was probably going to be loud enough to wake the werespider. He opted to start sifting through the nearest stack of boxes instead.

The first box was full of clothes, dated garments he couldn't imagine Crimson wearing, stuff better suited for some hippy-dippy love child of the seventies rather than the goth/punk aesthetic the werespider favored. Demons, especially old ones, were often chameleons, changing with the times to blend into society to better trap their prey. Maybe the werespider had once worn tie-dye and bellbottoms and had since moved on to some sort of weird alternative grunge style.

Jasper started to search the next box, but his hand came in contact with something soft and wet, and he jerked it back, knocking the box to the floor. Rotted papers and books and cloth tumbled to the ground, along with a bundle of some of the biggest and ugliest spiders he'd ever seen. A particularly large one scuttled towards him, and he squished it under his boot, feeling the crunch even through the thick sole. He shuddered, having had enough of boxes for the time being, then shook his disquiet away, heading for a door across from the bathroom.

The light streaming from the cracked bathroom door was yellowish and did little to illuminate the room across the hall. Jasper tried the worn crystal doorknob and found it unlocked. With caution he toed it open, his flashlight beam cutting ahead of him.

The room was dusty, disused, the walls covered in floor-to-ceiling bookshelves of heavy, dark wood, full to bursting with menacing-looking tomes. A large antique desk was pushed against the far wall, not far from the boarded-up window covered in rotting green velvet curtains.

The books interested him—they were not unlike many of the books back in the library at St. James, which were filled with all sorts of information on demons. The desk could be promising as well. This room hadn't been used in some time, but if the werespider had an old address book stowed away, that would at least be *something*.

Jasper took a step into the room, the floorboard screeching at his weight. He stepped back, certain both that the werespider would have heard him and that the floor was bound to collapse beneath his feet. The floor held and the door to the attic remained closed. After a moment of waiting, Jasper ventured back in, placing his feet carefully so the boards merely whimpered rather than screamed.

He reached the desk and opened the top drawer. It was empty except for a single piece of yellowed paper, its edges curled up from age. Two words were written in flowing cursive: *Fuck You.*

Jasper didn't have time to wonder what its purpose was—a heavy *click* sounded from the drawer as he opened it, and the room came alive with a vengeance. The wooden sides of the bookshelves exploded with a crack, and half a dozen curved blades, easily four feet long if not more, burst outward, slicing across the room. Books flew, hitting the floor with thuds like muffled gunfire. A particularly deadly blade came at him, and Jasper acted only on instinct, leaping backwards so that his back was against the wall, the blade slicing through the air in front of his face. On the back swing the blade hit the flashlight out of his hand, sending it spinning crazily through the air, the beam bouncing around until a different blade struck it in the air, breaking it. Darkness fell around him, blinding him. The blades continued to swing—he heard them even if he couldn't see them. Pressed against the wall, Jasper thought he'd just stay there. The blades couldn't go indefinitely, right? It might have been a good idea, but on one of the returns, the blade moved closer, cutting a slash in the thigh of his jeans, slicing the skin above his knee. Jasper hissed in pain and cursed. He had to *move.*

The darkness left him blind. He tried to remember the layout of the room: how many paces across was it? Was there any furniture other than the desk? How many blades were there? And who the fuck would put something like this in their house? It was like something from an ancient pharaoh's tomb, or a trap a serial killer with a lot of time on his hands would make.

Jasper could linger no longer; before the blade could swing back and remove the leg from his body, he moved, throwing himself forward into a low roll, pausing with his back to the side of the desk. He listened to the sound of the blades cutting through the air around him, trying to gauge where they were. One passed by so close that the air tickled his ear; he rolled into the space it had just inhabited, jumped to his feet, and ran, twisting and hoping he'd stay lucky.

The door was open the barest of cracks. Jasper threw himself against it, burst into the hall and promptly hit the wall, his palms smacking against the drywall, sending cracks running through it. His heart was pounding and his breath came out in pants, the adrenaline catching up with him now that he was out. In the room, the blades continued to swing.

Once his breath was a little more even, Jasper took stock of his injuries; the worst was the cut above his knee, though there were a few others, and he'd banged himself up pretty good in his haste. Better than getting cut in half, anyway.

A sharp, sudden snap of applause made him jump, and Jasper whirled around towards it, finding its source instantly. Crimson stood in the hallway, shoulder leaned against the wall, legs crossed at the ankles. He clapped slowly, the faint glow of his red eyes standing out of the shadows. "I'm impressed, hybrid. Thought for sure I'd be feedin' the stray cats your insides tomorrow."

"What the hell is that?" Jasper burst out before he could think better of it.

Crimson shrugged, slipping his hands into the pockets of his jeans. "Told ya not to touch my stuff." He was acting casual, but Jasper was sure it was just that: an act. There was tension held in his loose frame, evident in his sharp gaze. Jasper felt pretty tense himself. Stupidly, he had not brought any weapons with him. He didn't even have the flashlight, which could be used as a club in a pinch. The werespider didn't appear to be armed, but Jasper didn't want to have to find out for sure. Even unarmed, the werespider was dangerous. "What were you lookin' for?"

"What? Nothing. I, uh, couldn't sleep. I thought I'd read something. I didn't think the library would attack me."

Crimson made a soft, noncommittal noise. The glow of his eyes seemed to deepen, and Jasper did his best not to react negatively, not to give him reason to attack.

Finally, the werespider spoke. "You're bleeding."

Jasper looked down at his left leg, where the biggest cut was. Blood coated his jeans from the knee down. "Yeah," he said lamely.

"You planning on bleeding out in my hallway, or you going to do something about it?"

Jasper couldn't tell what the werespider was thinking. He'd caught Jasper red-handed and he didn't seem pleased, nor was he furious. If anything, he only seemed curious, his gaze considering.

All at once Crimson shrugged and turned away. "There should be some bandages under the sink in the bathroom. If you decide to die, do me a favor and do it in the basement. I'm goin' back to bed." The shadows swallowed him up, his steps silent as he went down the hall.

The noise of the swinging blades in the other room stopped, leaving only the creaking of the house around him. Jasper watched the space where he'd last seen the werespider, half-expecting him to reappear and finish the job his house had attempted, but he did not. The pain in his leg demanded more of his attention, and he shuffled into the bathroom, locking the flimsy lock behind him. It would do nothing to stop the werespider if he wanted to get in, but it was better than nothing.

Just as Crimson said, a roll of bandages was under the sink in an ancient first aid kit. Jasper took off his jeans. Under the fluorescent lights, the cut on his leg looked ghastly. Six inches across, it was thankfully not too deep, though the smeared, sticky blood made it look worse. A cabinet was in the corner, and Jasper was surprised to find it stocked with clean dark towels. A pile of dirty rags seemed more likely. He took the first aid kit and an armful of towels and sat on the edge of the claw-foot tub to wash the wound. His blood swirled pink and red down the drain. Once washed, the cut was not as bad as he had anticipated. Stitches were probably called for, but the idea of sewing his own skin made him feel light-headed, and the only needles he could find had long ago given in to rust, so he settled for wrapping it tightly with the roll of bandages.

Jasper pulled his ruined jeans back on. The whole ordeal left him shaken. His walk back to the attic room was full of limping, his eyes darting around the shadows that seemed to grow deeper around him. Returning to the attic was almost a relief. After all, he was pretty sure the only thing that would kill him would be Crimson, and a quick glance showed him back in his bed, appearing asleep. Jasper settled on the edge of the second bed, as far away from the spider as he could get. His pistol went under his pillow. He was too tense to sleep, the very idea preposterous. Instead, he dug his old, dog-eared copy of *To Kill a Mockingbird* out of his backpack, leaned his back against the headboard, and read the familiar words, one eye on the spider the whole time.

#

Crimson slept soundly through most of the day, barely moving and never making a noise. If Jasper didn't know better, he would have thought the demon was dead. Finally, when it was nearing dark, Crimson dragged himself out of bed, not to do anything interesting, just to make some coffee.

By this time Jasper was starving. There was no food in the house except the few unappealing cans he'd found in the cupboards, and he was hungry. When he mentioned it to the spider, he seemed uninterested, shrugging his shoulder and sucking back on a smoldering cigarette. If Jasper wanted, he said, he could have a drink or a smoke, but that wasn't what Jasper wanted. Eventually Crimson rolled his eyes at him and stood up from the couch, leading the way through the house and out the door. Jasper wasn't too surprised when they returned to Rascal's.

The bar served food, so to speak, and Jasper put down a burger of questionable origins and a few glasses of Coke, the werespider grimacing distastefully at the display. "I don't know how you stomach that," Crimson said, the tip of his cigarette glowing, delighted to ignore the no-smoking sign behind his shoulder.

"I don't know how you stomach *that*," Jasper countered, meaning the cigarette. He'd read the phrase "smokes like a chimney" a dozen times in books, but this was the first time he'd seen it executed in real life.

"Try one," offered the werespider, sliding the pack across the table.

"No, thanks." He slid it back.

Crimson shrugged. "Suit yourself."

They didn't go back to the house until the early hours of the morning when the sun began to threaten its rise. Crimson seemed good and drunk and talked endlessly but not about anything Jasper thought was valuable. Once again, when he got home, he shrugged off his jacket, hung it by the door, hooked his holsters on his bedpost, well within reach, and then fell into bed, seeming to fall asleep.

Jasper stayed up for a while longer, but he was tired, and all that yammering had given him a headache. He fell asleep, his own gun not an arm's length away.

#

Crimson woke up before dusk the next day and chased his coffee with a shot of clear liquor, offering Jasper one too. The Hunter declined. Crimson offered him another cigarette, and again he said no.

"You're no fun, half-breed."

"Please don't call me that."

A wicked grin spread across Crimson's handsome face. "Alright, hybrid."

Jasper's hands tightened into fists. "Look, I'm not a demon, so if you could stop with the implication that I am…"

"I don't get why it bothers you so much," said Crimson.

"Demons kill people for food," Jasper explained, though this was only a small part of it.

Crimson laughed as if Jasper had just told him a fantastic joke. "Oh, I see. Killing a person for money is just so much more noble."

"I kill *people*—" he said the word to appease Crimson, though what he really thought was *things* "—who deserve it. I don't deal in innocents."

Crimson arched an eyebrow, eyes gleaming. "And how do you judge innocence?"

Jasper frowned. He knew the answer, of course. Humans could be bad, but they were out of his jurisdiction. Demons were bad by definition. But he couldn't tell Crimson that. "I would just really appreciate it if you'd stop calling me 'hybrid,'" said Jasper, in lieu of an actual answer.

"You got it, killer." Crimson grinned.

Jasper sighed. He thought he preferred hybrid.

#

Jasper expected the next day to be like the day before and was thinking maybe this was all a big waste of time. The spider didn't do anything except drink and smoke and talk, usually without any input on Jasper's part and never about anything that could be considered remotely useful to St. James. Surely there were better things for him to be doing. Charlie was wrong.

They went out after dark, and Jasper figured they were going back to Rascal's, but they passed the bar and continued through the neighborhood, going up and down streets at random, occasionally looping back around to pass through an area twice. After an hour of this, Jasper asked him what they were doing.

"I'm checkin' for those vampires, or anyone else stupid enough to come pokin' around." Crimson gave Jasper a pointed look, punctuating it with a wink so quick Jasper wasn't sure if he imagined it. Jasper's hunch hadn't alerted him to anything demonic while they were walking around, other than the dull ache the werespider gave him, so he thought the coast was clear. Crimson came to the same conclusion. "What a waste of time," the werespider said, echoing Jasper's thoughts. Crimson elbowed him in the side, the gesture so familiar that Jasper tried not to bristle visibly. "Let's go have some fun."

"What kind of fun?" Jasper asked, suspicious. He was sure he and the demon would have different ideas for the definition of *fun*.

Crimson smiled, all straight white teeth and movie-star charm. "Well, it'll be fun for me, anyway." Jasper didn't like the sound of that.

He wasn't exactly surprised when they found their way to another bar, just disappointed by the spider's predictability.

The club music reached them first, its generic blown-out *bum-baba-bum* grating on Jasper's nerves already. Rascal's would have been better—the jukebox had the Stones and Nirvana and the only person he'd seen try to dance there was Crimson. The music brought forth visions of too many, too drunk bodies tucked in tightly to a too small space.

The building was brick and stout; a hammered metal sign hanging crookedly over a chipped red metal door read "The Crystal Ballroom." Jasper regretted coming along.

If Crimson sensed his displeasure and apprehension, he did not acknowledge it. He flashed his eyes briefly at the bouncer in a shirt several sizes too small for his bulging muscles, and the two of them entered.

The volume of the music doubled, tripled, the bass thumping in

Jasper's chest like a second, sick heart. The smell hit him next: hot and sweaty bodies, sweet, sticky alcohol, and hairspray, so thick it was like a cloud. A low-ceilinged hallway painted entirely black led them to the club proper, where the two stories opened up into a high-ceilinged room, a giant disco ball hanging in the middle, spinning in a cloud of smoke that swirled and danced around it. Below that were the people flowing and crashing together like river rapids, out of control yet somehow natural. Jasper thought there was even more of them until he realized one of the walls was made entirely of mirrors, reflecting the crowd back at itself. Crude messages, drawings, and phone numbers were scrawled across nearly every part that could be reached, reminiscent of a high school bathroom. The bar was low and black, lit from underneath by green neon, giving those near it a radioactive quality. Bright lights pulsed through the gloom, punctuated randomly by nauseating bright colors: red, yellow, blue, pink. Jasper rubbed his temple.

"Wanna dance?" asked Crimson, smiling as bright as the pulsing lights.

Jasper bristled, his shoulders raised. "No." He didn't even like being here; he couldn't imagine dancing alone, never mind with Crimson.

"Didn't think so." Crimson pushed through the crowd, and Jasper debated following him or turning around and going back to the house. He didn't have a key but was sure he could easily break through one of the windows on the ground floor (most of them were broken already anyway) and get in that way. Surely there was nothing useful to do here. Other than the general anxiety a crowded place like this gave him, he felt no demon presence. Did he really want to waste another night watching the werespider get drunk?

Jasper sighed, pushing his hair back from his face, and followed him. When he found Crimson, he was not alone. The werespider was standing next to the bar, a half-finished drink in his hand, talking to a Native American guy in skintight jeans and a lime green tank top that fit like a second skin and left a sliver of his toned stomach visible. A small woman (she barely looked Jasper's age) was holding the second man's hand, her wide brown eyes staring at the dancing people, swaying slightly to the music. As Jasper approached, she looked over at him, and he realized he'd been wrong: there were other demons here. At least two.

He almost needed to shout to hear himself over the sound of the thumping bass. "Hey," Jasper said, standing awkwardly on the outside of the little group.

"Hey yourself," said the man he didn't know, grinning and moving closer to Crimson to allow him space in the circle. Jasper didn't think he was a werespider, he felt different than Crimson did, but he wasn't sure exactly what he was. If forced to guess, he'd put his money on werewolf. He had that predatory animal way about him.

"You're barkin' up the wrong tree, Alan," Crimson said mildly, tipping back his drink. "Jasper doesn't like demons."

"Give me five minutes and a dark room and I could change his mind," Alan said.

Jasper resisted the urge to zip up his jacket as the demon raked his eyes up and down his body, and glared at him instead.

"While I'd like to see you try, you'd better not. He's very sensitive."

"I am not," Jasper insisted hotly, proving Crimson's point.

Crimson waved a hand dismissively in his direction and turned the rest of his attention to Alan. Setting his empty glass on the bar behind them, he trapped Alan in the cage of his arms. Alan looked delighted to be caught. "I'll take you up on that dark room," Crimson said, hands going to the werewolf's hips. "We're gonna need more than five minutes, though."

Alan grinned, wide and mischievous. "Abby, stay with Jason."

"Jasper," she corrected, her voice soft and dreamy, as if she were somewhere far away from here.

"Sure, whatever. Stay with him. Me and Charlotte will be back later." He and Crimson entered the crowd and quickly disappeared. Jasper didn't need to follow them to figure out what they were up to. He wasn't an idiot.

Abby slipped her small hand into his, and Jasper jerked his away as if her touch had burned him. The demon didn't seem to take offence or even notice.

"Wanna dance?" she asked, her voice barely there beneath the beat.

"No."

She merely stared at him with her wide, empty eyes, and Jasper assumed she couldn't hear him.

Leaning closer, he shook his head, speaking louder. "No, thank you."

Still giving no indication that she understood, Abby kept staring at him. It was starting to creep him out. He tried to ignore her and waited for Crimson to return, but found the room was too warm and too loud. Twice Jasper was jostled by thrashing bodies, though he was standing nowhere near the dance floor. This was a stupid idea.

He turned to the bar behind him and tried to get the tender's attention. "Can I, uh, just get a Sprite or 7 Up or whatever?"

The woman behind the bar had pink and purple hair, several hoops in different parts of her face, and a thick application of eyeliner. She looked at him for a beat too long, reminding him of the werewolf that hung by his side, before she turned to get his drink. What she put before him was dark red in color and garnished with an orange peel. It was decidedly not Sprite.

"Uh, I'm sorry, but I think you got my drink wrong."

"No, I didn't," she replied. "You did."

Before he could question her further, she was gone, leaving the dark red drink for him. He took a small sip. It was sweet and dry and definitely almost entirely alcohol. He took another drink. Damn, that went down easy. These things were dangerous. He had to keep his head. Jasper set it down on the bar and looked at the crowd.

Twenty minutes later Abby asked him again if he wanted to dance. The club was hot and smelled of booze and too many bodies. "Let's go outside," he suggested.

Abby put her hand back in his, and this time he let her. She was small, and Jasper could easily imagine the crowd taking her away.

They fought their way outside, where the air was cooler and clearer. Jasper dropped her hand. The pressure that had been building at the back of his head eased. He took a deep, even breath, letting the night air clear his mind.

"So, uh—" Jasper turned to look at the werewolf, who was staring at him with those creepy, empty eyes "—have you known Crimson long?"

"A while."

Jasper was going to ask her a question about Crimson's other friends, who they were and what they did, but another question seemed more important in the moment. "Has he always been a dick?"

Abby nodded gravely and then leaned forward to look down the street as if watching traffic. It was late and this wasn't the best part of town, so the road was empty except for a taxi parked with their light off halfway down the next block. She stepped back suddenly, her shoulder jarring Jasper's arm. He grabbed her shoulders to keep her from falling to the sidewalk, and just as quickly let go.

"What are you doing? Are you drunk or high or something?"

Abby shook her head as if to clear it rather than in answer. "It begins tonight," she whispered, touching her fingertips to her own lips.

"Excuse me?" Was it possible for werewolves to have a stroke? Maybe she'd had way too much of... something. Jasper didn't know enough about drugs to know what effects they'd have on a regular person let alone a demon.

"The doctor," she said, looking at her fingertips and then, catching sight of him behind her hand, at Jasper.

"Do you need a doctor?"

Abby shook her head, and this time Jasper was pretty sure she was saying no. She frowned, two little lines appearing between her dark, thin brows, and grabbed his hand urgently. Jasper was too startled to pull away.

"The doctor," she insisted. "He screams. There are monsters in the light and innocents in the shadows, and their faces run with blood. It's already started... Crimson doesn't know."

"What doesn't Crimson know?" The werespider's voice surprised him, and Jasper pulled his hand out of Abby's, stepping out of her limited reach. Crimson and Alan had finished whatever it was they had been doing (Jasper didn't care to wonder about the details) and had found them outside, the beating bass following them out into the street until the door fell shut behind them. Crimson had a fresh cigarette in his mouth and an arm thrown across Alan's shoulders. His voice was light and carefree, but as he narrowed his eyes and blew out a cloud of pale smoke, he looked anything but.

Jasper's mind stalled. He didn't have a sweet clue what Abby was talking about, but as far as things Crimson didn't know went, he could think of something that would have a bullet in his head pretty quick. "Abby was just... telling me a story."

Crimson quirked an eyebrow, looking unimpressed. "Oh yeah? I'd love to hear it."

"Um, well," Jasper began, but Abby cut him off.

"The doctor," she said, "he's—"

"Oh, I know this one!" Alan interrupted. Out of the flashing colored lights of the club and into the yellow streetlight Jasper now saw just how blown his pupils were, black and wide, swallowing most of the deep brown of his irises. "So there's this doctor—nah, wait, there's two doctors, and they fuck, right? One's a surgeon and she asks the other one if he's an anesthesiologist, and he's all like, 'Yeah, man, how'd ya know,' and she says, 'Cuz I didn't feel a thing'!" No one laughed. Alan shrugged. "Yeah, well, I guess Abs tells it better. Hey, you guys wanna hit up Moonlight next? I think it's Leather and Lace night."

"Um," said Jasper. It sounded even worse than The Crystal Ballroom, and The Crystal Ballroom was pretty bad. "If it's all the same, I think I'll head back to the house."

"You're just no fucking fun, huh?" Alan asked lightly. "What about you, Legs? Are you comin', or are you goin'?"

Crimson removed his arm from around Alan's shoulders and considered, blowing an impressive smoke ring and snubbing the butt of his cigarette out under his boot. "I'll go home too."

"Boo, you whore. Fine. Be boring. Just give me a cigarette before you go." Alan took the smoke that was offered to him, leaning in close for Crimson to light it. "Well, have fun. Don't do anything I wouldn't do." He winked at Jasper and took Abby's hand.

After they walked away, Crimson turned and started back towards his neighborhood. Jasper jogged after him.

"So." Jasper broke the moody silence. "That guy—Alan? He's your, uh, boyfriend?"

Crimson laughed once, the sound harsh and mean. "He's not my boyfriend. He's nobody. Why're you askin'? Interested?"

"No." Jasper shoved his hands into his pockets, warmth blooming across his cheeks. "I told you I'm not into that."

There was that mean laugh again. "Whatever you say, man. Whatever. You. Say."

Chapter Six

—

Werespider Family Values

The gunmetal burns freezing cold against his palm. He adjusts his hand on the grip and stops to shake out his numb fingers. In all the excitement he's forgotten his gloves. They're probably lying at the foot of Adam's bed, where he tossed them in order to fight with the tricky lock on the window so they could sneak out.

"We must be close," Adam whispers. "What's your hunch say?"

A feeling deep in his gut leads them forward, pulling them along like a fish on a line. "We're close," says Jasper, and he is rewarded with Adam's dazzling smile. Jasper grins back, bumping their shoulders together. "You ready?"

"Born ready," says Adam. He slaps Jasper's shoulder, his palm lingering long enough that Jasper imagines the touch warming him through, chasing away the chill of the November night.

Ahead in the distance is a scream. It is human only in memory.

They run towards it.

#

Jasper jerked awake, hand already outstretched for his gun. His fingers encountered only empty air. He sat up, heart racing, still grasping like the weapon would appear. Then he became aware of the dusky sunlight as it filtered through the half-closed curtains and caught on the table between the two beds. Someone had moved the Glock there, putting it just a little out of reach.

"You talk in your sleep," said the werespider. He was in the kitchen, the coffee machine bubbling as he let a cupboard slam closed. He pulled himself up so that he was sitting on the counter, knocking his heels against the cabinets and half-watching Jasper with that weird, unsettling stillness. Oh God, what had he said? There were a million things he didn't want the werespider to know, but he didn't exactly look ready to rip his lungs out.

Jasper pushed the comforter off himself, the sweat cooling on his body. "No, I don't."

The werespider's steady gaze didn't leave him. "Who's Adam?"

Jasper was saved from answering when a soft, insistent buzzing sounded from the jacket Crimson had left by the door. He was up off the counter and on the other side of the room in a flash.

Cell phone pinched between his shoulder and ear, he gestured with his thumb to indicate he needed to take the call, and then dipped out of the room, even as he spoke a "Hello?"

By the time he got back, the coffee had finished brewing, but he ignored it, grabbing his jacket instead. "I'm gonna go for a walk."

"Where to?" asked Jasper.

"Out."

The Hunter grabbed his backpack. "I'll come with you."

Crimson pulled his jacket on and dug a pair of sunglasses out of one of the many pockets. Jasper couldn't tell with the dark glass covering his eyes, but he thought Crimson was giving him one of those looks again, like he was trying to make sense of him. "No, thanks," the werespider said eventually.

"Why not?"

"Because I'm having a demon problem, and I don't want to intermix that with babysitting duties," growled Crimson.

"I'm good at demon problems," said Jasper, choosing not to bite back this time.

"Are you always this needy and annoying? Or do I just really bring it out in ya?"

Crimson was the most annoying, attention-seeking man he'd ever met, demon, human or otherwise. "I was just trying to help."

"Will you stop pouting if I let you come?"

Jasper chanced an optimistic smile and nodded.

"Fine." Crimson grabbed his holsters and strapped them on, fixing his battered leather jacket to hide them. Without another word he turned and disappeared down the stairs.

Jasper wanted a cup of coffee, but it didn't look like the

werespider was going to wait up. He grabbed his weapons and pulled his jacket on, jogging after him.

The afternoon was bright and sunny. Jasper was delighted. Crimson was irritated. When they passed under the shade of the trees lining the crooked path, the red gleam of his eyes could be seen through the black lenses of his Wayfarers. It was three p.m. and the sun would not set for many hours.

"So, what are we doing?"

"A friend of mine is in trouble," replied Crimson.

Jasper thought of the werewolves they'd spoken to the other night and frowned. "What kind of friend?"

"The helpless kind." Crimson walked at a quick clip, pausing only to glance in the windows of parked cars. "He's gotten himself into a sort of hostage situation with my cousins."

"Your, uh…" Jasper hesitated. "Werespider cousins?" He wasn't expecting that. The werespider was supposed to be alone.

"Look, man, it's really complicated." Crimson stopped beside a parked Buick and drew a coil of nylon string from an interior pocket of his jacket. "Stand closer to me and try not to look so much like you're stealing a car."

"I'm not stealing a car."

Crimson gave him a sarcastic thumbs-up. "Really excellent. You're doing great, kid."

Realizing he wasn't going to be deterred by something as simple as the law, Jasper shoved his hands in his pockets and leaned against the door, blocking the view from oncoming traffic. The nearest pedestrian was all the way on the other side of the street, near the crosswalk, but it still felt like every passenger in every car that drove by knew exactly what they were doing. "Will you at least hurry up?"

Crimson gave a noncommittal grunt. He tied a slipknot in the center of the string and pushed it into the car via the door crack then gradually worked the two ends down along the crease until the knot appeared on the other side of the windowpane. After a few more seconds, the open noose was around the locking knob. Crimson pulled both ends tight and gave them a hard tug. The slipknot closed around the stem and there was a quick, clicking *pop*. He opened the door and held it for Jasper. "Get in."

"I thought you were the only werespider in New York," said

Jasper, reluctantly scrambling into the passenger's side and reaching across the driver's seat to unlock the door. Crimson climbed in and immediately began messing with the steering column. He ripped the plastic covering almost all the way off and produced a small penknife from his sleeve. He was in the middle of stripping a wire when his gaze swiveled suddenly and curiously in Jasper's direction.

"Why do you say that?"

Oh hell. Why had he said that?

"I've just never seen any others," he improvised. Then, not wanting to pursue the conversation any further, he added, "Why would your cousins kidnap your friend?"

Crimson squinted at him suspiciously over his dark lenses and seemed about to say something, but a buzzing sound inside his jacket stopped him. He twisted together the two stripped wires he was holding, and the old car rumbled to life. Throwing it in reverse, he snatched the phone out of his jacket, flipped it open, and barked into the receiver, "Seriously, Sid, fuck off for like five seconds, okay? I'm on my way."

The car lurched back, narrowly avoiding the one parallel parked directly behind them. Crimson shifted into drive and stomped on the gas, propelling them forward into a cacophony of angrily blaring horns and shrieking rubber.

Jasper grabbed the belt over his shoulder as the momentum of the car pushed him down into his seat, and quickly snapped the buckle in place, but felt no safer. Crimson was entirely focused on barreling through traffic at a speed that felt both dangerous and unnecessary and hadn't answered his question. "So, since you're not going to like… elaborate or anything, I'm going to guess they took this guy for leverage," ventured Jasper after several moments.

Crimson tapped a finger to the tip of his own nose and nodded in Jasper's direction with half a grin. "Wow, I sure am lucky, having an attractive ace detective like yourself along. Here all this time I thought you didn't have a clue."

Jasper's cheeks burned. He opened his mouth to ask if he thought he was being funny (his tone implied yes) or if he was being dead serious (it was difficult to judge), and nearly bit his tongue off as the demon slammed on the brakes. The front tires locked, and the tail end of the vehicle swept around with a shriek. The vehicle came to rest alongside the curb with a jounce, but Jasper didn't feel like his stomach had caught up to the halt until after he'd gotten his seatbelt unbuckled. Crimson was halfway out of the car and moving with purpose. Jasper closed his door and jogged after him.

The air outside tasted hot and smoky with the afterburn of the tires. He caught up to Crimson in only a few steps. "I hate to ask, but there's a plan or something you're forgetting to let me in on, *right?*"

Crimson reined up. "Oh yeah. The plan. Uh, well… See, what we're going to do is go into this big building over here—" he made a sweeping gesture across the vacant parking lot beside them, to the large factory hunkered on the other side "—and then we're going to get my friend, Alcander, and then we're going to leave."

For his entire life, Jasper had thought of a good plan being the absolute difference between life and death. When he went on a mission, he had plans for his plans and backups for those, and if all failed, he had an eye on every exit sign available. "That… can't be your entire plan."

"Well," said Crimson, "it hits all the important bits. We just do whatever it is we need to do to accomplish all of those things in that order. Oh! But I should tell you, Alcander's really small." He made a gesture to indicate just how small, but surely must have exaggerated. His level palm was held barely above the height of his own elbow. "Dark hair. Pale. Really pale. He doesn't get out much, and he's scared of everything except his own shadow. So no shooting him. Anyone else is fair game."

"What if something goes wrong?" pressed Jasper.

Crimson's eyes glinted behind the shaded lenses. "We can only hope." His pocket buzzed again. He raised an eyebrow at Jasper. "I can't waste any more time with you. Come with me, stay here, go back to the house. Whatever. Your choice. But I have to go. Now."

Jasper had a hundred more questions, not the least of which was how many werespiders might be in there, but Crimson started across the cracked and faded pavement before he finished speaking. In a brief moment of fantasy, Jasper imagined just standing and watching him enter the building alone, then going back to the house and pouring himself a fresh cup of coffee. It was probably still hot. He would sit out this terrible plan, as he could have chosen to do thirty minutes ago before he'd insisted that he tag along. Crimson would either rescue his friend or he wouldn't. If he lived, the mission would proceed unhampered. If he died, good riddance.

Except…

If he died, he would take everything he knew with him. If he lived, Jasper felt like he'd never hear the end of it. He pushed his fingers through his curls, twisting at the ends and glaring after the retreating shape of the werespider as heat waves baking off the pavement rippled his shrinking silhouette.

If he went and risked his life in aid of the werespider *right now*, Crimson would almost certainly have to trust him. If, that was, they both lived.

"Fuck." Jasper sighed. He checked to make sure the safety on his gun was off and then started after him.

"This is a bad idea," he muttered out of the corner of his mouth when they were standing together in the long shadow at the foundry's base. It was constructed of sun-bleached brick and positioned well back from the main drag, like the owner had just forgotten about it during the Great Depression, and no one else had bothered with it since. He didn't see any movement in any of the windows, nor atop the towering roof; he felt the demons—dull and heavy in the middle, sharp and prickly on the outside of the sensation. Four, maybe. Or five. And at least one of them as strong as the demon beside him.

Yellow strips of caution tape stretched around the perimeter. Crimson plucked at one with a faint smile. "Al's way of dissuading visitors." He lifted it, gesturing him through, and Jasper ducked underneath, the demon letting the yellow tape fall behind them.

The entrance was nailed shut. Either of them could have torn it down, but not without making so much noise they would alert the whole building.

Keeping right up against the façade, they circled around to the loading bay on the opposite end and found one of the battered tin doors wedged permanently open. They stooped to peer inside.

Little could be seen beyond the end of the door's outline—a sliver of yellow-white sunlight in a vast square of darkness. "The little blonde one's name is Ivory," whispered Crimson. "She's the alpha. I'll pay attention to her. You pay attention to everything else. Okay?"

Jasper nodded an affirmative. While this was a better plan than the absolute nothing of five minutes earlier, it still wasn't great. It would have to suffice.

They slipped into the building together, with Crimson taking point since he could see clearly in the dark. The receiving floor was empty, but at the other end of it an unlocked door led to the assembly room. Here, broken skylights let in grayish beams of sunlight, revealing the shapes of large machines corroded beyond recognition. The scent of rot was set into the scattered pallets and forgotten crates, and it permeated the entire room. It reminded him a bit of Crimson's house, overfull and cluttered in a way that seemed intentionally confusing.

There was so much to look at that he almost didn't see the woman, except for the sensation he felt the moment she was in proximity.

She was straight as an arrow with long, fair legs and slender feet that tapered into sparkly silver polished toes. Her pale hair was straight and silky, brushing near her thighs as she watched her feet dangle from the railing of an overhead catwalk. A diamond anklet twinkled in the misty gray light.

She noticed them when they noticed her, and reclined on her hip with the banister casually held. "Oh, Crimson, darling, it's not meant to be a date. You didn't have to bring dinner."

"Oh boy, here we go." Crimson sighed. "Cut it with the ominous bullshit and just give me Alcander, okay?"

Ivory smiled coyly. "That's not part of the game."

"Ivory, darling." He spoke through gritted teeth, a rumble underneath his words. "You're the only person I know who can make eternity feel like forever. And not in a good way." He was aiming one of his revolvers in her direction but hadn't yet moved to fire. "I don't wanna play. Go bother one of the others."

"I remember when you used to be fun." Ivory sighed. She slid off the banister, taking no care of the way her dress fluttered around her bare thighs, and bounced as she landed ballerina-like on the balls of her feet. She was standing very close to Crimson now, but he still didn't fire. "Before you got all wrapped up in this... mortal nonsense." She drew a step closer. "You can't keep living out here alone like this. You're losing touch with reality." She delicately touched the muzzle of the revolver with one finger, steering it a bit to the side, out of her face. "*And* going soft."

Jasper cleared his throat pointedly. "We're actually roommates now, so he's not really alone or anything."

Ivory blinked at him like she'd forgotten he was there. Her nostrils flared again, and a curious smile spread across her face. She raised her eyebrows at Crimson. "Is this why you don't want to play? Because you're in the middle of another game with this half-blood mortal?"

"Ivory, listen to me very carefully." With Crimson it was always hard to tell whether any emotion was genuine, so Jasper couldn't be sure if his concern was feigned, but he seemed in some confused way like he was trying to help her. His voice was flat and firm and lacking its usual theatrics. "You're out of balance. You're acting psychotic. I've got too much going on to deal with you right now. So give me back Alcander and leave."

Ivory grabbed hold of his lapel, leaning into him. "I like the new voice. You sound just like them."

Crimson peeled her fingers away and pushed her hand firmly down to her side. "Don't fuckin' touch me."

The female werespider's smile faded. She turned away from him, sulking. "Maybe you've forgotten how this works, Crim. You don't get to decide whether you want to participate or not." Her opalescent blue eyes focused with renewed interest on Jasper. He was trying to follow the only instruction Crimson had given him, which was to ignore her and to watch for trouble. He could feel the other demons nearby but couldn't pinpoint their locations; they stuck to the deep shadows, out of sight. Silent. "Neither do your friends."

Ivory took a menacing step in his direction, and Jasper toggled the muzzle of the gun towards her. "Stay back."

She stopped. "You smell strange."

Jasper wondered if all werespiders were this rude, or if it was just this bloodline. She took another step closer and Jasper's jaw clenched. His finger twitched. He held steady.

"I see why he's drawn to you," continued Ivory. "Ashy darkness all around—you glint through the shade. Shining. Faceted. Like a diamond."

"Uh," said Jasper. He looked awkwardly at Crimson, who only shrugged. "Thank you?"

"Distractions like you are no good for the game." Her shape blurred. He heard the rapid patter of her footsteps and on impulse drew his silver short sword instead. She drew twin sharp sais, long thin blades with pointed, curved wings above the leather-wrapped handles. The wing of one sai hooked under his blade, stopping the point inches from his face. She was gone before he had time to aim to fire. For a second too short to measure, he tried to follow the white blur of movement with his gun but could never get enough of a lead on her to ensure a hit. Then she was back, striking at him with both blades as he scrambled to keep the sword between him and the sais.

"You're fast," she commented. A flurry of movement, Jasper spun on his heel to keep her in his sights. The blades glanced off one another. Jasper stepped carefully, adjusting to defend a second time. There was no room to try for an opening.

The blades clashed again, this time locking at the hilts. She gave hers a twist, and his own sword was wrenched from his grip, clattering as it hit the cracked concrete floor.

She turned immediately from him, raising her blade as if she anticipated she would now have to defend. In truth, Jasper was expecting the same thing, wondering for the entire time why Crimson had not yet intervened.

The reason became apparent in the next moment as they both realized the same thing at the same time.

Crimson was no longer there.

"Fucking prick," breathed Jasper.

"You snake," hissed Ivory.

#

The game was as old as time. It had grown and it had changed both in scope and objective, the loose set of rules warping and morphing to let it evolve and adapt. To lose was to lose everything, and even victory often came bittersweet.

Though, at the crux of the matter, there was no winning and no losing. That would have indicated an end; the game always continued.

The foreman's office was above, lit like a beacon. A trap, obviously, but one that compelled him.

The maze of machinery on the floor below was silent and still. He could smell the others though, their unique scents intermingled with

Alcander's familiar one.

Crimson took two tentative steps across the catwalk. A barrage of poorly aimed gunfire erupted from his left and right, and he dipped quickly underneath the handrail, letting himself fall to the floor below.

Ivory's angry voice echoed behind him. He thought fleetingly of the half-blood again. It was a shame he was going to lose him. All of Ivory's nonsense about auras aside, he was interesting. A small curiosity in a world without mystery. A question without an answer. In many respects, the female werespider was right. Even on his worst days, the mortal was entertaining. Easy to rile up, but quick to cool, and sharp underneath his quiet exterior.

Crimson liked him.

But Alcander was part of his pack. The only one left. And thus, the only one who mattered.

There was a flicker of movement on his right. "There," whispered the Spider, and for one bloody moment all other thought was discarded. He knew only feral rage.

The werespider's name was Knox. Knox Ivory. Technically, he was his nephew, though he only considered this after he finished pulverizing his skull against the sharp corner of a circuit breaker box. There were little wisps of blue in his blood-matted black hair. The red soaked into the suede of his vest, turning it a deep, dark purple, like a fresh bruise. Crimson slammed his head once more into the box, then winged him over the conveyor belt.

Where Knox was, Tybalt was never far behind.

If the other half of Ivory's brood ever learned how to master a gun, Crimson had a feeling he was going to be in big trouble. Luckily for him, Ty never took well to ranged weapons, and he had ample time to step out of the way of the heavy battle-axe as it came crashing down from an overhead swing. He fired at the opening under his arm, and then it was Ty's turn to be lucky—lucky that gold-plated bullets were difficult to make and expensive to buy, and lucky also that Crimson was too lazy to bother with either scenario.

The lead still tore through him, striking both lungs and probably grazing his heart. He shuddered down to one knee with his fingers still wrapped around the axe. Crimson twirled the gun in his hand, catching it by the barrel, and brought the grip down on the back of the demon's skull with a resounding CRUNCH. Blood splashed against the sandalwood. Tybalt's grip relaxed. The axe clanged to the floor in the same moment its wielder did.

This wouldn't stop them for long, but Crimson didn't have the heart to put them down in a more permanent way. They could hardly be blamed for Ivory's decisions.

"That any sorta way to be treatin' your relatives, Crim?"

He looked up from the slumping form of Tybalt. The door to the foreman's office was open. Yellow light spilled down the grated stairwell and glinted off the curved blades of the scimitars—one silver-plated, the other gold. Crimson knew these swords, and he knew the man who was holding them.

Time had changed Obsidian in the purely cosmetic ways it often changed their kind. His dark hair was woven back into a plaited braid, with a faded stars and stripes bandana covering his brow. His eyes were as dark as Crimson's own, but smaller and meaner, his skin a slightly deeper shade of bronze. Two or three weeks of stubble cast a shadow down the sides of his face to his chin, where the facial hair grew longer and denser and forked into two short braids. He was dressed in a light denim vest held together by a patchwork of fabric squares and old band logos. Black fingerless gloves and dark blue jeans.

Crimson lowered the gun. "You look ridiculous."

Sid's mouth fell open. "*Me,* ridiculous? What're you s'posed t'be? A fuckin'... gothic cowboy?"

"And what are you doing with your voice? You got peanut butter on the roof of your mouth or something?"

"Says the guy who sounds like Humphrey Bogart fucking James Cagney. Why don'tcha go ahead an' call me a 'wiseguy,' Crims? I haven't heard that one in a few decades."

Crimson smiled despite himself. "Alright, that's it. Get your big, square Frankenstein head down here so I can punch you in the face."

Sid pointed with the tip of the gold-plated blade. "I ain't comin' down there. You c'mon and bring yerself up here."

Crimson sighed. He remembered he had liked this game once, back when the others were still alive. Maybe he even still would if circumstances were different, but involving Alcander was no fair.

Somewhere behind him, there was a loud, angry screech and the crackling crunch of sprouting legs. Their more beastly forms had voices as distinct from one another as their human shapes, albeit with much less exact forms of communication. Crimson recognized Ivory's and knew it meant his time was now up.

"Alright, man. If you insist." He fired twice at Obsidian.

The scimitars flashed and glinted with the clang and spark of whizzing lead meeting enchanted steel.

Stop playing around.

The voice was right, as usual. As the deflected bullets *pinged* away, Crimson drew the other revolver and unloaded in Sid's direction as he ran towards him. One of the shots ricocheted and caught him in the thigh with a hot sting.

The spider surged to the forefront of his mind. He tasted venom and felt a low rattling at the center of his being. Mild irritation blotted into fury.

Crimson turned and leapt upwards, grabbing hold of the metal scaffolding with one hand and pulling himself on top of it, putting himself halfway up to the foreman's office. The space only allowed for two steps back, and he took them before running forward to throw himself upwards, twisting in midair to get an extra little arc of height. The tip of one blade passed close to his eye with a searing blaze of pain that crossed his eyelid and skewered upward in a blinding gush of black blood, but his feet still found their way underneath him. As the tips of his boots touched the concrete, he lined up his shot, and as the heels settled down, he fired.

Obsidian's blade swiped a diagonal path in front of him, but this time the bullet outpaced the blade. It struck him in the gullet, where his supernaturally reinforced bones were thinnest. The round passed through in a spray of blood, and for a split second, Crimson imagined it must have struck his brain stem.

The swords slipped out of Sid's hands. He stumbled a step back and Crimson fired again, this time at his stomach. He heard him thumping backward down the stairs, and ran for the lighted office before he could decide whether the other spider would be getting back up.

"Alcander?" His scent was everywhere, most prominently in the thick, dark-reddish splotches splashed underneath a chair in the center of the room. It was vacant now, but the heavy iron cuffs still attached to its arms said more than he liked. Crimson called his name again, this time before he could stop himself.

A door at the back of the office, near but not quite behind the abandoned desk, was slightly cracked.

Crimson strode towards it and jerked it open, almost ripping it from its rusted hinges.

He sighed, relieved. *"There* you are." He stooped down to pick up the shape huddled on the floor.

Somewhere (behind him, maybe below him) Crimson heard a very soft click and smelt a very brief wisp of smoke.

Careless, murmured the Spider.

Then came the explosion.

#

That fucking prick.

In that moment, Jasper was almost as mad at himself as he was at the werespider. He should have known better than to trust him even a little.

Ivory came at him again, and Jasper felt the burn of her blade slicing the back of his hand. He moved fast enough to avoid losing any digits but not fast enough for his liking. He fired off another shot, which Ivory twisted to dodge; in the same motion he drew a knife from beneath his coat and threw it, seeing with satisfaction as the blade—unfortunately only silver-plated—sank into her shoulder. His satisfaction was short lived. She ripped the blade out with a shout and looked at him with blood-red eyes.

Fuck this. Jasper was not going to get himself killed for the werespider, especially not after he'd abandoned him in a warehouse full of demons. Keeping the female in his sights, Jasper started to inch his way back towards the entrance. Two large rooms were between him and the outside, and after that a long stretch of parking lot between him and the car. Ivory was fast, but there was only one of her, and if he could hold her off (or better yet, *kill* her), he was sure he could make it.

Even as the options for escape began to form in his mind, the sound of gunfire from the room beyond reminded him they had come here to find someone who was in trouble. Very *real* trouble, if this female werespider was anything to judge by. Crimson deserved whatever happened to him, but did the person he'd come here to save deserve it as well?

Jasper wanted to believe so. But he wasn't *sure*.

"What's wrong, little hybrid? Scared?"

More gunfire.

He feinted toward the exit, and Ivory came running after him, determined to cut him off before he could reach the door, but Jasper was already going in the opposite direction, his eyes shining white with the effort. He sprayed a short burst of suppressing fire behind him, and, with a screech and a sound like a dozen bones breaking, the woman pursuing him burst into a gigantic white spider. Her eight long, thick legs ended in deadly points, and her fangs were dripping with dark black-red venom. He'd never seen a werespider before, not in real life.

Jasper was so distracted by the giant spider on his heels that he did not see the other werespider until he was nearly upon him. The Hunter only had time to see a flash of red eyes, outstretched arms, and teeth bared in a snarl before the spider, still in his human form, grabbed him, hands fisting into his jacket. The spider tried to pull him from his feet, and the two of them grappled for dominance. His back hit a tall piece of machinery, the rusting and rotting metal screeching at the impact. It was so precarious Jasper was sure it was going to fall on the two of them, but the demon's grip was unyielding, slamming him back again.

The Hunter slugged him in the jaw, once, twice, three times, and the werespider's grip slipped just enough for him to yank his jacket out. Jasper took several steps back, away from the new spider and the hunk of metal, raising his gun as his eyes searched for Ivory.

There. She was coming at him, a ghost in the shadows, made of snapping teeth and spiny legs. He aimed to fire—

A light was coming from nowhere and everywhere all at once, flaring like a muzzle flash turned up to eleven.

The explosion threw him on his back, the resounding *bang* hitting his eardrums as his back hit the floor, sucking the air from his lungs. For a moment he couldn't breathe, couldn't see, couldn't move. And then the light faded, returning him to the dark factory, the ringing in his ears fading to a tolerable squeal. He looked around, getting his bearings.

The great white spider was scrambling towards him at an alarming speed. He rolled over, got up on his elbow, and, using it as a support, steadied the gun, and squeezed the trigger.

The cartridge clicked empty. There had been no opportunity to reload.

Her fangs bore down towards his face even as something else dropped from above.

The creature's many legs bowed outward. Her abdomen hit the cement and her fangs struck the floor, cracking away chips of concrete. Jasper pushed himself away from the pool of viscous fluid that the pressure milked from her fangs.

A smaller, darker spider was latched on at the back of her thorax, his long, banded red-and-black legs braced on the floor as he strained to tear her head off. She twisted onto her back, wrapped her stouter white legs around him like a cage, and wrested him free long enough to regain her footing, but the other came scuttling back with force, and the two clashed together with a shared, echoing screech.

Jasper made it back to his feet, slapped a fresh magazine into his gun, and ran toward the thrashing tangle of legs and fangs.

He had never seen *any* werespider except in pictures, which he realized now was nowhere near the same as the real thing. Their size was surprising, and the way they moved made him want to crawl out of his skin.

The distinct red markings patterned throughout the otherwise jet-black coloration of the smaller spider seemed to speak for themselves. Given their human sizes, he would have thought Crimson would be bigger than Ivory, but that wasn't the case. The white spider was noticeably larger and stronger. She lashed at him with her legs and fangs, opening gory wounds in his black hide. Crimson was fighting back, getting a few shots in of his own, their many-legged bodies rolling and fighting and hissing together, but as the fight went on, it became apparent to Jasper that Crimson would lose.

Golden bullets were expensive and hard to come by, but Jasper had connections and wasn't going to put himself in a werespider's space without some protection. His standard ammunition was a mixed load of lead, iron, silver and, yes, gold. He was a little concerned that he'd hit Crimson, the pair of them were so entwined, though not concerned enough to hold his fire. Aiming for the largest part of the white spider, he unloaded.

Several shots missed, the spiders were too quick, but a couple hit home with a spray of scarlet, shocking against the white. Judging by the unearthly screech the spider that was Ivory gave, he thought one of them was gold.

The segmented legs drew close around her torso. She scuttled back crab-like, wheeled around, and fled for the shadows, leaving a trail of bright blood in her wake. The air was still thick with ash, and he lost sight of her very quickly. He looked towards Crimson... and swore loudly, jumping a step back despite himself.

It was lucky he had unloaded into Ivory. *Anything* that size would have been terrifying to have in such close proximity, but the spider was a special case. A gigantic monstrosity that seemed to have scuttled directly from an arachnophobe's worst nightmare. As it stood on the tips of its toes, the creature's two largest eyes were nearly level with his own. A smaller pair tapered back on either side.

It made a soft sound that contained no words but still sounded like a question. The lower half of its almost-face was two great, curved chelicerae with sharp translucent tips poking out of the tail ends. In addition to the crescent-shaped mark he saw earlier, there was a splash of red in the space just above its huge eerily glowing eyes and patterned throughout its long legs. The little spines tufted near the edges of the second set of eyes were likewise red. It chittered again, still with that upward inflection.

Jasper realized he'd squeezed the trigger of the gun twice, just on reflex.

The spider reared back with its front legs raised. Before Jasper had time to properly panic about what was certain to be an incoming strike, there was a crackling sound. The front legs shortened, the spines lying back then falling flat as the blackened skin underneath lightened to bronze. The fangs slipped grotesquely upward and receded into an upper lip that already seemed too human. While the hair covering the rest of the creature thinned, the tufts on its head grew longer, thicker, and softer. The spare legs bent inward like broken branches. They seemed simply to fold themselves out of existence. In a span of seconds, the spider was no more.

Crimson stood before him, entirely naked. His smooth bronze chest and toned arms were covered in open wounds and still-bleeding gashes. Jasper's gaze slid down to his muscled abdomen to the dark hair beneath his navel and then, cheeks burning furiously, skipped away. The white spider did not re-emerge from the shadows.

"Alcander," Crimson said flatly. Jasper followed his gaze. A small shape was huddled at the top of the stairs, unmoving, unbreathing. If this was Alcander, Crimson *had* exaggerated his height, but only just.

In the surrounding darkness there was another screech.

"Get him," said Crimson. "*Hurry,*" he added, striding away from Jasper to pick something off the ground. His long leather jacket. Somewhere nearby something heavy and metal, suddenly disturbed, clanged against the floor.

Jasper sprinted up the steps, grabbed hold of the unconscious man, and hefted him off the floor. Up close, he was almost certainly dead. There was no color in his face unless you counted the blue-black of the veins that shone through his pale skin. Yet he stirred slightly. In the dark it was hard to tell, but it seemed his eyelashes parted a sliver.

"Jasper?"

At the realization that the man recognized him, he felt a cold chill, like icy fingers creeping down his spine, but that was not all he felt. A peculiar little twist he knew too well, strangely soft, hesitant, almost uncertain. And then the realization that this man was no man at all.

His lips moved again, trying to make words, and this time fangs showed.

A fucking vampire.

Behind him, he heard the twirl of a cylinder and the unmistakable *click-click* of a hammer being struck. Then a booming crash. "Knox and Tybalt," called Crimson, but Jasper couldn't tell if it was an explanation, or if he was trying to reason with the others again. Angry at being misled but unable to complain, he scooped the vampire the rest of the way up and made for the exit.

Chapter Seven

—

The Good Doctor

The three of them booked it out of the warehouse and to the car Crimson had left running in the parking lot. Jasper had barely thrown the vampire in the back and gotten in the passenger side before the werespider stepped on the gas, firing them out into traffic, leaving the burning smell of tires in their wake. Jasper slammed his door closed.

"You just *left* me back there!" Jasper exclaimed, bracing his hand against the dash as they tore around a corner. "That bitch nearly killed me!"

"But she didn't," Crimson pointed out. He'd gathered most of his clothes, including his jacket and shirt and jeans, but was missing his boots. For the first time Crimson turned the full force of his brilliant smile at him, and Jasper couldn't help it, he was smiling back, thinking it was no surprise at all that Crimson could get almost anyone to give him almost anything. Realizing what he was doing, Jasper looked away, checking the side mirror to see if they were being followed. If they were, he couldn't see them, and he didn't keep looking for very long.

The wound on the back of his hand was bleeding pretty good, so after Jasper managed to get his seatbelt buckled, he dug around one-handed in his backpack, pulling out a cloth roll of bandages. It would have to be cleaned later, but for now Jasper just wanted to stop the bleeding. He wrapped his hand until he couldn't see the blood through it and tied it off with his teeth.

"So what the hell was that about?"

"That," said Crimson, "was the traditional werespider game of

Hostage. You should really just be glad she didn't wanna play War."

"She tried to *kill me*," insisted Jasper. And not just him. Crimson too.

"Yeah, Ivory plays for keeps."

"Are you hurt?" asked Jasper, because it felt like he should ask, not that Crimson had asked him.

"Oh yeah." The jacket was torn at the shoulder. A thick, dark layer of scabbed and bruised flesh could be seen through the popped seam. Puncture wounds on the side of his throat leaked a diluted mixture of clear venom and blood. Presently, they stopped and began to scab as well. "Mostly just the one on my face." It was a black band of poisoned blood on his forehead, a souvenir from the scuffle with Obsidian. He kept pawing the streaming black blood away from his eyes with the back of his hand, like a cat trying to clean its face. "I didn't expect him to take a shot at my head, y'know? I mean, Ivory, yeah. That's her prerogative or whatever. But *Sid*. I've known him for millenniums. Usually he's not such a fuckin' dick."

"Oh," replied Jasper. It took a moment for this off-the-cuff comment to sink in. Charlie said that records of the werespider started surfacing in 1840, so he knew he'd been around for nearly two centuries, which was a longer amount of time than Jasper wanted to imagine living. But… "Millenniums?" he repeated. "Plural?"

"I think he was mad cuz I said he had a Frankenstein head," continued Crimson. "But in all fairness—"

The man in the back seat groaned softly, and Crimson turned the radio down. "You alright back there?"

No response.

Jasper twisted around in his seat. Vampires came in all shapes, sizes, and colors, but he had never seen one that looked quite like this one. As Crimson had described, he was very small and somewhat delicate looking. At present, he was wrapped in a lab coat stained with grime and dark splotches of vampire blood, a pair of plastic goggles pushed up on his forehead, the band tangled in messy strands of dry-looking hair. He groaned again with the motion of the vehicle and tried to roll over.

The trash underneath him crinkled.

The back seat was a cluttered mess of empty fast-food bags, crushed tin cans, soda-caked Styrofoam cups, and used napkins. One of the napkins was stuck to the vampire's sallow cheek. He tried to brush it away, but when it continued to stick, his eyes slowly came unclosed. They were the pale grayish pink of a summer orchid in bloom, the whites darted with shocking red veins. They slowly took in the surrounding vehicle. The mounds of scattered trash, the young man twisted around to look at him from the front seat, the cigarette-scarred suede with bits of stuffing fighting through the burn marks.

With an ugly gagging noise, he sat up suddenly and quickly ripped the napkin off his cheek. Then scrambled into the corner of the seat, where the majority of the mess had earlier fallen out of the car. He was attempting to simultaneously move a pile of crumpled newspapers out from underneath him while also grasping blindly for the seatbelt over his shoulder. The swerving dance of rapidly cycling acceleration and deceleration as Crimson wedged the car into every open slot ahead of them and jumped between lanes of traffic like he thought he was in a race wasn't helping matters.

The vampire asked a dazed question, but his voice was too soft to hear over the chortle of the old engine and the rumble of New York's rush hour through the open windows. Jasper cranked the radio all the way down to silent and leaned cautiously closer. "What?"

The vampire stilled but for the external swaying of the vehicle. He was gripping the buckle of the seatbelt so hard that the tips of his porcelain-white fingers turned even whiter. "Where am I?"

"Relax, Al, you're safe." They came to a section of extreme congestion, and Crimson was forced to slow and inch along with other angry-looking motorists.

Alcander finally managed to snap the buckle.

Cursing, Crimson threw the car in park, popped open his door, and started to climb out.

Jasper realized what he was doing and grabbed his elbow. "Hey, you can't just leave a car sitting in traffic."

"Why not? It's not mine."

"Well, because! You just can't. It's in the way—you gotta at least pull to the side or something."

Crimson shook off his arm and got out of the car anyway, opening the back door and pulling the vampire out after him. Behind them a driver laid on their horn. Crimson gestured to the extremely frail-looking demon clinging to his arm for stability, then flipped the guy the bird.

Jasper grabbed his backpack and, with an apologetic shrug to the guy now trapped behind the Buick, followed the pair of demons.

They walked several blocks, taking turns at random and cutting through alleys and parking lots. Crimson basically carried the vampire, holding the smaller demon under his arm, pressed close to his side. Jasper didn't think Alcander was a fan of that based on the shaking and panicked whispers he heard from him, but Crimson did not let him go.

"Hey, where are we going?" Jasper asked. Crimson ignored him, turning down yet another alleyway. Jasper tried again, louder this time. "Crimson, where are we going?"

"Dunno 'til we get there."

"Seriously?"

"I'm not dealin' with those two again today. I'm too fuckin' old for their shit."

"Why don't we just go back to your house?" The way Crimson talked about it, the house was a death trap. Remembering the swinging blades he'd narrowly avoided being chopped in half with, Jasper agreed.

The werespider shook his head. "No good, they know too much. Better to lie low somewhere they can't be bothered to look."

They entered the lobby of a small hotel, where he shoved the vampire towards Jasper and told them both to wait while he got them a room. Both the Hunter and the vampire began to protest, but the werespider was off to shine his eyes at the pretty brunette behind the front desk before they could get too far.

"Are you, uh, okay?" Jasper asked after a moment.

The vampire was hugging himself tight, visibly shaking. He was even paler in the fluorescent lights, his veins dark beneath his paper-thin skin. The bloodied lab coat and goggles made it look like he was wearing a Halloween costume. Mad scientist/vampire. Jasper saw now that he had several wounds and gashes on his face and neck, as well as some on his arms and chest, based on the blood darkening the white coat like ink. They should have healed by now or at least been on the way, but they remained open and seeping, and when the vampire glanced quickly at him, he saw that his eyes were still pink. The vampire looked away immediately, almost as soon as their eyes met, and sidestepped to put some space between them.

"I am alright." He stole another glance in Jasper's direction, then away again. "Thank you for asking."

"We haven't really been formally introduced." He held out his hand to shake. "I'm Jasper."

Alcander looked down at his palm like he had just offered him a dead fish, and then crossed his arms over his chest. "Sorry, it is nothing personal. I just do not like to be touched."

"Oh," said Jasper, snapping his hand back down to his side. He'd hunted vampires nearly his entire life. They were usually very sensual creatures. *Usually* being the key word.

This one seemed to be exhibiting symptoms of severe blood dehydration, which he'd only ever seen happen to vampires in captivity. Usually such demons were vicious, bloodthirsty things, incapable of rational thought and driven by killer instinct. Again, *usually.* "Sorry."

"It is alright." He smiled weakly, his lips pressed together to hide the fangs. "Alcander Owen, MD. Most people just call me Al. Since you fall into that category, I guess you can too." The warmth in his voice was surprising, considering the outward chill of his demeanor.

"You used to be a doctor?" asked Jasper, his eyes going again to the bloody gash on his cheek. For a split second, he thought of the small strange werewolf he had met in The Crystal Ballroom just the night before.

"I *am* a doctor," replied Alcander.

"Alright, kids." Crimson came strolling back from the desk with two sets of keys twirling on his finger. "The bad news is I could only get the one room, so now I'm stuck with the two of you. Good news is, the keys are actually keys instead of those little card things." He dropped one into the breast pocket of Alcander's lab coat, then flipped the other back into his palm and put it in his own. "Oh, and the lady at the front desk says that your, uh… cosplay is really good. Am I sayin' that right? Cos-play?"

"I would really like to lie down," said Alcander.

"We're on the twentieth. You need me to carry you?"

"I can make it the twenty feet to the elevator," replied Alcander.

"Oh." Crimson looked uncomfortable. "I'll meetcha up there, then."

The two went their separate ways. Jasper didn't feel like climbing twenty fucking stories, and he couldn't understand why Crimson would either, so he opted to go with Alcander. The elevator had to stop several times, letting passengers on and off at almost every level. When they made it to the room, the door was already cracked open, and Crimson was already inside, sprawled out on the furthest bed and sipping a small bottle from the minibar while he channel-surfed.

The room was like the majority of hotel rooms. The matched double beds were covered in navy blue comforters with lighter blue sheets and pillowcases. The walls were a bland, inoffensive beige, beset above each wooden headboard with pictures of pale sunflowers. A varnished nightstand with nothing more than a grayish phone, a pad of paper, and a menu stand separated the beds, a double-headed light fixture just above it. There was a small mirrored closet beside the bathroom, near the door, and a long dresser at the head of the room, upon which rested an old tube television. In the corner, a slightly dusty air-conditioning unit labored next to a small lumpy love seat, its back to the drawn vertical blinds of a large, long window roughly the length of the room.

Jasper thoughtlessly dropped his bag on the free bed, but then felt peculiarly guilty when Alcander limped past him and collapsed on the love seat.

"Not even gonna take a shower, Al? Wow, you really *must* be sick."

The vampire didn't respond, his entire focus seemingly consumed by clumsily attempting to undo the laces of his shoes with hands that shook too hard to keep a stable grip. Crimson's smile faded. He grabbed one of the pillows off his bed and dropped it on the arm of the couch. "I'll keep watch. You get some sleep, yeah?"

"Yeah," mumbled Alcander. Without another word, he lay back on the love seat, then rolled over so that he was facing in towards the upholstery.

"So," said Crimson, throwing himself back on the bed, "drinks and movies?"

"I think I'm actually gonna have a shower," said Jasper. "And, uh... I'm kinda beat, so..."

"Yeah, yeah, I get it. I'll just sit here in the dark. Alone."

Jasper sighed. "You're so dramatic." He grabbed a fresh change of clothes out of his bag. "I'll watch *one movie* with you. *One.* And zero drinks. Then I'm going to bed."

#

The next day, Alcander did not wake.

He was still curled up on the couch where he fell asleep. When Jasper gently prodded him to try to wake him, he felt stiff and cold, and he did not stir in the slightest. Crimson tried the same tactic (a little less gently) and then swore. "He always does this to himself. I hate it."

"What's wrong with him?" Jasper immediately wished he hadn't asked. He already knew the answer, after all. He'd seen it in the holding cells before. After the bloodthirsty animalistic rage, the next stage of blood dehydration involved a comatose state resembling death. The professors called it "suspended animation" or sometimes "emergency hibernation." In this way the vampire could continue to survive even though it was on the cusp of starvation.

"*This* is what happens when an idiot vampire decides he's too noble to spill human blood," replied Crimson. "I told him that synthetic blood was a lousy idea."

"But that's a *great* idea," insisted Jasper. "If a vampire could survive on synthetic blood, it wouldn't be nece—did you just say Alcander doesn't drink human blood?" He couldn't believe this. A demon could wear many different masks, from the friendly to the monstrous. Some were more mild-mannered, and others more cautious, but when push came to shove, the demon in them always won out. "At all?"

"He's been clean for ages. Course, all that means is that he's no longer capable of taking care of himself. One little skirmish and he's a fucking potato." Crimson jerked the comforter off the bed and threw it angrily over him, tucking it tightly to the contours of his small frame and pulling the hem up so it covered his hair. He was muttering under his breath the whole time, but not in any language Jasper knew. He only caught the last bit. "For a genius, you're sure pretty dumb."

Crimson lit a cigarette as he rose. "Keep an eye on Al for a little bit. I'll be back."

Jasper immediately did not like the sound of this. "Where are you going?"

"To solve the problem."

"We passed a hospital on the way here." He and Charlie had spoken numerous times about how Jasper was going to have to deal with the demons' vices in order to stay in their good graces, but now that he was faced with actually doing it, he felt like he had undergone no preparation whatsoever. It was one thing to talk philosophically about the "greater good," another to look it dead in the eye and then stand aside to let the smaller evils go unnoticed. "You could probably steal a few units of blood and—"

"We're a little past that. Al hasn't had a drop of real human blood in, like, ten years. He's *dying*. If he sleeps much longer, he won't wake up."

"Vampires sometimes hibernate for hundreds of years," argued Jasper. "Besides, it won't be any faster to—"

"Alcander is not *Dracula*," said Crimson flatly. "Healthy vampires *can* survive in hibernation for a long, long time, but Al isn't healthy, and Sid and Ivory did a lot of damage. He needs warm, fresh blood. Not some lump of goo that's been stagnating on ice, in a plastic bag."

"But—"

"Jasper, this isn't a debate. Al *has* to feed. I am going to go get him food. End of story." He made for the door but paused with his hand on the knob. "I don't have to tell you that if ya hurt him, I'll hunt ya down and kill ya, do I?"

The werespider was a great deal more dangerous than he let on, and a great deal more reckless than seemed maintainable. Jasper suspected it would be wise to take the threat seriously. "I'll keep an eye on him until you get back, but I don't want anything to do with this afterwards."

"Deal," replied Crimson, and then he was out the door.

#

Crimson stood on the other side of the door, just out of view of the peephole, listening carefully.

The half-blood had come out of nowhere, and he asked an awful lot of questions. The werespider was more than a little suspicious about his motives: why he was here, why he had chosen to stay, what his stake was in all this. He claimed to be a mercenary, and he had the battle prowess to back up that claim, but not the disposition.

Yet he seemed harmless. Hell, better than harmless. Helpful. *Nice*, even.

Nice was never a good sign. Crimson would know. *He* was nice, after all.

Crimson waited outside the door for several more minutes, poised for the other to cut and run, to make some telling phone call, to give himself away.

He finally did hear the sound of Jasper's voice, but it didn't take the form of the panicked phone call he was expecting. Brow furrowing, he leaned closer and listened more carefully, certain he had heard incorrectly. "*Maycomb was an old town, but it was a tired, old town.*" He knew this from somewhere. A book? He remembered the copy of *To Kill a Mockingbird* he had seen the half-blood carrying or reading on numerous occasions, and the pieces clicked into place.

He's reading to him.

Crimson chewed the inside of his cheek, thinking. If it was a ploy, it was an elaborate one. Unlikely, but not impossible. He shook his head. Whether he was on the level or not, Jasper would have to be crazy to do anything to endanger himself right now. That included harming Alcander.

Still, it would be better not to stray too far, just in case.

He made for the stairwell.

It was late in the evening, and on a weeknight besides. Even if it weren't, he doubted he would have encountered anyone on the stairs. The mortals had gotten so lazy that many of them couldn't climb two flights, let alone twenty, and certainly not voluntarily.

When he reached the ground floor, he opened the door and looked out across the lobby.

The receptionist at the desk was different than the one who had checked him in. He found this a relief. The other had been too nice, her smile too sweet, too genuine. Maybe this one was nice too, but he didn't plan on finding out. Now was the time to clear his mind, not clutter it up with nonsense questions about whether the woman on the other side of the room was the best candidate for prey. A fox may as well debate which hen deserved to live or die.

Taking a breath, he centered himself and felt the strange preternatural magic somewhere within radiate up through his vocal cords and onto his lips. "Excuse me? Miss?"

The woman at the desk looked up from her magazine. Her hair was long and curly with unevenly bleached ends that suggested it had once been short and blond. She stood up with a standard customer-service smile already on her face. "Can I help you?"

"Yeah, could you lend me a hand?" His voice was saccharine sweet, neither too loud nor too soft. "My buddy and I were having drinks and he kinda overdid it. I think he's okay. I just need some help getting him down the stairs."

She smiled. "You guys should use the elevator next time. It's dangerous to take the stairs anyways. You never know who could be hiding there." She scrawled a note that read "back in 5" on a piece of notebook paper, folded it at the base so that it would stand upright, and started in his direction. Her smile had changed. Less customer-service friendly, more genuinely intrigued. "We'll have to be quick. No one comes in at this time of night, but I still gotta watch the desk."

"It won't take long," Crimson promised. She was within arm's reach now, but Crimson didn't reach out or grab her. He smiled his best smile, leaned closer, and looked deep into her light brown eyes. The expression melted from her face. She stared back up at him, frozen, unblinking. Up close, underneath the concealer, her eyes had the tired look that invariably found its way into the gaze of every nightshift worker. "Sleep," said Crimson.

Her knees buckled. She swayed and fell against him. He scooped her up in his arms and started back the way he had come. "Sorry, sweetheart, it's nothing personal."

#

Jasper decided to read to Alcander, mostly to keep his mind off Crimson and what Crimson was doing. It only partially worked, serving to distract him from checking the clock on his cell phone every thirty seconds, but not to quell the uneasy tightness in his throat and chest. It felt like he had wandered into a bad dream. He tried not to think about it.

After what was undoubtedly the longest fifteen minutes of his entire young life, there came the sound of a key rattling in the lock, then a loud, insistent knocking. Jasper set the book aside and went to the door to look through the peephole. Crimson was on the other side. Something was bundled in his arms. Jasper saw long curly hair, ruby red lips, the soft curve of a cheekbone. He flinched.

The knock came again, much longer and angrier. "Coming!" said Jasper, even though he was already standing right in front of the door. It couldn't be delayed any longer. He grabbed his backpack and shoved the copy of *To Kill A Mockingbird* inside. Throwing the deadbolt open, he jerked open the door, still taking great pains not to look too carefully at the person the werespider was carrying.

"I decided to go with—"

"Don't." Jasper didn't want to know any more details, feeling like he already knew too much. "I'm gonna go for a walk. I'll be back later." He cut around the demon still standing in the doorway and walked to the elevator at the other end of the hall. He didn't breathe until the doors had pinged shut and the lift was moving downward. Then he breathed fast and hard.

He couldn't stop imagining the vampire's fangs sunk in the woman's throat. She would die right there... and then he would have to go back to the room and sleep right where she'd been murdered, like nothing had ever happened.

He needed to call Charlie.

His cell phone was in his hand and he was dialing the number when it occurred to him he didn't know what he would say. That the werespider was behaving exactly the way they had expected him to? That wouldn't change anything, would it?

The elevator came to a stop and the doors whooshed open to reveal the vacant lobby. *Completely* vacant, he noticed, as there wasn't even a clerk attending the desk. Head down, Jasper walked quickly out into the street.

Chapter Eight

—

Old Friends

Jasper wasn't familiar with this part of town, so he picked a direction and went with it, walking until he found a coffee chain with its lights on. He could count the people inside on one hand. Three girls sat at a table on his left, sitting close together and drinking chocolatey frozen drinks that Jasper wanted to try even though his teeth hurt just thinking about it. The girls looked over at him when he entered and quickly turned back towards each other, talking low and fast. On the opposite side of the café was a homeless man, his head resting on his folded arms, a small coffee sitting beside him. He did not stir.

Jasper went to the counter and looked up at the menu. The options were a little overwhelming. While he was sure he'd love a large caramel-mocha frappawhatever with whipped cream and sprinkles, he decided to keep it simple. The single barista behind the counter asked him what he wanted, and he ordered a medium vanilla-flavored coffee, taking it to a table near the window.

He dug his novel out of his backpack and started to read, looking up a moment later when the scraping of the chair opposite him drew his attention to his visitor. One of the girls sat down on the other side of the table. She smiled at him, looking nervous. She had long dark hair and a tight white sweater. Jasper smiled back.

"Hi," he said.

"Hi. Um, so, my friends and me were wondering… Well, we come here a lot. Like, a lot a lot. And we've never seen you before, so…"

"So… do I come here often?"

The girl laughed, a blush appearing on her cheeks. "Well, when you say it like that, it sounds really lame."

"It's not lame," Jasper said, smiling. "It's... cute. And no, I don't come here often. First time, actually. But I think I like it here. Maybe I'll come back."

The girl smiled back at him, that blush still coloring her face. She was pretty, and he was thankful for the distraction she offered. "I'm Tiffany," she said.

"I'm Jasper."

Sudden movement drew his attention to the other side of the café. The homeless man, who Jasper thought was sleeping, was now standing, and though he was wearing dark sunglasses, Jasper was sure he was looking directly at him. His hair was dirty and lank, hanging past his ears in mats that looked more gray than blond. His clothes were in the same sorry state, looking like they'd been worn for weeks without a wash, faded with dust and filled with tears and holes. He wore a green army jacket that looked far too big for him, with what looked like blood dried on the collar. Jasper's stomach, which had been uneasy since he left the hotel, twisted horribly, pulling a gasp from his throat. The man—no, no, not a man—smiled, his lips pulled tight against his teeth.

"What's wrong?" Tiffany asked, looking over her shoulder at the other man. "Do you... know him?"

"I gotta go," Jasper managed, grabbing his bag from beside his chair and rushing out the door. *Please don't follow me, please don't follow.*

Jasper was so distracted that he wasn't paying attention to where he was going and ended up running into someone on the street, shoulder jarring shoulder. He stuttered out an apology and went to turn away, but strong hands grabbed his shoulders, holding him in place. "Hey. Hey, what's going on?"

Jasper's rushing mind cleared enough that he finally saw whom he'd run into. Crimson was still holding his shoulders, frowning at him. Jasper wondered dizzily why he was here and not with Alcander. Was he looking for him? Spying on him? Jasper was surprised to find he was relieved more than anything to have him here.

"We gotta go," Jasper insisted, pulling out of the werespider's grasp. When Crimson did not immediately follow, he grabbed the sleeve of his jacket, pulling him after him. They rushed down the street and around a corner; Jasper kept looking back to see if they were being followed. Soon they came to the entrance of a park, not Central but one of the little ones scattered around town. Jasper had gotten himself all turned around, but he thought that if they cut through here, they'd be able to get back to the hotel. He wanted badly to get out of the open.

Very little of the city's light reached them once they were under the dense canopy of trees. Jasper liked that about the parks in New York, that it was almost like stepping into a whole different world, one that could almost be wild if not for the asphalt walkways and well-kept grasses. Of course, he liked that during the day. At night the lack of light left him nearly blind and he had to rely more on his other senses. The sounds of the city were muted but still there, partially blocking any sounds that might come from the park. For the first time Jasper acknowledged the value in having a demon on his side—the darkness wouldn't blind him, and his hearing was probably fine enough that he would be able to discern any noises Jasper couldn't hear.

"Okay, hold on." Crimson came to a halt, and since Jasper was still holding onto his jacket, he had to stop too. "What's going on? You're completely freaking out. It ain't the feeding thing, is it? Because I told you that—" The werespider froze, sniffing curiously at the night air. His eyes narrowed, a hint of red showing through. "It smell kinda like a shallow grave out here to you?"

"Please, can we just go?" Jasper looked again over their shoulders, back at the streetlights and the buildings. He didn't see anything, but that didn't mean nothing was there. He wished he were calmer; he couldn't make any sense of the knots in his stomach.

"Not 'til you tell me what's going on."

"Crimson, please. I wanna get out of—ah." Jasper broke off with a soft hiss; the pain in his stomach spiked, but that was only part of it. He couldn't remember not having this sense, the innate ability to be able to sense demons. Charlie had never been able to give him a straight answer when he asked about it, but Jasper figured it was some recessive kind of psychic ability or magic. He could even usually use the sense to tell what sort of demon was near and how close. Vampires felt a little different than werewolves, and now that he knew Crimson a bit better, he thought he could tell apart werespiders as well. This feeling, though not entirely unfamiliar, was of something else, something he hadn't encountered in nearly three years. Something he hadn't encountered since Seattle.

But it couldn't be. That thing was dead.

"Fuck," the Hunter cursed softly as if pained. Jasper drew his gun without thinking, holding it with a loose, sure grip. The trees weren't as thick here as elsewhere; some of the second-degree light from the city illuminated part of the area, turning the leaves silver and gold in the afterglow. Movement at the tree line caught his sight, and he swung up his gun, firing in one fluid motion. The shadow, the figure, whatever it was, was quick, darting out of the line of fire, across the path to the opposite tree line. Jasper lined up another shot—

The figure stopped before he disappeared, hesitating. The light caught on his hair, turning it white. Jasper's finger was on the trigger, but he couldn't move a muscle. The figure's head turned towards him, pitch-black eyes focused on Jasper's. A slow grin grew on his face, showing a dozen pointed silver teeth. "Jazz?"

"Jazz?" echoed Crimson. "Friend of yours?"

"No."

"I'll be damned," said the demon. "It really is you. How long has it been? What are you doing here?"

"Sure seems to think so. Maybe you should get a closer look."

"Shut up," Jasper snapped, though it was difficult to know whom he was telling off, Crimson or the other demon, the one who was taking a step towards them. Jasper raised the gun again, pointing it at the demon's chest. He wouldn't miss twice.

The demon frowned. "What are you doing, Jazz? Don't you know who I am?"

"No," Jasper repeated.

"It's me. It's Adam."

A crack spilt down through Jasper's spine. "*No.*"

"Alright, kids, break it up." Crimson was not stupid enough to step entirely in the way of Jasper's gun, but he did step forward, moving so that Jasper was behind his shoulder, partially blocking him from view. "I think it's time for you to take off." His eyes flashed blood red, and he moved his coat so the demon could see the heavy revolvers at his sides. "This is the only warning you get. Leave now or I'll kill you before Jazz even has a chance."

The demon hesitated and seemed to look at Crimson, but it was hard to be sure with those fathomless black eyes. Jasper remembered them before they looked that way, bright and sparkling blue, full of life and light that shone with good nature. The gun shook just slightly in his hand and he felt sick. How had this happened? How did Adam *find* him?

"It's got nothing to do with you."

"Sure it does. I'm the guy who's going to be disposing of your body in about five seconds." Crimson's posture changed, back straightening, shoulders squaring. "Five. Four. Three…"

"Crimson, don't." Jasper finally managed to speak through the suffocating ball of guilt in the back of his throat.

Crimson shot him a glare. "So you're friends after all, then?"

"We aren't friends."

"Don't be like that, Jazz," whined Adam. "I just wanna talk to you." He took a ghoulish step forward, still grinning. His teeth were horrible, like a thousand razor blades crammed together, nothing at all like the smile Jasper remembered from before. Easy. Carefree. Kind. "I feel like it's the least you could do, since you got me killed and everything."

The werespider beside him rumbled like a dog about to snap. Adam paid him no mind. He was almost close enough to reach out and touch him, but not quite. He held out his hands, palms up. "Are you really gonna shoot a guy with no gun?"

"I will," said Crimson. The werespider drew like lightning striking, with the boom and crash of gunfire as the thunder that followed. Jasper didn't see the bullet, but he saw the cavernous hole it left in Adam's chest. Adam staggered, almost catching his balance, which was when the second and third shots struck him on the inner shoulder, spinning him almost all the way around and leaving room for the fourth shot, which hit him square in the back and dropped him at last to his knees. Crimson thumbed back the hammer and advanced towards the kneeling demon with the gun pointed at the back of his head.

Jasper should have been glad, but in that moment all he felt was blind panic. He was going to have to see it happen all over again, was going to be involved again, responsible for it. Again.

"Crimson, stop." He holstered his gun and forced his legs to move. On the ground, Adam gave a watery laugh. He turned onto his hip and stared up at the revolver with his jet-black eyes. Crimson squeezed the trigger twice just as Jasper got hold of his wrist and jerked it sharply away.

Two scorching holes appeared in the grass behind Adam. He barely blinked. He planted his feet firmly on the ground and threw himself up onto them, then started to lurch away in wide, stiff-legged steps. The bushes rustled. Twigs snapped. And he was gone.

Crimson shouldered Jasper off him with a rapidly clicking hiss that came from his chest and reverberated behind his clenched teeth. His dark hair seemed darker and spinier, prickling like hackles. For a fraction of a second Jasper considered drawing his gun again, not because he was angry with him, but because he was afraid of what he was about to do. Then the light in his eyes dimmed. He breathed out through his nose. Just like that, the demon fell away and left behind nothing but an irritated-looking Crimson. He clicked open the revolver's cylinder, carelessly spilling the spent casings in the grass, then reloaded the gun and shoved it in the holster. "You shouldn't have stopped me."

"You're probably right," agreed Jasper. "But I had to."

"You wanna tell me why?"

"No," Jasper said, only to add a beat later, "He was my friend. We used to work together... before. I... I thought he was dead."

Crimson made a small thoughtful noise in reply, and though Jasper didn't look at him, he could feel the werespider's eyes on him, calculating.

"You need a drink," Crimson decided.

He nearly laughed at Crimson's single-mindedness. "No, thanks," Jasper said.

"Wasn't really a question, kid." Crimson slapped his shoulder but not light enough that it didn't hurt. Jasper glared at him and was ignored completely. "C'mon, let's get outta here."

Crimson led the way out of the park and down the street they'd just come from. He pulled out a pack of cigarettes from one of his jacket's many pockets and tapped out two smokes, handing one to Jasper and lighting the other one, the flare of the ember illuminating his profile. He passed the lighter over, and Jasper lit his, though it took him a few tries. It couldn't make him feel any worse, he reasoned, and he breathed in the smoke, like how he'd seen Crimson do it. It filled his lungs and burned his throat. He coughed several times, blinking back sudden tears, but caught his breath and tried again, taking in a little bit less this time. After a few puffs it actually felt good, some of the knots in his stomach relaxing, a dizzy, heady feeling in his mind. A tingling sensation rushed through his limbs and made them feel surprisingly light. He still thought it tasted pretty bad.

Jasper spent much of the walk looking over his shoulder to see if they were being followed, but it seemed as if Adam was gone. For now. Jasper still didn't know what his old partner was doing here in New York. It was a popular city for demons, but it was also well populated with Hunters, something Adam should have been smart enough to be wary of. He'd come here despite the dangers. Why? Was he here on his own, or did he have help? Was it just bad dumb luck that he found Jasper, or did he come looking for him? Jasper smoked the cigarette down to the filter.

The summer night was warm, but Jasper shivered under his jacket anyway. The buildings around them eventually grew more and more familiar, and when Jasper saw the hotel they were staying in, he assumed that was where they were going, but Crimson continued down the street and around the corner, entering a door Jasper almost missed. It was so nondescript it blended into the building around it.

While Jasper had the ability to sense demons, it seemed as if Crimson possessed a skill in locating dive bars no matter where he went. This bar was a fair bit less charming than Rascal's, which was saying something. Tinny country music played over blown-out speakers, and everything seemed to be made from pale, ugly wood: the booths, the tables, the bar, the stools. No one pretended they were here to have fun. The bar's few patrons sat alone, each nursing tall beers in chipped mugs. Crimson strolled in confidently (there was no bouncer at the door for him to turn his shining eyes on), rapping his knuckles on the counter to get the attention of a gray-bearded man cleaning a glass with a dubiously clean rag, his eyes on a big old tube TV mounted in the corner. The picture was so bad Jasper wasn't sure what the man was watching.

"Four shots of tequila. Top shelf."

The bearded man grunted what might have been a laugh and took his time setting down the glass he was cleaning, taking the half-empty bottle of tequila from the back of the bar, and pouring four shots into four different sized shot glasses. Crimson tipped one back easily, the glass clinking decidedly against the worn wood of the bar. He looked at Jasper expectantly.

Jasper slid the shot nearest to him closer, frowning at the clear liquid. Crimson made it look so easy. Jasper brought the shot to his lips and drank half of it. Immediately the taste burned his tongue and all the way down to his stomach. He hissed through his teeth, it was either that or coughing, and he was certain his eyes were tearing slightly when he said, "That's fucking disgusting." The werespider shrugged, finishing his second shot like it was nothing more than water.

Jasper finished his shot with a grimace and pushed the last one closer to Crimson. The werespider didn't argue and took it, tapping the empty glass on the bar top. The tender had gone back to his dirty glass and old TV and was slow refilling them.

"So, what? I'm guessin' ya wanna talk about it? The whole—" he smiled here, unfriendly "—friend thing."

Jasper didn't think it sounded like he wanted to listen, and he didn't really feel like talking about his dead partner. "Not with you, no."

"Thank the gods for small favors, eh?" The bartender returned to fill their glasses. Crimson took another shot and motioned for it to be filled again, carelessly tossing one of those movie-star smiles his way.

"It's pretty shitty of you," commented Crimson lightly when the tender was gone.

"What?"

"You. Shitty. Being such an asshole to your so-called friend back there."

Jasper was dumbfounded. His mouth opened and closed, searching for words. The knots in his stomach twisted like angry snakes. "That wasn't my friend. It was something else."

Crimson ignored this. "Just because he got himself turned into whatever the fuck he is, you don't want anything to do with him? I don't even see what the big deal is. It could be worse. He could be DEAD."

"He *is* dead!" snapped Jasper, right as the swell of John Denver's "Country Roads" faded to silence. The bar was more dark than light, but Jasper still shrank a little and raised a hand to half cover his face.

"Can we not talk about this? I just *told you* I didn't want to. So drop it."

"*Fine.*"

They sat in surly, uneasy silence for several moments, listening to the overhead speakers crackle, now some new country song, one Jasper didn't recognize. The werespider beside him had started spinning his pocket watch on the counter. Watching Crimson try (*actually try*) not to talk was very surreal, like watching a small hyper child try to play "the quiet game." Jasper searched desperately for some topic of interest. A comment or a question that would steer the demon's attention elsewhere, but he was so mad it was hard to think.

"You know," said Crimson, too soon. His eyes were still down on the pocket watch, watching the silver spider stamped on its front as it danced in a spinning circle. "I just think it's kind of a little weird is all. I mean, here you sit, all cozy and friendly with me." If he were actually paying attention, Crimson would have seen there was nothing "cozy" or "friendly" about Jasper right now, and that there hadn't been since he decided to feed a living human to his vampire buddy. "Meanwhile, your actual best friend shambles himself back to life, tries to say hi, and then you go and get him shot? That's shitty, man."

"You're the one who shot him!"

"Well, it didn't look like you guys were planning on swapping phone numbers, so yeah. I figured you were gonna tell me he was trying to lure you into a van or just into a kinda dark corner so he could bash your head in. I didn't know you were avoiding him just cuz you're a fuckin' bigot."

Jasper thought about that chilled night three years before. A creature with razor teeth, Adam's terrified blue eyes fixed on his, their hands clasped desperately, the way his partner, his best friend's blood steamed hot in the night as he bled out. Crimson had no idea what he was talking about.

"I'm going back to the hotel," he said, quietly because otherwise he would scream. He slid off the barstool. If he had to listen to another word from the werespider's bitter mouth, he was going to lose it.

"He's still a person, you know." There was a red gleam in the spider's eyes to match the white shining in his own.

"Just shut up, okay? Don't talk to me."

The werespider rolled his eyes and went back to his drinking. Jasper left the bar, heading back to the hotel. No one came after him in the night.

Chapter Nine

—

Suspicious Minds

It wasn't until he was standing outside the room that he remembered he didn't have a key. Jasper knew the vampire didn't trust him, so he went back to the front desk to be let in, but the attendant still had not returned. Nor had anyone else. He waited around for a while to see if she would come back, but she didn't, and Jasper felt even sicker thinking about it. He went back to the room to try his luck.

He knocked on the door.

There was no answer.

He knocked again. "Hey, uh, Alcander? It's Jasper. Can you let me in?"

"Where's Crimson?" came the muffled reply.

Jasper tried the knob, but it was still locked. "He's down the street, getting drunk. Can you let me in? I don't have a key." Silence answered him. Swearing to himself, Jasper grabbed hold of the knob and shook it, rattling the door in its frame. He just wanted to get inside and lie down. Why did these fucking demons have to make everything so hard? God, he wanted to go home. "I'm not going to hurt you, bloodsucker. Just let me in!"

Jasper wasn't surprised when this tactic didn't work, but he was still pissed about it. He had half a mind to go back to the bar, shoot Crimson dead, and dig the key out of his wallet. Instead he went back to the lobby to fume and wait.

Jasper tried not to think about Adam and failed. He tried to distract himself with his book but couldn't focus. Twice he took out his phone and started to call Charlie to tell him… something, he was never sure what. He wanted another cigarette, but he didn't want to leave the lobby.

Crimson strolled in an hour and a half later. He wasn't stumbling but was obviously drunk. Jasper could smell the booze on him when he walked over.

"You still here?" Crimson asked. He was smiling in a way that reminded Jasper of a scowl.

Jasper ignored the snide remark. "I don't have a key. The vampire wouldn't let me in."

"There's gotta be a joke there," Crimson said as Jasper followed him back to the room. "Something 'bout an invitation." He unlocked the door with his key and they both went in. The vampire was sitting on the furthest end of the couch, his feet pulled up underneath him. He looked cautiously at the pair but seemed relieved that Crimson was back and not dead in some alley.

If Jasper expected to find evidence of what had happened here, he didn't. Everything was as neat and tidy as it was when they checked in, maybe even more so. Alcander looked healthier, his skin flushed and hair shiny. His clothes were different, neat and clean, not a spot of blood on them. He, at least, had the good grace to look guilty about what he'd done.

Crimson lifted his hand towards Alcander in greeting and then disappeared into the bathroom. The sounds of the shower running came soon after.

Jasper went over to the bed furthest from the door and sat down to undo the laces of his boots. This put him almost directly behind Alcander. The vampire didn't like it, and he got up and moved, sitting on the edge of the other bed. Jasper noticed he sat as far away as he could, his hands on his knees, his feet on the ground. As if he would be able to get away fast enough. As if Jasper couldn't kill him before Crimson could come out and stop him. Al couldn't fight to save his life (literally). It wouldn't be hard. A silver bullet or a sharp enough knife. Destroy the brain or the heart and that was enough. Jasper thought this without any real intention, he just couldn't help it. It was habit. The vampire didn't have to fear him; he wasn't planning on hurting him. At least, not yet.

"Could you please turn on the television?" Alcander's voice was soft and submissive, a gentle inquiry.

Jasper glanced at him still poised on the edge of the bed like he might bolt at a moment's notice, and then looked at the nightstand between the two beds, at the remote that sat in plain sight.

"Uh, sure, go ahead." Jasper nodded to the remote.

Alcander looked very uncomfortable, wiping his hands on the knees of his pants.

"What is it?"

"A remote control is amongst the dirtiest things in the home. In a hotel it's dirtier than the bedsheets, the floor, and even the toilet. On average they are covered with more than 1.2 million CFU per square inch. It's *disgusting.*"

Jasper wasn't sure what CFU meant, but he was sure he was missing something. Was the vampire worried about *germs*? There were some demon diseases, but they were extremely uncommon and not transferable via hotel TV remote. "You're a vampire," Jasper explained.

"Yes, I am aware of that."

The two of them stared at each other until Jasper finally relented. "Whatever." Rolling his eyes, he picked up the remote. "What do you want to watch?"

"The local news, please."

Jasper found the channel and leaned back against the wooden headboard, watching the screen. Maybe it would distract him from his thoughts or, even better, maybe it would be so mind-numbingly boring he'd just fall asleep. There was a story about a fire that almost burned down a beloved bakery, the dark-haired newswoman getting misty-eyed over burnt pastries, followed by a short report on gunfire and possible gang activity in the park a few blocks away from the hotel. The news had moved on to a story about a new subway entrance on the west side, but Jasper spoke anyway.

"That was Crimson," he said. "The gunfire. And me too, I guess."

"Why?" Alcander turned to him, alarmed. "Did Ivory find us again?"

The Hunter shook his head. "No, it wasn't her. It was... someone else. Someone I know. Knew."

"A demon?"

"No," Jasper said quickly. "Well... he didn't used to be, anyway. He's something else now." He ran his hand over his face, scrubbing his jaw, rubbing the back of his neck.

The vampire's posture changed. He pulled his feet up onto the bed and crossed his legs underneath them, turning his front more towards Jasper as he straightened his spine so that he looked a little taller, a little surer. His hands still rested on his knees, but they no longer moved anxiously. He was looking at Jasper indirectly, from the corner of his light eyes. Jasper frowned and glanced away.

"Who was it?" Alcander asked in that gentle voice of his. Against the soft rhythm of the shower, it was almost like music.

"Adam," Jasper whispered with a shiver. He pulled the sleeves of his jacket down over his hands. "Adam Mallory. He was my friend, my partner. Years ago, in Seattle. We knew each other since we were just kids, went to school together." The aforementioned school was the Hunting Academy, Adrian of Nicomedia Academy, in Seattle. He and Adam were top of their class, and when they both graduated early, it just made sense that they should stay together. Jasper laughed once, abruptly, the sound like choking. He looked back at Alcander still sitting on the opposite bed with his hands resting on his knees, and looked away again.

"It was my fault. How he died. It was my idea."

"Your fault and your idea are entirely different things."

"It feels like the same thing." Jasper's throat felt tight. His eyes felt hot. "I convinced him to take on a job. It was too big for us." But what had actually happened was that they had decided to go after a mark that hadn't been assigned to them—a powerful, unnamed creature, otherworldly in its design, elusive in its behavior. It left no scent and showed no aura, but Jasper had been able to feel the thing a mile off, and he was certain he and Adam would prevail where others had failed. "We were stupid. Stupid kids."

Alcander said nothing.

"I thought he was dead. I was sure of it." He remembered Adam's shaking body and how quickly it went still. He wished he could forget. "And I moved away from there, to move past all that, or whatever. The *trauma*—" if words could have eye rolls, that one would be spinning in its socket "—of it all. And then somehow he finds me? But he's not Adam anymore, he's some—he's some *thing*."

Alcander was quiet. "I'm sorry you feel that way," he said eventually. He seemed on the brink of saying something else, but the shower shut off in the other room, and he shut his mouth, returning his attention to the screen.

Jasper wiped his hand over his eyes, sniffing back the tears that managed to escape. If Crimson saw, he knew he'd never hear the end of it. Luckily when Crimson came out of the bathroom, he didn't seem to be paying much attention to either of them. Wearing just jeans and still preening his damp hair, he went and dug through the closet in search of a shirt, pausing only long enough to tell Alcander to "turn that boring shit off."

Jasper turned it down a few notches but didn't change the channel. "Well, what do you want to watch?"

Crimson grinned. "What's on the pay-per-view?"

Jasper scowled, but his heart wasn't in it. "Don't be gross."

There were only two beds, but a wordless glance from Crimson sent Alcander back to the couch. The werespider tossed a pillow at him, and he caught it with a demon's ease, though truthfully Jasper found it hard to think of him as a demon. He was scared of remote controls, for Christ's sake. Crimson pulled a black T-shirt over his bare torso and fell back on the bed where Alcander had been. He reached to the nightstand and switched the light off.

"Sleep tight, hybrid—"

"*Jasper.*"

"—we're leaving tomorrow."

"What?" Jasper turned the light back on. "What do you mean, leaving?"

"It's getting awful hot around here, what with my family and your friends. I'm thinkin' we should get the fuck outta Dodge."

"And go… where? Like, Jersey or something?"

"Or something," agreed Crimson, turning the light off once more. It might have been a trick of the light from the television, but his eyes shone red in the dark. Jasper was sure he'd never get used to that. "I want to leave early, so get some sleep."

"Whatever." Despite the warning in his chest, Jasper turned his back to the werespider and closed his eyes.

#

"Alright, Doc," said Crimson, an hour after Jasper had gone to sleep.

He and Alcander were seated in a booth at the in-house bar, far to the back of the dining area. Crimson's shining eyes assured that they could get whatever table they wanted, and that any mortals in the area would keep from pestering them. "Talk to me. Whatcha find out?"

Alcander was very uncomfortable in public. Too many people, too many contaminants, too many variables. The corner of his paper placemat was wrinkled, and he tried to smooth the crease. This little task seemed to take up the entirety of his focus. "You talked to him, didn't you?"

Crimson slipped the placemat out from underneath his fingers and swapped it for his own. "Sure, I talk to the hybrid all the time."

"Not him." Alcander found other imaginary problems on the table. Packets of sugar that needed to be rearranged in their holders by color, a listing of the daily specials that needed to be straightened on its menu stand. He'd wash his hands raw after this. "His friend. Adam."

"Oh," said Crimson. "Him."

"Why do you say it like that?" asked Alcander.

Crimson frowned. "You're not gonna like it." Alcander gave him a look, and Crimson sighed, pushed himself into the corner of the booth with his back against the wall, and kicked his feet up in the empty space beside him. "I scared the shit outta him before I knew he was important, so he didn't really wanna tell me much. Way he tells it, though, our little lost lamb upstairs is actually more of a wolf in sheep's clothes. He said they used to be hunting buddies."

Alcander's brow creased. "That's nonsense. Places like St. James do not hire nonhumans."

"You know, Al, that's just what I said," replied Crimson. "I said, 'Bullshit,' and he goes on to tell me this crazy story about how he and Jasper chased down this... frankly made-up-sounding demon. And how it killed him. And how the agency buried him."

"If he had been buried by a bunch of Hunters, they would have put him down as soon as he woke up."

Crimson scratched the side of his throat, ruminating. "Well, it's a little vague. I don't think they knew he was comin' back. Way he told it, he was in the ground for a while."

"More than a night?" asked Alcander.

"Try more than a week," replied Crimson. "I think they *embalmed* him, Al. He *reeks*. You ever smelled formaldehyde after it's been marinating in a corpse for a month or two? I probably did him a favor, putting so many holes in him." There was something he wasn't saying, but if he didn't say it now, Alcander knew there was no reason to bother with trying to push him. Once the werespider dug his heels in, he couldn't be moved, not with a stick nor a carrot. "I dunno, man," continued Crimson. "The kid does have a sore spot when it comes to the whole demon thing, and he acts sketchy as hell any time we're on the wrong side of the mortal law. It's pretty *weird* for a freelance mercenary…"

"You said that demon did not like him," said Alcander. He saw the conclusion Crimson was working himself around to, and Crimson was right; he didn't like it, mainly because he knew Crimson's preferred way of dealing with Hunters who crossed him. It was much the same way he dealt with *anyone* who crossed him, which was to say that, if Crimson had his way, he'd shoot Jasper dead while he slept, and never think of him again.

Alcander took issue with this, not only because the half-blood had saved his life, but also because he simply couldn't believe Jasper could be a *Hunter*. Hunters were almost as single-minded as religious zealots and even more self-righteous. Crueler. "Perhaps he fabricated the story in hopes of vengeance," offered Alcander. "Though I fear to say that what Adam told you bears a… striking resemblance to what Jasper told me."

Crimson raised an eyebrow. "Which was?"

"That they worked together. Took a mission too big. Adam was killed." Alcander ran out of things to fuss over on the table and started picking at his cuticles instead. "He seemed to believe… he was no longer Adam." It was a common enough misconception among humans, that a demon reborn was purged entirely of his human nature.

"See, that seems pretty Hunter-y to me," said Crimson. Alcander opened his mouth to protest (he did not want to sit quietly in this restaurant while Crimson strolled upstairs and put half a dozen bullets in the half-blood's sleeping body), but the werespider held up a hand. "But you know what *doesn't* seem Hunter-y? He let him *go*. I was going to kill him, and Jasper stopped me."

"And to you that means…?"

"I dunno," repeated Crimson. "Did you find out anything with that… contraption of yours?"

The "contraption" in question was his computer, which was still back home in the warehouse. He hadn't had the opportunity to grab it when the other werespiders dragged him out of the building, but he had done a fair amount of research on the half-blood prior, first at Crimson's request and then, as his prying returned more questions than answers, to satiate his own curiosity.

"St. James has no files on him," said Alcander. "According to what little I could find elsewhere, he attended a human high school in Seattle. Graduated two years early. Both parents deceased."

"Could they fake that?" asked Crimson.

Alcander shrugged. "It would be difficult, but St. James is a very powerful organization."

"Yeah, I guess you're right," said Crimson. "Maybe we should get rid of him, just to be safe."

Alcander leaned slightly across the table, lowering his voice to just above a whisper. "If you lay a hand on that human without proof, I am never going to speak to you again."

Crimson looked more amused by this threat than anything, a big grin lighting up his features, reaching all the way to his brown eyes. "Whoa, Doc, check you out. There's a little vamp in you after all."

"I am *serious*, Crimson."

"Yeah, yeah." Crimson was still grinning. "Don't get your fangs all in a twist. I like the little brat too, alright?" Alcander wasn't surprised that this was true, but he was surprised to hear Crimson vocalize it. "Here's what we'll do. The Summer Solstice Tour is in the next few days, down in Florida. The three of us will take a nice little vacation, far, far, far away from St. James, and we'll see how he reacts. And I'll, uh… try to push his buttons a little along the way, see if I can figure anything out. Hell, maybe if we're lucky, someone in the Summerlands will have a clue about what he is."

"What if he *is* a Hunter, though?" asked Alcander, his voice very soft.

Crimson shrugged. "His friends are gonna have a helluva time finding his body all the way in the Summerlands."

#

Jasper had been checking in with Charlie regularly. Since the werespider had super hearing and they were rarely separated, it was mostly through coded texts. So far, he hadn't had much to report other than the fact Crimson hadn't killed him yet. When he and the vampire snuck out in the middle of the night, Jasper decided to give his father a call.

Charlie sounded tired when he answered the phone, which made sense since it was three thirty in the morning. "Hey, Jazz," he said, "you okay?"

Jasper was struck with a sudden and intense pang of homesickness. "Yeah, I'm okay."

"You sound strange."

"Just tired." He knew he should tell Charlie about Adam, but he also knew what would happen if the Hunters found out about his ex-partner. Even though he knew it wasn't really Adam anymore, even though he knew he'd probably hurt people, even though it was his job to stop things like him, he didn't want Adam to be hunted down and killed, didn't want his death on his conscience once again. "I think the spider wants to leave town."

"Why do you think that?"

"Uh, well, he told me so. Says it's getting too dangerous between the Hunters and his family. Have you guys found them yet?"

"They're very evasive. We've got a good team, though. McKracken, Thurman, the Neilson brothers. We're hopeful. Are you going to go with him?"

"I should, right? I mean, if he's running scared, he's probably going to somewhere or someone he trusts, right? Could be an actual lead."

"Where are you going?"

"Uh, I'm not sure. He hasn't told me yet. Maybe he hasn't even decided. The guy's hard to gauge sometimes."

"You'll let me know when he does, right?"

"Right." There was a lull in the conversation, and Jasper thought he heard something in the hallway outside the room. It could have been anything. Another guest. Room service. "I should go; they could be back any minute. I'll text you."

"Are you sure you're alright?"

Jasper almost started to tell him about Adam but stopped himself.

Whatever happened to him wouldn't be his fault again. "I'm fine. It's just... hard, being on edge all the time. And I don't have much to show for it."

"You're doing great," Charlie assured him. "It'll be worth it, I just know it. Just keep it up. He trusts you enough to take you with him, that's amazing. I'm sure he'll open up even more. You've got this, Jasper."

"Thanks, Dad."

"I'll let you go. I love you. And let me know where you're going."

#

"Florida," said Alcander.

The two demons got back late, but where they went or what they discussed, Jasper did not know. He lay in his feigned sleep with the gun clutched under the pillow, waiting for one of them to make a move. Crimson went back to the bed and Alcander back to the couch, and from there, as far as he could tell, they both went to sleep.

Crimson was still asleep now. Jasper heard Alcander trying to wake him first, but Crimson only responded with rumbling growls before dramatically cocooning himself in the comforter and stuffing his head underneath the pillow. So much for his so-called "early start."

Jasper felt like doing much the same thing, but Crimson was so mean about it that he felt a little bad for Alcander. He resigned himself to getting up without a fight. "Crimson thinks it's our best bet, since his cousins won't expect him to flee south," continued Alcander as he started remaking the bed that Jasper had just vacated. Something about just letting the vampire pick up after him didn't sit well with Jasper. He grabbed the opposite corner to help.

"Yeah, but Florida though? It seems kind of like a dramatic reaction to me. I mean, is it really necessary to—"

"What does it matter if it's necessary?" mumbled Crimson from underneath the pillow. He lifted the edge, peering out with his shining eyes, a small frown on the corner of his mouth. "You've got no friends here and you don't own any property. What's it matter where you are?" There was a trap in these words, and Jasper decided to take a detour around it.

"It doesn't. It just seems far. I've never been to Florida."

"All the better reason to go." Crimson yawned. He tossed the pillow aside and sat up. Jasper hated the neat way his hair lay in smooth, silky waves even right when he woke up. "You don't have to go, but if you decide to stay behind, you'd better keep your mouth shut."

"I didn't say I didn't want to go," Jasper said. "I just don't understand why *there*. Do you, like, have a place to stay there?"

"Nope. But it's the furthest south I can go without leaving the country. I guess if you prefer Mexico…"

Jasper felt a twist of sheer panic at the idea of being that far removed from the influence of the agency and shook his head. "Florida's fine. Are you worried we'll be followed?"

"Sid's a fantastic tracker, and Ivory's gonna be real pissed about that golden bullet you put in her. She don't like to lose." He kicked back the blankets and climbed out of bed. "But she gets bored of her little games pretty quickly. She'll mope around New York a bit, then go off to bother one of the others. And then if I'm *really* lucky, I might go two, three hundred years without having to see them again." He yawned. "You'll be dead by then."

Jasper frowned. Florida was a long way away. It was miles out of his jurisdiction, though Hunting groups were known to work cooperatively across borders without much fuss. However, there was no way to guarantee the Hunters from Florida wouldn't interfere with their operation, nor would there be any easy mode of escape should things go wrong.

"I'm going to go see if there's coffee. You wanna come with? They're probably still serving breakfast."

#

A cluster of uniformed officers, one plainclothes detective, and an extremely hyperactive photographer were gathered in the hotel lobby around a nervous-looking man who kept wringing his hands and fretting at his mustache.

Jasper and Crimson were almost to the double set of doors that led to the dining room when the detective looked up and spotted them. "Hey! You two!"

They both turned, Jasper reluctantly, Crimson with a convincingly feigned "who me?" expression on his face. The detective came striding towards them with a steno pad under his arm and a pen behind his ear. He stopped right in front of them, glanced down at the notepad and then back up at them. "You're... Thomas Reed? Twentieth floor? Room 2011?"

"That's me," said Crimson. "Is there a problem?"

"We aren't sure yet," replied the detective. "Last night, the receptionist, uhh... Andrea Huston, abandoned her post. She hasn't been seen since."

"Yeah, I thought it was a little weird I couldn't get anyone at the front desk last night," said Crimson. "Jack got locked outta the room for like *two hours*. Real shit service. Wouldn't recommend it."

The detective's eyes narrowed at him slightly, but Crimson only smiled. "Is there some way I can help?"

"We have security footage of the two of you coming and going from the hotel around the time of her disappearance. Actually, we have footage of *him* coming and going." He pointed at Jasper. "*You* just show up, but we can't find any video of you leaving. Isn't that weird?"

Crimson shrugged. "Yeah, I guess. I don't know how it coulda missed me though."

"Maybe you left via another route?" suggested the detective.

Crimson laughed. "Oh yeah, sure. Maybe I *jumped* from the twentieth floor. Or maybe... I dunno... this is just a guess but, uhh..." He pointed at the corner of the room, where a single camera hung facing out across the lobby, pointed towards the front desk. "Maybe your top-of-the-line security system from 1975 just *missed* me."

The detective looked back at the hotel owner, who shrugged weakly. "We aren't the Four Seasons, Detective Mercer. We have one camera in the elevator and one in the lobby, and that's it."

"Ah yes, the elevator," said Mercer. "There's no footage of you in there either, Mr. Reed. Yet... you're on the twentieth floor."

"Stairs are fantastic for cardio," replied Crimson, then, "Am I under arrest, Detective Mercer?"

The man took the pen from behind his ear and wrote something in the steno pad, then shook his head. "No, Mr. Reed. But... let's just say you're a person of interest."

Crimson grinned. "Well, there's something we can agree on. Now… if you don't mind… Jack and I had a late night last night, and since we couldn't get any *room service*—" he shot a withering glance over at the owner "—we're pretty hungry. Feel free to drop in if you think of any more questions, yeah?"

"Don't leave the city," said Mercer, unsmiling. Either Crimson wasn't using his glamor, or this guy was the sort of human who would be green-lighted for the Hunting program at St. James.

"Sure thing, officer," said Crimson. "Jackie?"

Jasper was using his entire focus to remain calm and attentive towards the officer, and it took him a second to realize *he* was "Jackie," but when he did, he nodded and dipped through the double doors with the werespider.

"Fuckin' flatfoot," muttered Crimson as the doors swung shut behind them. He grabbed a stray newspaper off a vacant table and dropped down into a chair near the buffet.

Jasper *had* been hungry, but after the encounter with the officer, he found he had somewhat lost his appetite. He still went and piled a plate with bacon, eggs, and two pieces of toast smeared in butter. He poured so much milk and sugar into his coffee that it barely resembled coffee anymore, then went back to the table, where Crimson was reading comic strips with the sort of serious face someone reading about the stock market might have.

After a long, drawn silence where Jasper did little but pick miserably at his eggs, he said, "I can't believe it doesn't bother you at all. That girl didn't deserve that."

Crimson glanced up at Jasper, then at the plate in front of him. "You know pigs are as intelligent as a three-year-old human child? And the cows they use as slaves to make your delicious butter make best friends? Don't even get me started on the way they treat chickens."

"What're you, an animal rights activist now?" Jasper didn't like what the werespider was implying.

Crimson shook his head. "No way. I think you should eat whatever you want to eat." He flipped the newspaper closed, folded it in half, and stood. "I also think pots should be careful about calling kettles black."

Chapter Ten

—

Highway to Hell

Alcander said it would be a lot easier crossing the country in a car that wasn't hot. Crimson said going the legal route would be "way less exciting" but relented at the rent-a-car outlet when, after some tricky fraud on Al's part, they green-lighted him for a racy 2003 S-Type Jaguar in all black. It was blissfully more spacious than the Buick and drove like a dream in comparison. The fact that it didn't smell like two-week-old french fries and dirty socks was just icing on the cake.

Alcander didn't drive and seemed uncomfortable even being *in* the vehicle. So that just left Jasper and Crimson and roughly eighteen hours of congested interstates, backcountry byways, and toll roads, all of which seemed to be in an eternal state of construction.

The sticker on the dashboard insisted that the car wasn't meant to be smoked in, but even Jasper had to admit they had to ignore it. If they had to stop every fifteen minutes for Crimson to smoke, they wouldn't reach Florida for weeks, and frankly, as the temperature rose steadily from hot to hotter to sweltering and swampy, he didn't want to get out either.

Being trapped in a car with two demons on a cross-country road trip should have been a personal Hell for Jasper... but he was surprised to find it wasn't. Al barely spoke except to comment on landmarks they passed, the little bits of trivia droning from the back seat like a built-in tour guide. And Crimson's style of driving, which was terrifying in the close-knit traffic of the inner city, felt much smoother and safer on the interstate, and in a car that didn't feel like it was about to rattle apart if it broke sixty miles per hour.

There was a CD player, but they had no CDs, so they passed the time flipping between radio stations as they listed in and out of range, oftentimes so quickly that the song playing didn't even have time to complete. Jasper was surprised when, time after time, the werespider stopped on frequencies playing classic rock. The second time he stopped for the opening riff of The Rolling Stones' "Paint It, Black," Jasper couldn't help but ask, "So, uh... You're a fan of old-school rock, huh?" He didn't know why he hadn't expected them to have this in common. He assumed that much of the way the werespider presented himself was a very elaborate act. The voice. The clothes. The smile. Underneath the skin, a mindless, malevolent predator was puppeting around this once-human body like an anglerfish.

But it didn't *feel* that way.

"Well, yeah. Of course. You have any idea what music was like *before* rock 'n roll?"

Jasper couldn't help but grin. "I don't like to think about it for too long."

"Yeah, well, consider yourself lucky. I had to live it."

They had to stop periodically, partially because Jasper needed to eat, use the restroom and stretch, partially because Crimson was incapable of going more than six hours without a drink, and partially because of Alcander's sporadic panic attacks. All of the rest stops were eerily similar with poorly lit bathrooms and dusty chocolate bars, the clerks all dead-eyed and uninterested. The racks of magnets and postcards always showed the same faded pictures, the magazines out of date and thoroughly read over. All of them seemed to have racks of T-shirts with pictures of Arizona despite the fact that Arizona was on the other side of the country.

"Check it out," Crimson said, tossing a plastic bag into Jasper's lap as they pulled out of a rest stop in Richmond, Virginia, the highway a dark stretch ahead of them. The Hunter glared at him but looked anyway. Inside were a couple of packs of Marlboros, a handful of BIC lighters and, most interestingly, half a dozen CDs. Jasper grabbed some and flipped through them. *Best of Led Zeppelin. The Essential Billy Joel. Queen's Greatest Hits.*

"Hey, no way. This is sweet." Jasper ripped open the plastic wrap on the Queen CD and put it in the player. He was getting tired of surfing channels and listening to local radio ads.

"I found 'em behind a shit ton of gospel albums," Crimson said. "And those lighters are for you so you'll fuckin' stop stealin' mine." It might have been touching if he hadn't almost certainly stolen everything in the bag.

As the music played, the last of the tension seemed to float out the open windows into the warm night air. Jasper tapped his foot to the beat until halfway through "Somebody to Love" Crimson started singing, his fingers tapping out the tempo on the steering wheel. His singing voice was much better than it ought to have been considering the thick New York accent it usually carried, smooth and sweet as honey. A little surprised, Jasper watched him in the passing headlights of other cars, still wearing his sunglasses even though the sun had set hours ago. A smile tugged at the corner of his mouth and he joined in, hesitantly at first. He wasn't as good a singer as the werespider. Eventually he didn't care.

Jasper knew all the words to "Bohemian Rhapsody," but Crimson could hit every note, which he hadn't thought anyone but Freddie Mercury could do. He had a story for every song, sometimes about the band, where he had seen them, where he had been the first time he heard one of their songs. At one point, as Jazz was putting in the third CD, Crimson asked him why he was so into classic rock. "Aren't you a little young? What are you, sixteen?"

"I'm eighteen," Jasper corrected. He thought about telling a joke or shrugging the question off. Crimson seemed to have been pretty honest with him. He decided to be honest too. "My dad was really into it. I have all his old records, and I've listened to them all the time since I was a kid. I never knew him, he and my mom died when I was really young, and it just sort of... made me feel close to him. That and it literally, actually *rocks*."

"How did your parents die?"

"Car crash," Jasper explained.

"Imagine that," said Crimson. "A rare, possibly undiscovered breed of demon killed in something as boring as a human car crash." Jasper opened his mouth to tell him to shut up (seriously, why did he always have to ruin everything?), but Crimson continued, "You're lucky no one got their hands on you when you were just a baby. You'd be living in a lab or a research facility by now."

"C'mon, Crimson, stop with the exaggerations."

"I'm not exaggerating," said Crimson. "I don't know what you are."

"That doesn't mean *nobody* does." He had asked Charlie numerous times, especially around the age of thirteen, when his eyes had first begun to glow white. Charlie convinced him it was some sort of latent psychic ability, but he hadn't known it affected his scent until he was sixteen and started working regularly in the field. Prior to that, he hadn't had much interaction with people outside the academy in Seattle. There was Adam, of course, but he was the son of another hunting family; his parents both worked there alongside Charlie. Usually psychic abilities begot a track in the magical division, but Jasper had no talent for magic and had pursued combat instead.

If he was some sort of demon hybrid, someone at St. James surely would have noticed. Right?

"That's fair, I guess." Crimson glanced at him out of the corner of his eye. "I'm sorry about your parents."

"Thanks," replied Jasper. Though he didn't believe the demon could possibly care, it was very civil of him to pretend. "And it's okay, really. Like I said, I never really knew them, and I had a great adoptive father. It really doesn't bother me."

Crimson made a thoughtful noise. "It would bother me." He steered them down an exit ramp, bringing them to a truck stop. This one sported a twenty-four-hour diner as well as a gas station. He tossed Jasper the keys as he climbed out of the car, throwing his sunglasses in the driver's seat. In the back seat, Alcander was just waking up. "You wanna fill up the tank, grab something to eat?"

"Where are you going?" asked Jasper.

"For a walk," replied Crimson.

"Where to?"

Crimson sighed, running his hand along the back of his neck. He was still wearing his long leather jacket despite the rising temperature. "Why you gotta make things so difficult?"

The stop was fairly busy, with lines of semitrucks parked along the back lot and a smattering of family vehicles parked in the front. The muffled sound of a child screaming for no good reason reached them from one of the cars. Beyond the parking lot, there was a wooded area, not quite dense enough to be called a forest, and apart from the interstate, there was no sign of civilization for miles in either direction.

At first, he didn't understand where Crimson could possibly be going. His human pantomime was so well refined it made it easy to forget or to ignore what he was, but the sheen in his eyes brought it back instantly. Jasper shot a glare at him. "Are you going hunting?"

"We're stopping for dinner," said Crimson, the glimmer in his eyes starting to brighten. It seemed to alter him from the ground up, the monster showing through the mask. "We aren't all so lucky as to have it served to us on a platter." He blinked, and just as quickly as it had shown, the light was gone. "Would ya rather have me lose my fuckin' mind behind the wheel?"

"No," said Jasper softly. He looked out across the parking lot again, at the semis in their eerily silent lines, their steel bodies glimmering in the bright lights around the stop. He looked back at Crimson. "How do you choose?"

Crimson shrugged. "If I wait a bit, they usually choose for me." He stepped past him, heading towards the back lot. "If not, there's always convenience. Keep an eye on Al, would you?"

Jasper found this answer less than satisfactory, and he started to go after the werespider to tell him so, but Alcander, still looking half-asleep, rolled down his window. "What are we doing?"

Jasper watched Crimson wander to the back lot, his hands in his pockets, looking as if he really were just going for a stroll, his only intent to stretch his legs after the long hours in the car. He disappeared around the corner of the building, and Jasper turned away, trying not to think about it. "We stopped to get something to eat," he said. He almost asked if Al wanted anything before realizing what that would mean. "Come in with me."

"Um…" The vampire looked towards where the werespider had gone, then reluctantly back at Jasper.

"You can stay in the car if you really want."

"Um… no. I will go with you." He followed Jasper into the diner, sticking right beside him the whole way. It reminded Jasper vaguely of a much younger version of himself on the rare occasions when Charlie took him grocery shopping.

They were seated at a booth in front of the window. Alcander seemed bound and determined to touch nothing and kept his hands folded firmly in his lap as the waitress took their orders. The vampire ordered coffee, Jasper a grilled cheese and fries with a cup of soup on the side.

"So, uh…" Whenever he was around Alcander, Crimson had been there too, so they had spent very little time together just one on one. He felt like he should talk to him, if only to distract himself from the probable homicide occurring in the woods. "Is it like… rude to ask how old you are?"

"I will be turning seventy-six in October," replied Alcander. Jasper's expression must have given away the fact that he was trying to do the math in his head because the vampire added gently, "I was born in 1929."

"Oh." The age was not surprising, exactly. Jasper knew there were lots of vampires who were older than that in New York, but the problem with vampires was that there were so fucking many of them. Most of the vampires Jasper had met (murdered) were younger because the young ones were stupider. They were reckless, and their recklessness drew attention to them. Many didn't even live to see thirty. "Are you from New York?"

"Boston," said Alcander. Another patron passed close by their table, and Alcander shifted deeper into the booth, eyes darting uncomfortably to follow the man's movement until he was well away from them. Perhaps this wasn't the vampire who had escaped St. James with Crimson after all. "Born and raised."

"How'd you end up in New York?"

The vampire's eyes went down to his hands. "Sorry, I do not like to talk about it."

"That's alright," said Jasper.

The waitress arrived with Jasper's Coke and Alcander's coffee. She told them their food would be around in "two shakes" and then was off again, this time to clean up the dirty dishes at the table across the way. Jasper noticed that whoever had dined there hadn't left a tip. He wondered if the person made it back to their vehicle alive.

"Did you go to college?" He looked awful young to have been a doctor in his human life, older than Crimson, but young nonetheless, in his early twenties.

Alcander glanced up with his eyes, though his head stayed down. A faint smile flitted across his lips. "That is generally how one attains a doctorate, is it not?"

"I didn't know if you guys had like... some sort of supernatural school of medicine or something."

"Ah, yes," said Alcander. "Good old SSM." This one had a sense of humor too. He wondered if they all did. "I went to Harvard. Early admission." Alcander took a measured sip of his coffee. "Did you go to school?"

"I graduated when I was fifteen," said Jasper, though he wasn't sure Al would consider the program he had graduated *from* to bear any resemblance to actual school. "From high school, I mean."

Maybe he imagined it, but for the briefest of moments it seemed the vampire looked relieved.

"Me too," he said after a moment.

That would explain the medical degree, Jasper supposed, but not why the werespider was so fiercely protective of him. The waitress was back with his food before he could inquire further. Now that it was set in front of him, it seemed like an extravagant amount for one person. The grilled cheese was two layers high, the fries beside it heaped in a ridiculous mound. He picked at it tentatively while Alcander drank his coffee and stared out the window.

It was nice to finally have a little silence, but he was still almost grateful when the bell above the door jingled, and Crimson came strolling into the diner. As before, there was no evidence of his crime anywhere on his person, but there was a noticeable difference—a fullness in his lips and softness in his face, his complexion now slightly darker, as if the flush of blood underneath had also refreshed his melanin.

"Hey, tall an' good-lookin', you 'bout done?"

A lot of food was still left on the platter, but Jasper started to rise anyway. He didn't want to be anywhere near here when the werespider's victim was noticed missing. He'd already covered for the demon once during an interrogation and decided never to have to relive that experience again. "I'll ask for a to-go box."

"Nah, don't worry about it." Crimson dropped into the booth across from him, his arm slung up over the back. "No rush."

Jasper hesitantly sat back down. He was surprised to see the waitress again, already right by the table, her smile extra-bright and her professional demeanor suddenly giddy.

"Hey there." She spoke directly to Crimson, not so much as glancing at either of the others. "Can I getcha anything?"

"A large cup of the house blend to go, and the bill, please."

"Sure thing, sug," replied the woman. Again, Jasper might have imagined it, but he was pretty sure the werespider's eye twitched a little.

"You wanna take a picture?" asked Crimson when the waitress had gone. "It won't actually last longer, but I wager it might be a whole lot more convenient for me."

"What?"

"Well, cuz then you could leer at *it* instead," explained the werespider in a faux-earnest voice. "And it'll be just about as likely to transform into the actual devil."

Suddenly self-conscious, Jasper returned his gaze quickly to his food. "Whatever, I wasn't *leering.*"

"I dunno. Seemed pretty leery to me. Whaddya think, Al?"

"I think you need not go so far out of your way to push his buttons," replied Alcander, tersely but not rudely.

Since Jasper was so determined to look anywhere but the werespider, he couldn't see his reaction, but he heard it in a soft chuckle, and for the rest of the meal Crimson was hardly obnoxious at all. He even grabbed the bill when it came around. After staring at the numbers on the receipt for exactly no time at all, he dropped a handful of wadded cash in the center of the table, then set the check facedown on top of it.

"What are you doing?" Jasper asked.

Crimson's eyes went from him to the pile of money, back to him. "Is it not enough?"

"There's like a hundred bucks here."

"So... too little? Too much?"

Jasper peeked at the check. The total came to just under twenty dollars. The waitress had jotted her name and number down in the margin. The *i*'s in *Trixie* were both dotted with hearts, and she had drawn a little winkie face after her name. Jasper's eyes rolled before he could stop them. "Jesus Christ, dude. That's like an eighty-dollar tip."

"Which is...?" He looked towards Alcander.

"Too much," supplied Alcander. "You should leave three dollars and ninety-nine cents in addition to the nineteen ninety-five that was the initial cost, for a total of twenty-three ninety-four."

"Well, you don't have to be that weirdly specific about it," said Jasper. He straightened out a few of the bills and saw that he was wrong. It was more than a hundred dollars. One of the bills was a fifty. "I mean, twenty-four bucks would be alright."

Crimson looked at the pile of cash as if it were the bane of his existence, then shook his head and climbed out of the booth. "Doesn't matter. It's not my money." The implication had the cash out of Jasper's hand immediately. "She can have it," continued Crimson, starting towards the front of the diner. "Buy herself a new pair of shoes. You two comin' or what?"

"Yeah," said Jasper.

Trixie reemerged into the dining room as they were making their exit. He hadn't noticed before, but she was wearing a ratty pair of sneakers with holes near the toes. The sole was starting to come off the back of one heel.

Outside, he looked curiously at Crimson.

"See, you're doin' it again," accused the werespider almost immediately, but this time Jasper recognized the comment for what it was. No more or less than a playful tease.

"I wasn't leering," said Jasper, and this time it was the truth.

#

It was midafternoon when they arrived in Miami. Jasper was driving, which, considering the traffic, was probably for the best. Jasper liked the Jag and didn't want to leave it in the middle of the street, where someone else would most definitely take it. It would be hard enough to give it back to the rental agency, but the New York plates stuck out this far south, and though Jazz didn't think Crimson's family would actually follow them down here, he guessed they shouldn't help them along. Maybe the next car they got could have satellite radio.

They moved forward a few feet. It was hard to gauge the city through the windshield of the car, but it looked alright to Jasper. The sky was a clear, bright blue, and he even caught a few glimpses of the ocean between glass buildings. The windows were down, letting in the smell of salt breeze, exhaust, and wet, and letting out the cold air-conditioning. It was hot, hotter than Jasper had anticipated, but he'd take heat and humidity over cold any day. "So where should I head?"

"The fuck if I know," said Crimson. He was sitting low in his seat, his dark sunglasses covering his eyes. The sun glared back at him through the gaps in the skyline, and he flipped his visor down for extra protection. "Just pick a hotel."

"Do you really not have a place to stay?"

"Says the kid who begged to live with me."

"I did not *beg*," argued Jasper. He would have said more if the subject were not so dangerous. He turned back to a safer one. "What's our budget?" Jasper had just under two thousand dollars with him, in cash. The bills were spread about his person: in his wallet, of course, and hidden in different parts of his backpack, rolled up into balls of socks, and even tucked underneath the soles of his boots. He also had a credit card, just in case, stuck behind his fake driver's license.

Since he was supposed to be a down-on-his-luck mercenary, he didn't flash his funds around, but in their travels Jasper realized Crimson's grasp on things as unimportant as money was very weak. This was probably a side effect that came with stealing everything, but he didn't even remember to take the change when Jasper gave him money to actually purchase cigarettes. Alcander, he thought, would take more notice.

They didn't know how long they were going to be here, and Jasper was worried if they weren't careful, they'd run out of money. Crimson could just flash his eyes and his charming smile and get them a room, but it was the principle of the thing.

"Ask Al. He's the millionaire."

"Al lives in an abandoned factory," Jasper pointed out doubtfully.

"He lives *under* it. Very important distinction." That didn't seem any better to Jasper. "There's some space there, pull up, pull up. Gods, you're an awful driver. This is literally killin' me."

"Are you, like, actually a millionaire, Al?" Jasper was sure this was another one of Crimson's overexaggerations.

"In a manner of speaking," Al replied. "I have many skills that companies are more than happy to pay me for and quite a lot of time on my hands. Do not worry about the hotel; money really is not a concern. Just please make sure it is clean and quiet and not too heavily populated. If you can see if they—"

Crimson threw his hands up dramatically. "Shut up, Al! I do not want the last thing I hear to be your obsessive-compulsive bullshit."

"You're not dying, Crimson," Jasper said. In front of them a car pulled forward, revealing the opening to a vacant side street. "We're almost there." Jasper didn't know where it led. He took it anyway.

#

The hotel was larger than the last they'd stayed at. Alcander had a bank card under a false name, and a false ID to match, but he was waiting for Crimson, who was distracted by a small bridal party that was taking pictures in the lobby. After the long drive, Jasper didn't feel like waiting for him to (a) get tired of flirting with the bride or (b) get punched by the groom. "Here. I'll do it."

"Thank you," said Al, letting Jasper take the card, careful that their fingers did not touch. They checked in under the name of "Andrews." Alcander signed all the paperwork, and the woman at the desk gave them their keys.

After the hours and hours spent in the car, the very idea of a bed was almost too good to be true. Jasper barely looked at the room before striding over to the closest bed, dropping his backpack by the foot of it, and throwing himself down onto its white puffy bedspread, boots and all. He'd slept a little on the ride down but realized now it was not enough.

His jacket had come off several states ago and had been shoved into his backpack when the heat became too much for the leather, and he reluctantly sat up now to take off his boots. The AC was on and the room was cool. "I'm gonna take a nap," he said, peeling back the top layer of blankets. "Wake me up in an hour."

Chapter Eleven

—

The Summerlands

"Hey, get up." Jasper woke to Crimson shaking his shoulder. "We're gonna be late."

"Late for what?" Jasper yawned. Crimson was still shaking his shoulder, and he reached with one arm to push him away.

"For the festival," explained Crimson.

This explained nothing. There had been no mention of a festival. He'd asked Crimson if he had plans a dozen times on the way down. He yawned again, rubbed his eyes, and blinked slowly. "What's going on? Are you a dream or something?"

Crimson arched an eyebrow. "I knew you dreamed about me, Jazz."

"I meant to say nightmare," Jasper corrected himself. His eyes were still groggy with sleep.

Crimson gave his shoulder another shake.

"Quit it." Jasper reached past the werespider to pick up the clock on the nightstand and get a better look at the numbers. It was just after eleven p.m. He couldn't believe he'd slept for so long. "What festival are you talking about?"

"Well, you know... the one I, uh..." He paused, thinking, then, "Oh yeah, the one I decided not to tell you about. Hmm... Well, I changed my mind. The Summer Solstice Tour will definitely be much better with you than with Al."

Jasper had no idea what the Summer Solstice Tour was, but he reckoned that since he had never heard of it, it was probably his job to investigate. That was why he was with Crimson in the first place, after all. Let the demon run to every hidey-hole and secret safe house in Miami.

"Give me a second to get dressed and, like, take a shower." He was still dressed in the clothes he fell asleep in, but he'd worn them in the car all day and had been looking forward to a long shower when he woke up. Considering Crimson's hurried manner, he settled for a quick five minutes. He didn't know what to wear, but Crimson was just wearing a black T-shirt and dark jeans, his jacket held over one shoulder with a careless finger, so Jasper figured the faded Zeppelin shirt and his regular jeans were fine. His own leather jacket was necessary to hide his pistol and to act as armor against any attacks that might come. Then they were out the door, hand raised in a brief farewell to Alcander.

The night was humid, but without the sun beating down, it didn't feel so bad. "What happens if we're late?"

"We don't get to go," said Crimson with a shrug. He was swinging his pocket watch at his side from its thin silver chain, the circles loose and fast. "I think we'll make it though."

Jasper had given up on being answered in anything but vagaries. He decided that whatever this tour thing was, it couldn't be worse than Ivory, whom he *also* hadn't bothered to tell him about. At least he hadn't just slipped away while he wasn't paying attention.

Yet.

As they moved through the streets, the number of pedestrians around them began to multiply. Many of them were dressed conspicuously in colorful shawls and long sweeping robes, bejeweled on their hands and necks and ears. A small woman with a black cat curled around her shoulders jogged past them, calling back to the man behind her that they needed to hurry because they were going to be late.

He was beginning to get an uncomfortable feeling. Not the sort that would indicate demon activity, but more of an uneasy sensation of disquiet. His heart was racing, and cold sweat prickled at his temples, his hands clammy. It felt like a small wild animal scrambling around in the back of his mind, desperate to escape. His first instinct was to turn around and run in the other direction, but, not wanting to be left behind, he persisted on, through a pair of open copper gates, long gone green from the elements, and up a long stepping-stone path, now very congested.

"I feel kind of weird," he told Crimson.

The werespider waved it away. "It's just part of the glamor. Keeps the normals from accidentally wandering in with the rest of the crowd. It'll let up when we get inside."

The path led to a large house, three stories tall with a balcony that overlooked the sea. The scent of salt and burning spice was thick in the air. They mounted the stone steps and passed through the archway.

The interior of the building was one great silver circuit, with thick black arches situated at the compass points. They stretched overhead to unite at a great square clock that hung at their heart like a lantern. There must have been well over two hundred people packed in the room, and more kept rushing in, pushing those already assembled into a claustrophobic lump. Jasper was corralled along with the rest. As the flow of people pushed and jostled them as close to the center of the room as they could, he reached out and grabbed Crimson's wrist. "Don't ditch me again."

"No promises," said Crimson, and Jasper scowled at him. "Okay, so, crash course, when that clock up there strikes midnight, the festival will be *here*, but only for a second. When it's *here*, we have to jump on. So when I say jump, jump. Okay?"

"Yeah, great, sure." Jasper had no idea what the flying fuck he was talking about, but the second hand was less than a minute away from midnight. "Anything else?"

"Well, we have to be back at this *exact spot* at midnight *tomorrow night* or we'll be trapped in the festival until Yule."

"Wait, what?" He did not want to risk getting trapped in whatever "the festival" was until whenever Yule was. "What if I don't jump?"

"I mean, that might be okay. If your kind regrows its kneecaps." The clock overhead began to chime loudly. Its hands spun in frantic circles. Its face pulsed with purple light. "Don't hold your breath!" shouted Crimson over the ear-shattering chimes and the excited cheering and whooping from the crowd. He turned his wrist so that they were holding hands, fingers twined together. "You'll feel like you wanna, but if you do, you're definitely gonna puke!"

Jasper glanced around for an escape route, but there were too many people. The last chime faded with a booming echo, and

Crimson's fingers tightened in his. Jasper heard a faint, strange chord of harp-like music and the sound of flutes. "*Jump*," said Crimson, and the entire group went up as one.

At the top of his jump, their surroundings changed. It was like the festival was a lightbulb that had just been flipped on. First it wasn't; then it simply was.

He felt the sudden hard jar of earth beneath his feet and stumbled, only Crimson's hand stopping him from falling. His stomach was still tossing and, though he could see just fine, his eyes were still adjusting to the vision that appeared before him.

"Yeah, I know it's not very fun," admitted Crimson. They were near the foot of a grassy knoll, surrounded by a sparse smattering of trees. Just over the crest, yellow-orange hues meshed into the starry lavender sky. He could smell the smoke of the bonfire and hear the excited chatter of voices, the musical lilt of woodwinds and strings. "I hate portal travel. I think we can get some herbal stuff on the way in for the nausea."

It wasn't just the portal travel that was making his stomach nervous. It was everything. The situation, the portal, the occasional stray demon amidst the greater bulk of the spellcasters. The air felt thicker and smelt like a gigantic garden in full bloom, giving the forest a strange, giddy, dreamlike feeling. It was probably the excess of magical energy, he supposed. Or maybe simply the forest itself.

The people around him began to move away as they became aware of the greater amount of space. Jasper pulled his hand from Crimson's. "Where are we?"

"This is the Summer Solstice Tour," explained Crimson as they joined the throng of people working their way up the slope. "Some people call it the Summerlands. It's a little pocket dimension the spellcasters colonized, oh... I don't know, five... six hundred years ago. Every equinox, entrances crop up all over the world, so they have a big festival for people to visit. Lots of spellcasters retire here. Well, all the good ones anyways."

Holy shit. Charlie's crazy plan was actually working. Of course, he had anticipated it would work out in *some* way, *eventually*. He just hadn't expected it to happen so quickly, nor so extravagantly.

"We're at the Elven Star Port." Crimson pointed over the sea of bobbing hats, headscarves, and hoods, to a small boulder resting at the base of the hill. A seven-pointed star had been carved into its face on all four sides. "Don't forget. If we get the wrong one on the way back, we'll end up in, like, Hong Kong or something."

"Noted," said Jasper.

At the top of the hill, a banner floated over the path without the aid of support poles, the word WELCOME fluttering, cycling through more languages than Jasper could identify. Beyond, the path widened to encompass the festival, which stretched beyond the line of sight.

They stopped to get drinks at a small stand not far from the entrance. A troupe of garishly dressed performers were playing lively music within earshot of their picnic bench while several others danced wildly around a huge multicolored bonfire. The shadows they cast seemed to move with a life of their own, not quite mimicking their counterparts.

The drinks were glowing, Jasper's the bright fluorescent blue of a bug zapper, Crimson's go-light green. Crimson assured him the glow was merely cosmetic and it would quell the uneasiness in his stomach, so he gave it a shot.

It was ice cold and as sweet as raspberry lemonade, with an underbite that made his tongue tingle and completely cleared his sinuses. By the end of the first glass, he felt drunker than he had ever felt in his life, but also elated, energetic. They had a second glass over a substantial number of cigarettes while they watched the people come and go. By the third drink, Crimson decided he was going to go dance in the spinning circle around the bonfire. He asked Jasper along, and Jasper felt so amped up he almost said yes, but something withheld him. He shook his head.

"Suit yourself," said Crimson.

He waited until the werespider was gone, then pulled out his phone. The experts in the magical research and development wing would kill for a few snapshots of this place.

The screen was dark. For a few minutes, he tried to get it to turn on, holding down the "on" button, taking out the battery and putting it back in, even banging it once on the bench. No good. Either it had gotten fried during the jump, or there was some sort of warding charm to prevent people just like him from taking photographic evidence. Maybe it was for the best. Crimson was just starting to warm up to him, and he didn't want to do anything to arouse his suspicions.

Slipping the phone back in his pocket, he went and ordered another drink, this one a mellower, rosy shade of pink. It was weaker, and he nursed it while he kept an eye on the demon. He planned to stay focused.

His plan didn't last very long.

#

Time passed in a blur. Jasper was no longer sure exactly how many drinks he'd had, but his pack of cigarettes was empty all too soon.

Crimson had surely come better prepared. Jasper made his way around the circuit of dancers, searching their strange faces for the werespider's familiar one. Clusters of people stood around the outside of the ring, drinking and smoking and chatting, some of them tangled together in intimate poses that made Jasper's skin prickle hotly.

Through the crowd, he spotted Crimson. The werespider was standing in a small circle, smoking with a dark-skinned woman in a skull mask, a patchwork nightmare of a man in a tweed jacket, and a scantily clad blonde woman in high heels and snakeskin.

As he watched, the woman in the skull mask smiled, laughing at something and slapping Crimson's shoulder, shaking her head. Her eyes were bright blue, shining out of the sockets of the mask. Something about her tickled the back of Jasper's mind, but he couldn't place her.

"Crimson darling, don't be so *gauche*," she was saying as Jasper approached. "You simply *must* come to the auction. Everyone who's anyone is going to be there."

Crimson drew on the cigarette, held in the smoke for a moment, and then puffed it out with a laugh. The light from the fire gave the cloud a strange, soft pink cast. "Yeah, that's exactly why I'm not goin'."

Jasper tossed back the last of his drink and plucked the cigarette from between Crimson's fingers. "Hey, let me hit that real quick." He brought the cigarette to his lips and inhaled. The smoke was sweeter than the harsh tobacco flavor of the Marlboros he smoked. He took another longer, deeper hit to get a better sense of the flavor. It tasted almost like candy.

Crimson watched him with a bemused expression, one eyebrow raised, a crooked smile pulling the corner of his mouth. He cleared his throat. "You know that's not a cigarette, right?"

"What do ya mean?" It looked like a cigarette and burned like a cigarette, but he supposed, trying it again, it didn't really taste like a cigarette.

Crimson took it back, taking a quick hit before passing it over to the woman in the skull mask. She breathed in the smoke, eyes burning like blue fire. She winked one of them at him and spoke briefly in a language Jasper couldn't identify.

The patchwork man laughed once, a short sound like nails in a meat grinder.

"Now, Morg," scolded Crimson, his voice as mild as a dreamy stream, lofty as a cloud, "be nice. He couldn't have known."

"He will know soon enough." The pinkish smoke wreathed the woman. There were little fissures and cracks in her mask, the ivory faded and stained with time. It was impossible to pretend it was made from anything other than human bone. She took another hit and passed it to the man, who inhaled until the smoke escaped through the stitches on the sides of his throat. He laughed again, horribly and stupidly.

Jasper's eyes widened, and he looked to Crimson with accusation. "Was that... drugs? Did you give me drugs? You have to *tell* people shit like that."

"Hey, man, you took it without askin'."

"*Crimson.*"

"Alright, don't get your panties all in a twist." The werespider put an arm around his shoulders and turned him, walking him away from the small group. "You aren't gonna freak out, are you? You barely had any."

Jasper was currently in another dimension, surrounded by spellcasters and demons and generally people who would probably want to kill him, a werespider his only connection here, and had just smoked... what? Some weird magic pot? He thought he had a pretty good reason to freak out.

Yet, as Crimson walked him over to the outskirts of the party, where lush trees with dark blue-green bark sat clustered together in a small wooded area, their thick, heavy branches muffling the sounds of celebration, Jasper didn't feel like he was freaking out. He felt relaxed, loose, if a little light-headed. He breathed in the clear night air and didn't know if he'd ever breathed anything as pure and as sweet.

"I'm not freaking out. It's just, like, you shoulda warned me or whatever."

"Well, I'll warn you that you're about to have a fantastic time." Crimson grinned. Crimson and Jasper both had widely varied opinions on what constituted "a fantastic time." He would have said so, except the idea seemed to become entangled somewhere between his mind and his lips. The world seemed sharper and brighter, like the details had been held underneath a magnifying glass. "Besides, no one ever died from a few huffs of hallucinistem."

"It is nice here," he admitted. Charlie would certainly be pleased. Well, not about the drinking or the smoking or the weed. But a secret pocket dimension full of spellcasters and demons? Finally, something interesting. He leaned against the nearest tree, looking back at the party through the branches, his eyes eventually settling on Crimson. The light of the giant bonfire waned here, the sky, seeming stuck in a permanent twilight, casting his profile in purple light. "It's really... pretty."

"Oh yeah, it's great." Sometimes Crimson's grin seemed so genuine that he wanted to believe it was real. "Now, what do you wanna do first? The wild bats are friendly. Sometimes you can get them to let you ride them. There's dueling in the coliseum right now. Or we could check out the bazaar."

"I don't really like flying," replied Jasper, much less on a wild bat.

"And the duels don't get any good until the finals," said Crimson. "Guess that leaves shopping. Let's go."

The festival was spread across a large area of land, interspersed between patches of wood and larger clearings with foot trails leading the way. Crimson dragged him up a slope, weaving his way around the vendors and food stands that sat atop it.

His eyes didn't know what to take in first, but he was trying very hard not to stare. The myriad of strange sights and sounds came from every side. To his right a vendor in a long snakeskin suit tried to hail them over to purchase what looked to be baby dragons in cages made of iron and bone. To his left, a woman with bright pink hair was having a very stern talk with a gigantic, lumpy creature that was elsewise indescribable. Crimson excused them around a cluster of creepy doll-like children who all spoke as one, and then cut through an opening in the tree line.

Here the woods gave way to a large open plaza hemmed in by extra-bright green hedges. Stands and tents were erected every few feet with signs posted in front of them in various languages. Brightly colored flags and ribbons were strung between them, lit with small paper lanterns. "Maybe we could find somethin' to cover up your aura. People are starting to stare."

"They are?" Jasper had noticed a number of eyes turning in their direction as they made their way through the festival, but he assumed it was mainly because of Crimson, who couldn't seem to help but make himself the center of attention. Now that he looked, he saw the gazes were more targeted. He wrapped his arms uncomfortably around himself and tried not to look at anyone. "What's so fascinating about it anyhow?"

"I dunno, man. Can't see 'em. Your scent though—"

"Yeah, I know I smell weird." He didn't know why every demon he met felt like it was necessary to bring this up, but it was getting on his nerves.

"It ain't like that," said Crimson. They started to work their way through the throngs of people. Jasper usually didn't like crowded spaces, and he especially didn't like them when people kept openly gawking at him, but he still felt surprisingly calm. "You actually smell kinda amazing. Like, y'know that scent in the air on a sunny day in fall? It's kind of like that."

He stopped in front of a particularly gloomy-looking stand draped in faded and holey gray fabric, where the table was covered in glowing rocks and statuettes. A thick black candle smoldered with a steady stream of black smoke, casting the stooping hooded figure on the other side in dimmer light. It tilted back its head, nothing but shadow beneath its hood, and gargled out a question.

Crimson said something back in the same archaic language. After a short debate, Crimson removed a cracked stone coin from his pocket and held it out to the vendor, who took it in two craggy, clawlike hands and turned it over several times, then reached under the table and drew out a small silken satchel. It filled this with a mixture of small gemstones and paper-thin bronze coins, then passed it to Crimson.

As he accepted the satchel, the hooded shape made a loud snuffling sound. Its head turned towards Jasper. It croaked another guttural question.

"Hey!" Crimson snapped his fingers at the thing, drawing its attention away. He shook his head curtly, an open scowl making his pretty face look harder, older. The stream of sharp, angry words that came from him were in an ancient language, impossible to understand, but his tone was one of anger.

What was that about?

The thing lifted both hands in the universal signal for *calm down*.

Crimson muttered something in the language, then nudged Jasper away from the stand with his elbow. "So yeah, something for auras, definitely."

"What did it say to you?"

Crimson's hand went to the back of his own neck. "He wanted to know if you were... I mean, I don't want you to take this the wrong way."

"I can't take it any sort of way if you don't tell me."

Crimson stopped by one of the stands, picking at the odds and ends there. "He wanted to know if you were for sale."

For a moment, the world shrank to embers. Sudden anxiety surged through the heady feeling of the hallucinistem. "Jesus."

"I told him to go fuck himself, if it makes you feel any better. Well... actually what I said, it doesn't really translate that smooth. But that was the general gist."

"Did he say why he wanted to, um... buy me?"

"Something about white light. I don't know."

"Oh." Ivory had said something similar and she wasn't exactly the first. There had been seers and psychics at the academy who brought it up, although none of them had ever tried to *buy* him. The topic made him uncomfortable. He didn't want to think about it. "You sold it *something* though," said Jasper. It wasn't a question.

"Humans experiencing trauma let off bursts of harmless psychic energy. The coin absorbs and stores that energy so it can be later refined." Crimson spun the satchel the witch had traded him for the coin as he glanced over tables strewn with trinkets and herbal bundles. "Some of the old-timers still trade in them. I'd been carrying that one for almost twenty years, so it was pretty valuable."

Ah. So he was trading in human suffering. Every time Jasper thought he was starting to kind of like the guy, he gave him reason not to. Jasper dismissed it. There was no good reason to fight with him here and now, and they obviously needed the money.

At another stand, a small goblinish man offered them a pocket-sized tin of flowery reeds that he claimed would dim an aura when consumed. "You chew one every two hours, you seem perfectly human." His voice was earthy and textured, like moss. Crimson selected a small glass jar of pasty salve, a pile of hand-rolled cigarettes, and three vials of some sort of powder, then paid the man with two gemstones, and handed the tin to Jasper.

Jasper looked doubtfully at the reeds. They were about the length and width of a cigarette, with tufts of fuzzy purplish flowers all the way from top to bottom. Better than a dozen were in the box, meaning there would be several spare, but he had never taken anything to alter his aura before and couldn't help noticing Crimson hadn't inquired about side effects. Across the way he caught the eye of a stall vendor, a man with a pointed black beard and dark, fathomless eyes. It was hard to tell, but he was pretty sure he was staring at him. Jasper plucked a reed from the tin and chewed it cautiously. Its bitter taste made him wince, and he wished for another of those glowing drinks just to wash the taste out of his mouth.

At the next stand they found a sweater woven from arctic dragon fur and lined with "rare sea serpent skin" supposedly capable of keeping the wearer warm and dry even in harsh climates. Crimson bought that too, along with some sort of weird, crooked tusk he claimed was for Alcander, half a dozen small boxes of rare tea leaves, strange coffee grounds, and a pound of what Jasper could only guess was more hallucinistem, fluffy pink dried herbs. Then, finally, a soft brown leather backpack to throw it all in.

"Don't you want anything more, uh… magicky?" Jasper asked.

"Nah, man. Magic was more my ex's thing." Crimson didn't quite meet Jasper's eye, preferring to poke at the feathers on a large dreamcatcher at a nearby stand. Maybe it was just the hallucinistem working on him, but the strings and feathers seemed to absorb light, like the reverse of a glow, and when the werespider touched it, the shadows near his feet drew around him while the light bent away. "I was gonna give him the coin for his birthday, but, well, it didn't really work out."

"Sorry about that, man. Breakups suck." Not that Jasper really knew. He could count the number of dates he'd been on without even using all of his fingers on one hand. He was never all that interested in the whole "relationship" scene, and the girls he knew didn't seem to ever be his type.

"We didn't break up," said Crimson. "He was murdered."

The lady tending the table noticed him playing with the merchandise and spared Jasper the awkwardness of having to inquire further by pointing sternly at the "no touching" sign painted in bright red lettering to the immediate left of the dreamcatcher, then shooed them both away.

The hallucinistem must have had a delayed effect, because it was only just now that the full effects really began to solidly hit him. His limbs felt heavy and relaxed, and the already sharp edges of the world grew more intense. He felt tired, but in a good way.

They took a break in a lofty tent draped with shrouds and tapestries and misty with hookah smoke. Jasper soon found himself lying on a low chaise lounge, tangerine orange with butterscotch yellow stripes, with Crimson sitting on a mismatched pillow on the floor beside him. The spider was smoking from a tall, wide-bottomed glass cylinder. It was half filled with water, with heated stones piled on the top, and bubbled when he inhaled through the rubber tube attached near the base. The sound was soothing. Like water in a stream. Not that Jasper hung around many streams in Manhattan.

The small line of circus elephants patterned on the shroud above him marched in spiraling circles that seemed to rotate into eternity. Some waved balloons as they marched, while others rolled beach balls or rode on tiny trikes.

"Magic?" Jasper asked.

Crimson looked up, squinting. "Are they moving?"

"Yeah."

"Nope, that's the hallucinistem." He blew a puff of smoke over Jasper. The tendrils curled and spun in wispy images that only took full form even as they twisted into new shapes, more intricate and fascinating than the silly cartoon elephants. "Don't worry. It'll wear off soon."

"I'm not worried," Jasper said. He should have been, a little bit, but between the heavy feeling in his limbs and the smoke clouding around them, dancing in the air, he couldn't really be bothered. He stretched out on the chaise lounge, his boots hanging off one end, his head pillowed in his arms at the other. Crimson offered him the hookah and he shook his head. He felt good right now. Like, really good. Better than he could ever remember feeling. He didn't want to push it, and just watching the smoke swirl around him was enough.

Crimson leaned his back against the side of the sofa and breathed the smoke out through his nose. *Like a dragon*, Jasper thought. The blueish smoke hung around him like a cloud. Crimson was talking, as he usually was, but Jasper found it difficult to distinguish words from one another, all of them blending together in the smooth song of his voice. The air was hazy between them, thick enough that it was almost a real, substantial thing. Jasper lifted a hand, trailing his fingers through the smoke. It drifted away, made of nothing after all. Still, it seemed to cling to Crimson, spinning tendrils caressing his jaw, his cheeks, the shiny black of his hair. Jasper reached out again to move it away, the tips of his fingers brushing Crimson's hair. It was soft and silky and warm to the touch. Jasper touched it again, smoothing a lock back behind his ear.

And then Crimson stopped talking. He turned his head to better look back at him but said nothing, just met the half-blood's green eyes with his brown ones, a question held there.

Jasper sat up, the motion making him a little dizzy, and ran a hand over his face, tugging his fingers through his own unruly hair. "I'm kinda hungry. Do they have any, like, normal food here?"

"Sure," Crimson said slowly. His eyes were still on him, curious. He took another long hit from the tube and then set it aside as he exhaled. "Well, close enough to normal anyway. You like seafood? I've heard the serpent sushi's to die for."

"Maybe just a cheeseburger," suggested Jasper.

"Well, they don't really have cows here," said Crimson. "But I'm sure summer buffalo couldn't taste all that different. They export a ton of it this time of year."

The food court was out along a huge shallow lake. Several small craft were adrift in the water, which was a dark gray-blue and smooth as a mirror. The tables were packed, so they crawled out on the stones above the shoreline. Dawn had broken while they were resting in the lounge, though this dawn was like none Jasper had ever seen. The sun was a shining lavender beacon, and the sky never grew blue, but pinkish-purple, with wispy clouds that hung low like smoke.

The summer buffalo burger wasn't bad—seasoned with spices and extremely juicy, with a warm bun that had a slight crunch, and a reddish sort of lettuce that tasted vaguely like fry sauce. Crimson bought one too, but only so he could tear it up and toss chunks down at the waterline for the long-bodied baby serpents that nested there. A particularly bold one crawled halfway out of the water to snatch a piece that had fallen short, then backpedaled rapidly into the pool with the meat clenched in its beak. It was cute in that awkward sort of way ugly things often were, head too big for its slender body, eyes too big for its head, and malformed legs too small to be of any real use. Crimson said that next summer it would migrate out to the open ocean (of which this planet was primarily comprised) and there it would shed its baby skin, along with its silly little legs, and then, if it survived, grow to an enormous and terrifying size.

Jasper felt steadier with the protein in his stomach absorbing some of the alcohol, and the glass bottle of crystal-clear water that came along with the food rejuvenated some of his energy, which was good because they spent the rest of the day bouncing from one attraction to the next, only stopping for drinks (and once, another burger) along the way.

On the outskirts of the fair, Jasper cautiously stroked the ears of a giant fox bat as big as a horse, while it nibbled on an oversized apple and stared at him with big puppylike eyes. In the afternoon, they saw two full-grown sea serpents fighting for territory from the deck of a small boat a safe distance away, and afterwards walked a hedge maze where, for a small fee, one could sample exotic fruits by plucking them directly from the bushes. By the time evening came, they had added an assortment of odds and ends to Crimson's backpack, including two pounds of summer buffalo jerky, which Jasper decided he liked after all, and a smattering of exotic spices he thought he'd use if he ever learned how to cook. They went to every inch of the place except for the barren stretch on the other side of a craggy pass Crimson called the "Summoning Circles," which he seemed determined to steer clear of.

They were strolling along the path with the moon high in the sky overhead and no particular destination in mind, when somewhere far off a trumpet began to sound. "That'll be the closing ceremonies," said Crimson. "They're basically like the world's greatest magic show if it were also a rock concert. C'mon, it'll be fun."

Beyond the rise, a depression in the forest floor made a sizable valley, at the bottom of which a stage had been erected. There was no seating, but people were sitting along the slope on blankets and pillows and in folding chairs and gathered around the stage.

Jasper had never been to a concert before, much less a magical concert. The stage was large, made of raw unprocessed wood, the dark blue-green bark showing through, looking like it had simply grown there on its own rather than been built. Instead of traditional spotlights, several pillars were topped with bright flames in different colors, casting light on the stage and gathering crowd. As they approached, the band—a motley crew who didn't look like what Jasper thought rock bands looked like (though one of them looked like they were literally made out of rocks)—took up their instruments and began to play. There were no speakers that Jasper could see, yet the sound was loud enough to easily be heard across the field.

"They're pretty good," Jasper said over the music. It reminded him a little bit of Rush, but somehow with more drums and even weirder.

"Wanna get closer?"

"Um, okay." The crowd was thicker and livelier near the front. Jasper hooked his arm into Crimson's and smiled. "Just don't ditch me. For real, man."

Crimson looked down at their arms and smiled back. "I won't. For real."

#

The show ended with a literal BOOM, the performers vanishing in a multicolored blaze of glittering smoke. He wished his phone worked here so he could record some of this stuff. He had no idea how he was going to file a report for this when it was all over.

The crowd screamed and jumped excitedly, some of them shooting small wisps of harmless light at the stage. Crimson said that was like throwing roses, then added that they should probably move before everyone started to leave and the whole thing became "a clusterfuck." They had moved further away from the stage over the course of the show and opted to take a shortcut through the woods to avoid the crowd. Since the entire situation was unsafe, Jasper decided not to bother asking whether this was safe or not.

The trees muted some of the sound from the valley. The woods were surprisingly more comfortable than he'd thought they would be. There were no curious stares here, nor rambunctious conversation; it was almost quiet. He felt mellow and calm amid the cool colors and sweet-smelling air. Crimson was trotting along ahead of him, going on about one of the women who'd been on the stage. Jasper was only half-listening. He knew he should probably listen carefully to everything the werespider was saying, but he said so much half the time, and so little of it about anything, that it was hard to pay attention. The wood was denser here, the canopy more so, and he was more focused on keeping from stubbing his toes in the dark.

"Did you hear that?" Crimson stopped short and Jasper bumped into his back.

"You're not about to tell me these trees are alive or something, are you?" Jasper didn't know whether he was joking or not, and neither did the tone of his voice.

"Of course they're alive, Jasper. They're *trees*."

"Shut up, you know what I mean," replied Jasper, but Crimson became very still, his head cocked to one side, with his luminescent eyes focused off in the middle distance. He looked suddenly in the opposite direction and then, without words, started off in long strides.

As they got closer, Jasper heard it too. Jasper was light-footed by trade, and Crimson by nature, but whoever was moving towards them was not. He heard him snapping twigs and stumbling on roots, the short, ragged sound of his breath. The noises were coming towards them at an angle. Crimson moved suddenly like a viper striking, reaching out, grabbing hold of whoever or whatever it was, and dragging it from the foliage.

It was a seemingly human man in a red shirt. It was difficult to tell much else with him squirming and struggling uselessly against Crimson's grip. Jasper squinted through the darkness and drew a little closer, then grabbed Crimson's elbow. "Put him down. He's hurt."

Up closer, he saw the red he glimpsed was not fabric, but blood, a shocking amount.

Crimson let the man drop too suddenly for him to have a chance to catch himself, and Jasper missed catching him by an inch, so he hit the forest floor on his hip. He dragged himself backwards, away from the pair, until he lost his energy and stopped at the base of a hewn stump. The light found him clearer here, and now Jasper could see the symbols and sigils carved in neat rows on his torso and down his arms. He was older than he'd thought—silver streaks in his dark hair, lines on his tanned face, the scraggly shadow of a beard on his chin. Forty-something, maybe.

Crimson shrugged. "Smells human to me." As if this were not obvious.

"It's alright." Jasper took a few steps closer. "We're not going to hurt you."

"He musta been over near the summoning circles," said Crimson. He hadn't moved to help, but was listening again and watching the surrounding trees. "Probably got loose. There'll be someone looking for him. Let him be."

The man didn't seem to hear them. He was holding one hand cradled in his lap, shaking. When Jasper was within grabbing distance of him, the man looked up, startled. "Please. Let me go. They're coming. I have to go. I have to—"

"Good gods, I'm not gonna listen to that." Crimson sighed. He swept in beside Jasper, took hold of the man's chin to angle his face up, and looked him carefully in the eye. "Be calm."

All expression went out of the man's face. The shaking eased, and gradually he went from gasping for breath to breathing normally. Crimson let go and looked at Jasper. "There are people headed our way. You'll hear them soon."

"We should get out of here." Jasper shrugged off his jacket and offered it to the man. He merely looked at him with blank eyes, so Jasper leaned forward to lay the jacket over his shoulders. He was reaching for his hand to pull him to his feet when he saw that two of his fingers were missing, the stumps still lazily pumping blood. He grabbed his elbow instead. The man swayed on his bare feet.

"Can you walk?" Jasper asked. He thought he heard something in the woods back the way the man had come from, and a glance showed the orange glow of a torch through the tree trunks. "Or run?"

"Uh," replied the man.

Overhead, an owl perched on the bough of a nearby tree.

"Little late, I think," said Crimson.

The owl hooted loudly and one of the voices called, "This way!"

"There's definitely too many of them," said Crimson. "They're coming from over there too. *Just let him be.*"

Seeing that Crimson had no intention of helping, Jasper pulled on the man's arm. "Run."

But the man did not move. He was listlessly watching Crimson. God damn the stupid glamor.

"*Crimson*," hissed Jasper.

Twigs crackled underfoot.

The owl hooted and ruffled its feathers.

"*Fine*," Crimson growled back. His glaring eyes flickered to the mortal. "*Run.*"

The man moved so suddenly he almost jerked Jasper's arm out of its socket, though once he was moving, Jasper caught up and passed him easily. The sounds were closer now, and Crimson was right—they were all around them.

The shape of a tall, robed figure burst into view, and Jasper veered away as wisps of fire ignited at his heels. They ran around a fallen trunk, losing sight of the caster as they lost sight of them. He and the human dove in a small copse of trees. Crimson was with them all along, but he didn't follow them into the copse, preferring instead to stand right out in the open, rocking boredly from heel to toe with his hands in his pockets. Jasper swore under his breath.

Before he could figure out how to get him out of the open, two men appeared, running on foot in their direction. Jasper crouched, gesturing for the human to stay silent while he watched through a break in the boughs.

"Hey! You there! Demon!" The taller of the two men jogged right up to Crimson. He stooped over, his hands on his knees as he panted. "Did you see a human come through here?"

"About yea high? Drenched in blood and reeking with the unmistakable scent of mortal terror?" asked Crimson politely.

The shorter of the two snapped his fingers. "Yeah, that's the guy."

"He went out towards the coliseum." He pointed back the way he and Jasper had come.

The taller one seemed to finally catch his breath. "Thanks," he said, and they both took off again.

Crimson glowered at Jasper through the trees, his gaze finding him quickly even though he was hidden. "You're gonna get us killed."

One to talk, thought Jasper. Somewhere nearby, the owl hooted again, louder this time. It probably belonged to a sorcerer a good deal wiser than the two nitwits Crimson had just fooled.

"We gotta keep moving," Jasper told the newcomer. The glamor appeared to have faded. He was shaking again, and when Jasper spoke suddenly, he took a sharp intake of breath, as if startled. "Hey, don't be scared. I'm Jasper and that's Crimson. We're going to help you, okay?" This was said almost pointedly in Crimson's direction. "What's your name?"

"M-Maxwell. Max."

"Hi, Max. We gotta go, okay?"

Max's eyes were still dazed, but he nodded as if he understood. They picked their way clear of the copse, and the three of them started to move away from the approaching sounds. The owl hooted irritably, hopping after them, from branch to branch.

"How much time do we have left?" Jasper couldn't tell how long they'd been there. It felt like forever and also like no time at all.

Crimson took his watch from his pocket and looked at it. It seemed to work fine here even though Jasper's phone wouldn't even turn on. "About ten minutes."

"We can make that."

"We could make it a lot faster without the human," replied Crimson. Presently, Max's foot caught an exposed root. Despite his bitching, Crimson caught him and strung his arm over his shoulders, stooping slightly to heft him up on his hip and then breaking into a flat-out run.

The owl screeched and plunged from the boughs with its great white wings spread and its talons outstretched. Jasper drew his pistol and spun to take the cursed thing out of the air, but even as he raised the weapon, there was a blinding flash of light. Then…

Pitch darkness.

He tried to blink his vision back into focus, but all he could see was an inky blackness. Something snatched at him out of the shadows, and he struck it with the heel of the gun's grip on reflex, connecting hard.

A voice that was unmistakably Crimson's swore a vile string of curse words and insults, too quickly to truly understand. The darkness was impenetrable. He couldn't even see the demon's eyes.

"I can't see anything." Jasper tried to keep the panic from his voice. He wasn't like Crimson; he couldn't easily fall back on his other senses when he found himself suddenly without his sight. His demon sense was useless against a spellcaster that was otherwise human, and he couldn't hear well enough to allow him to fight blind.

The werespider's hand grabbed his empty one, tugging him after him. Jasper's boot caught on the uneven ground, but he righted himself and tightened his grip. "It's a spell," Crimson growled. "Don't you know anything? Fight it off."

Jasper's specialty was in demons such as Crimson—vampires and weres, things that had once been human but now weren't—not in sorcerers and the like. He wasn't used to dealing with magic, but now did not seem like the time to get into it.

He tried to focus on clearing his mind, shaking the spell off, all while still running blind through a forest. There was a low whistle and they were suddenly moving in a different direction, the whooshing boom and throwback heat of a fire somewhere near where they had just been. His shoulder crashed into a tree, jarring him. He would have fallen if Crimson let go, but the werespider's grip was an iron vise.

Branches whipped from all sides, cutting into his arms. One branch hit him good and hard across his face, and he tasted blood from his split lip. This seemed to be enough to snap him out of the spell, and the world returned to him just as quickly as it had disappeared, like a light switching on.

They were still in the forest, the trees closer and taller and darker, blue-black. Crimson seemed to know where he was going, but Jasper suspected he was only going on impulse and necessity. Jasper spared a glance over his shoulder to see a figure—he could not tell if it was a man or a woman or otherwise—literally flying after them, the great owl at its side. The spellcaster threw out its hand, and a tree that was awful close for comfort burst into flames.

They sprang over a fallen tree trunk, the firelight casting their shadows out ahead of them. Beneath the nearer sound of spitting and crackling flames was the chatter of voices and laughter. A clock began to chime in loud, even keels.

Crimson swore.

The forest gave way suddenly to a steep decline, the lavender sky open above them. He could see the disc now, and the large number of people gathered on it. A few looked up in their direction.

Loose gravel slid underfoot. A whoosh of fire burst at their heels, spitting shattered hunks of stone into the air.

The chime clanged for the fifth... or was it the sixth time? The face of the clock began to pulse, its hands spinning.

They hit the base of the hill and veered to avoid a second burst of flame. Crimson threw in an extra burst of speed, and Jasper was surprised to find he could keep up just fine, but so could the spellcaster. He felt fingers grasp at the collar of his shirt, the scrape of long fingernails on flesh.

"JUMP!" screamed Crimson as the last chime split the air, and Jasper sprang forward with all his might.

Chapter Twelve

—

All Accounted For

They leapt forward instead of straight up in the air, and when they came through on the other side, there was nothing to slow their momentum. They landed in a tangle of arms and legs amid several magic users who hadn't quite gotten their feet. Jasper's gun clattered to the side harmlessly.

Crimson was laughing as he stood and brushed himself off. "Holy shit, man. You're crazier than me."

The exhilaration of having so narrowly escaped had Jasper grinning as well. He was no stranger to close calls, nor was he accustomed to coming by them so frequently. "I can't believe we made it." He picked up his gun and made sure the safety was back on. There was no sign of the spellcaster who was chasing them. They must have been stuck in the Summerlands.

Jasper remembered their reason for fleeing said spellcaster and looked for Max, finding him struggling to his feet near a few disgruntled spellcasters, still wearing his jacket. Jasper helped him up. "Hey, Max." He tried to speak softly. The man was still shaking and scared, weak from blood loss and shock. "It's alright, it didn't follow us." They should get out of here quick anyway. What if the caster had friends?

"Our friend can help you," Jasper said.

Crimson took one look at Max covered in blood and filth from stumbling around the forest, and sighed, though his smile was still there, sparkling in his eyes. "Al's gonna be pissed."

#

Max was well enough to walk, but only because Crimson put him under again. Jasper didn't like the way the werespider carelessly wielded his hypnotism, but he had to admit it could come in handy. Max must have been in excruciating pain and well on his way to a fatal case of shock, but the hypnosis seemed to keep both problems at bay.

They made it back to the hotel in good time, considering the circumstances. Crimson headed for the stairwell and Max tried to follow him. Jasper caught his arm, glowering at Crimson. "What are you doing? He'll never make it up all those."

Crimson frowned but, looking at Max, had to concede the point. "It's kinda small for three people, isn't it?" he asked when the lift arrived and Jasper stepped on.

"Uh, not really." There were more spacious lifts, surely, but these were larger than the ones at the agency, which had obviously been installed back when people were smaller or something. Jasper put his hand out to hold the door. "Come on, you're drawing attention to us."

"Gods, you call me dramatic," huffed Crimson, but he stepped on and put as much distance between him and the other two as possible, standing in the corner with his fingers wrapped around the rail behind him. Soft jazz music played as they ascended. The doors only opened once, for a suited businessman with a roll-along suitcase at his heel. "If I were you, I'd wait for the next one," growled Crimson. It only took one scathing look for the man to agree.

The doors slid shut. The music played on. Jasper cleared his throat, trying to hide a small grin with his fist. "So, uh, you're scared of elevators, huh?"

"Fuck you, Craig, I'm not *scared* of elevators." Jasper's eyes went to the deathlike vise-grip he had on the handrail, and the werespider quickly let up, but his fingers left indentations in the cheap metal. He shoved his hands in his pockets instead. "I just don't like being cooped up in these things. There's nowhere to go."

It was kind of funny, but Crimson was obviously very sensitive about it, and Jasper didn't want to antagonize him, though he couldn't stop from smiling. The door opened again, this time to their floor, and Crimson was the first one out, Max trailing after him like a puppy.

Alcander wasn't as angry as Crimson predicted he would be. When they came into the room with the injured human, he fired off a quick series of questions, which Crimson answered with a shrug and the short explanation that they had "found him in the woods." Jasper thought it was a pretty sorry explanation and went into some more detail, the spellcaster, the chase, the suspected ritual. Max began to shudder and shake more violently, and Al seemed to make up his mind on the matter, leading the human into the bathroom.

"Are you hurt?" the doctor asked, and Jasper realized he was talking to him. The tip of his tongue traced the cut on his lip. It wasn't very deep. He could take care of it and the other cuts along his arms easily.

"I'm fine. Just help Max."

Alcander said he'd do a much better job of helping Max if he had any sort of medical supplies. Jasper dug his first aid kit out of his backpack. It was a little better than a standard first aid kit but still rather sorry when you compared it to Max's injuries. Crimson offered him the jar of salve he had purchased in the Summerlands, and, though Alcander looked extremely uncertain, he took it nonetheless.

Al told him to take one of the sheets off the bed and cut it into strips, which he did, and then he told him, in a curt, firm voice, that he could leave the room. Jasper thought it was a nice way of telling him to get the fuck out of his way.

Since the bathroom was occupied, Jasper had to make do with the mirror on the closet door, washing off his face and his arms with a bottle of water from the mini fridge and what was probably a clean T-shirt. None of the cuts were deep enough or wide enough to need stitches. It was good they didn't actually fight the spellcaster. It could have been a lot worse.

"Thanks for helping me get him out of there," said Jasper, looking back at Crimson through the mirror. He hadn't been certain he was going to.

"Yeah, well, I promised I wasn't gonna ditch you, so you didn't really give me much choice." Crimson shrugged as he tossed his backpack and jacket onto the bed nearest the window. "Besides, I figure this makes us even. You helped me out with Alcander. I helped you out with Mark—"

"Max," corrected Jasper.

"Whatever." He climbed onto the bed. "I'm gonna get some sleep. Wake me up if..." He paused, presumably to think of acceptable reasons for waking him. "Just don't wake me up. I'm sure it'll be fine."

Having been awake for the entire festival and considering the recent excitement, Jasper could have gone to bed too, but he wanted to make sure Max was going to be alright. He waited up.

It was more than two hours after Crimson had gone to sleep that Al finally emerged from the bathroom, drying his hands on a white hotel hand towel. It was noticeably less white than it had been before, and Jasper was a little surprised to see the vampire holding onto something so filthy so tightly.

"Is he—" Jasper started to ask, but Al gently interrupted. "He will be fine, Jasper. I've patched him up as best I can. That salve seems to be helping. He has lost a lot of blood, though. I am afraid there is nothing I can do about that with my current resources. He will need rest and plenty of it. Could you please bring him out?"

Alcander was a vampire and should have been strong enough to carry the human on his own, but Jasper didn't argue with him. Turning off the movie he was watching on low, he went to get Max. He was lying in the bathtub, a folded towel beneath his head serving for a pillow. Asleep, his chest rising and falling slowly under the white strips of sheet, graying hair pushed back off his face. The stumps of his missing fingers were thickly wrapped, red already coloring the white. When Jasper lifted him from the basin, his eyes fluttered under his bruised lids, but he did not wake, not even when he brought him to the main room and laid him on the second bed.

There were four of them now, and only two beds and one couch. The beds were big enough for two, but Max needed as easy a rest as he could get, and Jasper didn't want to crawl in beside Crimson. The werespider was being nice to him lately, especially at the festival, but he seemed like the sort of guy who could easily get the wrong idea. He'd probably wake up on the floor anyway, so he resolved to sleep there tonight. Al could have the couch. It was the least he could do to repay him.

Jasper grabbed the extra pillow from Crimson's bed. His mind felt fuzzy from tiredness and the leftover alcohol and hallucinistem in his system. He glanced at the empty space beside the werespider, plenty big enough for him, and at the werespider himself. His eyes were closed, dark lashes resting against his cheeks, hair rumpled in a way that looked very deliberate and messy. Jasper thought of the smoke-filled tent, the ghostlike memory of his hair at his fingertips. He turned away, threw the pillow onto the floor between the beds, lay down, and tried to sleep.

#

"Crimson?"

The vampire's voice was a soft hiss, pulling him unwillingly away from the deep darkness of slumber. He kept his eyes closed, feigning sleep.

"I know you are awake," said Alcander.

Crimson sighed. Godsdamn his vampire ears. The werespider rolled over, squinting at the other demon, then sitting up and tilting his head to listen to the soft snore of the half-blood lying on the floor at the end of the bed. Al finicked beside him. "Did they know?"

"Will you shut up?" Crimson tossed back the blankets and climbed out of bed. He gestured for Alcander to follow him. They slipped out onto the balcony, Crimson easing the sliding glass door shut behind them and preemptively lighting a cigarette as an excuse in case the mortal should wake.

"Well?" It was unusual for Al to be so impatient.

"Well nothing."

"Nothing?" Ah, skepticism. There was the Alcander he knew.

"That's what I said. Nothing. Nada. Bubkes. Should I think of other synonyms? Zilch."

"I get it. Can't we talk inside?" He was obviously uncomfortable on the balcony, his back pressed against the glass.

"No." Crimson perched on the handrail, hooking his ankles around the bars. The buildings were shorter here, and the air tasted strange, so similar to New York, yet so different. "He'll hear us."

"If what you say is true, there is nothing to hear," replied Alcander. "Who did you talk to, anyway?"

"Lots of people." Crimson tapped his ash to the parking lot

below. It was packed with sleek, expensive cars, too clean and too new. Everything was always different from how he remembered it. "I saw Morgaine." He almost didn't mention it.

"*Morgaine Onyx?*" The vampire hated Crimson's association with the blood mage—their ideological philosophies rested on opposite ends of a spectrum—but Crimson couldn't help it; he had precious few friends to begin with and couldn't afford to go kicking them to the curb any time they had a problem with one another.

Not that he was sure he considered Morgaine a *friend*, exactly.

"What did she say?"

"Just the usual magic folk gibberish," replied Crimson. "Nothing important. I also got Jasper high outta his fuckin' mind and drunk to boot. Didn't let anything slip. If he's really stagin' some sting, he's pretty good at keepin' it under wraps. He did get a little weird about that human in there, but that don't seem abnormal for him."

"So then, you don't believe him to be...?"

"A Hunter out for my blood?" Fleeting thoughts of the hookah tent, Jasper's fingers trailing through the ends of his hair. Then of the vampires in Brooklyn wisping into ash. Of Adam, wildly rambling nonsense, his strange ratlike black eyes darting. Nothing made sense. "I dunno. We'll have to see. If you're uneasy, I can stay up again, keep watch."

Alcander shook his head. "I will do it. I need to keep an eye on Max anyway." He shifted antsily from foot to foot. "Could we—"

"Yeah, I think we're good." Alcander shouldn't have to deal with this. "Go on inside. I'll be there in a minute."

\#

It hadn't occurred to Jasper to ask Max where he lived while they were running for their lives from the spellcaster, and he was happy to learn the next day that he was from Miami. He lived in a small house in Buena Vista, by himself, and had been abducted from his own bedroom one night after working at his accounting firm just a few blocks away. That had been two weeks ago.

As far as Jasper could gather, his abduction was random. He wasn't any sort of magic. The most important thing seemed to be that he was alone. No wife or kids, both parents deceased. Any family he had lived on the other side of the country. There didn't seem to be anyone who would miss him.

Alcander wanted to watch over him for another day before letting him go home. Already he looked leagues better thanks to Al's care and the magic salve Crimson had bought in the Summerlands, but it would have felt like a waste for him to have survived the ordeal just to die due to an infection.

Jasper went out and got more medical supplies and more takeout than two people could possibly eat. It was the first time in a long time that he shared a meal with someone who actually ate food. It was nice. He'd kind of missed it.

The day after that he made the mistake of mentioning that if they had a car, they could drive Max home, and Crimson was out the door before he could stop him. He was back within half an hour with an old hatchback and a shit-eating grin. The car was obviously stolen, but with the damage already done, Jasper saw little need to make a scene and got in the front seat after helping Max into the back.

At his house, a cute little one-story on a street of cute little houses, Jasper insisted on helping Max inside while he ignored Crimson's eye rolling. He wrote his number down on a sticky pad and stuck it on the fridge, telling Max to call him if he needed anything. Max thanked him and gave him a business card with his number on it, though the human wasn't sure if he would still have a job after being gone for two weeks without a good excuse. Somehow, he didn't think being kidnapped by magicians who tried to sacrifice him to their blood god would work.

Chapter Thirteen

—

Date Night

The next few weeks passed in a blur. Jasper all too quickly grew accustomed to sleeping in and staying up late, so much so that he could hardly recall what it was like to have spent the better part of his life rising with the sun, if not earlier.

Most of their evenings were spent barhopping. Jasper learned poker and pool and the names of more mixed drinks than he had known existed. In the predawn hours, before sleep, Crimson liked to watch movies. These were often the sort that included lots of fast cars and large explosions, but he had an obvious soft spot for the old black-and-whites. Bogart and Cagney. Welles and Robinson. Jasper preferred books and music to the more visual forms of media, but he warmed to the films and, gradually, liked them as well.

Alcander never left the hotel. Never even left the room. During the second week of their stay, Crimson brought a laptop back from one of their outings "to keep him from going crazy," and Alcander seemed delighted for probably the first time since Jasper had known him. He was far less sulky from then on, though he was still sometimes skittish around him.

When the barhopping lost some of its appeal (or when Jasper grew tired of waking up hungover almost every single day), they explored the city's other attractions, first the mundane human ones, then those of a slightly more supernatural nature.

The city was not as booming with demon activity as New York was, but there were a small number of secluded haunts and even a supposedly haunted house, where Crimson swore the creepy sounds and mysterious gusts of cold wind were nothing more than an overzealous mage trying to make a mint off dumb tourists.

Once, Crimson told him he was going for a walk and insisted he not follow. It wasn't hard for Jasper to figure out why; his skin had the washed-out look of a faded picture taken in sepia tone, and his dark eyes were more often the shade of rust than of chocolate. When he came home, however, he seemed healthier than ever.

Jasper tried not to think about it. He tried so hard, in fact, that he *didn't* think about it. Then it was back to the bars and nightclubs and pubs.

"No way," said Jasper, one night midway through the third week. "I know how this goes. You convince me to go into this obnoxiously loud club, you hang out with me for like five minutes, you run into some pretty girl or handsome guy, and then you ditch me with a retarded werewolf."

"Abby's not retarded," said Crimson. He nudged him with his elbow. "And that's not the way it's gotta go. Maybe this time you could meet some pretty girl and ditch *me*." This was absolute bullshit, of course, but Crimson seemed surprisingly earnest. "Do people still use the word *wingman?*"

Jasper smiled weakly. "Only in the movies, Crims."

The club was as obnoxious as he had anticipated, but before long Jasper was too drunk to care and *just* drunk enough to ask a girl to dance. Fortunately, she was drunk enough to agree.

Her name was Lindsay, and she had short, spiky blond hair and a nose ring, and though Jasper was sure she was very obviously too cool for him, he was delighted when she gave him her phone number and asked him to text her.

"Am I supposed to wait three days or something?" asked Jasper the next day, when he was squinting at the smudge of ink on the back of his hand in an attempt to make out the blurry digits.

"If she's actually interested, three days is gonna feel like an eternity, and if she isn't, then you could wait a year and it'd still be too soon."

"So, then I should text her now," Jasper decided.

Crimson snatched the phone out of his hand.

Jasper's heart flew into his throat. Charlie rarely contacted him without his having been contacted first, and always from a different burner phone with a code word to make certain it was safe, but he didn't want Crimson anywhere near that phone. He reached for it. Crimson lifted it over his shoulder and put a hand flat on Jasper's chest to hold him at bay.

"No way, she'll think you're a fuckin' stalker." He wasn't actually looking at the phone, just trying to keep it away from him. Jasper relaxed. Crimson held up a finger. "One day. Contact her in the evening, and don't try to make plans for the same day. That's obnoxious."

"I guess if anyone would know anything about being obnoxious, it'd be you," said Jasper with a grin not entirely ingenuine. "Now give me my phone back."

"You could get it back yourself if you weren't so short."

"I am not short." Jasper was a hair over six feet tall, not much smaller than the werespider. "You're just freakishly big."

Crimson winked. "You should see the rest of me."

Alcander sighed at them from behind his laptop. It seemed like the only times he was away from the thing were when he was sleeping or bathing. "Will you *please* just give him his phone back?"

"Yeah, yeah." Crimson dropped the phone in his outstretched hand. "Let me know if your hot date has a cute friend. If you're lucky, we can go together, and I'll make sure you don't screw it up."

As it turned out, Lindsay did have a friend, and they had plans to go clubbing over the weekend. Lindsay said she was sure it would be alright if he and Crimson joined them, which was somewhat of a relief. It would be less awkward to go in a group, even if it meant it wouldn't be exactly the same as what he considered a *date*. So, three days later, he found himself standing in a club, scanning faces in search of hers. She spotted them before he spotted her, and she stood on the footrest of her barstool, waving them over.

"Hi!" she yelled. She had to yell. It was the only way to hear anything in these places. She kissed him quickly on the cheek and grinned, holding his gaze for a long moment before making a sort of "oops" expression and drawing away. "Sorry! I almost forgot!" She gestured beside her to a tall, shapely woman in knee-high lace-up boots and an off-the-shoulder black dress. She was a little older than Lindsay, but not by much. "This is my friend Cindy!" She and Crimson were already looking at each other, both in surprised delight.

"Holy shit," said Crimson. "Is Cindy short for Cinderella? Because you look like a *princess*."

"Wow," said Cindy. Her hand went to her lips, trying to cover a grin. "That was really bad. Do you say that to every girl named Cindy?"

"Not yet. Should I start?"

She shook her head, still smiling. "Probably not."

"I'll keep that in mind," said Crimson. "I'm Johnny." He offered her his hand, and she took it with a firm shake. "Do you wanna dance?"

"Sure, why not?" They both took off into the crowd, and Lindsay grabbed Jasper's arm.

"C'mon."

He and Crimson had shared two drinks at the in-house bar back at the hotel before coming, and though he didn't exactly feel drunk enough to dance yet, he felt buzzed enough to try. If only to appease Lindsay. He had been completely trashed when they'd done it before, and he remembered little else but brief flashes—standing on the back patio with dozens of other people clustered together like cattle while he tried to clumsily light her cigarette, doing Irish Car Bombs at the bar, the touch of her nails on the back of his neck, a peal of Crimson's laughter, a loud pulsing rhythm with a chaotic under beat that seemed to permeate the entire night. It seemed like he had been able to feel that rhythm in his body, and he hadn't had to think much about how he moved to it, but now he felt unsure.

He tried to remember everything Crimson had told him about dancing ("The most important rule," he said, "is loosening the fuck up.") and moved to the beat. For all the grace he had in a fight, on the dance floor he struggled to keep the rhythm and just hoped he looked too cool to care rather than entirely hopeless.

If Lindsay had a problem with his dancing, she hid it well, giving him a smile as she raised her arms above her head, shaking her hair. She looked very pretty under the flashing lights, so he took a chance and kissed her, quickly and gently, on the lips. "Sorry," he said almost immediately. "I just thought—"

She grabbed the front of his shirt and pulled him closer, getting up on her toes so she could press her lips more firmly against his. As they drew apart, the song tapered off. Lindsay smiled at him and pointed towards the bar, a question in her expression. He nodded and took her hand. It was easier for him to get through the crowd than it was for her, so he led the way.

Cindy and Crimson were already at the bar, though they looked a lot less thrilled with each other than they had earlier. Crimson leaned on his elbows with his arms folded on the counter and glared down into his drink. Cindy said something to him several times, but he barely seemed to be paying any attention to her.

When he and Lindsay approached, Cindy stood suddenly, grabbed her purse, and marched over to Lindsay. "We're going to the bathroom."

"Oh… kay…" said Lindsay and was almost immediately dragged away. She shrugged helplessly at Jasper over her shoulder and trotted along behind her friend.

Jasper stumbled over and hopped on the stool beside the werespider. "She kissed me."

"Oh, yeah?" asked Crimson. He half-raised his glass in Jasper's direction and gave him a nod. "Congratulations." He threw back the rest of the drink and clapped the glass down on the bar.

"She's really cool, right? Like *really cool*."

"Yeah, she seems great," agreed Crimson. Jasper blinked at his unenthusiastic tone, and Crimson must have read the expression on his face because he cracked a smile. "I'm not being sarcastic, Jazz. I'm really happy for ya. I just don't really like Cindy all that much. Not my type. Think I'm actually gonna take off here soon."

"You're going *home*?" It was strange how quickly a place could seem like "home" sometimes. "It's barely midnight."

"Yeah, I already told Cindy I had to go soon. She's really susceptible to the pheromones or something. She's already getting all weird and possessive; plus she keeps calling me *sugar*." This time he was sure he didn't imagine the look of disgust Crimson made at the endearment. "Must be a Southern thing. It's *really* annoying, and I *really* don't wanna deal with it."

"I'll go with you, then." He didn't want to be left alone with the girls. He barely knew them. Besides which, Crimson was acting weird, and though he definitely thought the werespider could stand to be knocked down a peg or two (or three or ten or twenty), he didn't like how quiet he was being.

"Thanks, kid. But I'll be fine. You should stay. Have fun. Give us somethin' to talk about back at the hotel."

Only it didn't give them anything to talk about back at the hotel because by the time Jasper got back, the werespider was already in bed. He woke up briefly when Jasper turned on the TV, and vaguely watched whatever was playing, but drifted off again before long.

When evening came again, Jasper was up before Crimson, which wasn't unusual. He shot a quick text message to Lindsay, telling her he'd had a really good time and that he hoped she had as well, then took a quick shower and ran to the nearby diner for breakfast. It was the only place close to the hotel that served pancakes in the afternoon, and it was usually quiet. He texted Charlie a coded message to let him know things were well and that he'd contact him with a full report once he could be certain he could do so without risking Crimson or Alcander nosing in, then deleted his history, finished his late afternoon breakfast, and went back to the hotel.

Alcander was up now, but Crimson still wasn't. He grumbled in his sleep when Jasper closed and bolted the door.

Jasper checked the time.

It was after five p.m., and though the sun was still up, usually he would be awake by now. Taking a seat on the edge of the bed, he grabbed a dollar-bin paperback from his backpack and tried to read, but the book didn't hold his attention long. He went over to Alcander instead. "What you up to, Al?"

Alcander snapped the laptop closed. "Nothing."

Jasper couldn't help himself. He felt suspicious and it showed before he could stop it.

"I was, uh… just checking on something. It isn't important." He set the computer aside, fixing his attention on Jasper. "Do the two of you have plans tonight?"

"I'm not sure," said Jasper. "What about you? Big plans?" He tried to joke.

"I was thinking perhaps I would just stay in." Alcander made a joke of his own. The vampire was an oddity he could not understand or explain. In all the time they spent there, he never once left the room, and he had no idea what he did when maid service came around to call—maybe just hid out on the balcony or in the closet or something. Not that they really needed maid service, since Al spent almost as much time cleaning as he did fucking around on the laptop. He was gentle in a way that defied words, soft spoken, but intelligent and thoughtful, and, vampire or no, Jasper liked him.

"Are you still working on that formula? For the synthetic blood?"

"It is difficult without a lab, but yes. It has all the chemical components, but I am afraid there is still something missing."

"Can you guys really not just eat, like, animal blood?" That was what they fed the vampires they had in the holding cells at St. James, and though they often grew weak, it kept them alive. Jasper didn't mention that for several reasons.

Alcander very nearly scowled. He drew his lips back down over his teeth, holding them in a straight line. "Animal blood is also lacking. You can technically drink it, and it will not kill you, but you run into a similar problem as with synthetic. Something is missing. And animal blood is just *disgusting*. Do you have any idea what percentage of other bodily fluids can be found in that?"

"Point taken," Jasper said quickly. "Uh, please don't tell me." He was still suspicious about what was on that laptop and wondered if he'd ever get a chance to look at it. It didn't seem very likely considering Al's relationship with the thing.

"I apologize," said Alcander. "It is just..." He struggled for a moment. "There are demons like me, who can survive through makeshift means, but all we do is *survive*. It is hard and it is miserable and obviously... *obviously* it is not for all of us. If I could find a way to replicate the blood in a way that was as functional and as desirable as the genuine article, I could end all of this. Neither of us would have to sacrifice our needs. No one would have to die."

The agency had made many attempts to cure both vampirism and lycanthropy, but he did not know of any attempts to simply feed the demons in some other way. When a fox kept raiding the henhouse, you dealt with the problem by shooting the fox, not by leaving out kibble.

Even with such a solution in circulation, he doubted if the population at large would accept it any better than meat enthusiasts accepted veganism. Still... it was a noble goal, and with Crimson around to protect him, he might even survive long enough to succeed.

Unless...

A sensation of horror sank through him like an anchor through the sea.

Unless both of them ended up dead or locked in a cage at St. James.

"What about magic?" suggested Jasper, hoping his voice was not noticeably strained. He couldn't do magic himself, but casters weren't hard to come by in the city. "You've got money. Couldn't you just hire a consultant... or...?"

"If the casters could magic up a flesh and blood alternative, they would be marketing it in droves by now," said Alcander. "Anyway, I do not have the right sort of currency to hire a powerful witch or warlock. And the Hunting Agencies are always indoctrinating the reasonable ones early on."

"But you've tried it?" asked Jasper.

"I've looked into it," said Alcander. "And worked with magicians where I could. If such a spell exists, no one knows it."

Jasper frowned slightly but shrugged, trying to school his expression into something more pleasant. "I'm sure you'll figure it out."

The vampire nodded. "Thank you."

He seemed from there content to keep to himself, but Jasper wasn't done. "Hey, Al?"

"Yes?"

"When we first met..." He paused, glancing towards Crimson. The werespider seemed sound asleep, but he could never truly tell. "You, uh... recognized me, didn't you?"

Alcander looked nervous. "What do you mean?"

"You said my name right as you were coming to." The vampire probably didn't remember, but Jasper still did. "How come?"

Alcander shifted uncomfortably and started to fidget with objects on the end table. "It was nothing, really. Crimson mentioned you to me, your name, where you had come from. He wanted to know if your story was legitimate." Jasper was glad Charlie had deleted his records from the servers at St. James, building him a separate file to reflect his cover story. All Alcander would have found in his files was an exact mirror to the story he had told Crimson at Rascal's. "That was a while back though," added Alcander. "You should not worry about it. We know you would not harm us."

"Of course not, Al." With that, Jasper went back to his paperback, frowning.

Chapter Fourteen

—

New Friends

It took no small amount of effort, but he finally convinced Crimson to leave the hotel room. The werespider said he didn't want to go to a bar. Or a club. Or a movie. He'd promised earlier that they would go to the beach, and when Jasper suggested it, he seemed resigned to the fact that they would actually have to go *somewhere*, and agreed.

They found a mostly deserted stretch of coast not far from where they were staying, and walked together just above the high-tide line. The climate was far too hot during the day and humid even in the evening, but with the cool mist of the sea spray, it was quite pleasant.

Eventually, they reached a dock, and Jasper decided it would probably be even nicer out over the water. Crimson followed him down the slick wooden walkway with the same extreme lack of enthusiasm as he'd had for the last two days, and when Jasper sat down at the end with his feet dangling over the side, just above the water, he followed suit.

The waves crashed and receded. Crashed and receded. After a while, the silence began to press. When it finally grew too heavy, Crimson spoke in a soft voice, nearly inaudible over the waves. "I'm, uh… sorry about what happened with Ivory." It hadn't been so long ago, but in the panicked race of the past month, it seemed to have attained a daunting distance, forgotten almost. Another life. "It was just…" He stopped. "I really thought…" He stopped again. Struggled. It was bizarre to see him, *Crimson*, at a loss for words. "It was so *weird*, y'know? I was sure—*fucking sure* you weren't on the level."

The werespider was looking out across the water, not towards him, and when he spoke again, Jasper was grateful that it was so. "I'm glad I was wrong."

Jasper should have been excited to hear him say this, but he found he wasn't. He watched Crimson absently flick a stray pebble out across the water.

Then the werespider turned to him and held out a hand, as if to shake. "Friends?"

"I thought we were already friends." Jasper tried for a light, joking tone but fell short. He cleared his throat with a cough and took Crimson's outstretched hand. It was warm and smooth in his, his grip firm and sure. "Friends," he agreed. He was thankful for the cool sea breeze because he wasn't feeling so hot right then.

"Alright then, it's a deal." Crimson let go of his hand and reclined instead on his palms, looking up at the sky, but then seemed to remember something. "No take backsies." The light way he said it suggested he was kidding. What Jasper actually knew about Crimson suggested he was not. Jasper made his lips smile back in a way that mimicked mild amusement, and then looked out across the water instead.

"I'm tired," said Crimson after a while.

"You slept all day," said Jasper. It was barely eleven p.m. "And most of yesterday." Considering the amount the werespider usually slept (barely at all) this was extravagant. He wondered if werespiders got sick. Maybe it was the climate or something.

"Yeah. I know."

"Do you want to go swimming or something?"

Crimson perked up slightly. "Sure."

Jasper looked back down the length of the dock at the beach that stretched behind them. It was dark, but between the light coming off the city and from the half-full moon, he could see enough to believe they were alone. Way, way down the stretch of white sand, he saw the orange glow of a fire. It was far enough away that he did not worry. Jasper got to his feet and unzipped his sweater, dropping it to the worn wood beneath them. He was more careful removing his pistol, throwing the sleeve of his sweater over it before pulling off his T-shirt and dropping it on the pile. Next came his boots, his socks stuffed inside them.

He was undoing the button on his jeans when Crimson spoke. "Any excuse to take your clothes off in front of me, huh, Jazz?" He'd been so sullen that the joke was almost welcome.

"Shut up," Jasper said mildly. He did wish he didn't blush so easily; it wasn't very good for his street cred. At least it was dark. "See those rocks over there?" He nodded to the coast.

"The caves?"

Jasper couldn't see well enough in the darkness but was sure the werespider was right. "Yeah, the caves. I'll race ya." He stripped the rest of the way down to his boxers and, without waiting for Crimson, who was still fully dressed, coat and all, he jumped into the water.

It was warmer than he thought it would be, and beneath its surface the world was reduced to darkness and swirling, weighted silence. It helped clear his troubled mind.

He resurfaced to Crimson's swearing. "You're a fuckin' cheater!" He threw his jacket back onto the dock, and Jasper turned and started paddling in the opposite direction as quickly as he could. He was almost at the mound of stones and was stretching out his hand to haul himself up when something snagged his ankle and dragged him back. He twisted around, kicking, and saw Crimson. "Now who's cheating?" Planting his foot firmly on his chest, he pushed him back and slipped his hold. His back bumped against the stones and he flipped around to scramble quickly up them, his feet slipping and sliding on their slick, polished surface. A short distance upward, the ground levelled out to create a narrow shelf.

Crimson climbed up beside him. "Looks like you're slowing down in your old age," Jasper mocked gently and was pleased to see him smile, though he wished he wasn't.

"Don't let it go to your head. I let you win." The werespider pushed his wet hair back, sending trails of water running down his finely muscled back and chest.

Jasper looked away, at the moving water below them. The silence that stretched before them was more comfortable than the previous. Crimson dangled his long legs above the water, catching the soft crest of a wave with his toe, and Jasper rested his chin on his bent knee, noticing that even this small distance out revealed more stars in the sky.

"I like it out here," said Jasper.

"Eh…" said Crimson. "It's alright. I liked it better when it was all frontier. Sad about the natives, though. The seventeenth century here was almost as depressing as the fourteenth one in Europe. I didn't think there'd be any of them left by the time your people were done."

"Hey now, 'my' people didn't make it over here until the 1800s." He said it lightly, playfully. He, in fact, hadn't come here until 1987, when he was two. He'd been born in Ireland. His father was of Irish descent. His mother… well, signs pointed to her having been something else entirely. He wished he knew what. "And we had it almost just as bad as everyone else."

Crimson raised a cynical eyebrow.

Jasper grinned. "Well, that's what I hear, anyway. It's not like I know for sure. I wasn't exactly there."

"I was," said Crimson. It was strange to think about.

"Can I ask you a question?" Jasper asked.

"What's one more?"

"How old are you exactly?"

"*Exactly?* Fuck if I know, man."

"Well, then, roughly." He found it a little hard to believe he could forget how old he was, but he supposed that Charlie was only in his forties and he always had to stop and think about the answer.

"You wouldn't believe me."

"Sure I would."

For a moment it seemed like Crimson wouldn't answer. Pulling his gaze from the ocean, he looked at Jasper. "Three thousand. Give or take a few decades. I can't really keep track anymore."

Jasper had to stop himself from calling bullshit. Three thousand years was a number he couldn't fathom. How could a person live for three thousand years? Why would they *want* to?

Crimson was still looking at him, reading the expression of disbelief.

"That's… a long time," Jasper said finally, and Crimson sighed, looking back out at the water.

"You have no idea."

Chapter Fifteen

—

Best-Laid Missions

Jasper had been to this bookstore a couple of times, sometimes with Crimson and sometimes alone. It wasn't anything special, one of those chains with multiple stories and a coffee shop built in. The stacks were full and organized by genre and then by author. Something was comforting about being surrounded by stories; Jasper needed some comfort now.

He found an empty section of the store, tucked in a corner with the sociology books. A plastic wicker armchair with a missing pillow was between two bookshelves, and Jasper sat there, knee bouncing anxiously as he took out his phone. He flipped it open and closed a few times, going as far as bringing up his father's number before snapping it shut again.

There was no point delaying it.

Jasper called Charlie and listened to the phone ring. It seemed to ring for a long time, though in reality it was only three or four times. Normally talking to his dad calmed him down, but when his father's deep and even voice spoke a single "Hello?" he brought his thumbnail to his mouth and worried it with his teeth.

"Hey, Dad," he said. "It's Jazz."

Charlie's voice brightened. "Jasper, hello! Happy hunting?"

"Um, well, about that." Jasper took a deep breath. "Uh, so about the mission... I think... it's kind of a bust."

He heard the sound of a door opening and closing, muffled over the cell. "What do you mean?"

"I mean... well, I've been hanging out with the guy for a while now and, I don't know, I just think we were wrong. He's... he's a loner. He doesn't have a pack, and from what I've gathered, most of his allies and friends are either dead or we already have 'em in the cells. He's alone, man. Total dead end."

Charlie was silent on the other end of the phone. Jasper imagined him in his apartment study, the wall of windows looking out at the Manhattan skyline, shades half-drawn to cut the glare from the late afternoon sun; the bookshelves full of history and demonology books, spines worn by time and touch; the large desk in the middle of the room that he sat behind, leaning thoughtfully back in his chair. Jasper bit his thumbnail down to the quick.

"A dead end," Charlie said finally.

"Yeah. A dead end. Really, I don't think this guy knows anything important."

"You don't? You haven't been with him that long. How can you be sure?"

"It's been more than a month." It felt even longer. Everything felt different now, like he was seeing things clearly. *He* felt different. He remembered first meeting Crimson and how much he disliked him. It had been instantaneous, instinct, habit. He was a demon and that was all that mattered. Now Jasper saw more important things: Crimson was rash and brave and quick and funny. He knew every Stones song ever recorded and had a story for every topic and occasion. He was almost predictable in his routines until he wasn't, and Jasper was always surprised by what surprised him, like how he could play the piano as well as Billy Joel or Elton John, or that he was so scared of elevators he would rather walk up forty stories than ride in one. Even when Jasper was mad at him, which wasn't uncommon, he liked him, and behind his sneers and moody silences, he thought Crimson liked him too.

He hadn't felt this way since Adam.

They were friends.

He could not explain this to his father.

"He's lonely, Dad. He fell for it, easy. He thinks we're, like, best friends or something." The words tasted bitter. He was trying so hard to sound removed from it. Just another job. "He's told me a bunch of shit, but none of it is useful."

"What about that vampire? Alcander Owen?"

"He's an agoraphobic vampire with anxiety. He can, like, barely function. I really don't think there's any sort of lead there."

"So what exactly did you have in mind as a course of action?"

While Charlie was both his boss and his guardian, it rarely ever felt like he was giving orders. He listened to Jasper and valued his opinion, even when his opinion was less than perfect. Jasper almost breathed a sigh of relief. "Cut our losses and abort the mission?" he suggested.

There was a beat of silence slightly too long to be anything but a surprised pause. "That's really what you think would be best?"

"Yes, it really is. Whole thing was sort of a waste of time."

"Alright. Well, in that case, we'll call it." Charlie's voice sounded mildly disappointed. Jasper was glad he didn't have to hide the fact that he was smiling. He opened his mouth to tell him he would be on the next flight home, but Charlie wasn't done. "We can send someone from the Miami branch to help you put them down if you need them."

The shock of his statement was like a punch to the heart. "What?"

"Unless you're *certain* you can handle them on your own." Charlie mistook his question. "I know there's only two of them."

"No, I-I don't think that's necessary."

"It's no trouble. I'm sure they'd be happy for the action. There isn't much down there other than witches, and they tend to know their place better than demons. I know you're capable, but there's no need to be reckless."

"No, that's not what I mean. I just... I don't think we have to kill them. I mean, they're out of New York, isn't that enough?"

There was another silence, this one impossible to read. If Jasper were in the room with him, he would be able to tell what he was thinking. He chewed his nail again, tasting blood.

"What are you saying, Jasper?"

"I'm just sayin'... that I-I think we can just leave them alone. They aren't hurting anybody."

"Oh, they aren't, are they?" Charlie's voice had turned in a direction Jasper wasn't used to hearing, especially directed at him. "How often do they have to feed? Once or twice a month? What do you think happens then? Jasper, you know this. It's basic. They kill people; that's why we kill them. To save people. How many people do you think the werespider's murdered in his time? Hundreds? Thousands? Double that with the vampire. They have to be taken care of."

Jasper's breath felt caught in his chest. Charlie was right, Jazz knew what demons did to survive. He knew that they should be stopped, that he should want to save as many people as possible. It just wasn't as simple as that anymore. Crimson was a person; Al was a person. They were his friends, as fucked up as that might be. He wanted to protect them too.

"Jasper." Charlie's voice, firm.

Jasper realized he hadn't said anything. "I just don't think—"

"There is nothing to think about! Jesus Christ, Jasper, what's wrong with you? Has he gotten into your head, is that what's happening here?"

"He isn't in my head," he snapped. And he wasn't—Jasper knew how demon hypnosis worked, and he knew how to fight it. It had never worked on him anyway; he never felt the pull other Hunters described when a vampire tried to compel them. Crimson had never turned those shining eyes on him anyway, not since the very beginning. "I just don't think it's right. They aren't monsters, they're—"

"Enough! I want you on the earliest plane back. The Miami branch will finish this if you can't. Now tell me where to find them."

Panic stabbed at his chest. "No."

"What did you say?"

"I said no." Jasper's voice shook, but he continued anyway. "No, I won't tell you, and no, I won't kill them."

"Jasper Daniel Craig," he warned.

"I gotta go. I'm sorry." He hung up the phone. It rang immediately, and he ended the call. When it rang again, he shut it off.

The stacks of books, which had been comforting to him moments before, now felt suffocating, too close and too heavy. He needed to get out of here. He wasn't sure where he was going to go, he just needed to get out. He needed fresh air. He needed a cigarette.

Jasper headed for the stairs that led down to the lower level, but as he rounded the corner of an aisle, he froze, like an animal trapped in the headlights of an oncoming car. Crimson was standing there, holding a book open in front of him. He was in the political science section, which felt like the most ridiculous place to find him. He probably didn't even know who the president was. The werespider looked up at Jasper and replaced the book. His face gave nothing away.

"How long have you been in here?" demanded Jasper. He wasn't ready to deal with Crimson and couldn't tell what the demon might or might not have heard. "Were you following me?"

"I followed your trail here, yeah," replied Crimson, all innocence. "But I wasn't like... stalking you or whatever."

"You could have texted me if you wanted to know where I was. You didn't have to—to track me."

"I didn't know it was such a big fuckin' deal," replied Crimson. If he expected some sort of signal as to what he had or had not heard, there was none.

"It's just weird." He fought to keep the anger from his voice. Maybe it was all as innocent as it seemed. Maybe he was just overreacting.

Crimson languidly raised an eyebrow. "Alright," he said. "Noted." He put his hands in his pockets, surveying him with a tilted head. "You okay? Your heart's beating really fast."

The demonic hearing was no fair. Crimson could do it to him, but he could not do it to Crimson. "It tends to do that when a person is angry, which I am." He wasn't, really. Well, in a way, he was. But not at Crimson.

"Why?" asked Crimson. The other patrons were starting to look at them now, though neither of them had raised his voice much above a conversational tone.

"Because it's *rude*, Crimson. And it's an invasion of privacy. And it..." He wavered. "It makes me feel like you don't trust me." This was all some version of the truth, just simplified to an abridged version that ignored the crux of the matter, which was that he was scared, not angry. He wished he could tell him but knew he couldn't. Not ever.

"Oh," said Crimson. He rubbed the nape of his neck, his expression surprisingly sheepish. "If ya wanna know the truth, I'm real bad at texting. And I didn't think people talked on phones anymore."

Jasper's heart beat a little slower. He hoped like hell he wasn't lying, but at this point he'd take any out he could get. "People don't talk on cell phones anymore," he agreed. It seemed like he could scarcely remember a time before text messaging. "But you can call me." This was the most ridiculous argument he'd ever had in his life. He made for the door.

"You don't want a book?" asked Crimson as he followed.

"I don't have any money," said Jasper. Then he turned suddenly on his heel, grabbing the book Crimson had just picked up out of his hand and setting it firmly back on the shelf. "I don't need you to steal stuff for me."

"Maybe it was for me," said Crimson, but he didn't try to take it again.

Out on the sidewalk, Jasper lit a cigarette. He looked up one side of the street and down the other. Was there some way Charlie could find him here? Was it worth alarming the demons? If he told them, they would almost certainly want to know how he knew, and he doubted if he could explain without running the risk of getting murdered in the process.

He looked at the werespider. "Hey, uh... You wanna get out of town?"

"Why?" asked Crimson. "Should I?"

Jasper coughed on cigarette smoke. "I was just thinking maybe we could try for the other coast this time."

"Yeah, sure. Maybe we could all go to some out-of-the-way log cabin, deep in the woods, where no one will hear us scream. That the plan?"

Alarm bells rang in Jasper's mind. He tried to keep calm. "What?"

Crimson cracked a smile. "You know I'm just fuckin' with you, right?"

Jasper smiled nervously. "Yeah, I know."

Crimson turned away, starting down the street. "I was thinking we would probably head back to New York soon. I figured you would come with us, but if you've got your own thing going on—"

"No thing," said Jasper quickly. "I just thought it might be fun."

"Not with Alcander tagging along it won't." Crimson hesitated. "I really should get him back home. I'm gonna give it another week or so. Ivory'll have gotten bored by then. She's probably already off bothering someone else. But we could go on another trip afterwards if you want."

The sentiment was nice, but it wasn't what he wanted to hear. He couldn't very well argue about it either. "Alright," said Jasper, resigned. "I guess we'll see."

Chapter Sixteen

—

The Joan of Arc Institute

It took a few days to locate the demons and the rogue Hunter who was with them. It was less that they were particularly good at hiding and more that the Hunters had a lot of city to sweep and not many agents to search. The Miami agency was more involved in controlling and monitoring the state's rather large spellcaster population than in hunting demons, who tended towards colder climates.

They had psychics who could sense auras and minds, and had spellcasters who could find anyone with an incantation so long as they had something of personal value to the person or creature they were tracking. With a population of over five million people and an area covering more than eighty-five miles, it looked like they were facing a pretty big job just to track down three individuals.

It was Ryan Bowie's idea to use the Hunter's ID photo and a facial-recognition program he'd been working on to scan the security feeds of the larger hotels in Miami. Their feeds were uploaded as they were recorded into a company's servers, which he'd easily found and gained access to. From there, he said, it was mostly a waiting game as the program scanned the footage from the last few weeks. It could take up to five days, assuming they got a hit at all. Otherwise it would be back to the drawing board.

The program had already been running for nearly a full day.

"How old is this kid?"

"Eighteen. The picture's from last year. Shouldn't have changed so much that the program can't pick him out." Ryan was leaned back in his chair, his feet propped up on the desk, legs crossed at the ankles, a Rubik's Cube spinning in his hands. The glow of the computer's multiple monitors could be seen in his eyes, which stayed focused on the flickering images of the cycling security feeds. In the corner of the leftmost screen was the Hunter's picture: short, curly reddish-brown hair and almost startling green eyes stared back out at them from a freckled face.

Selena Chase frowned. She, along with most of the room's six members, was dressed in simple Hunter's garb: a long-sleeve black shirt, fitted close to the body, thicker through the chest and arms; dark pants that were resistant to tearing and staining; and heavy-soled leather boots. Her hair was dark and cropped into a short, straight bob. She tugged absently at a strand of hair, tucking it behind her ear. "That's an awful long time for someone his age to be alone with a demon." Hell, she couldn't imagine doing it. Jasper Craig was either very brave or very stupid for trying. Knowing what most Hunters his age were like made her think he was probably both.

"Two demons," Colt Summers corrected. "The vampire, remember? Alcander Owen. New York didn't have any files on him, not so much as a picture."

"So what?" Stefan wasn't interested in the vampire. They were commonplace, everywhere (never mind that he'd never fought one). You couldn't go one block in New York City without running into one (never mind that he'd never been to New York). "He's a nobody. The werespider, Crimson Apocalypse"—he said the name like it belonged to the front man of the coolest, hardest metal band ever— "he's going to be fun. He's like five hundred years old, at least, dude. And werespiders, they can use superpowerful, like, hypnosis. Persuasions. Stronger than a vamp's. They're basically psychic."

"They aren't psychic." Constance Singer *was* a psychic, able to sense and read auras across and through buildings. It was a gift and she had worked hard to hone it, pushing herself greater distances, trying to read the intentions of the targets, find out what they were about to do, almost like mind reading. "It's their pheromones. It's chemical. Fucks with your brain, makes you stupid, and that makes *them* convincing. It's different."

"Same results," Holly Alder put in softly. It didn't matter much what you called it, hypnosis or mind control, it all was a sort of magic, and every kind of magic had a reaction, a foil. She'd had some time to work on something to make their team immune to the spider's powers, but as for the other Hunter...

"It's hard to tell what Craig's going to be like." Selena had dealt with a few vampires and familiars in her career. The vamps were spooky—so quick that if you blinked at the wrong time, they could kill you, with those pointed fangs and eyes that glowed red in the dark, and that horrible hissing—but familiars always scared her more. They were still human, but they didn't think like humans anymore. Any human in their right mind would want nothing to do with those life-sucking monsters, but familiars were always completely enamored with their vampires, caring more about them than they did their own lives.

She'd seen a female familiar, around her own age, physically attack a Hunter who had just dusted her vampire, screaming this awful scream like she was being ripped apart as she tore at his face with her nails, grappling a knife from his belt to stab him over and over in the chest and throat. There was no choice other than to shoot her dead before she could attack someone else. But Selena had seen the opposite too, familiars who were dried husks of people, who stared unseeing with glossy eyes, skin pale and sunken, ashy as if they were turning to dust. Familiars whose hearts still beat and whose blood still flowed but were otherwise gone forever.

Stefan was partially right, werespiders often did have stronger hypnotic powers than vampires. Selena wasn't able to find any documentation on prolonged exposure to a werespider's presence but could imagine what the results could be. "Hopefully he can still be reasoned with. If he'll come to our side, that's great, but if the demon has him too far under, we'll have to take him out of the fight—dose him with something, knock him out. Hopefully they can bring him back after." She didn't sound entirely convinced.

The computer beeped, and Ryan set aside the Rubik's Cube, kicked his feet down off the desk, and scooted the rolling chair closer as he reached for the wireless computer mouse. "Hey, check it out. Looks like we got a match."

Selena leaned over his shoulder to look at the screen as Ryan slowed the footage down to normal speed. The others clustered around his chair.

The hotel lobby was modern and open, done in bright whites and sharp blacks, showing a cluster of black sofas and chairs by the floor-to-ceiling windows on one side of the room, and a large black piano next to the in-house bar on the other. The camera view showed part of the reception desk and the main entryway, through which two figures came in. The glass to the outside was dark, and the time stamp indicated it was very late, past four in the morning. Based on the pair's less than steady steps, it appeared as if they'd been drinking. There was no audio, but the darker of the two figures had his head thrown back as if in laughter. The second figure—a young man with reddish-brown hair—was grinning, his face turned towards the other, completely captivated by him. He wasn't looking towards the camera. Selena leaned forward to get a closer look, and a moment later the second figure turned, pointing to something off-screen, and she saw that it was him. Jasper Craig.

"When is this footage from?" she asked.

"Two nights ago." Ryan was typing furiously on one of the keyboards while the video continued to play on the screen. Jasper and the other figure, who could only be the werespider, walked past the reception desk and through a doorway that led to the stairs. "They're at the Larchmont. I'm scanning the more recent footage, see if I can find them again. I don't know the name they're under, but"—he turned a second screen towards them, showing footage from the same night but a different camera, this one on one of the floors, showing the pair of them entering a room—"they're on the thirty-third floor. Room… 3317." More typing, Ryan's fingers running smoothly over the keys. "Under the name Andrews. Looks like they're still checked in."

"Make sure they're still there."

"Yes, ma'am." He turned the screen back and jumped quickly through the feed, speeding through much of the day until the door opened again, showing Jasper leaving, this time alone, and returning with large paper cups of coffee and a white paper bag from a deli or coffee shop. Later he and the werespider left together and returned several hours later. They never saw the vampire leave at all. It was currently midafternoon, and the most recent footage placed them inside the hotel room.

"Unless they left through the window, that's where they are now."

"We should kick down the door and blow them the fuck away."

Stefan was the second youngest member of the team at twenty-one, though he often seemed younger due to his hotheaded temper and crude language. He was an excellent warrior though, his results inarguable. If it came to a fight, which Selena suspected it would, she wanted him there, but if it were up to Stefan, they'd go in guns blazing.

"The Larchmont is right downtown, and it's a pretty popular place this time of year," Colt explained, and Selena was thankful to have a second that was so in tune with her own thoughts. She cast a grateful look at him and he smiled her way. "It's too dangerous to try to do anything at the hotel. Maybe if we could somehow draw them out?"

Ryan was still cycling through the footage of the hotel, going backwards in time at a speed that was hard to follow. "It looks like the Hunter and the spider go out every night. Sometimes all night, sometimes for just a few hours. Usually together, but sometimes not. The only footage I can find of the vampire is from check-in, three weeks ago." He slowed the feed down, showing the Hunter talking to the receptionist and sliding some papers over to the vampire, who signed them, holding the pen with a tissue pulled from a box on the counter. He was smaller than the Hunter, with long dark hair pulled back into a low ponytail. Ryan switched to the hallway footage to show him entering the room. "Doesn't look like he goes anywhere."

"We could get the other two first," suggested Constance. "Follow them when they go out, take care of them somewhere less populated. Come back for him. Six of us and one vampire? Simple."

"We can do it tonight," Stefan said eagerly.

"Tonight," said Selena, "we'll do surveillance. Follow them, see where they go. And we'll have someone check on the vampire too." She checked her watch. "Everyone, go rest up. We'll meet back here at 1600 and go over the plan."

#

Judging by the way they usually stumbled in in the early morning, they suspected the Hunter and the spider spent most of their nights drinking. Holly was only twenty, which left her out of this particular surveillance duty. She and Colton would go with Ryan to the hotel; Selena, Constance, and Stefan would trail the others.

A restaurant was directly across the street from the hotel, an expensive Italian place called El Cielo. The patio was full when they arrived at sunset. Selena bribed the maître d' to seat them there anyway. They ordered dinner and ate slowly, watching the hotel across the street, but after an hour there was no sign of them. They ordered dessert, picking over it for as long as possible. The wait staff was growing impatient with them, there were other customers who wanted the chairs, but they remained, ordering a round of drinks though they only drank water.

"Where the fuck are they?" Stefan demanded, annoyed by the inaction. He took a drink of his beer, which had gone flat and warm, and pulled a face.

"Maybe they're staying in tonight?" offered Constance, though she didn't sound very happy about this idea either.

Selena checked the time. Based on the footage, the two of them usually left the hotel between seven and ten p.m. It was just after ten now. They'd wait for a little while longer, but if they needed to, they would come back the next night and wait again.

They were just about to call it a night when Ryan's voice spoke via an earpiece. "We got Craig in the lobby." A pink motorcycle came roaring up to the hotel, and she covered her other ear, homing in on the sound of his voice. "And the werespider." The woman riding the motorcycle parked it along the curb, then pulled her matching pink helmet off, revealing short blond locks that stuck up unevenly. She had an athletic build, without much in the way of curves. If not for the color of her motorcycle and helmet, Selena might have easily mistaken her for an attractive young man. The woman flipped her cell phone open and pulled off one leather glove with her teeth so she could type more easily.

Moments later, Jasper Craig appeared. He waved at the woman, then held up one finger with an apologetic look, and leaned back through the held door, presumably to call out to someone in the lobby. The music on the patio and the traffic on the street was too loud for Selena to make out words, but Ryan told her he was talking to the werespider, who had just shown up in the lobby. When the message was communicated, he jogged down the steps and gave the woman a quick peck on the lips. While this was happening, Crimson strolled outside. He waved at the woman as she and Craig parted, then cupped his hands around his mouth to yell over the traffic, "I'll catch up with you guys in a little bit."

"Sure thing!" Craig yelled back.

The woman hung her helmet from the handlebar of the motorcycle, then, with a quick farewell wave towards Crimson, grabbed Craig's hand. The two of them started down the street and Selena swore under her breath. Should they follow Craig or stick with the werespider? Crimson was still standing in front of the doors, watching the other two go as he tapped ash from the end of his cigarette. Selena had a split second to decide and she picked accordingly.

"Square away the bill," she told Constance. "Then come after us right away."

She and Stefan both rose casually and made for the gated exit while Constance subtly gestured to their waiter for the check.

The Hunter and the human were in no great hurry, and he was thankfully tall enough that they could spot him even over the crowd of tourists and civilians who milled about. The two Hunters walked together, several meters behind their prey and on the opposite side of the road, taking turns pausing in front of storefronts and pretending to look at the merchandise while the other kept watch.

A dark-haired woman in a red tube top with a short black miniskirt and matching stiletto heels was waiting in front of the club. When she saw the other two, she upturned her hands in a "what the fuck?" sort of gesture, then stood on tiptoe to try to see over them. Craig said something to her as they approached, and she rolled her eyes, huffing, but followed them both into the bar.

"Pretty sure the werespider just stood that girl up," said Stefan into the mic. He whistled long and low right into the microphone. "Girl who looks like that—he really *must* be evil."

"Hush, Stefan," Selena said sternly, but not unkindly. Crimson said he would be along later, meaning he could show up at any moment. They needed to get inside and out of sight before he came trotting up right behind them. Maybe if they were lucky, they could even get ahold of Craig and try to talk (or force) some sense into him before the other could interfere.

Like most clubs, it was loud inside. It was a bare-bones sort of place, the floors made of concrete that was already drenched and sticky with spilled beer. There were high-top tables near the entrance, but very few people were sitting at them, and since there was no official dance floor, people were also dancing in between and around them, with the greater number of patrons clustered in the big open space not far from the bar. The trio was at the bar, ordering drinks.

Stefan and Selena climbed up a staircase that led to a second level, overlooking the rest of the club, and stood close to (but not quite against) the railing.

Constance showed up not long after and casually danced her way onto the floor, blending into the crowd and flowing with the energy of the room in a way that only an empath could.

Craig and the girls fought their way to an empty corner of the room, where they stood in a small circle, drinking, occasionally swaying to the music, yelling in the direction of one another to be heard. After about half an hour, when they were all three starting to get good and drunk, they moved out with the rest of the crowd, though Craig didn't seem exactly thrilled about it. He wasn't there long before he excused himself back to his corner and left the girls to dance together.

Selena looked towards Constance, who looked directly back at her almost at the same moment. She playfully slapped the chest of her current dance partner and then moved away from him, losing him in the crowd. She kept the rhythm all the way over to where Craig was standing and texting.

#

Constance wouldn't have been able to lose Craig if she wanted to. His aura stood out from the crowd, a vibrant and almost glaring white among the pale pinks and blues and greens of the other club-goers. She'd never seen anything so bright before.

She danced her way closer to him, her 24-karat-gold-capped heels keeping easy balance, even on the sticky concrete. He didn't look up from his phone until she was nearly touching him. "Hey," she said.

"Um, hi." Craig looked at her, his phone still held in his hands. His eyes went over her shoulder, scanning the crowd.

"Not crazy about dancing, huh?" Even with her high heels, she was still several inches shorter than him, though underneath her pink sweater, her arms were strong and sinewy, and the long legs below were just the same. He watched her from the corner of his eye and didn't reply. She felt his reluctance holding him back. She mimicked his stance, leaning her back against the wall, and pulled her long black ponytail over her shoulder, twisting the end around the tip of her finger. "What are you doing over here all by yourself?"

"I'm waiting for someone," he said, leaning a little closer so she could hear him but just as quickly leaned back. She knew she wasn't exactly a supermodel, but the disinterested vibes coming from him still surprised her. Maybe she wasn't his type.

"Your girlfriend?"

Another wave of hesitation. "I don't have a girlfriend," he said after a moment. "I'm waiting for my friend." He went back to his phone, frowning at whatever he found there. She tried to angle her head so she could read it, but he flipped it closed and slipped it into the front pocket of his jeans.

"I'm Constance," she offered.

"Jasper."

She couldn't get him to budge and was thinking about giving it over as a lost cause when a cold, dissonant feeling sank down through her. She and the Hunter looked up at the same time. The werespider was just emerging from the short hallway that led to the club proper. Like most demons, his aura was shadowy black and seemed to wisp around him in smoky tendrils. Near the center of him, close to his heart, was a flicker of red. She felt strength and age, but great pain also, and perhaps even madness. She drew her mind quickly back, afraid he would notice her Seeing.

His gaze went in her direction, but it passed over her, settling instead on the man beside her. She wasn't trying to Look, but sometimes the sight had a will of its own, and she felt the changing waves of energy. Interest. Excitement. Warmth. Beside her, the feelings of anxiety softened.

Crimson came right up to them. "Hey, Jazz." He clapped him on the shoulder, and where the two met, their auras blended and shifted to gray. Red wisps of light raced through the black like pulses of a heartbeat. "What're you doin' over here? Decorating the wall?"

"I was worried about you," said Craig. The guilt showed only in his mind.

Holy shit, thought Constance.

"I'll catch you later," she told Jasper. "Glad you found your friend." She slipped between him and the werespider, waited until they had both looked away, and then ascended the stairs to the landing.

Stefan was pouting in a crummy-looking booth that looked as if no one should ever have eaten in it at any point. Selena was still standing near the railing, holding an unsipped glass of whiskey.

Constance kept her arms firmly at her sides and kept her step very even and casual. She walked up to Selena, tugged on her sleeve, and the two of them excused themselves out onto the fire escape, which was designated for smoking, while Stefan kept an eye on the other two.

"What is it?" asked Selena. The music could still be heard, but it was somewhat quieter with a door between them.

"The werespider is in love," said Constance flatly.

Selena's eyebrow went up.

"Okay, yeah, I might be exaggerating a little, but he pretty clearly likes him. *A lot.*"

"What about Craig?"

Constance frowned. "I think he's under pretty good. I couldn't get a good read on him, but as soon as he saw the spider, he... changed. He was happy to see him." She shook her head. There was more, but it was difficult to explain auras to people who couldn't see them. The way their auras had blended together, that red spark between them, worried her.

"You think it's his persuasion?"

The other option was too awful. How could a Hunter possibly care for one of those *things*? "I've never met a familiar, but yeah, I think so."

Selena nodded, but kept her own counsel for now, and then touched her earpiece. "Bowie, we've got eyes on both the werespider and the familiar. How's it going with the vampire?"

There was no response. Constance picked up on Selena's sudden worry, and they shared a glance. Then Selena's cell phone began to vibrate. She answered quickly, on the first ring.

"Selena." Ryan's voice was quick and serious. "We're having some technical difficulties on this end." Beside him, his computer screen was bright blue. White text in neat lines broadcasted a nonstop repeating error message, thousands of times per minute until the core memory finally ran out and the whole works crashed. "The whole system's overloaded."

"A bug?" guessed Selena.

"I'm not sure," said Ryan. "But the comms are down, as is the security feed."

"Keep trying to restore communications," said Selena. "We'll keep you posted via text message."

They got back inside, and Stefan glowered at them. "Took you long enough. I gotta piss like a racehorse."

This was hardly surprising considering the amount of time they had been following the two of them, though it was agitating. "Make it quick," said Selena.

Stefan nodded and went down the stairs. Underneath them was a small alcove leading to a little hallway with a "ladies" sign on one end and a "gentlemen" sign on the other. The men's room was getting crowded by this time of night, and he shouldered his way to a urinal. Surveillance was boring; they had them right there in front of them, what were they waiting for? If Stefan were in charge, the demons would be dead already, and maybe the Hunter too. The way he'd heard it, familiars were just as bad as demons, and any Hunter stupid enough to fall under their spells was hardly a Hunter at all.

He washed his hands, drying them on his pants since the paper towels had already run out. He was headed to the door when Craig came in, an absent smile on his face. Stefan made sure his shoulder slammed into his as he passed. Craig turned and glared at him, the cheap light fixtures making his eyes seem to flash.

"Sorry, bro," Stefan sneered. "Didn't see you there."

"Uh, well, you're excused." Craig turned to walk away, but Stefan just couldn't let him.

"Nice jacket. You know this isn't a leather bar, though, right?"

Craig halted. Beside the werespider, he looked to be an average height, but up close he was quite large—taller than Stefan, with the build of an Olympic swimmer or sprinter. He looked back at him, the glare still held in his eyes. "Do you have a problem, man?"

"Yeah, I think I do." Selena chirped in his ear and started to let him know that communications had been restored, but her voice cut out halfway, replaced by a loud burst of static feedback. He touched his ear, wincing slightly. The other man was staring at him with narrowed green eyes. He glanced down, glanced back up. Stefan wished he'd try something, but he was still.

The first few chords of "Sympathy For The Devil" by the Stones briefly sounded, and Craig took his eyes off him just long enough to retrieve the phone from his pocket.

Stefan opened his mouth to ask whether that was his boyfriend checking to make sure he hadn't drowned in the toilet, when another burst of static interrupted his thoughts. Selena was still trying to get through. "I gotta go," said Stefan.

Chapter Seventeen

—

Pressure

The Hunter left the bathroom, and Jasper was *sure* that he was right in his assumption. Once he'd really gotten a good look at him, it was impossible not to see the signs—the heavy pair of combat boots, the flinch of microphone feedback, the way he was built and how he carried himself. He'd been paranoid for days, always looking over his shoulder, but he was *right*, though he got no satisfaction from this.

They had to get out of here.

"Hello?" The music was so loud he could hardly hear Alcander on the other side of the phone. He jammed his finger into his other ear to block out some noise. "Al, what's going on? Are you alright?"

"I think so," said Alcander's voice, soft, hesitant. "For now." There was a pause, then, if possible, his voice grew smaller. "Is Crimson with you? He won't answer his cell phone, and I need to speak to him."

"He's in the other room," said Jasper. "Is something wrong? I can give him a message or… Are you in some sort of trouble?"

There was a tense, drawn pause. Jasper thought of the probable Hunter he'd just run into and felt sudden, racing panic. "Is somebody *with* you, Alcander?"

Silence.

"Al?"

"I'm here." He was obviously scared. "Alright, I'll tell you." But he didn't, not right away. Jasper wanted to scream at him to hurry the fuck up. Crimson was alone in the other room, and where there was

172

one Hunter, there was almost always bound to be more. "Someone has patched into the hotel's surveillance system, and they have been using it to track your and Crimson's movements. I have waylaid them for now, but I have reason to believe they are Hunters."

"Jesus Christ, Al, why didn't you lead with that?" Jasper strode quickly back into the main room. The crowd was denser than it was before, and fucking Crimson had wandered off and lost himself in it during the five minutes they were separated. Jasper looked frantically around, searching first for the werespider's familiar face, then for the less familiar one from the bathroom. Neither jumped out at him. "Al! Are you still there?"

"Yes."

"You should have just *told me*. I coulda been looking for him this whole time. Why didn't you—"

"Because they are here for you," said Alcander. And just like that, all sound seemed suddenly muted. He could only hear Alcander's voice—small and scared and strained. "I followed the patch backwards to them. The details on the electronic report are fairly slim, and I am still decrypting it, but... it is you, isn't it? Undercover mission. Rogue operative. You are supposed to kill us."

Charlie had altered the details of his file when he went undercover, so he had never been concerned that the smart little vampire could find him that way. Obviously, he'd found some sort of mission briefing, probably issued to the Miami Hunters via Charlie.

He could deny it. That was what he wanted to do. But Alcander was not an idiot. He'd know. He already knew. Jasper looked around again, scouring the crowd with trained eyes. "God, don't tell Crimson. I'm not going to hurt you guys. Al, you know that, right?"

His gaze went up and trailed the balcony. He saw the black-haired girl who had spoken to him earlier and, not far away, the Hunter, both of them pretending to be very engrossed in a very serious conversation. Jasper thought "pretending" because the way their lips moved, they were speaking in regular, conversational tones, which they couldn't have heard with the noise of the club unless they were both talented lip-readers. So that was two. At *least* two, plus (from what he knew about typical hunting teams and considering the information from Alcander) whoever was there from tech, and (since it was Florida and half the fucking population seemed to use some form of magic) probably someone from the magical division as well. So four.

At least four...

Where the blue fuck is Crimson?

"Are you okay, Al? They're not there, right?"

"I have traced the IP address to a building in Coconut Grove, just over five miles away. I am sure they are bouncing the signal; it could be from almost anywhere. I am trying to get a better point on it."

The vampire was talking low and fast, panic building. Jasper felt a stab of sympathy and guilt. He shouldn't have left him alone. "I'm not going to let them hurt *you* either. *Either* of you." Alcander hadn't even done anything to warrant it.

"What about when they try to hurt you?" murmured Alcander.

That was a good question. He compartmentalized it. There were many bridges that needed crossing before he came to that one. "Stay in the hotel room. *Call* me if anything happens. And keep calling Crimson. I can't find him." Keeping a weather eye on the two Hunters above, he hung up the phone and started to elbow his way through the crowd. This was a nightmare. God, he could really use a...

Cigarette.

He felt so stupid he could have screamed. He looked around for the "smoking" sign. There wasn't one, but a bright red "EXIT" sign was posted above a fire escape door. Some cheeky young artist had crookedly spray-painted "& Smoker's Lounge" in drippy, yellow lettering off to the side of it. He wove his way in that direction. Above him, a thirtysomething woman with short-cropped black hair and a blue dress descended the steps a little *too* casually.

He went straight for the fire exit. It was propped open with a doorstop, a sliver of the night outside showing. He burst through the door, the words already coming out of his mouth. "Crimson, we have to... go...?"

A very drunk-looking man in an old letterman jacket blinked blearily at him with an unlit cigarette hanging from the corner of his mouth.

Moments ago, he believed that his heart was racing. Now, he saw that he was mistaken. Hands clenching at his sides, he spun around and marched back into the club. He was making a beeline for the staircase. He didn't know what he was going to do when he got there, just that he had to do *something,*

That was when he noticed the short-haired woman standing against the wall and looking pointedly away, near a beaded curtain. It was so close to the smoke machine that he hadn't noticed it earlier. His eyes darted up to the other two. They were out of sight now, no longer near the railing. Then back to the lady in blue. Was she one of them? As inconspicuously as he could, he made his way over to the curtain and brushed the beads aside.

The room beyond was lit almost exclusively by old neon signs, some of them from brands long expired, and wallpapered in napkins with scribble art. Keeping his back to the wall, looking first ahead and then behind, and then ahead and then behind, he reached for his gun and inched down the short, low-lit corridor. The sound of bass thumped in the walls, the ceiling, under his feet, and in his chest. There were raised voices up ahead, but making out individual words through the music was impossible.

He stopped near a bend at the end of the hallway and stole another glance quickly behind him. Then he turned on the flashlight on his phone and shined it into the dark corners at either side of the door. The woman hadn't followed him. At least, not yet.

Laying his palm on the backstrap of his pistol and shining the light ahead, he rounded the corner all at once.

The gun was halfway out of the holster when his eyes finally understood what he was seeing, and he quickly let go.

A large group of young women were nestled around a table, playing some sort of drinking game. One of them was wearing a little plastic crown with spikes fashioned to look like cartoony penises. Right smack in the middle of the group, with a pile of shot glasses already heaped in front of him, was Crimson.

"Heya, Jazz!"

It was a miracle he didn't crush his own cell phone, he was gripping it so tightly. "What are you doing?"

"Samantha's getting married next week," said Crimson, and all of the very wasted ladies cheered and "whoo'd" like this were new information they hadn't heard before. "We're playin' Never Have I Ever. I'm losin' real bad."

"Who—" began Jasper, but that wasn't the question he really

wanted to ask. "Why—" he began again, but that still wasn't the question. In fact, there wasn't any question. "We have to leave." He grabbed the back of Crimson's chair and wrenched it away from the table. "*Now.*"

The group of women "aww'd" and "how come'd," but Crimson was on his feet in an instant. "What's up?"

It was entirely too much to explain. "Al." That was a good enough summary, and it would definitely get him moving, away from the Hunters, back to the hotel, and back to Alcander, but what he would do when he got there and fully understood the truth, Jasper did not know. At least Al would be taken care of.

The red in his eyes shone as brightly as the neon signs around them. He took off at a quick clip, not quite jogging, but neither walking. As they were nearing the end of the hall, Jasper remembered the woman. "Wait. I think there might be Hunters. In the club."

Crimson rounded on him without breaking stride. "You think or you know?"

"I'm pretty sure," said Jasper. "Almost positive." At least that was true. "I counted at least three."

"What about Al?"

"I... I don't know. He sounded scared, but he didn't say they were there."

Crimson took hold of his hand, pulling him back into the club proper. "C'mon."

The woman with the short hair was gone from her previous place on the other side of the curtain. Jasper looked around for her again, but his eyes found Lindsay and her friend before they found any of the Hunters.

"There you guys are!" Lindsay yelled over the music, grabbing Jasper's other hand and pressing a sloppy kiss against his lips. "You disappeared. I thought you bailed! Come dance with me!"

"Lindsay, we gotta go." He pulled his hand from hers, his gaze darting around the club. He saw the man he'd encountered in the bathroom, glaring right at them.

"Yeah, let's get outta here," Lindsay agreed. "We can go to my place! My roommate's at her parents' this weekend, so we can be alone."

A different sort of panic rose in Jasper's throat. "I—uh..." He looked away from the Hunter, casting Crimson a look.

"We're gonna need a rain check, babe," Crimson said. "It's my brother. He's a bit of a basket case—thinks people are after him, watching him through his webcam and shit. Jazz here is the only one who can talk him down when he gets nuts. We'll catch up with you tomorrow."

"Oh," Lindsay looked disappointed, but she bought it. "Okay. Well, I hope everything works out okay."

"Thanks," Jasper said, unsure if he spoke loud enough to be heard. He raised his voice. "Get home safe." He hoped the Hunters wouldn't follow her but couldn't worry about that now. They had to get back to Al.

Crimson led him through the club. Jasper had never been on the other side of the Hunters and found he was terrified. He knew exactly what they were capable of. They knew where they were staying; they knew where they went out. God, he'd been so stupid. He should have argued more with Crimson, convinced him to go somewhere else. But he hadn't wanted to leave. No, he had been having too much fun, and he'd met a girl who seemed to like him, and he was such an idiot.

The night was muggy but still cooler than the crowded club behind them. Jasper wiped the sweat from the back of his neck. It wasn't far to the hotel. "They know where we're staying. Al said they were watching the security feeds. We have to get him and go."

"If Al's been fuckin' around with their security-whatevers, they probably think *we* know, don'tcha think? And if *they* know that *we* know, they're gonna expect us to react like we know, y'know?"

"Crimson, I have no idea what you're trying to say to me right now. We have to leave."

Crimson's eyes flickered. "It's the middle of the night, we don't have a car, and even if we got one, they're expectin' us to run. How far do you think we'd get? *Are there* only four of them? Or are there six? Or eight? Or ten?" He was talking quickly and quietly now, his voice barely above a whisper, his lips hardly moving. "They could be all around us right now. They look just like everyone else."

Jasper looked behind them and saw the girl who'd been talking to him—Constance—walk out of the club, pause at the curb, and then cross the street.

"What are we going to do?" Jasper asked.

"We just act like we don't notice them," said Crimson. "Because if we *did* know, we'd obviously run. If we *don't* run…"

"Then they think we're still in the dark." Jasper understood.

"A trap only works when you don't see it comin'." He paused, lit a cigarette, took a drag and handed it to Jasper. "You like plans, right? Let's make a plan."

#

Jasper was suspicious of everyone in the lobby, from the pair of women having drinks at the in-house bar, to the middle-aged man reading a magazine, to the receptionist who smiled at them from behind the front desk. They took the stairs, and though Jasper went as fast as he could go, he could tell Crimson was impatient with the speed. Jasper told him to go ahead, to check on Alcander, but Crimson only told him to hurry up.

The door was bolted when they reached it. "Al, it's us," Jasper began.

Crimson leaned around him, slamming his fist against the door with three booming knocks. "Open the fuckin' door, Doc!" A few seconds later the door was opened, and the vampire let them in, closing it quickly behind them.

#

"Did anyone come by the room?" asked Crimson as he entered. "A maid or…"

"No," said Alcander. Crimson didn't know why he bothered asking. No new scents were in the room. "I never let them in. They leave everything by the door in the morning."

"The cameras?" asked Crimson.

Alcander pointed stiffly to the laptop that sat open on the bed. "They are down right now." Something about the way the vampire was acting wasn't sitting right with him. "The staff is working on getting them back up. I'm not sure—"

"Can *you* bring them back up?"

Alcander clicked his tongue against the roof of his mouth like this was a stupid question. Maybe it was. For all he knew, the things ran by magic, as well as electricity. "If I bring them back online, the hotel and whoever is patched into them will have access to them too."

"Yeah, yeah," said Crimson. "That's fine." Or he thought it was anyway. They were already in the room, after all. No one to see them come, and if Alcander was here, then (he assumed) he could also make it so no one would see them go.

Alcander walked over to the computer and hit several keys. The image on the screen shifted to a view of the hotel lobby. A woman in a blue dress entered through the front door. She paused at the front desk to ask a question of the attendant.

"She was at the club," said Jasper. Externally, the half-blood looked quite calm, but in the otherwise silent room, the sound of his heartbeat was deafening. When Ivory Goldwin had come tearing at him on eight legs with a mouth full of fangs, it had beat faster than this, but only just. "She was following you."

"Guess it's our turn, then," replied Crimson. He wondered if the clerk was her contact, or if she was just trying to blend in. More likely, she was asking him if he had seen them. While she was lingering near the desk, two others entered. A young man and the long-haired girl Jasper had been watching. Something about the girl didn't sit right with him either—he'd seen her before Jasper keyed him into the fact that she was a Hunter, but not *long* before. The trio started moving towards the elevators before he could quite suss out where and when. "Can you…?"

"On it," said Alcander. The view switched to an overhead camera inside the lift. Gods, these mortals hid the little electronic spies everywhere these days. And to think this country claimed to value "privacy." What a pain in the ass. He watched the three of them. The youngest woman was standing in the corner of the lift, her ponytail draped over her shoulder, twisting the end absently around her finger. "They are coming to this floor," continued Alcander.

And then it clicked, and Crimson whirled on Jasper. "Tying up loose ends, Jazz?" He remembered where he'd seen her now. Jasper had been talking to her when Crimson got to the club, and she'd cleared out as soon as he arrived, a full twenty minutes earlier than he said he would in his text message. "You had me goin' for a bit there, I'll give you that."

"Crimson," said Jasper, very slowly, very deliberately, "you're being very paranoid right now."

That's just what a Hunter would say, said the Spider.

It's also probably what a normal person would say, said Zahir, his human half. *Considering what you just said.*

"You would say that," said Crimson aloud.

Jasper wasn't looking directly at him but rather at a point just over his shoulder. "I told you I'm not a Hunter."

"Tell me again. And this time fuckin' look at me when you say it."

Jasper's eyes flicked to him and then quickly away, towards Alcander instead. What was that about? Just as quickly he was looking away again, not at either of them. The half-blood clenched his jaw so hard a muscle in it jumped. "I'm not a Hunter," he said, forcing his bright green eyes to focus. "Anymore." He flinched from Crimson's flashing eyes, but he didn't turn tail and run. He was either very brave or very stupid. "Look, Crimson, let me explain. I... I haven't been entirely truthful with you."

The words hit him like hollow pangs, though they really shouldn't have. This outcome was always in the cards, yet he felt blindsided. Betrayed. "No fuckin' shit," Crimson muttered. He bit down on his tongue to keep from saying more, to keep from shouting. The half-blood was doing the very thing he'd been trying to get him to do for weeks, and he didn't want him to get scared and clam up.

"The night we met, I told you I wasn't a Hunter because you would have killed me otherwise." Jasper's hands were still held carefully away from his weapon, a small tremor in the tips of his fingers.

Crimson risked glancing away from the Hunter, to the laptop on the bed. The view was taken from the hallway now, and the other Hunters were moving in their direction.

"I thought that'd be it, y'know?" Jasper's voice drew his attention back to him. Crimson moved all at once, crossing the short distance between them in the blink of an eye and seizing the front of the Hunter's jacket with a low growl.

"Crimson, don't!"

He ignored Alcander. "Stop buying time. *Talk*."

"You were nice to me," said Jasper, now in a breathless rush. "It's hard to get undercover operatives situated on the other side. My dad—*Charlie*, he thought it would be a good way in. So… he sent me to you."

"Great," said Crimson. The Spider came to the forefront, a layer of flesh the only thing separating him from his more beastly form. "Now I'll know who to address the body bag to."

"Crimson Apocalypse, that is *enough!*" He wasn't accustomed to hearing Alcander raise his voice to him, even when he was angry, and he looked in his direction despite himself. This inadvertently brought his gaze to the laptop. The Hunters were on their floor now, but they were stopped at a door almost all the way at the other end of the hall. It opened and they passed inside.

Wait…

That didn't make any sense. They should be coming *here*, to help Jasper.

Perhaps they just don't want to blow his cover, suggested the Spider.

That doesn't make any sense, you jackass. He warned you about the Hunters. Remember?

Alcander seized his elbow, tugging on his arm. For all the good it did him, he might well have been wrestling with a steel girder. "Crimson, let him go!"

Tell that dipshit vampire to fuck off. He's crazy!

He's your best friend.

"I wanted to tell you." Jasper, terrified green eyes starting to well, gripped Crimson's wrists, speaking almost as quickly as Alcander, talking over him, apologies tumbling from his lips as he tried to explain himself.

Crimson could hardly hear either of them through the internal screaming match between the two halves of his mind. He let go suddenly, taking several leery steps back. "Both of you shut up for a second!" He didn't know whom he was talking to—Alcander and Jasper, or Zahir and the Spider, but either way it worked. Jasper and Alcander both lapsed into silence, though Alcander took a step between them. His fangs were showing, a glimmer of red underneath the gray making his eyes pink.

"I can't believe you're siding with a Hunter right now," he told the vampire. Especially when at least four others were just down the hall.

"If you would actually *listen* instead of jumping wildly to conclusions, you would know that he is not a Hunter," replied

Alcander, a hiss below his words. He looked over his shoulder. "Jasper, it is okay. You can tell him the truth."

"I was trying to," said Jasper in a small voice, barely above a whisper. He paused, clearing the watery sound from his throat, and started again. "Look, I didn't know you guys, alright? Once I got to know you, I knew I couldn't go through with it. So I called Charlie. I told him I had to quit. I *didn't* call those Hunters here. I swear—to God or on my mother's grave or on whatever else you can think of— I am not with them. I'm on your side, Crimson. *Yours.*"

Crimson glowered at him. "You need to leave."

Jasper made a small sound of distress, but nodded miserably, and went towards the closet to get his backpack.

"Leave the bag," added the werespider. Perhaps all that Jasper said was true, but a turncoat could flip back to his original colors with the ease of a chameleon, and he didn't need the Hunter adding his arsenal to theirs. He was dangerous enough all on his own. "I'll give you five minutes to clear out of the building. Don't stop and chitchat with your Hunter friends." He gestured towards the laptop. "I'll know if you do."

"They're not my friends. They're here to take me back," said Jasper. His heart sounded like a bongo drum. "To St. James."

"Yeah, well, they can have you," replied Crimson, though some of the venom had gone out of his voice. He chanced another look at the screen. There was no movement in the hallway, but he was sure they were watching. "You'd better get moving. Clock's ticking."

"Crimson, *please*—"

"Kid, if you knew me like you think you know me, you'd know you should take your chance to run while you've still got it."

"But I don't want to go back!" A note of panic, too pitchy to be false. Jasper pulled the sleeves of his jacket down over his knuckles and folded his arms over his chest. "I mean... I want to stay with you."

Crimson's eyes widened very slightly, the red wisping out of them like a candle suddenly extinguished.

"I don't know what I can say to make this better," continued Jasper. He laid a hand on Alcander's shoulder, steering him gently aside. Alcander went, but not without a pointed glare at Crimson, and Jasper took his place, now reaching for Crimson's wrist with both hands. His heart was beating so fast, Crimson could feel the pulse in his fingertips beating against his own. "I should have told you. Right away. But I couldn't." His throat clicked. "I was scared of how you would react. I fucked up. I *know* I fucked up, but you've got to believe me; I would never hurt you *or* Al."

Crimson opened his mouth, sure that the words would just come out, like they always did, but this time they didn't. He took a deep breath and pressed his eyes closed as he exhaled. He held them closed until he felt the pressure in his temples. Then he opened them again.

Jasper's startling green eyes stared up at him, a high flush in his cheeks bringing out his freckles and complementing the soft pink of his lips. He didn't want to think about what the Hunters would do to him, didn't want, even, to think of what they had already done to him—this beautiful, powerful, unique, but painfully naive creature, crafted into a killing instrument probably before he was even old enough to drive a car. Hunters were not kind to familiars, and if Jasper thought Crimson's reaction to treachery was bad, he would be in for a terrifying shock when St. James had him back in their clutches.

Don't. You. Dare.

"Please," said Jasper again.

"Yeah," replied Crimson. "Okay."

You fucking idiot.

Obviously, Jasper expected a bigger or much different reaction than this, because the words seemed to take a second to process. He made a small sound, half sigh of relief, half gasping laugh. "Really?"

"Yeah, sure. Why not?" There were about a million reasons, but as he'd figured out in the Summerlands, none of them felt quite as strong as the bittersweet twinge in his chest when Jasper smiled at him. It was stupidly optimistic, gambling his and Alcander's lives on what amounted to a crush, but he couldn't help it. He liked him. "Besides, who else is gonna help me with these godsdamned assholes? Alcander? Not fuckin' likely."

Jasper laughed again, the sound surer of itself. "God, thank you." He squeezed his arm again, his hands folding around Crimson's, holding it tightly. "Thank you." There was that smile again, relieved and hopeful and maybe something else. Jasper let go all too soon, turning away for the moment it took him to wipe his eyes with his sleeve. His heart began to slow.

"Okay," he said, the tremor fading from his breath, his voice losing its near-hysteric tone, smoothing out some. Jasper looked at him, giving him a tentative smile. Crimson felt himself smile back.

He hoped he wasn't making a huge mistake.

"Okay," said the half-blood again, like he was still convincing himself. His eyes flitted away, guilt evident in them, looking to Alcander and to the computer screen, which now showed the empty hallway. "Can you go back with that thing? Find out how many we're dealin' with? We've got a plan to make."

Chapter Eighteen

—

Happy Hunting

It was early afternoon when Alcander cut the feeds for the second time. They timed the moment deliberately, waiting until the hotel was at its busiest so they could attempt to blend in with the crowd of guests coming and going. Three of the five remaining reeds would be used to mask their individual auras and, with any luck, once they were amongst the crowd, it would be easy to slip away undetected.

Jasper believed the Hunters valued their secrecy enough to try to avoid causing too much of a scene, but knew also they could be very clever when it came to finding ways around being detected by civilians. It wasn't much of a plan, and more of a gamble than he preferred, but it would have to suffice.

Jasper, Crimson, and Alcander moved out into the hall, Crimson taking point and Jasper following in the rear, with Alcander in between them.

The elevator was too dangerous; if the Hunters had some way of stopping it, they would be trapped and, frankly, selfishly, Jasper didn't want to be stuck in a lift with two panicked demons should something go wrong. Not that he thought they would harm him, more that it simply didn't seem like his idea of a good time.

They made for the stairs at a run. Crimson reached the door at the end of the hall and was shouldering it open when the door Jasper was tasked with watching popped open a sliver. "Behind us," hissed Jasper, his voice soft so only the demons would hear.

#

The demons had been quiet all night. Ryan, his eyes heavy with sleeplessness, sat at his computer, at the desk near the window, and watched the identical lines of unmoving doors, the empty hallway. Holly and Constance were sharing a room four levels down, and Stefan and Colt were two levels below that.

Constance's assessment of Jasper was grim. She didn't think it was a good idea to contact him and attempt to coerce him out of the demons' company. It was Selena who decided they would attempt to capture him instead.

Holly and Constance set the trap days ahead of time—a warding charm on the twenty-eighth floor, one in the stairwell and one in the elevator. They'd only held off thus far to make certain they had all their ducks in a row. They intended to spring the trap late at night, when other patrons were unlikely to interfere.

Selena was suspicious of the pair's behavior, and she decided they would keep an eye on them every waking moment. So Ryan was doing just that, but it was boring, and he found it difficult to focus for hours and hours on what was essentially nothing. He rubbed his eyes and stood up, stretched his arms and cracked his bones, then turned towards Selena, who was sleeping in the bed nearest the window, to tell her it was her shift.

"Hey, Captain, you wanna..." He did a double take. The feed went black very suddenly. A moment later, it went blue, with the same error message he'd received the other night. "Shit," said Ryan. "Captain, wake up!"

Selena was up and out of the bed like she'd fallen asleep with a syringe of adrenaline under her pillow. "The cameras?" she guessed.

"Yeah, they just went—"

With the newer comms acting so buggy, they had switched back to good old-fashioned radio. "Teams Beta and Delta, be alert." She made for the door, opened it a sliver, and used a compact mirror from her pocket to check the hall. At the far end, the reflection of moving shapes could be seen heading towards the stairwell.

Three moving shapes, to be exact.

The vampire never went with them. Not in all the time they had been here. They were either running or taking him hunting, and either way, it was unacceptable. "Targets are on the move. Singer, Alder, take preventative measures."

This was hardly ideal, but if the three of them made it out of the city, it was very likely they wouldn't be able to find them again, and Selena did not want to take the risk. Gesturing curtly for Ryan to grab his weapon, she stepped out into the hallway and ran after them.

#

Crimson was tearing down the stairs in leaps and bounds, only pausing occasionally to throw a snarl over his shoulder for Alcander to "keep up." Jasper called from behind to let him know someone was following them, and Crimson looked back towards Alcander, opened his mouth to yell at him for the third time, and ran headlong into... something.

It *felt* like a brick wall, but unlike a brick wall, it was invisible, and the impact came with a surge of electricity that wrapped him in its arcs and threw him backwards. His back slammed into Alcander, taking the feet out from underneath him. Jasper threw on the brakes, skipping on the tip of his toe for two steps before catching his balance on the railing.

There was the sound of feet on the steps above. The short-haired woman, now in a long blue coat nearly the same color as the dress had been, pointed her gun over the railing above them and squeezed the trigger several times, but all three of them drew back against the wall, out of line of sight.

She was only a few levels above them, and if she bottlenecked them here, with the Hunters no doubt approaching them from the other levels, Crimson was pretty sure they were going to die. He looked up, scanning the wall until he found what he was looking for. "Smoke detector." He pointed to it, and the way Jasper understood immediately what he was trying to say was something that *could* be taught, but only with years and years of training. He dropped his backpack on the floor, ripped the zipper open, and grabbed one of the half-dozen bargain-bin novels he'd collected at various gas stations and rest areas on their way to Miami. Crimson, Zippo already lighted, held the flame to the pages, and they plumed with brilliant orange flames, black smoke rolling off in clouds. Crimson dropped the Zippo, clasped his hands together to make a foothold, then boosted Jasper up to the little white circle high on the wall.

The Hunter rounded the last bend in the stairs just as the fire alarm began to wail, her gun already raised, Crimson squarely in her sights. Jasper fired before she could, and she threw herself behind the railing divider. The half-blood jumped down, firing once more for cover, and Crimson drew his gun, turning to look first towards the door beside them, then down the stairs.

"Jasper," called the woman's voice, "we're here to help you. Put the gun down and step away from the demon."

#

"I thought you said they were in the stairwell," hissed Constance's voice in Selena's ear.

Selena's brow crinkled. She and Ryan, both crouched around a bend in the staircase, shared a doubtful look with one another, and then Selena, despite herself, peeked around the corner.

A bullet whizzed past her head. The plaster on the wall behind her exploded.

She touched her radio. "They're right here. Can't you See them?"

"I see three energy signatures," replied Constance. "Three *human* energy signatures and a bunch more on the way."

Selena swore under her breath. They were masking their auras somehow. It wouldn't help them while they were corralled on the landing, but now, more than ever, it was imperative they catch them before they could leave the building. "Jasper, listen to me, no one wants to hurt you."

She subtly gestured to Ryan, giving him the signal to ready the tranq gun. Below them, there was the BOOM of a large-caliber revolver, the werespider trying to further incite panic. She heard a cry and felt a bolt of panic as she recognized Colt's voice.

She touched her comm. "Summers, are you hit?" There was no answer. Panic gripped her chest. "Colt! Answer me. That's an order!" But Colt did not answer.

On the stairs above them, she heard the doors burst open, the sound of voices. The sound of panic.

#

"Help!" yelled Crimson, and at first Jasper was confused, because he'd never heard him sound so frightened and helpless in all the time he'd known him, and because he thought he was talking to him. Then he saw the large group of people emerging on the landing below them, right where the two male Hunters were hiding. "We're trapped! They're trying to kill us!"

To their right the door burst open as well, but the shield was still in effect there, and though the door passed through it unhampered (much as Crimson's and Jasper's bullets did), the organic material of the human bodies trying to shove their way through it did not. Instead there was just a static burst of electricity and lots of frightened and confused screaming. Constance was wedged between them and the forcefield, trying to quell the panicked press of bodies and even seeming more than a little frightened herself.

The civilians were panicking, what they had probably thought to be a harmless glitch or routine drill having suddenly turned into a probable shooting from what (to people attempting to leave the twenty-eighth floor) seemed to be an inescapable, possibly on-fire hotel. "Holly! Holly, for fuck's sake!" Above and below them, the Hunters were overrun with angrily grasping hands that tried to seize their weapons or cast them over the railing.

A high, shrill voice cried several words over the clamor, and the shield suddenly gave way, unleashing the flow of bodies from every direction. Crimson snatched for Constance's arm as she struggled to right herself. His fingers closed around her elbow. She came jerking to his side with an expression on her face that was still forming fear, and before she had time even to scream, Crimson grabbed her belt in his free hand, swept her up off her feet, and threw her over the railing like she was a rag doll.

Her bloodcurdling shriek echoed alongside the screech of the fire alarm, through the surprised swell of silence, only to stop mid-scream with a solid, heavy thud. The spell of the werespider's voice broke, and with it the mindless mob mentality faltered as well. Then there were more screams, lots of them, mounting into a cacophony that seemed too big and loud for a space so small.

Some of the mortals wheeled around on a dime and ran back the way they had come. Others lunged past them and down the stairs like their lives depended on it. A few tried to rush them, but Crimson shouldered and batted them harmlessly aside. When this didn't deter them immediately, he drew his gun and fired straight up, which signaled an end to the mortals attempting to get in their way.

"Hallway," said Crimson, and Jasper agreed. He grabbed a hold of Alcander, who was making an admirable effort to squeeze himself into the wall, and dragged him along in the wake left at Crimson's heel.

They emerged in the corridor just as the majority of civilians were making their exit, either back towards the elevators or onto the stairs, but one young woman (not much older than Jasper) still stood, her eyes shining with furious tears. She cast her hand towards them, fingers bent in the shape of talons.

A wide arc of electricity splayed from her palm. Jasper threw himself and Alcander to the floor. The hairs on the back of his neck bristled, and he felt a static tingle in his teeth. The thin blue-white beams crackled over them and left charred wounds in the cream-colored plaster. Orange embers glowed and smoked at their heart, a single small flame flickering near the tail end of the blast, gone almost as quickly as it had bloomed.

They were barely back to standing when she brought her palms together with a shouted word, and the carpet ripped itself out from beneath their feet, rising like a serpent as they sprawled backwards. Jasper landed in a roll, stopping upright on his heels and toes, Crimson already looming beside him.

Another burst of electricity tore the raised rug asunder, narrowly missing Jasper and striking Crimson on the inside of his shoulder. The force spun him around and slammed him against the unfinished floorboards below. He surged back to his feet with a snarl and then lunged down the hall in a serpentine pattern, ignoring Jasper's cries for him to wait.

"Behind us!" shouted Alcander.

Jasper turned in time to see him pull the stairway door closed. It started to rattle and bounce immediately, the thin metal rail slipping in Alcander's grip. Something heavy impacted against the small rectangular half window. It shattered; the shine of gunmetal shone through.

Jasper had a split second to make a choice, and he chose to grab the rail beside Alcander, his eyes shining white as he wrested the door firmly closed. A shot fired, close enough that his ears screeched, and he gritted his teeth, twisting the metal rail so that it crossed the doorframe, effectively barring it. For now.

He grabbed Alcander's shoulder and turned him towards the hall, giving him a shove to get him moving. They'd have to find another way down.

#

Like all demons, the spider was fast, and this one had incredible reflexes, running and turning and twisting out of the way. Even when the electricity managed to hit him, it barely seemed to slow him. Holly backpedaled, throwing bursts of lightning left and right with one hand, trying to turn his gunfire aside with the other. Then suddenly he was right on top of her. His fist impacted against her sternum, and her ribs cracked with a crunch. She coughed, choking on blood, and the demon swung again, this time slamming across her jaw. Black spots burst across her vision and she crumpled to the ground. The spider brought his boot down on her rib cage, smashing it open like a rotted pumpkin. Her body convulsed for a spare few seconds, blue sparks jumping between her fingers, and then was still.

#

Three down. Jasper should have been horrified by the mechanical way he processed this information. How different was this from hunting, really? It was easy to think of it as nothing more than another mission. *Three to go.*

Most of the rooms and hallways were vacant, but there were a few stragglers, people who assumed the alarm was for everyone except them, just now poking their heads out of their rooms. Jasper, Crimson, and Al ran past them, to the other side of the hotel. There wasn't a second set of stairs, which Jasper thought was some sort of fire hazard, but they did find the staff service elevator. The Hunters probably didn't have access to this one, but even if they did, it wasn't like they had many other options. Crimson might have been willing to jump out of a window at twenty stories, but Jazz and Al were not.

The closest the service elevator took them to the exit was to housekeeping and laundry, on the third floor. From there they could re-enter the stairwell, and by now the largest part of the crowd was out, though this was still not ideal. It would have been easier if they could have gotten out with everyone else. With Crimson, it seemed, plans often went astray.

They paused by the door, where Crimson listened, his head cocked to the left. He gave a miniscule nod, looking at Jasper with blood-red eyes. The half-blood checked his clip, readjusted his grip, and nodded in return. Crimson kicked open the door, and they went into the stairwell, heading for the lobby.

Something hit Jasper just below his collarbone as they emerged into the large vacant room. He jerked backwards, ducking out of the line of fire and behind the reception desk on impulse, dragging Alcander with him. Looking down, he saw the yellow feathered end of a dart sticking out of his chest and pulled it out. The barest remnant of a vibrant green liquid remained in the vial. *Shit, shit, fuck, shit.* He tossed it aside. It was better than getting a bullet to the chest, but already he felt woozy and light-headed.

On the other side of the counter, he heard a vicious snarl rip through the air, followed closely by a scatter of automatic gunfire and a man's scream cut suddenly short. Taking a deep breath, he made to stand.

Alcander grabbed his wrist to pull him back down. In his fear he almost looked like a proper vampire, his gray eyes nearly red, his fangs showing, but Jasper was not afraid. Al was harmless.

He held up the dart. "That was a large dose of midazolam. In a few minutes you will be unconscious. You'll be an open target out there."

Jasper pulled his wrist out of the doctor's grasp. He knew he was right, but... "They'll kill him. I have to try." Eyes shining white with determination, he rose and made his way around the desk.

The body of one of the male Hunters was sprawled on the floor, eyes wide and staring, looking almost at Jasper. His throat was gone; Jasper saw the white of his spine through the blood that spread across the floor. Maybe ten feet away Crimson was in battle with the woman in the blue coat. She had a sword, long and thin, its edge emblazoned in gold. Crimson was dancing around her, avoiding her slices and jabs. She was quick, very quick, but Crimson was faster. Still, she sliced at him, and as Jasper watched, the blade came down and across his shoulder. He imagined more than heard the sizzle of flesh.

Crimson hissed, a harsh animal sound.

Jasper started towards the pair of them but was pulled from his feet, hitting the hard tile floor gracelessly. The tranq slowed his reaction time enough so that when his elbow hit the ground, his gun went flying across the floor, far out of reach. The ceiling spun above him. The Hunter from the bathroom the previous night brought the butt of his pistol down, hard across his lips. A sharp, eye-watering sting, then a numb tingle that fanned across his entire face. His cheek smacked the tile. He tasted blood. "You stupid shit!" Fingers clenched around his throat, knees pinning his chest, a hand raised the gun to come down on his face again.

Jasper felt a bright, surging energy pulse through him. He did not think, just grabbed upwards with both hands, one on the man's chin, the other on the back of his neck near the base of his skull, fingers splayed and twisted through his dark blond hair. His eyes were glowing white. He saw their reflection in the wide, surprised blue eyes of the man above. He grimaced, baring teeth coated in blood, and twisted the Hunter's head briskly to one side as hard as he could muster.

A crack, like the snap of dry twigs, but louder and crunchier; the sound reverberated down Jasper's arms. The Hunter's eyes glazed. With a puppetlike loll, he slumped over sideways and hit the floor beside him, a tendril of blood dripping from his lips, nostrils flaring desperately for several seconds before suddenly becoming still.

The energy deserted him almost as quickly as it had come. Groggily, Jasper made his way back to his feet. His ears were ringing, and all other sounds seemed very distant, as if they were playing on a television in another room. Jasper squeezed his eyes shut. He swayed and reached up to steady himself, stumbling against the grand piano. A single low flat note pierced the ringing silence in his ears. There was something he was supposed to be doing. Something important. He needed his gun. Where had it gone?

He wasn't aware of the moment his legs buckled beneath him,

only opening his eyes in time to see the lobby twirl around him in a dizzying mess of light and color. The impact of the floor never came. Instead, bafflingly, he felt like he was floating, the weightless sense of flying, cool air against his face. He opened his eyes, unaware of having closed them again, and saw above him Crimson's pretty face, an ugly slash marring his cheek, gushing black, smoking blood. Jasper reached to touch it, wanting to ask if he was alright, but the darkness at the corners of his blurred vision persisted and descended, pulling him the rest of the way down.

Chapter Nineteen

—

Going Underground

Jasper didn't wake all at once. Slowly he became aware of a tapping sound, far off but constant, insistent. He wanted to ignore it, wanted to stay in the quiet, safe dark of his slumber, but now that its perfect silence was disrupted, it left him, pulling him back to consciousness.

He became aware of rough fabric under his cheek; of cool, stale air in his nose; of warmth against his back and around his waist.

He opened his eyes.

It was dark, so dark that at first, he couldn't see anything at all, and panic shocked through his chest, ripping away any last remnants of sleep that clung to him. He sat up, blinking in the darkness. Details came into view: he was in an unfinished room, the walls wooden skeletons, some with drywall, most without. A white washer/dryer set nearly shone in the shadows of one corner of the room next to a large basin sink. A bulky wood-cased television sat in the other. A big throw rug covered most of the floor, its color indistinguishable, and on top of it, not far from where he sat, the surface of a polished coffee table reflected the barest amount of light coming in from a tiny rectangular window high up on one wall, the only one he could see.

Where was he?

"Jazz?" Something brushed his wrist, and he jerked his arm away even as he recognized the voice.

"Crimson?" The muted red glow of his eyes, a demon's version of night-vision goggles, looked over at him near the head of the bed. Not so long ago the sight of such things would twist his stomach

195

with poison feelings of hate, but now he felt only comfort.

"Where are we?" He tried to remember. Everything was so blurry, an adrenaline-fueled collection of snapshots. Some were more focused than others, and he wished they weren't. A spray of blood, bright red against polished white floors; his own hands wrapped around the neck of one of the Hunters, the hard snap of bone.

A wave of nausea rolled over him and he closed his eyes.

"We're at that human's house. Max." Jasper didn't say anything, so Crimson continued. "There's iron beams in the basement." In the dark he could hardly be seen, but Jasper felt him gesture to the ceiling above them. "Makes it crazy hard to track with magic." Jasper's silence persisted, though the other gave him ample time to respond. "You've been out for a few hours."

Jasper opened his eyes and looked around the dark room again. A new horror crawled into his heart. "Where's Al?"

"Al's fine." Crimson's voice was uncharacteristically soft, melodic almost. The werespider sat up beside him on the bed—no, wait, it was a futon, Jasper felt the hard metal bar through the lumpy mattress—and gently touched his shoulder, kneading the muscles there. Jasper leaned into it without thought. "He was down here too, but he wouldn't shut up about service or connection or whatever the fuck it's called, so I sent him upstairs before he had an aneurysm or woke you up." Crimson's hand moved, rubbing small circles between his shoulder blades. The pressure was calming, reminding him of when he was very young, and his father would rub his back to help him sleep after a nightmare.

This felt like a nightmare.

"I'll get the light." Crimson moved to get up, and Jasper grabbed his arm, holding him back.

"No!" The sound of his own voice surprised him, louder and rougher than he expected. When he spoke again, it was quietly, as if to make up for shouting. "No. Leave it off. Please."

"If that's what you want." Crimson settled back on the edge of the futon. "Whatever you want."

Jasper released his arm, rubbing his hands on the thighs of his jeans. The basement wasn't terribly cold, but he couldn't suppress the chill that shook him. Crimson put his hand between his shoulders again, and Jasper closed his eyes, curling his hands into fists.

"Can I get you anything?" asked the werespider. "Water? Food?"

Crimson was being painfully nice. Jasper was used to his teasing and his goading and his sarcastic comments. He felt almost confused by his tenderness. He didn't deserve such kindness, not after the way he'd lied to him, nor after the way he'd almost gotten them all killed. Crimson should hate him.

He opened his mouth to say that, no, he didn't need anything, but the words didn't come out. In their place a sob choked him.

Jasper had never killed a human. And though he had come to believe there was little difference between the dozens of vampires he'd killed and the Hunter in the lobby, it weighed on him differently. At least the Hunter had been in self-defense. He just hadn't expected it to be *so easy*. Once he picked a side, he fell right back into his training. Once his hands were around the Hunter's neck and he saw how simple it was to end him with a nearly effortless twist of his wrists (that was even with the tranquilizer in his system), he didn't even have to think about it.

The werespider didn't say anything, just closed the gap between them, then pulled him into an embrace, Jasper's face against his shoulder, Crimson's cheek against his hair. He didn't ask what was wrong, didn't try to say it was going to be okay. He just let Jasper cry, the sobs shaking his body while Crimson rubbed his back and held him close. Jasper, who rarely felt small, felt small then, but with Crimson's arms around him, he also felt safe, cared for. Fingers clinging to his T-shirt, he held him back tightly and breathed in a shuddering breath. Even with the jacket gone, the scent of leather was still there, as much a part of him as his black hair and flashing eyes.

Eventually his sobs gave way to shaking, heaving breaths, which then turned to hitching periodic sighs and whimpers, and then to sniffles. Jasper noticed he'd all but soaked Crimson's T-shirt at the shoulder and rubbed uselessly at it, with a small and miserably uttered, "Sorry." His throat ached, and his eyes felt itchy from too many tears. His horror and sorrow were still there, hollow and faraway holes in his heart and belly. Mostly, now, he just felt tired.

Crimson shook his head. "You don't ever gotta apologize to me for a few tears, Jazz. Whatever the cause."

Jasper swallowed hard, the click in the back of his scratchy throat audible. "I'll take that glass of water now, if you're still offering."

"Sure thing," said Crimson, then bellowed up the stairs, "Hey! Alcander!"

Jasper sighed. Well, it was nice while it lasted. "Don't do that." He rubbed hurriedly at his eyes with the back of his hand. "I'll get it myself. It's not like my legs are broken."

"Can't," said Crimson. "Iron beams, remember? I gave Al the last of the reeds, and he's so meek, he probably already shows up as a mortal."

"Crimson, I am standing right here." Alcander was halfway down the steps, a lime green ceramic mug in his hands.

"Yeah, I know," said Crimson, and Jasper elbowed him sharply in the side.

Alcander scowled, but descended the rest of the way, flipping the light switch as he passed. He offered the mug to Jasper, who accepted with a sincere (if raspy), "Thank you, Al." He took a small sip, then a much deeper one. The water soothed the ache in his throat and seemed to temper the fever in his skin.

Alcander crouched in front of him, his pale pink eyes scanning Jasper's face. "How are you feeling?"

"I'm okay," said Jasper. "Really. I've been through worse." Though he didn't know that he had. "Where's Max?" He wanted to thank him for letting them stay at his place right out of the blue. And make certain he was actually okay with the danger that was implicit in such a choice, and not just wandering around upstairs in some half-hypnotized daze à la Crimson.

"He is making dinner," replied Alcander.

Jasper looked suspiciously at Crimson, and he raised both hands. "Hey, don't look at me. He volunteered."

"He is very friendly."

Crimson snorted. "Well, he ought to be after we nearly died saving his skin."

Jasper hadn't helped Max because he wanted him to owe them, it was just something he had to do. The thought of trying to explain that to Crimson, even after he'd been so nice to him, sounded exhausting. He finished the water and set the empty mug on the coffee table. With the light on, he could more clearly see the basement, noting the pink plastic-covered insulation between the wooden frames of the walls, the closed door at the bottom of the stairs that he hoped was a bathroom, and the large metal sink by the washer and dryer, with a faucet that dripped steadily, the source of the constant tapping sound. A big ugly red leather armchair was pushed under the stairs next to a few neatly stacked boxes, but other than that and the futon, there wasn't any other furniture. There was also no clock on any of the walls, or the lack thereof, so Jasper wasn't sure what time it was. The small window showed nothing but darkness, seeming darker now with the light inside.

There were much worse places to be, but Jasper was anxious to find out when they were leaving.

#

Max had spent his first week back wandering quizzically through the rooms of his house, numbly searching for the sense of connection he'd once felt to the place. For the most part, he was hollow, empty, only circulating around the house habitually, as if somehow, someday, he would remember why he used to bother doing so. This bleak feeling was interrupted only by sudden bursts of choking panic. They came from nowhere, lasted however long they lasted, and went as they pleased, often with neither warning nor trigger.

Then he lived in perpetual terror of their approach. One seemed to lurk through every door.

Barring college and a rental apartment in his early twenties, he had lived in the old one-story house for his entire life. It was his father's house. His parents had been married on the front porch. Their wedding picture was still on the mantel over the fireplace, sitting in the same place it had sat for nearly fifty years. The living room still had its original moldings, though the hideous wallpaper had been stripped and replaced with flat blue paint. He'd painted it himself.

It was, and had always been, his home.

It now felt suspiciously like a tomb.

During the second week, he'd relocated himself to the basement. The futon down there wreaked hell with his back and hip, and on the nights when he did manage to sleep, he woke feeling largely like someone had spent the better half of their night kicking the shit out of him, but it was better than the living room, where he could still see the trails his fingernails had left on the hardwood floor. And a far cry better than the bedroom, whose door he had not opened since the day Jasper and Crimson dropped him off.

It came down to two facts.

One, the house no longer felt safe.

Two, there was literally nowhere else for him to go.

He couldn't even go to work anymore. Hadn't even *tried*.

During the third week, the police showed up, seeming shocked, baffled, and then, finally, angry to find him just hanging out there, like he had never left. He wondered who might have reported him missing, but no one came to mind. Someone at work, perhaps. Or maybe one of the neighbors. It was really too depressing a question to ask outright, and he didn't feel like having a complete mental breakdown in front of the Miami beat cop who came to check on him. He gave the officer some half-assed explanation about how he'd simply decided he needed to get away from it all for a while, and how there was really no need for any alarm.

The cop went away, and Max slunk back into his house.

During the fourth week, he'd taken it into his mind that he was going to put the house up for sale and move. Definitely out of Miami, maybe even out of Florida as well.

That was when the demons showed up.

Despite all the evidence to the contrary, it had started to feel to Max like the entire thing was a hallucination. Their presence—there and real and tangible—was a relief.

The news they brought with them was less so. They were being hunted, and it looked a great deal like they would need to run. Crimson, his arms and hands crusted in drying blood, was carrying Jasper and hadn't so much as asked if they could come in, as he elbowed his way past and told him they were staying. But that was okay. Max would not have argued even if they had given him the opportunity.

They were downstairs now, the murmur of their voices carrying up through the cracked basement door, into the kitchen, where Max was slicing carrots into even, chunky pieces. He swept them into the pot with the flat of the blade, then started on the onions. By the time he had the pot simmering, the tone of the voices downstairs was no longer low and serious but playful and joking.

He set the timer on the stove, then sat down on the couch. The quiet bubbling of the stew combined with the dreamlike murmur of voices below lulled him, and the terror that lived like a scrambling rat at the back of his brain seemed at last to take a break from its gnawing.

He was asleep in minutes.

He awoke to the sound of the timer, panicked about nothing in particular but panicked nonetheless.

The annoying beeping noise stopped almost as quickly as it began, before Max could make it off the couch.

The vampire, Alcander, was already at the stove, giving the pot a few perfunctory stirs before neatly ladling the thick stew into two identical bowls. He was wearing a gray turtleneck, a loaner from Max that was a full size too large. His shaggy hair, still damp, was tied loosely back at the nape of his neck, fangs hidden in a gently encouraging smile. "I have been keeping an eye on it for you. I hope you do not mind."

"Not at all," said Max. "I should be apologizing to you for falling asleep."

"You looked like you needed it. How are you feeling?"

"Okay, I guess. Apart from the nightmares. And the panic attacks. And the pain. But that's mostly from the futon, I think. Except for my fingers. Or, uh… the lack thereof." He hadn't yet made it a full day without forgetting they weren't there, and must have burned himself half a dozen times in the last month, reaching for the handle of a skillet or frying pan, only to have it slip through his phantom fingers and go toppling from the stove. He was lucky the wok hadn't broken his foot. "But… other than that…"

"You need rest," repeated Alcander. "But food first, I think. Why don't you come eat with Jasper? I am sure he could do with a human's company right now, and he has been asking about you."

"I'd be happy to," said Max. *He* could do with *any* sort of company right now, human or otherwise. He placed the bowls on a small carrying tray, added a half loaf of fresh-baked bread and a sleeve of store-bought cookies on the side, then followed Alcander downstairs.

#

The door at the top of the stairs opened again, and Max appeared there, though it was difficult to see him from their position on the futon. The smell of whatever he had cooked reached Jasper first, and despite his anxiety and troubled mind, he felt hungry.

Max looked better than he had a month earlier, when Crimson and Jasper found him wandering in the woods. His long-sleeved flannel covered a majority of the scarring, excusing a few jagged runes etched into the side of his throat. The scabbing had peeled away, leaving white ghosts of slightly puckered scar tissue. Some of the color had returned to his still-thin face, and his blue eyes were stained with dark, sleepless circles underneath.

He brought Jasper a tray with a bowl of thick, hearty stew and a thermos of coffee, with fresh chunks of bread, still warm from the oven, on the side. Jasper hadn't had home-cooked food in longer than he could remember, and he scarfed it down hungrily while they bounced ideas back and forth. Crimson believed they should return to New York, where the Hunters would be least likely to expect them. Jasper wasn't sure that was such a hot idea, but primarily because the idea of possibly running into Charlie out there quickly had his stomach twisting into knots.

"Maybe we could go somewhere else," suggested Jasper. "Someplace where there aren't so many Hunters."

"No such place," said Crimson. "Not in the States anyhow. You know how much money these people spend on their military. Anyway, I have connections in New York."

"Crimson, you don't understand," reasoned Jasper. "They know where you *live*." It hurt him to tell him this, almost as much as it had hurt him to admit he was a Hunter. More, in fact, because the place was obviously important to him. "They're going to be pissed that we killed those Hunters. They'll come after us."

"The house'll keep 'em out."

Jasper thought of the swinging blades in the old library, of Crimson's vague warnings. "A few booby traps won't be enough to stop a group of trained Hunters."

"There's a lot more than a *few*. You ever see one of those old movies where a bunch of explorers discover a pharaoh's tomb, so they all go down there, sniffin' around for artifacts, and then even though there's like twenty people to start with, only the hero and the dame make it out alive? It's kinda like that. 'Cept no one makes it out alive."

"You're being ridiculous. If I only managed to activate one—"

"You only managed to activate the one that was *set*," interrupted Crimson. "I don't keep them all active *all the time*."

"What? Why?"

"Because I get tired of cleaning up dead teenagers, mostly. You should see the mess the chandelier makes. Guts and brains all over the walls. And don't get me started on the trapdoors. Sometimes it's days before the smell works its way up."

Jasper flinched. How could the demon be so gentle one moment and then so cold the next? Sometimes he felt like there were two of him. "That's *disgusting.*"

Crimson grinned. "Wait until I tell you what the sconces do."

As this went on, Alcander was typing on his laptop in the chair by the stairs. He cleared his throat. "I don't believe the Hunters are going to be a problem."

Al was supposed to be the smart one. The day the Hunters gave up on a hunt was the day hell froze over. "What are you talking about?"

He turned the screen to face Jasper, though he could see very little from the other side of the room. "I do not know whether you would consider this good news or bad news, but if St. James is to be believed, you died in the same car accident that killed your parents." Before Jasper could properly form a response, Al continued, "The good news is that there are not any files on any of your... shall we say, more recent activities either. I don't see anything about the operation you and Charlie cobbled together. The file from Joan of Arc is still being drafted, but I see that it has been changed to exclude you entirely. They do not even mention that Crimson and I are from New York. It leaves gaps in the archive somewhat, but none anyone would notice unless they were looking for them. Seems to me like someone on the inside is looking out for you."

Jasper made a small noise of noncommitment. He supposed it was a good thing that the Hunters didn't know he existed. In fact, it was probably the best thing for their survival. The idea of his father systematically deleting every mention of his existence didn't make him feel so hot, though. He was too worn out to express this feeling, which was probably a good thing because he did not want to cry in front of Crimson again, no matter how kind the werespider had been.

"If you three need a ride back to New York, I'd be happy to take you." Max spoke up for the first time in the conversation. His voice was soft and slow, not quite a drawl but something akin to one. As Jasper understood, he had not gone back to work and had been living day by day on whatever nest egg he'd built while working as an accountant. "That is, if you want to go back."

"We couldn't ask you to do that, Max. You've really already done more than enough."

"Oh, it's no bother." He rubbed the stumps of the missing fingers on his right hand, his eyes not quite meeting Jasper's. "I don't have much to do around here except sit around and feel like I'm going crazy. I, uh… can't really sleep here anyway. Might be nice to get away for a few days. And I've never been to New York."

"If you wanna come with us cuz you're scared the boogeyman's gonna crawl outta your floorboards in the middle of the night, you can just say that," said Crimson.

Jasper threw another, much harder, much more pointed elbow in his side, punctuating the unspoken sentence with a glare.

"What? That's what it is, isn't it?" He looked towards Max, who only shrank a little in the armchair.

Jasper had known about demons his entire life. While other children were out playing tag and kickball, he'd learned fencing and marksmanship. After Saturday morning cartoons, he read hunting manuals from his father's study. He slayed his first live vampire when he was thirteen. Granted, it was under controlled circumstances, but the werewolf that came a year and a half later wasn't.

He couldn't imagine what it was like to one day simply wake up to reality and then have to live there while everyone he knew was still asleep. "We'd love it if you gave us a ride," said Jasper. "Crimson drives like a fuckin' asshole anyway."

#

The drive back to New York was not bad, insofar as such things went. The hatchback was slightly smaller than Jasper would have preferred, and slightly too slow to hold Crimson's bitching at bay, but with three drivers they made good time.

They were going to stay with Alcander for a couple of weeks until they could be certain the heat had died down and they weren't being pursued. The factory was an old ironworks, which had seen its last great boom during the Second World War and had fallen to ruin in the years since. Alcander said his older brother had worked there during the Great Depression. He wondered if any of the vampire's human family was still alive, then decided it might be rude to ask.

"The iron is good for shielding against tracking spells, and psychics don't See through it clearly," said Alcander as they wove their way through the dark in a single-file line. Like all vampires, Al could see in the dark almost as well as he could in the light, but he was carrying a small flashlight, a beacon for the others in case they should become lost. "The condemned signs and caution tape keep the humans away. Most of them, anyway." He turned sideways to squeeze through a gap between two large furnaces, careful not to brush the grimy machines. His small stature gave him that luxury, but it wasn't allotted to the other three. Chunks of jutting metal snagged at Jasper's clothing, and he had to stoop to keep from banging his head on the rusty supports.

On the other side, the space widened out just enough for the four of them to stand in a very close, nearly claustrophobic huddle. The only thing there was a blank space of wall. Using the handle of the flashlight to avoid using his own fingers, Alcander pushed open a small compartment hidden in the molding on the baseboards. This revealed a keypad. Judging by the dirt and grime around the fixture, it had not been used consistently in many years. Alcander made a face. "Max, do you think you could...?"

"Yeah, I got it. What's the number?"

"11131952," said Alcander.

Max entered the number, and the keypad beeped and flashed. There was a metallic *thunk* somewhere inside the wall.

"Okay, quick, before it times out, 0104051216081519."

The keypad *beep*ed twice more, then flashed green. A second loud *thunk*, and a rectangular seam appeared in the wall. With a hiss of air, it pushed itself outward, then rumbled softly aside, revealing a steel door. A glass lens mounted at the top of the frame shined a green light down as Alcander stepped beneath it. Gears knocked and clanked. Something that sounded like a chain on a spool rattled, and the door slowly opened inward to reveal a stone set of stairs that spiraled down into darkness.

"Lotta pomp and circumstance for a hole in the ground," muttered Crimson. "How'd Sid and Ivory get in anyhow?"

Alcander started down the stairs. "They didn't. Knox did. As far as I can tell, he broke his collarbone, probably his hips, and maybe one of his arms, and then slithered down the air duct." Overhead, motion sensors detected their movement, and the staircase lit itself in increments that mirrored their progress. "I will be putting bars over the vents tonight, I think."

An archway at the bottom gave way to a tiny foyer with concrete flooring, a coat rack, and little else. Alcander asked all of them to take off their shoes, then led them through a small door into the basement proper.

It looked more like a penthouse apartment in Manhattan than a finished basement. The walls and carpet were white, the matching furniture deep gray. Everything was as neat and orderly as Jasper expected it to be, knowing the vampire, excusing a smear of blood on the wall—a souvenir from the struggle with Knox, most likely. Crimson, who had obviously been there before, was gone from his side in a second.

"This is the living room," said Alcander to Jasper and Max. "The kitchen is through there." He pointed through an archway to the left. "As is my lab and my bedroom." He looked back towards Jasper. "You and Crimson will have to fight over the guest room." He gestured to the hallway that ran to the right, where Crimson had already gone. "Just please try to refrain from doing so physically." Jasper didn't think there was any danger of that. "There is a small library down that way, too, and a full bathroom. I'm afraid I don't have much in the way of food anymore. Since Michael died, there has been little use for the majority of the accommodations."

"Michael?" repeated Jasper. This name rang a bell, but he could not recall why.

"He and Crimson used to stay here quite often," explained Alcander. "As did his cousin and her husband." Alcander's voice was even and calm, matter-of-fact, but as was so often the case with the little vampire, his eyes gave him away. They seemed distant. Sad.

Jasper cleared his throat awkwardly. "I'd, uh… love to see the library."

"Of course," said Alcander. He showed him down the hall. On the way, they passed the guest room, where Crimson was digging for something in the closet. The adjacent door led to a large square room, where the walls were lined from floor to ceiling in neat rows of carefully categorized and labeled books. Additional shelving had been added in the center, making it look quite a great deal like a legitimate library. "I do not know if anything here will suit your tastes," said Alcander. "I have little interest in fiction, and most of the volumes are mine, but Nightwind, Michael, and Crimson kept some of theirs here as well, and Salem was fond of photography collections."

Upon closer inspection, Jasper noticed some of the stacks were labeled with their names, and Crimson's took up a whole corner almost to themselves. No wonder there were so few books at his house. They were all here.

"If you're into trash romance novels where the girl always gets the guy and they both live happily ever after, I think Mikey had about a thousand of them." Jasper jumped at the sound of Crimson's voice suddenly so close. He hated when he did that. They really needed to put a bell or something around his neck. "But if you're into trash romance novels where the guys tragically convinced he's Dracula, that'd be more Night's style."

Jasper smiled slightly. "What if I'm not into any sort of trash romance novels?"

"Hypothetically, you mean?" Crimson tilted his head to the left, thinking. "I've got all the classics. Well, all the ones that don't suck, anyway."

"I've never seen you read anything," said Jasper.

Crimson shrugged. "I'm really into movies this century."

Jasper noticed his hands were clasped behind his back, like he was holding something there. "What's that?"

Crimson drew a step back. "What's what?"

"Behind your back." He tried to lean around him, but Crimson turned slightly, keeping his front towards him.

"It's just a book. I was returning it."

"If it's just a book, why won't you let me see it?" asked Jasper, making another snatch for it even as he finished his question.

Crimson dipped around him, but Jasper caught a glimpse of the cover. A woman in a flowing dark green dress, the shoulders sloping so much that it looked about ready to fall from her swelling breasts, clung to a roguish, shirtless man with long dark hair. He grinned. "It's a fucking romance, isn't it?"

Crimson sighed. "Yeah, man." He set it on the shelf, not in any particular spot, ignoring the way Alcander's eye twitched. "You wanna come watch a movie?"

"Well, it depends." Jasper couldn't stop grinning, the picture of Crimson totally engrossed in one of those cliched will-they-won't-they romances was too good. "Are you gonna wanna watch some sappy romance movie?"

"You'd love that, wouldn't you?" huffed Crimson. "But no. I was actually thinking more along the lines of *Mockingbird*. It's just about to start." He pointed back towards the living room, where the couch was piled with blankets and pillows, no doubt excavated from the closet in the guest room. The television was already on, playing a commercial.

"Okay," agreed Jasper. "Sounds fun. You guys wanna—"

"No, thank you," said Al before he had even finished the question. Jasper looked towards Max, who, curiously enough, was not looking at him, but at Crimson.

"Max?"

"Hm? Oh. No. Thanks. I think, uh, I'll just hang out here and, uh, look over the books. For a while." He said this in a much more awkward way than Jasper saw cause for, fumbling over the words, looking more over Jasper's shoulder than directly at his face. Jasper curiously turned to see what Crimson was doing that was so damned interesting, but the werespider was just standing there, looking innocent. *Too* innocent. "I don't want to intrude," added Max.

"Oh... kay." He didn't understand how Max could believe he could possibly "intrude" on the relatively nonsocial act of watching a movie, but he wasn't going to argue with him. "I'll see you guys later, then."

The living room was comprised of a large sectional couch and an easy chair with a stand in between, white plush carpet, and a big flat TV almost as wide as the stand it was sitting on. Jasper climbed into the nest of pillows and blankets, putting himself in the corner of the sectional, with his legs stretched out towards the television. Apart from short breaks for food, he had been crammed in the hatchback for nearly eighteen hours straight, and it felt good to lie on something softer and more spacious than a car seat.

Plenty of room was left on the couch, but, after flipping off the table lamp, Crimson sat beside him, his legs curled underneath him, elbow propped on the back of the couch. It wasn't unusual for the werespider to prefer being near others, and Jasper didn't mind, so he made no comment.

He had seen the movie before and, as adaptations went, he thought it wasn't bad. He was having trouble focusing on it, however, the black-and-white images moving in front of his eyes without actually processing. Eventually, the film went to commercial. "So you used to stay here a lot, huh?"

Crimson shifted uncomfortably. "Yeah, sometimes." He plucked a singular piece of lint (probably the only piece that existed in the entire place) off the back of the couch, rolled it between his fingers, and then flicked it away. "The others were fond of Alcander."

Jasper thought of the pictures he had seen in the file Charlie gave him. Alcander wasn't in any of them, but there was a man and a woman in one of them—Salem and Nightwind, he supposed. And a younger man, with wavy brown hair and shining blue eyes. Crimson had asked about Adam and about his parents, listening to him ramble on and on about the details of his life that couldn't have been interesting to anyone else other than Jasper. He knew Crimson's mate had been a magic user, and he knew his pack died during a raid (though Crimson did not know he knew that). Yet he had never asked him much else about them, and he was starting to feel a little guilty about it.

"Do you still miss them?"

"Well, yeah." Crimson hesitated. "I loved Mike, but he was here and gone so fast, and I'm kinda used to that, so I got over it pretty quick. And I never got on so well with Sal. He was Nightwind's, like... thirteenth husband or something, so I always figured he'd be gone eventually, but I liked him, especially there near the end." He reached into his pocket, drew out his wallet, and flipped it open. The picture was not the same one he had seen in the file. It was much older. The werespider was sitting at a table, half a glass of whiskey held at an angle, the female werespider leaned over his shoulder, her arms thrown around him in a hug, cheek against his forehead. Her eyes were a strange shade of blue, almost violet, and maybe it was the lighting, but his were a shade he had never seen before. Burgundy. They looked happy. "Mostly, I miss Nightwind."

"Your cousin?"

The corner of his lip curled. "Technically. She was more like a sister, though. Except for when she was like a mother... or a daughter." He flipped the wallet closed and replaced it in his pocket. "She was made a year after I was, so we were together for most of our lives." He paused, ruminating. "She was my best friend."

"I'm sorry," said Jasper. He knew how it had hurt to lose Adam, who had been his best friend since he was five. For months afterward he would wake up, convinced it was a nightmare, that, somehow, he was still alive. Of course, in some ways his imagination had been correct about this. Even to this day, the other still haunted his dreams. If Crimson could be believed, he'd known Nightwind for nearly three thousand years. No wonder he spent most of his time trying to drink himself into oblivion.

"Not your fault," said Crimson. "You probably weren't even born yet."

"I'm still sorry. You shouldn't have to be alone." The commercial break ended, and the movie returned. Jasper glanced at it, then quickly back at Crimson. On impulse he seized the werespider's hand, drawing all of his attention. "You're not alone now. I plan on sticking around for a while."

Crimson gently cocked one eyebrow. "Yeah?"

"Yeah." Jasper squeezed his hand once and then let go, adjusting one of the many pillows. A small, nervous feeling settled into his belly, and he tried again to watch the movie. "Is that... okay?"

Jasper wasn't looking at Crimson, but he heard the smile in his voice when he spoke. "Yeah, Jazz, that's okay."

#

There was only one guest room, and Jasper could have easily taken the couch, but they intended to stay for a while, and Jasper didn't feel right forcing Max to sleep on the floor or crammed into the easy chair. Crimson said when he was growing up, his entire family slept in one bed, which wasn't so much a bed as a sack of straw, and he didn't see why Jasper needed to make such a fuss about their sharing. Besides, they could both smoke in the guest room, which was something they couldn't do in the rest of the house. The bed was a king size, significantly larger than the one they'd shared at Max's.

Jasper decided not to quibble. They were just friends, after all, and it felt ridiculously vain, assuming that the other was going to try something. Crimson could sleep with whomever he wanted. Honestly, why would he even be interested in Jasper?

Crimson didn't try anything, and after a few nights he was so used to the weight of him on the other side of the bed that he found he didn't mind it at all. The werespider was a very quiet sleeper, though he woke often, usually in response to some small sound too quiet and far off for Jasper to hear himself. It reminded him of the way a cat slept. And just like a cat, there were a few occasions (three or four) where he burst suddenly awake, seemingly at random, and in an utter panic. Once he even made it all the way out of the bed and onto his feet before Jasper reached across the mattress, touching his wrist and saying his name, bringing him back to reality.

Jasper had his own share of nightmares. Sometimes about Adam. Sometimes about the Hunters. His waking always woke Crimson (the werespider said it was because of the change in the tempo of his heart and the depth of his breathing), but Crimson never seemed to mind. He would lay a palm on his chest, assure him he was safe, tell him it was only a dream.

Alcander was often in his lab, and sometimes Jasper went to visit him. The room was filled with more machines and devices than he cared to count or attempt to identify. Screens poured digital readouts and flashed or pinged with results. One entire wall was taken up by a dry-erase board crammed with numbers and equations in neat rows, the lines differentiated by colors of marker.

Alcander was delighted to have him, and here, safe and surrounded by his machines, he talked excessively. Jasper only understood about a third of what he said, but he liked how excited and at ease the vampire seemed.

Max opted to stay "for now." He was the only one of them who could cook. Jasper, who had never made anything more complicated than boxed mac 'n cheese, hung around the kitchen during mealtimes, helping with small tasks and trying to learn a thing or two in the process. The reality was that there wasn't much else to do, and he had to figure it out anyway. There was no agency cantina to go back to, and he couldn't survive on fast food for the rest of his life, not unless he wanted "the rest of his life" to be about forty.

The days tapered together, his sense of time warped by the lack of sunlight and change.

Crimson cracked before he did.

"I can't be here anymore," he told him over coffee one morning (or… perhaps it was evening). "I don't know how he lives like this. I gotta go somewhere. Do something."

Jasper was a fan of the mellow vibe the place had, and of the routine he'd settled into. It was a well-needed rest from the absolute chaos of the month past, and with little more to do than talk, he came to know the others quite well, but as the days wore on, he found it lacking. It felt like time to go home.

Chapter Twenty

—

Sleepover

Aside from the spoiled food in the fridge, the house was just as they had left it. They were at Alcander's for less time than it had felt. Twelve days.

He had no idea how much he would miss fresh air and sunlight. He opened all of the curtains and all of the windows the attic had to offer and cracked the basement door to get a draft going through the broken windows downstairs. A thick layer of dust had built up in their absence, and the place was never that organized to begin with. He tried to clean it up and put it together as best he could without sparing too much effort.

Crimson wasn't a fan of it, but his complaining was mostly limited to snide remarks, and if he actually minded, Jasper was sure he would put a stop to it.

At first, both were still leery of spending too much time outside the house. Night after night went by, and no one came after them. Soon, it seemed perhaps no one would.

There still wasn't much in the way of food at Crimson's house, though Jasper picked up some snacks and frozen pizzas from a small grocery store down the road. He was tired of eating burnt, bland pizza and didn't feel like bothering Max (who still hadn't left Alcander's, and it was looking like he simply wouldn't) for a home-cooked meal. Crimson's first suggestion was Rascal's. They hadn't been in ages, so Jasper agreed.

The staff greeted Crimson like an old friend, commenting on his sudden disappearance. Crimson laughed good-naturedly and joked with them about his vacation, making the rounds through the bar and collecting free drinks along the way. When he was finally done (for the time being), they grabbed a booth, and Jasper ordered a burger and a beer, not having to worry too much about getting ID'd with the werespider at his side.

Crimson got up to talk to the bartender, who had just entered the bar, and Jasper took out his phone, checking his messages. He hadn't gotten any in a few days, which probably wasn't surprising since he only really had Crimson and Al (and Max) as friends. On the way out of Florida, he'd gotten Crimson to text Lindsay for him, telling her to lose his number, and after a flurry of angry messages, she seemed to have decided to do just that. Jasper felt bad. He had liked her, he thought, but there was no other way around the inevitable.

He expected to hear something from Charlie, though. He was dreading it, actually, but thought his father would reach out to him at some point, even just to tell him he was a horrible, awful person. He only received persistent silence, which was somehow worse than knowing what he actually thought.

Jasper drafted a message to Alcander, just saying hi. He wanted to get the vampire to see if any new information had cropped up about him. This not knowing was making him sick.

The message bounced back almost immediately along with another message telling him he didn't have service and giving him a number to call if he wanted to set up an account.

Jasper frowned.

It took him too long to figure out that his phone had been disconnected, now demoted to a glorified calculator/pocketbook insofar as its function. This probably also meant the agency credit card he was using to pay the bill had been cancelled, which was slightly less of a loss since he was too scared of them tracking his purchases to use it. He should have seen this coming—why would the agency keep his phone active? He'd said so himself, he wasn't a Hunter anymore, but he was still upset.

He didn't notice the werewolves join them until one crawled into Crimson's lap on the other side of the booth. Abby slid in next to him while Alan stuck his tongue down Crimson's throat. The scent of weed wafted all the way across the table.

"Heya, Charlotte," Alan said when he came up for air. "Where you been?"

"We went on a sort of vacation," replied Crimson. It was only half a lie.

"Hi, Alan," Jasper said pointedly.

"Jensen!" exclaimed Alan, too loudly and too enthusiastically. He climbed out of Crimson's lap, just barely, and sat next to him, basically hanging off his shoulder. He grinned a stupid, vacant grin. "Good to see you, man."

"My name is Jasper," Jasper said and shot Crimson a look, which the werespider chose to ignore.

Alan looked away from him as if he hadn't spoken at all, back to Crimson. "Well, next time you go on a vacation, you should let me know." His fingers curled through the ends of Crimson's hair, a lock twisted around the pointer finger, a gentle tug, not subtle. Jasper wanted to clear his throat or yell at him to fuck off, but he bit his tongue, glaring down with pale eyes at the sticky drink menu in front of him. "People have been asking about you," added Alan.

Across the table, Crimson stiffened slightly, the friendly, flirtatious smile wiping itself clean off his face. He and Jasper exchanged a glance.

"People?" asked Jasper. "What people?"

Alan laid a finger aside his chin and pantomimed being deep in thought. He did a poor job of it. Probably because he'd never had a deep thought in his entire existence. "Hmm... what was that guy's name? I just can't seem to remember. You know how forgetful I am."

"Alan darling." Crimson turned his face back towards his, leaning in close. "I have half a pound of hallucinistem in my pocket. If you want me to share, you'd better get to remembering."

Alan perked visibly. "An incubus. Half-breed. Brown hair. Big puppy-dog eyes." He grinned at Crimson. "He almost wore me out."

Crimson was not smiling. "His name?"

"It was Shane, I think."

The shot glass in Crimson's hand exploded. "Shane Robinson?" he asked through gritted teeth. Beside Jasper, Abby slowly reached for a twinkling, liquor-soaked shard and held it up to the lamp overhead.

"Yeah, maybe," agreed Alan, oblivious to the fact that Crimson looked like he was about to flip the whole booth over. "I don't really deal in last names, if you know what I mean. Speaking of, I hope you plan on sharing more than just drugs with me."

Abby rotated the shard of glass this way and that. A bead of blood began to develop on the pad of her thumb, but she seemed not to notice as she watched the iridescent patterns twinkle through the curved glass. "Sleepover," she said dreamily.

"Great idea, Abs," said Alan, and Jasper quickly looked at Crimson, glaring with every muscle in his face.

Crimson wasn't paying any attention to him though. He was mopping up the spilled drink with a napkin, barely looking at anyone, a frown on his mouth, in his eyes, between his brows.

"Can we crash at yours tonight?" Alan's hooded eyes promised things Jasper didn't even want to think about. "I'll make it worth your while."

This finally drew the werespider's attention. "You'd better," said Crimson, snapping out of the momentary fugue the name brought. His arm sank down around the other demon's shoulders, and Jasper felt a hot flare of anger. This was utter bullshit. He *did not* want to spend the rest of his night watching this idiot werewolf drool all over Crimson while his idiot sister sat around doing and saying weird, stupid shit.

"Let's go now. This place is lame." Alan climbed over the werespider's lap, out of the booth, pausing on his way to rub himself all over Crimson. His ass jostled the table, spilling some of Jasper's beer.

"Actually," Jasper said loudly after the display was over, "we came here for dinner. And then I think we've got plans. *Right*, Crimson?"

The werespider slid out of the booth. He shrugged. "No plans," he said, and in that second Jasper hated him. "Can't you eat something at home?"

"No."

"We'll see you later, then. You've got a key."

"Abs, you coming?" Alan plucked the shard of glass from her fingers and tossed it to the side, pausing to wipe the blood off her small hand with the hem of his stupid mesh T-shirt. "Or do you want to stay here for a bit?"

The last thing Jasper wanted was to be left alone at the bar with Abby. The werewolf spoke up before him. "I'll stay with Jasper." Short of pushing her out of the booth or climbing over the table, he was stuck.

Alan kissed the top of her head. "Sounds cool to me." He linked fingers with Crimson, who drew him to his side, and then they were gone. Crimson only paused long enough to speak to the waitress, indicating Jasper and Abby's table.

The two of them were barely out the door when Jasper's stomach clenched with a strange sensation he had not felt before, distracting him from his white-hot anger. The feeling was demonic in origin, he knew that for certain, but it was unusual. Warmer, lighter, tingly almost.

He looked over the back of the booth.

A wiry man in his mid to late twenties was standing at the bar, leaning on his elbow with his hip rested against the stool behind him. He was dressed in a '50s-style flight jacket, brown fur trim on the collar and half a dozen patches sewn on the sleeves and breast, some of them military in nature, most not. The jacket was slightly too large for its wearer, both too long in the hem and wide in the chest. It fell almost to the middle of his thigh and looked like it would swallow him up. Jasper had a strange feeling that he had seen him somewhere before but could not think of where.

He was speaking to the waitress; his hand lay over hers. A thick-banded ring, inlaid with a large ruby—too large, in fact, to be real—was on the pinkie of his left hand. He followed a gesture the waitress made and then, lifting his eyebrows, took off his glasses, polished the lenses on the hem of his shirt, and looked right at him and Abby.

Jasper turned quickly and sank low in the booth. Great. What new hell was this?

"Abby," he hissed, "stop staring."

The little werewolf had followed his gaze, but she did not have the sense of propriety to hide the fact that she was looking. "Shadow games," she muttered vaguely, and he bit his lip to keep from snapping at her to shut up.

It was too late anyway. The man was on his way over to their booth. Jasper suddenly became very interested in an old-timey painting of dogs playing poker that was situated on the wall just above their table. There was the sound of knuckles rapping softly on wood. He thought about pretending not to have heard, but fucking Abby was still staring.

He looked at the demon. He had a thin, angular face, accentuated by a short goatee, minus the mustache. On the side of his throat, the head of a black cobra was poised with fangs flashing, its neck trailing down to disappear into the collar of his jacket. He saw where the tattoo ended; the snake's tail curled around his wrist, over the back of his hand, tapering on his ring finger.

He was cute. Not in the traditional perfect-skin, perfect-hair, perfect-face sort of way, but in a more alternative way, like John Lennon or Brandon Boyd. He leaned on their table, palms flat, eyes fixed on Jasper. "Howdy."

"Hi," said Jasper.

"Can I join you?"

"Uh…" said Jasper, but it wasn't really a question.

The man slid into the booth opposite them. Crimson had left the bottle of Patron on the table. The man picked it up, read the label, then unscrewed the cap and took a deep swig.

"Can we… help you?"

The man brought the bottle away from his lips, grinning with a hint of mischief. "I hear tell you two might be able to help me locate a friend of mine." Still holding the bottle, he pointed at Abby with his pinkie. "Don't I know you?"

She stared at him blankly.

He nodded. "I'd recognize those big vacant peepers anywhere. *You're* Abby. And that must make *you*…" He paused. "Do you work with Alan or something?"

"Definitely not." He would have vomited the words if he could have.

"That's too bad," grunted the man. Jasper was *sure* he had seen him before. Something about his smile and that *tattoo*. "Face like that, you could retire before you were thirty."

Jasper rolled his eyes. He was beginning to understand why women hated men so much. "Who are you?"

The man reached across the table, offering him his hand. Jasper started to reach for it, but suddenly, faster than he had ever seen her move, Abby grabbed his wrist and forced his palm flat down on the table. She looked at him, wide-eyed, and shook her head once, hard. "No touching."

The man's amicable expression faded into a heavy scowl. "You're a clever little mutt, ain'tcha?"

"Abby's not a mutt," said Jasper. She wasn't clever either, but no need to split hairs. "Now, answer my question."

He took another swig from the bottle. "The name's Shane."

Jasper had started to expect as much, so his expression did not reflect the anxious uncertainty he felt. "What's your friend's name?"

Shane snorted. "That'd depend on the day of the week, probably." He leaned a little closer, tapping the label on the front of the bottle. "I know he was here. Did he go back to his house? Or did he go running off with fuckin' Marmaduke?"

A little of both, actually, thought Jasper, but did not say. "I don't know whom you're talking about," he said instead. Crimson obviously didn't like the guy, but he hadn't taken the time to say why, or what Jasper might be expected to do should he encounter him. "But I think you should go."

Shane drummed his ring against the table. Then he smiled widely. It reminded him of the way Crimson would sometimes smile and smile and smile, right until he lost his fucking mind and went ballistic on someone. "Alright." He started to get up. Stopped. "But if you see Crimson anytime soon. Say... tonight, could you ask him to meet me here? Saturday, eight p.m."

"If you know where your imaginary friend lives, why don't you just go tell him yourself?"

Shane laughed. "In his *house?* You insane? That place's a death trap." It was the laugh that finally gave him away, the way he threw his head back, the snake tattoo rearing as if to strike. Jasper remembered sitting in Charlie's office, looking through the small stack of old photos, lingering on a group image. It seemed so long ago. "Do I look like the stupid teenager in a horror movie to you?"

Jasper said nothing. As tempting as it was to bicker with the guy, it was obvious he shouldn't goad him on. He pressed his lips together, sending a scowl his way.

"Alright," said Shane. "I know when I'm not wanted. I'll let you two alone." Giving the waitress a wave, he walked towards the front of the bar. Jasper watched from the corner of his eye until he saw the door swing open and then fall closed. Then he flipped open his cell phone and started to dial Crimson's number. The phone was all the way to his ear before he remembered he didn't have any service.

"Damn it. Abby, *move*."

#

They were almost back to the house before he remembered he was pissed at Crimson, and then he was *doubly* pissed. He didn't even get to eat. He stopped on the stoop, digging in his pocket for keys, but not before glancing around to make sure (for maybe the fortieth time) they weren't being followed.

Shane was nowhere in sight, and other than the small, relatively weak feeling of the werewolf beside him, and the small, equally weak feeling of the werewolf in the house, he didn't sense any other demons. He had grown so accustomed to Crimson that his sense for him seemed to have become fatigued. It no longer reacted to the werespider with any sort of forewarning.

He got the door unlocked and went inside. When he got to the stairs, he realized Abby was still just standing out on the porch, tick-tocking slightly in the wind like a broken pendulum. Swearing, he marched over to her, grabbed her hand, and dragged her inside, slamming the door as loudly as he could muster without breaking it off the hinges.

The upper hallway had the lingering aroma of hallucinistem, a smell that could almost have been mistaken for cotton candy perfume if not for the slightly floral scent intermixed. He was in a frantic hurry, but when he reached the door to the attic, he stopped cold. The last thing he wanted to do was burst in the room while Crimson and Alan were still going at it. The very thought made his blood boil. Stupid Crimson. If he spent half as much time thinking with his brain as with his dick, he'd probably have cured cancer by now. And what sort of douchebag took his lover to the only livable room of what amounted to a *shared* studio apartment?

A narrow beam of yellow light gleamed through the crack at the bottom of the door. He leaned a little closer, listening for any telltale noise. No sound came from the attic, but a voice behind him inquired curiously, "Did'ja forget how to see the door?"

"Jesus fucking Christ!" He *hated* when he did that. He glowered at the werespider, who was half-dressed in only blue jeans, the belt still unbuckled, uppermost button popped open as if he'd just quickly thrown them on... or not quite gotten them off. About a foot to his right, a door was cracked, the room beyond dark. "You're not in the attic," said Jasper. He'd never seen Crimson go into any of the other rooms in the house except the bathroom, and then only to shower. Because of this, he just assumed they were veritable disaster areas, just like the rest of the house, and had avoided them for fear of falling through the decrepit floorboards or activating another trap that the spider assured him was waiting.

Crimson leaned close, as if to tell him a secret. Then, in a conspiratorial whisper: "This might surprise you, but Alan's not really very picky." He dropped the voice, straightening up with a shrug. "Neither am I, come to think of it."

"*Crimson*," Alan's voice whined out of the room behind him. "What is it?"

"Just Jazz trying to get himself shot in the face," Crimson called back. Belatedly, Jasper saw the werespider was holding one of his revolvers. Maybe he saw the way Jasper looked at it, because he laughed weakly. "Seriously, man, don't go around kicking doors in and shit. I am way, *way* too high for that."

"Shut up," said Jasper. "I need to talk to you."

"I'm a little busy. Why don't you and Abby go start a movie or—"

"*Shut. Up,*" repeated Jasper, loudly and firmly, and, for a wonder, Crimson did. "You know that guy you were talking about? The one who was looking for you? Shane?"

"Dirty little rat," muttered Crimson. "What about him?"

"He was at Rascal's. I just saw him."

Crimson took a step back, leery. "Gross. He didn't touch you, did he?" That was a bizarre question, made more bizarre by the harsh, angry way it was posed.

"No," replied Jasper. "But he did act extra special *super* weird. Sort of like how you're acting right now. There something you want to tell me?"

"Not really," said Crimson. "What did he say?"

"He wants you to meet him at Rascal's. Saturday. Eight o'clock."

Crimson was silent for a long, drawn moment, digesting the

information with whatever thinking capacity the drugs left him with. "I'm gonna rip his fuckin' head off." He shoved past Jasper, tore open the attic door, and went clambering up the stairs. This spilled additional light into the hallway, just enough for Jasper to get a regrettably good look at Alan as he came staggering out of the spare room.

"Christ, what's taking so long?" He would have been naked if not for Crimson's jacket. His arms were folded over his chest, holding the front shut but not, it seemed, all that intentionally. He walked over to the foot of the steps and yelled up them, "Y'know, some people pay really good money to fuck me."

Crimson came jogging back down the steps, pulling on a pair of black leather gloves as he went. "I won't be gone long." He stopped at the bottom of the steps and laid a kiss at the corner of Alan's mouth. He'd managed to get his pants the rest of the way on and put on a fresh shirt, long-sleeved. "It should only take… I don't know… an hour? Maybe two…"

Alan was clearly completely unaware of what was happening. To be fair, Jasper didn't really understand either. "What're the gloves for?"

"They're to help me strangle Shane," said Crimson matter-of-factly.

Alan stared at them dizzily. "Is he into leather?"

Crimson considered. "Yeah, but that's not why I need them."

"You can't touch him." Jasper understood. Incubi were uncommon in North America, often preferring more arid climates. The history of the species was dense, often confused with propagated folklore, and rarely with any sort of consistency. Jasper had learned about them in school, but knowledge that went unused was often forgotten. "Why?"

"He's a fuckin' incubus," spit Crimson. "He secretes like… LSD." Now that it was said aloud, Jasper remembered this about them too. It was never something he troubled himself with, however. If a vampire's gaze could not affect him, and a werespider's pheromones were rendered null, he always assumed the same would apply when it came to other species. "Gets in your pores," continued Crimson in a rapid, distracted voice. "Fucks you up. The saliva's worse. Might as well be crack cocaine. One minute you're about to hurl him off the

Empire State Building. Then he catches you in a kiss and next you know you're like 'oh, Shane, I forgive you. Let's adopt three cats and move to Miami fuckin' Beach.'" A quell of surprised silence met him, and he realized he had spoken aloud. He looked from one face to the next, looked away. "I gotta go."

"I'll come with you," said Jasper. He didn't want to be stuck here with the werewolves. Alan was a nightmare, and while he didn't exactly loathe Abby (as annoying as she was), he didn't like her either. Besides, the werespider was clearly in no state of mind to be picking a fight with anyone. His eyes were glowing red, as they always did when he was angry, but the irises were paper-thin slivers, barely showing around the swollen black pupils and hard to differentiate from the bloodshot whites. "Or... better idea... maybe you don't go while you're high out of your mind. How about that?"

"Yeah!" agreed Alan, grabbing his arm. "Stay here and be high with me. That'll be way more fun."

"I told you, I'm coming right back," repeated Crimson, angrily now.

"Unless he catches you in a kiss," said Jasper. "And then you get to move to Miami Beach. What are you going to name your cats?"

"Shane got to name all of them, and he took them when we broke up," burst Crimson. He rubbed two fingers across his brow, thumb kneading his temple, and then raked his hand back through his hair, tugging a few locks down into his face, the heel of his palm pressed to his forehead. "Gods, I hate him so much."

"He didn't follow us," said Jasper. "And he was afraid to come into your house." It wasn't hard to see why. The werespider's anger often came on like a flash storm, but even when his life (or Al's life, or Jasper's) was in danger, Jasper had never seen him take it so *personally*. "Stay here tonight. We'll deal with it tomorrow."

"Jerry's right," said Alan. "Anyway, that guy wasn't so tough. I mean, he fucked like a—"

Crimson clapped a hand over Alan's mouth. "Alright." He looked at Jasper. "*Fine*." He moved his hand, revealing the hopeful, half-there grin that was permanently affixed to the werewolf's face. "Go back to bed. I'll be there in a minute."

Alan hugged himself tighter, his smile widening. "Oh, I love when you're all commanding."

"*Now*, Alan."

"Yessir," purred Alan. Jasper felt like throwing up. Crimson had exceptionally bad taste in men. Actually, thinking of Ivory, in women as well. Alan slinked back into the darkened room, and Jasper looked away quickly but not quickly enough to miss the flash of his bare back and ass as he shrugged off the coat, letting it fall into a pile on the floor.

"I'm not going to tell you what to do," said Crimson. "But if I were you, I'd stay in the house tonight. Shane isn't above foul play. Actually, it's kind of right up his alley."

Jasper frowned but nodded. "Yeah, okay."

Crimson returned the nod, started to reach for him, and stopped. "I'll see ya soon," he said, then disappeared into the room, with neither thanks nor apology. The door fell shut behind him with a soft click. With no other recourse, Jasper took Abby upstairs, sat her in the armchair, and put on the television. He sat on the bed, chewing on leftover summer buffalo jerky and trying not to hear anything but the television, which he had tuned to an inappropriately loud volume. The surround sound rattled the trinkets stacked around the room any time the dialogue on screen went above a whisper. It was still better than the alternative.

The ashtray on the nightstand between the two beds was nearly full and his lungs were starting to hurt from smoking when the door at the bottom of the stairs creaked open and Crimson and Alan came stumbling up into the attic, still hanging on each other, but without the desperation they had previously.

The werespider's ears were more sensitive than his, and he cringed at the roaring sound of WWII helicopters as they alighted with wounded men harnessed in litters. Abby barely stirred for the entire duration of the movie and didn't speak at all, for which Jasper was grateful. He watched Crimson cross the room to grab the remote and turn the volume down. Alan was still hanging around the kitchenette. He checked a message on his phone, clicked his tongue against the roof of his mouth, and went over to the couch. "C'mon, Abs. We gotta roll."

"You're not staying here tonight?" asked Crimson. His voice was toneless, face unreadable, but he would not have asked if he did not want him to.

"Well, I would, but"—Alan flashed the phone at him—"duty calls. My alpha'll shit a silver brick if she finds out I turned down two hundred bucks an hour." He paused, assessing the werespider. "Of course, if someone were to, say… price match…"

"You want me to pay to *let you* sleep in my bed?"

"Time's money, honey." He drew a step closer. "We don't *have* to sleep."

"Phfftt, alright, get outta here, then," said Crimson, flopping down on the sofa.

Alan shrugged. "Worth a shot." Tossing Crimson's jacket in his lap, he laid a kiss on his temple, grabbed Abby's hand, and led her down the stairs. She waved vaguely in Jasper's direction, though she wasn't looking at him. The two appeared briefly on the black-and-white security feeds, walking away arm in arm from the stoop. Alan hopped the gate, then held it open for Abby, who drifted through like a specter.

"If I ever pay that werewolf to sleep with me, take me out back and shoot me," muttered Crimson, stretching out on the couch, his head resting on the arm.

"You *did* pay him," said Jasper. "With the drugs, remember?"

Crimson shifted uneasily on the couch and rolled over to look at him. "That's different. We were just sharing. And Alan sleeps with me all the time. For nothing. So…"

Jasper breathed a snort out through his nose. "I don't know why you bother with him at all. He doesn't even like you. And he's *mean* to you."

Crimson smiled with his lips and his teeth, but the rest of his face stayed fixed in a scowl. "Wow, are you finished?"

"I'm just trying to look out for you," said Jasper.

Crimson barked sarcastic laughter. "That's weird, cuz it kinda seems to me like you're being a jealous little bitch."

"Ha!" Jasper echoed the werespider's sarcasm, though even to his own ears, it sounded more grated. Harsher. "Jealous of *what*, exactly? Your terrible taste in men?"

"At least I have *some* sort of taste. What can I say, Jazz? We can't all be holier-than-thou virgins like you. *Some* of us don't walk around all day being terrified of our own sexuality."

"He said he was going to stay, and he didn't," said Jasper flatly.

"And now he gets to run off to fuck someone else, probably your psycho ex-boyfriend, and I have to sit here and deal with you pouting all night."

"You don't gotta deal with jack shit," spit Crimson. He sat up, swung his legs off the couch, and stood. "I'll sleep in the other room." He snatched the throw pillow off the couch and, without even looking his way, strode for the stairs. "Have a good fuckin' night." The door slammed with a resounding BANG that rattled the shelves even worse than the surround sound had.

For several moments after he was gone, Jasper sat on the bed, his heartbeat fast and hard, a peculiar-feeling lump set in the back of his throat. There were so many things he still wanted to say. It would have been easier if he had not left.

After another half hour of sitting on the bed, listlessly watching the movie as he had hypothetical argument after hypothetical argument in his own head, he got up and killed the lights. He turned the television off, found that without its latent noise, he seemed able to hear every creak and groan in the building, and then turned it back on and flipped through the stations until he found a *film noir* that seemed familiar in the way all old movies, even the ones you hadn't seen, always did.

He fell asleep to the low rumble of Humphrey Bogart and the clipped, nasal sneer of James Cagney.

Chapter Twenty-One

—

Devil in Disguise

When Jasper woke the next day, it was alone. He wasn't surprised since he had barely slept, having woken often and easily, sometimes for no apparent reason whatsoever. Against his better judgment, he looked towards the other mattress every time, sure that by that hour Crimson would have relented and slipped back into the room to sleep in his own bed. His expectations were wrong every time.

He made coffee, strong and black and bitter.

They had made loose plans to deal with Shane today, but that was before the yelling match. Besides, it was still early. Barely eleven. Be damned if he was going to sit around for the entire afternoon, waiting for the werespider to just blow him off again.

He took a quick shower, got changed, and took his backpack to walk to the library four blocks over.

He had never been to this library before and had to use the new ID Alcander had provided him with to open a fresh account. The towering rows of leather-bound books were like old friends, easing the pervasive feeling of isolation. He stayed for an hour and a half, during which time he picked only four books. On a good week, he could get through all four in four days. He'd drop by Alcander's and pick up a few more. He wanted to talk to the vampire anyway, check up on him and Max, see if something could be done about his phone, and find out if he knew anything about Shane.

It was only a ten-minute walk, but Jasper was in no great hurry. He bought a pack of cigarettes at a newsstand and loitered there, browsing the headlines while he smoked his first cigarette of the day, regretting he hadn't brought a thermos of coffee to go with it.

It was a quarter to one on the dot when he arrived at Alcander's. He twisted and turned and ducked his way to the back of the warehouse. When he reached the door, it was already open. Alcander and Max both stood there, framed by the light from below.

Alcander was wringing his hands nervously. "Are you... moving back in?"

"What?"

"I do not mind," said the vampire quickly. "You can certainly stay here."

"*What?*" repeated Jasper.

"Crimson just called," explained Max. "He said you took all your stuff and left, and you weren't answering your cell phone. So... we thought..."

Jasper felt a brief moment of satisfaction—Crimson had been worried about him—which quickly turned into something like shame. "My phone doesn't work anymore," he explained, which didn't explain anything. He adjusted his backpack and scuffed the heel of one boot against the concrete floor. "We, uh, had a fight last night."

Max stepped to the side, offering the staircase. "Do you want breakfast?"

Jasper smiled, just a little. "Yeah. Yeah, that would be great."

Alcander had an entire tote full of spare burner phones of every make and model imaginable. Jasper sat in the kitchen, listening to the sizzle of bacon, and tinkered with the settings on one. It was the first cell phone he'd ever had that did not flip open—flat and slim with an expanded number pad of tiny buttons that included letters, like a keyboard. He tried twice to compose a message to Crimson, but both ended up too long and complicated, muddled with an excess of thoughts too difficult to convey in the written word. Finally, he just sent a message that simply said, "Hey, it's Jasper. This is my new phone. I'll be home soon."

There was no response.

He wasn't surprised. Crimson texted in much the same way a seventy-year-old grandmother with failing vision might.

Alcander sat at the table beside him, his laptop popped open, fingers racing over the keys in a rhythmic *tip-tap-clack*, pausing only occasionally. He held down one key and struck another. "One moment." He disappeared into the lab.

"So are you like... staying here for good?" The question was directed at Max, who was sitting on the other side of the table, slowly eating while he read a pulp fiction detective novel from Michael's section of the library. "I don't mean that to sound like... judgy," Jasper added quickly when Max glanced up. "I was just wondering."

"Alcander said he could use an extra pair of hands around the lab. I think he's mostly just being nice," replied Max. "But he *really* doesn't like to go outside, and sometimes he does need things. And I need a place to live and a job, so it just seemed to work out."

Jasper thought it was probably a good thing for Alcander to have someone around. Someone to look after him and also maybe someone to look after. He liked Alcander's house, but he didn't think the vampire should be all alone down here.

When Al returned, he was holding a small blue passport. He set it in front of Jasper. "Alright, you should be all set."

Jasper tried to say "thank you" around a mouthful of eggs, nearly choked trying to swallow them, and then managed to get the words out. Alcander gave him a small patient smile and assured him it was "no problem at all." "Did you need anything else? Debit and credit cards?"

It didn't feel right to take Al's money, even though he had more of it than he could really use. But... Jasper's company credit cards had been canceled along with his phone, and he could count the dollars he had left on his fingers. He did a weird half-shrug, half-nod thing and scraped the rest of his food into his mouth so he could avoid properly answering. Alcander was up and gone before he could finish chewing, returning with a half dozen cards he must have already had prepared in the other room.

"Thanks," Jasper said again. He took his plate to the sink and rinsed it, then poured the final dregs of coffee down the drain and rinsed the mug as well. He set them both in the rack to dry, knowing full well that they would be gone over again, no matter how well or poor a job he had done getting them clean. "Hey, Al, do you know an incubus named Shane?"

Alcander made a face. "I hope you do not mean Shane Robinson."

"That seems to be the standard reaction," replied Jasper.

It was lucky that vampires could not develop frown lines. "Is he in town?"

"Yup."

Alcander snapped shut the laptop and steepled his fingers under his chin. The gesture reminded him of Charlie. "I suppose it was too much to expect that he would stay away."

"He comes around a lot, then?"

"Oh, every decade or so, when all else fails. You would do well to keep him away from Crimson. Those two are like nitric acid and hydrazine."

Jasper didn't really understand what that meant, but by the grave tone of the vampire's voice, he surmised they were two things that probably should not be mixed. "Any idea why he might be hanging around?"

Alcander tiredly turned up one palm in a lofty shrug. "Every con artist needs his stooge." He slid back his chair and stood, the laptop clasped under his arm. "I really should be heading to bed." It was nearly two p.m. Jasper was surprised he hadn't slept yet. "Sorry to run. Take care, Jasper."

"You too," said Jasper. "And thank you. For everything."

#

When he got back to the house, he found Crimson in the attic, awake. He was sitting on the bed with an impressive collection of knives and guns spread out before him. When Jasper entered the room, he looked up just long enough to nod in his direction, then looked back down just as quickly, his focus on sharpening the knife currently in his hand.

Jasper set his backpack down on the kitchen floor and opened the fridge to put away a handful of Tupperware containers Max had given him before he left Alcander's. He picked a book out of his bag at random and went to the couch.

He tried to read.

The only sound was the scrape of the blade against the whetstone, steady and persistent. The silence was louder than every cab driver in Brooklyn simultaneously blaring all of their horns during rush hour.

"Are those for Shane?" asked Jasper after a while. He didn't see how one demon (and a half-blood no less) could warrant such an arsenal, and regardless of what Crimson said, Shane hadn't done much more than ask for a meeting, but he didn't know what else to say.

Crimson grunted. "I guess. They needed it anyway." There was no follow-up. He set the blade aside and started on the next. Jasper tried to go back to reading.

"You figure... sunset? Or maybe we could go a little earlier," suggested Jasper. It seemed easier to pretend the argument had never happened than to address it directly. He had been sure Crimson would not see it the same way, would be screaming at him as soon as he walked in the door, but it wasn't so, and now it felt like there was no way to approach the topic. The other wouldn't give him an opening. "I got a pretty good sense for him at the bar. I could probably track him."

Crimson finished polishing the blade he was working on and set it down in a pile of its fellows. "I'm not actually gonna kill Shane, Jazz. I was just really high and really pissed, but I wasn't gonna do it. Not really. I mean, not unless he did something to deserve it first."

"Oh," said Jasper. He had seemed so set on it the night before. The way Crimson kept looking away made him feel like he wasn't telling him the whole truth. "You... don't consider someone drugging you so that they could force you to uproot your life and move somewhere else to be... like... enough?"

Crimson's hand went to the back of his neck, his gaze still avoidant. "I dunno? Maybe?"

Jasper sighed. "Crimson, if you're saying this because you don't want me to come with you—"

"I'm *saying it* because you *asked*," cut in Crimson, his voice suddenly as sharp as the newly polished blade. Jasper felt his own features harden in return. Crimson continued before he could reply. "I *still* need to figure out why he's hanging around. I definitely don't wanna wait until Saturday. So that leaves today. You said you wanted to come, so if you wanna come, do that, but if you changed your mind, it's, y'know, whatever."

"I said I would go," said Jasper. "So obviously I'll go."

"See? That right there? That's pissing me off. You're not obligated to go with me just cuz you said you would. It's not your civic fuckin' duty, and my life is not your godsdamned responsibility." They were cusping onto another argument, though it was not about Shane or anything to do with him, really.

"Why don't you just say whatever it is you're actually trying to say?" asked Jasper.

"Why don't you?"

Now that gave him pause. The answer was that he didn't really know himself. He bit the inside of his cheek, thinking. "You ditched me at the bar last night. You know I hate that."

Crimson stared at him, his expression one of disbelief. Actually voicing it aloud made him realize how petty it sounded, but it was more than just that. It was just hard to explain.

"You ditched me for that *werewolf*." He rephrased it. "I just thought we were going to hang out, and then all of a sudden he's there, and it's just like I don't even exist. Then Shane shows up, so I come running all the way back home to give you a heads-up, and you just take for granted—"

"Take for granted?" repeated Crimson, livid. "I don't know how to tell you this, Jazz, but me an' you didn't have *plans*. You were hungry, so I went with you to the bar. Alan showed up, and I decided I'd like to get laid. I told the waitress to put whatever you guys wanted on my tab. I figured you'd be there longer."

"You could have asked if it was okay if you brought him over," insisted Jasper, though his argument felt weaker now. "He's a fucking jerk to me."

"Well, shit, Jasper, it ain't like you give him any reasons to be *nice* to you." Jasper opened his mouth to retort, but Crimson raised both hands. "Y'know what? Forget about it. You hate him that much, I'll just not have him around anymore. We'll go all the way to his shithole apartment in Queens. It'll be fine."

That wasn't what Jasper wanted at all. Mainly because he thought Crimson deserved a little better than someone who just tossed him aside when he was done with him, and partially because that resolution somehow ended up with *him* feeling like the asshole in this scenario. He pressed his lips together. "Whatever."

"Alright," said Crimson. He replaced the knives in their roll bag, folded it up, buckled it, and tossed it on the floor beside the bed. "I'm gonna sleep for a while. We'll go in a few hours. Okay?"

Jasper nodded. "Okay."

#

Twilight was on the horizon when they set out across Crimson's territory in search of the incubus. He was not near enough for Jasper to sense him, so they headed back to Rascal's, where Crimson hoped to pick up the trail with his sense of smell.

Several people had come and gone since the previous night, but after a while the werespider seemed to suss it out and they were off.

At the end of the avenue, they pushed out into the surrounding blocks, whose demon occupation was scarce thanks to the severely territorial presence of the werespider. Crimson lost the trail at a crisscross of paths, where the demon activity was strangely high, but by then it didn't matter. Jasper could feel him. He was close.

So were at least half a dozen other demons.

The building was whitewashed, three-story, boxy and square. The lower level appeared to have once been some sort of barber shop, but it looked as though it hadn't been in use since the '70s. The windows were covered in yellowing newspaper, the candy-striped pole outside faded so badly that the red spirals, now pink, were hardly discernible from the white.

The front door was locked. A cop car idled on the other side of the street. Jasper dragged Crimson away before he could start bashing in windows.

The space between the building and the one next to it was claustrophobically narrow, too thin for even a trash can. There was a window on the second floor though, and it was open. The smooth sounds of old-school rhythm and blues wheedled their way down.

"Can you jump that high?" whispered Crimson.

"I could climb it, easy."

Crimson shook his head. "No good. Gives 'em too much time to hear us coming. Get on my back. I'll jump. You just have your gun ready in case."

Jasper climbed onto Crimson's back, feeling a little ridiculous. He wrapped an arm around the werespider's shoulders, his other hand holding his pistol. Crimson grabbed his legs and hiked them up to his waist. There wasn't time to feel embarrassed, but Jasper felt the heat on his face anyway as he squeezed his knees to Crimson's waist just in time for him to make the jump to the second floor, fingers finding purchase on the thin ledge. He pulled them both inside, and Jasper dropped quickly from his back.

The room was a small bedroom with a single bed and a tall, thin dresser but not much else. Someone was in the bed, and though Jasper wasn't sure whether they were a demon, he was sure they weren't human. He and Crimson made almost no noise as they came in, but the person turned towards them, sitting up in the bed, the sheets falling around their waist. Gently pointed ears showed through shiny blue-black hair, and silver eyes blinked blurrily at them. They seemed to realize the two of them shouldn't be there, and their lips parted, perhaps to call out to someone else in the house.

Crimson was by the bed before a sound could escape, grabbing hold of their sharp chin, his other hand cupping the base of their skull. With a quick twist and a short snap, the other slumped back onto the bed, looking almost asleep.

Crimson looked back to Jasper, eyes red as fresh blood. Jasper nodded and went to the partly open door, listening for movement. He could hear very little over the crooning of John Lee Hooker, and when he peered cautiously out into the hallway, opening the door wider with the muzzle of his gun, he saw no one. He nodded again to Crimson, and the werespider moved past him, into the hallway. They followed the sounds of music to an open living room.

Shane was sitting on an overstuffed sofa, his arms stretched out along the back of the couch on either side of him, boots rested on a mismatched ottoman. Above him, a female vampire perched like a cat, absently playing with his hair. Another was sitting on the floor by the couch, his cheek rested against the demon's knee.

Shane laughed when he saw them. "What's the matter with you, sugar? You know you don't gotta go breakin' into my house just t'get a word with me."

The vampires were all around them, and they were strong, Jasper could feel it. Among their number were also two werewolves; a ghoulish, eyeless creature with gray leather for skin; and a winged woman who, while still quite small, resembled an oversized fairy. Shane must have brought them from around the city. Or perhaps they had come with him from wherever he had come from.

There was no air-conditioning, the spinning ceiling fan above them doing little more than rotating the hot, stagnant air of the crowded room. Jasper's hands were sweating in the gloves Crimson had insisted he wear, and he felt the flannel sticking to the small of his back.

Shane looked extremely comfortable. "Anyways, me an' you already had an appointment. Or did your li'l errand boy over there forget t'give you the message?"

"I got your message," said Crimson. "And whatever the con is, I'm not into it. So take your collection of goons—" he spun a finger around to indicate the dozen or so people assembled in the room "—and clear out."

"Aww... Don't be like that, sug." Shane pouted. He shooed the vampires away from him and stood, putting his hands in the pockets of the flight jacket, resting easy on one leg. "You don't even know the play yet."

Jasper looked at Crimson. "Is this just, like... your whole life? All the time?"

"Basically," lamented Crimson.

"It'll be fun," enticed Shane. "Me an' you. Just like old times."

Crimson wavered, just a little, his dark eyes narrowed with a combination of anger and curiosity. "What are you up to?"

The incubus clapped his hands together, bouncing on the balls of his feet. "I thought you'd never ask." In that moment, he looked and sounded like a small child seeing a real live puppy for the first time. "I'm gonna rob a bank!"

Crimson groaned. "Oh, c'mon, man. You don't need my help for that. Just slip in early in spit in all the tellers' coffee or something."

"Gross," said Jasper pointedly.

"Not a *human* bank, y'big dumb galoot. The artifact one. In Jersey. Well... if you're mincing hairs, *near* Jersey."

"The one in the Atlantic Ocean?" asked Crimson incredulously. "That's gonna be a huge pain in the ass. I'm not doing it."

Shane drew closer. Alan hadn't been wrong about his big puppy-dog eyes. "But I *need* you. You're the only demon I ever met who could speak Atlantean, and besides..." Here he reached for his cheek, the ruby ring on his pinkie glinting in the light from above. "Who else can I trust to protect me from those big scary golem guards?"

Jasper didn't think. He just moved, wedging himself in between the two of them before they could make contact, pushing Crimson a step back in the process and sticking the muzzle of his pistol in Shane's chest. Around them, swords swished out of sheaths, hammers clicked, and the fairy-looking thing rose in the air, her dragonfly wings humming incessantly. "You need to back off."

Shane half raised his hands in mock surrender, a little giggle escaping him. "Whoa, take it easy, eye candy." He gestured vaguely for the others to stand down. Many of the weapons were lowered, but not all of them. "You're welcome t'come along too if that's what it takes."

"We're not interested," said Jasper.

Shane tilted his head so he could look around Jasper, at the werespider just over his shoulder. "Love the new model, Crim. Much more dashing than the old one. And those *eyes*. Never seen white before. Where'd you find him? Off world?"

"Don't talk to him," said Jasper. It was obvious the werespider had a weakness for this creature, though why was anyone's guess. Probably for the same reason he kept putting up with Alan. Or Ivory. "You can talk to me."

"Well, aren't you a regular knight in shining armor?" Shane laughed. "If you're half as dedicated in the bedroom, he must be fixin' to have a right proper wedding for the two of you. You're awful young though. How long you been together? Two... three months?"

Jasper was prepared for him to say a variety of things, but not that. "We're, uh... actually just friends."

Shane pressed his lips tight together, but the laughter could be heard rattling around inside him, his shoulders shaking with his attempts to contain it. It burst out in a quick guffaw, and he quickly put both hands over his mouth, but it still shone in his eyes. Finally, he got it under control enough to bring his lips over his knuckles. "Handsome *and* stupid. He's head over heels. You guys are gonna make a stunnin' pair. Really. And you don't gotta fret. I won't steal him from ya. It'll just be business"

"The answer is *no*," said Jasper. He had it all wrong. Crimson didn't think of him that way. If he had, he surely would have said something by now. Of course... he *had* said things, numerous times, in fact. Almost from the first time they met, come to think of it. But that was just Crimson. He was just kidding. He did that with all of his friends...

Except Alcander.

And Max.

And Abby.

Who were actually the only other three friends Jasper had ever met, excluding Alan, who shouldn't have counted for obvious reasons.

His heart fluttered.

Shane heaved a sigh. "Well, shit. I didn't wanna have t'do it this way, but ya aren't givin' me a lotta other options."

"Shane," warned Crimson, "don't."

Jasper glanced away for a fraction of a second, looking back over his shoulder towards Crimson. A touch on his jaw had him turning back around. His skin tingled where Shane's hand touched as it slid around the back of Jasper's neck to pull his face down towards him. Jasper got a close-up view of those puppy-dog eyes and of Shane's curled lips before the incubus pushed their mouths together, his hot tongue twisting around Jasper's. Their teeth clashed together, and Jasper realized with a jolt he was kissing him back.

Someone seized the back of his shirt, pulling him away. There was a string of familiar curses at his ear and scattered chuckles from around the room. Shane's laughter was distinct from the others, his dark eyes shining with it behind his thin-framed glasses. He held out his hands, his fingers curling in a beckoning gesture. "C'mere, lover boy."

Crimson gripped Jasper's shoulders hard, holding him back. "Say, why don't you go pick on someone more your own level, huh? Like a snake, or a jackal, or a pile'a burning garbage?"

Jasper felt strange, giddy. He wondered if this was how the incubus venom worked. Looking at Shane with his outstretched hands, his crocodile smile, he felt *something*. But he didn't feel like getting any closer to him or running off to adopt a bunch of cats.

His pistol had lowered, pointing down at the floor, and he

readjusted his grip. In one quick motion he brought the gun up again. There was enough time for surprise to register on Shane's face, but not enough for him to get out of the way before Jasper shot him point-blank in the stomach.

The effect on the room was delayed. Shane cried out, stumbling back to the couch, his hands covering the hole in his belly, the blood seeping through his fingers. He coughed, and blood sprayed from his mouth, speckling his lips. He smeared the tendrils away on the back of his wrist. "Oh, you shouldn't have done that, now, eye candy."

The female vampire rushed them first with the fairy thing buzzing a step behind. Jasper spun out of the way, ducking under Crimson's arms as the werespider reached for her and snatched her out of the air mid-leap. He threw her back into the fairy, and the pair of them crashed into the wall, the fairy's wings crumpled.

Jasper was already on the other side of the werespider, back against his. One of the werewolves moved towards them, thick black claws growing from his hands, dark hair spreading down his neck. Jasper shot out his right knee, and he tumbled down with fur still rippling along his spine and fangs still sprouting in his elongated snout.

The room erupted into a chorus of noise, voices shouting and metal singing and hammers snapping. A trio of shots rang out, the last one with a resounding *boom*. Crimson's revolvers were almost deafening in the small space.

They couldn't stay here. There were too many, too close.

They had blocked the door. Jasper couldn't blame them; it was smart, really. They were two against, what, twelve? Stuck in here, they could make quick work of the pair of them.

Crimson pointed his gun into the center of the group in the doorway, and from the side of the room a vampire came at him with a machete, intent on chopping off his arm. Jasper moved quickly, stepping in his path and firing off a shot that sent him spinning. He was still off-kilter when Jasper knocked him all the way to the ground with an elbow cracking first into his chest and then into his nose.

The gray-skinned thing grabbed at him, and someone tried to wrestle his gun from him. The gloves made it hard to keep hold of, but he managed, slamming the butt of his pistol against their head, stunning them long enough that he could pull one of the knives from his belt to stab at what he hoped were vulnerable spots of the gray-skinned thing—the stomach, the chest, the groin, and the neck. He didn't know what sort of creature it was, but it was vaguely human in shape, and after his onslaught it let him go, leaving thick gray slime where it touched him.

Jasper ran towards the door, the exit now open, slipping out of the reach of most blades. A sword swung at him and he danced out of the way; it sliced through the tips of his hair and landed across his shoulder. He was out of its range before it could do any serious damage, but it still burned.

The hallway was long and narrow, ending in a window that had a scenic view of a solid brick wall. Jasper ran towards it, firing as he went to blow out the glass. Crimson was right behind him, throwing open every door in the hall as he passed. Bullets blew through the panels, cheap wood flying.

As he reached the end of the hall, Jasper put his gloved hand on the sill, briefly feeling the bite of broken glass before vaulting through the opening. He turned his shoulder into a roll as he hit the concrete. They were only on the second story, and though he might have a bruise come morning, he scarcely felt the impact.

Crimson landed in a crouch in front of him, the long coat puddled around him. They both fired back up at the window.

A fanged face ducked away with a screech.

Out front of the building, a bell jingled softly. The squeak of a door long unused.

"Hey! White eyes!"

Jasper heard the shot even before he had turned his head to look at the speaker. From the corner of his eye, he caught sight of Shane standing at the opposite end of the alley, the muzzle of his gun flashing with a second flare.

Crimson's arm swept him aside, nearly knocking him from his feet. His shoulder blades struck the brick wall.

The werespider staggered a step back. Then another as the second shot impacted high on his collarbone. The gun on that side slipped from his fingers; the smooth white sandalwood, now soaked black and steaming, bounced on the cement, spun once on its grip, then fell flat. Crimson raised his left hand and Jasper his right, and both fired down the alley as one.

Shane dipped away, blood pouring from him like a spigot.

"Imma fuckin' kill you!" screamed Crimson at the top of his voice. "You hear me, you little godsdamned weasel?!" The spider moved underneath his skin, stretching it like a poorly fitted suit. The pupils and whites of his eyes were vanished entirely, and strings of venom stretched between his still-human teeth, now stained black. Still hurling threats, he tore after the incubus like an unleashed junkyard dog, and Jasper saw no choice but to follow.

At the other end of the alley, they caught a glimpse of Shane as he skirted around the hood of an idling car and made for the adjacent alley. Crimson fired again, heedless of the civilian in the car. The bullet went insanely wide anyway. Jasper saw the puff of shattered stone as it chipped off the corner of a building.

He didn't understand how Crimson had missed. They were barely twenty feet apart.

He squeezed the trigger again, but the gun clicked empty. Shane was already scrambling out of sight as if his life depended on it, which it did, because even without the gun, Crimson was bound and determined to follow. Jasper reached to grab the back of his coat, yelling for him to slow down, but his fingers slipped before they could find purchase, and Crimson went sprinting out into the road with the empty revolver still clenched at his side.

In the swell of oncoming headlights, the werespider missed a step. Then another.

The approaching vehicle threw on its brakes.

Crimson ignored it. So did Jasper. He jogged out into the road after him, shouting again for him to stop.

In what could be best described as a poorly executed stagger, Crimson crossed the yellow line. On the other side, he dropped like a stone. Jasper threw himself to his knees beside him, hand on his back, eyes focused on the corner nearby, sure that Shane would pop back out. It took less than a second for him to decide he wasn't going to return. All at once, the gears in his mind started winding in reverse, and all the emotions he could not feel during the heat of battle came roaring back.

He looked down at Crimson.

He was braced up on his elbow, coughing wretchedly, his whole body shaking. Smoke rolled out of the deep holes near his collarbone and on his chest. He had one foot underneath him and was trying to stubbornly push himself back up, but this only ended with a weak lunge. He would have thrown himself right back on the asphalt if Jasper did not catch him.

For all that, he was still talking, through panting breaths and hacking spits of blood and venom. "Imma kill him. Lemme go, Jazz. Imma *fuckin'* tear his *fuckin'* spleen out. Imma fuckin' kill him." He said it over and over again like a mantra as he struggled in vain against Jasper's grip, but his strength was failing. Already more of his weight rested against Jasper than on his own feet.

The driver of the car that almost hit them decided he had seen enough and, bearing wide, hit the gas. The car screeched by on their left, then swerved back to the middle of the road, taillights fading quickly in the distance.

A new pair of headlights was coming in the opposite direction.

Jasper quickly holstered his gun and strung the werespider's good arm over his shoulders. Keeping his elbow locked around his waist, he dragged him towards the other side of the road. At first Crimson tried to help him, matching Jasper's every two steps to his one, but he grew heavier and heavier with every breath, his words fading to rasped whispers.

Jasper got them to the sidewalk before they could get creamed by a passing vehicle, then readjusted his grip, putting his arm under Crimson's thighs and trying to lift him instead.

He was either much lighter than expected, or Jasper was much stronger than he knew, because he hoisted him up easily, but the sheer size of him was cumbersome, and Jasper had to widen his stance and stagger his step to keep from weaving when he walked.

He could not go back the way they had come.

He could not go the way Shane had gone either.

He could not stay near the road.

He lugged the werespider up the steps of the closed bank nearby, then cut around the railing, tramping through a small garden and past the drive-thru ATM. A parking garage was on the other side and, not knowing what else to do, Jasper bore towards it.

Chapter Twenty-Two

—

For You

The front of his shirt was soon soaked with the demon's blood.

The lowest level of the parking garage was full of cars, and people to go with them. Jasper kept away from them, pausing and crouching behind vehicles any time one drew near, letting them pass, moving again. There was no need to shush Crimson. He was quiet now. Jasper only knew he was still alive by the clench of his fingers on the collar of his shirt.

He took the elevator. He thought for the entire ascent how Crimson hated elevators. He wondered *why* he hated them and wondered why he had never asked. He tried not to think about how he was probably scared to die in one, and how that just might end up being how he went. He was so still now, barely breathing.

He hit the emergency stop halfway between levels and set Crimson down in the corner of the lift. Huddled beside him, trying to remain calm, he fumbled out his cell phone and clumsily selected Alcander's name from the contact list. His hands were shaking so badly he had to try twice. His thumb left dark bloody smears on the keyboard and screen.

Alcander answered on the first ring. "Hello, Jasper." His voice was light and airy, carefree.

"Al!" The name croaked out of him through the heavy pressure in his chest. "Al, you gotta help. It's Crimson. He's... I think he's dying, Al."

Alcander's manner changed dramatically. "What happened?"

"We went to find Shane." The whole story tried to spill out in one breath, but he stopped himself before he could properly begin. It did not matter *how* it had happened. Only one detail mattered. "He got shot. With a gold bullet. Twice."

Beside him, Crimson's chest fell and did not rise. Jasper's breath caught. He touched the side of his throat.

A pulse, slow and shallow, thumped once against his fingertips. He felt relief, but short lived.

"I don't know what to do. He'll never make it back to yours. Is there even a cure for—"

"Jasper, listen to me." It was the same curt tone he had used when Jasper was trying to help him back at the hotel room, when he'd brought him Max. "You need to get the gold out of him. By whatever means necessary. Don't do it carefully. Don't take your time. Just get it out."

"Okay," said Jasper. The direct order seemed to kick-start the Hunter in him. Switching the phone to speaker, he set it on the tile and drew his knife. The lump on Crimson's collarbone was situated closer to the surface, right up against the skin, which it had begun to burn through. Jasper shoved the point of the blade underneath and pushed the bullet. It wiggled but stuck in the widened gap made by the knife, as if it were fused to the bone beneath. A hot burst of sulphury smoke plumed right into his face. He squinted through the sting in his eyes and pushed until the bullet popped out and *pinged* to the floor. It was half melted, a bubble solidified over top of the lead underneath.

The one on his sternum was deeper. In the dim fluorescent light, he could barely see the sliver of precious metal glinting through the murky sea surrounding it.

When Jasper jabbed the blade there, Crimson sprang back alive with an inhuman screech. Black spines bristled in a fanning effect across his skin. Skeletal fingers, more claw and exoskeleton than flesh, gripped his wrist hard. "Crimson, it's just me!" Jasper cried out, then, in a slightly calmer voice, "It's *me*."

The grip loosened. The chittering noise inside gargled out. The werespider's terrified brown eyes fixed onto his, his fingers clasped desperately around the heel of his hand as blood streamed out of him. Suddenly, Jasper was sixteen, and the eyes he was staring at were blue, not brown.

Crimson's lips tried and failed to form words. Then his eyes rolled back; his grip relaxed. His head lolled.

This could not happen. Not again.

Not again.

He plunged the blade back into his chest, trying to wedge the stubborn bullet free. It came loose but wouldn't come out. The blade did nothing more than rattle it around, sending fresh plumes of acrid smoke up his way whenever it hit muscle.

He dropped the knife and shoved his fingers into the open wound instead.

The searing hot metal burned, and his digits slipped on the slick surface. He gritted his teeth, gripped tight, and ripped it free. It left scorch marks where there should have been fingerprints. He cast it aside.

"All! The bullets are out!" he yelled towards the phone. "What do I do now?"

"Look in his pockets," crackled the phone. Underneath the clipped words, he heard traffic, a siren. He hoped that meant Alcander was on his way. "There should be a small tin box. It looks sort of like an epinephrine kit."

Jasper searched in the hand pockets. He found the werespider's pocket watch, his cell phone, a pack of cigarettes, and his Zippo, among other odds and ends: loose coins and bits of string, a crumpled wad of mostly one-dollar bills.

"It's not here!"

"Check in *all* the pockets," insisted Alcander. Jasper didn't know how he could sound so calm. Maybe because he wasn't right here, watching his best friend die. "It's probably on the inside."

Jasper pulled back the lapel and looked. Perhaps because he had never inspected the jacket too carefully, he had never realized how meticulously tailored it was. The inside was like a magician's trick coat. Extra pockets were sewn along the in-seam, a zipper in the bottom of the hand pockets, small picks wedged in the collar, in easy reach of teeth.

"When you find it, inject it directly into his heart. His skin and bones are very thick, so you'll have to bring the needle down hard, as if you were stabbing someone."

"And that'll fix him?" asked Jasper, desperately feeling up and down the row of pockets. His fingers encountered something solid and boxy in a pocket halfway down, and he reached inside.

"No," said Alcander. "But it will give us time. And it might wake him up."

Jasper pulled the object out. It was a small tin can, just as Alcander had said. The box was labelled in neat, blocky, evenly spaced handwriting. It said "Crimson Cocktail." Alcander's idea of a joke.

Jasper popped the clasp and grabbed the syringe inside. The needle was thick and long, from decades earlier, and it made Jasper feel impossibly sicker to see it, but it was untarnished and clean, and if it would save Crimson, he would have stabbed it into his own leg.

"*If* he wakes up, *keep* him awake. Do not stop the bleeding—his blood is poison right now—but try to keep him warm. I will be there soon."

The line clicked to silence. Jasper's mind whirled. He hadn't given him an address. *He* wasn't even sure where he was right now. He couldn't remember the name of the road or any of the nearby stores. How the hell did Alcander expect to find them?

He took a breath to clear his head. If Alcander said he was coming, he was coming. He had to have faith.

He pushed up the hem of Crimson's ruined shirt and felt his chest for a heartbeat. It beat so slowly now that he had to wait several seconds. When it finally thumped, he pressed his thumb just above it. It was so near the hole in his chest, three inches away, if that. He lined up the needle, brought it up to the top of his reach, then slammed it down with all his might and pressed the plunger.

Crimson's eyes popped open with a wheeze. It must have hit close enough.

Jasper was so happy that, if he had let himself, he could have started bawling right there and then. He steadied the back of the demon's head and gently swatted his cheeks, trying to bring him more fully around. Crimson blinked at him blearily. Coughed wetly. "Jazz?"

"I'm right here," said Jasper. His vision doubled and blurred. A few hot tears finally managed to escape his eyes, and he did not know whether they were from fear or panic or joy. The heel of Crimson's palm clumsily brushed one away, leaving a smear in its wake. "It's okay," he told the werespider, grabbing his hand. "You're gonna be okay. Al's coming."

"You," murmured Crimson. There was no upward inflection, so it took him a beat too long to realize it was a question.

"Me too." Jasper would feel the pain of his own injuries later. Right now, his own body felt far away.

"Good," said Crimson when the words had processed. The focus slipped out of his face. Eyelids drooping, his chin sank back towards his sternum.

Jasper shook him. "But you gotta *stay awake* for me, Crims. I *need* you to stay awake. Do you hear me?" He shook him again, harder this time.

Crimson struggled himself away from unconsciousness, though it clearly took all his strength. His punch-drunk gaze swung back and forth. Refocused. "For you."

Jasper's heart clenched painfully in his chest. Shane was a manipulative monster, and Jasper shouldn't give a good goddamn what he said about anything, but now that the sentiment was there, he could not unsee it. The fixed adoration in his gaze. The romance in his words. The demon must have been in pain unimaginable, but still, his concern lay in Jasper's direction, like he was the one who was slowly dying from a poisoned sickness.

"Whatever... you... want."

"I want you to stay awake," repeated Jasper. He pulled down the sleeve of his shirt and wiped uselessly at the blood painted around Crimson's mouth. Underneath, his lips were ghastly pale. "I want you to live."

"Talk," rasped Crimson.

His mind went blank. For all he could think in that moment, he might have never had a thought in his whole entire life. "About what?"

"Just... talk..."

"Okay, okay." Al told him to keep Crimson warm, so he closed the front of his jacket. It barely felt like it would do anything, so, as carefully as he could manage, he pulled the werespider further into his lap, putting his back against his chest and wrapping his arms around him. It still didn't feel like enough. "You remember Adam?"

Crimson said something. Jasper thought it was "teeth."

"Yeah, sharp teeth and black eyes. He didn't used to look like that though. He used to have nice, normal teeth and blue eyes. He was very handsome." Jasper paused. He slipped a hand inside Crimson's jacket, feeling his chest for movement. The werespider's breath was shallow and rattling, but there. He waited to feel a heartbeat before he continued. "I knew him for a long time, for as long as I can remember. We were both from hunting families. We lived just down the street from each other our whole lives. His whole life. He was my best friend. I... I loved him." He waited again for signs of life. Crimson was still breathing, but every time there was a pause, Jasper was terrified he wouldn't start again. "Are you listening to me?"

Crimson's head rolled. Jasper thought he was trying to nod. He gave him a little shake until he spoke. "Yeah." His voice was too small. Where was Al?

"When I was seven, I asked him to marry me, because that's what you did when you loved someone, you got married. I even gave him a ring. It was blue raspberry flavored, his favorite. He said no. Boys were supposed to marry girls, not other boys. I told him I was just joking, and then I went home and cried all afternoon. Charlie wanted to know what was wrong, but I wouldn't tell him. I never told anyone, and I think Adam just forgot about it. I still loved him, though, I just kept it to myself. It was worth it to just be his friend."

Crimson made a small sound. It might have just been a moan or a gasp, but Jasper thought it sounded like he was agreeing with him. Jasper fought back a fresh wave of emotion.

"Al's gonna be here soon," he promised again, hoping he was right. He shook Crimson again, touching his chin to lift his face from his chest. "Hey. Hey, man, listen to me. You heard the one about the lesbian vampires?" Another uncertain sound in the affirmative. His eyes floated around the elevator before they found Jasper again. The half-blood couldn't tell if he was seeing anything. "Help me with the punch line, then. What did one say to the other? Same time...?" Another shake.

"Time next... month?"

"Yeah. Yeah, that's it." Beside them, Jasper's phone started to ring. Jasper picked it up before it could finish the first note. "Al?"

"I followed your phone signal to the building, but I do not see you. Where are you two?"

"In the elevator."

"Get down to the parking garage. Street level. We will get as close as we can."

The parking garage was packed, a less than ideal place to take Crimson, who was looking more and more like a corpse, but if that was what Al said to do, he was going to do it. As carefully as he could, Jasper got up and sent the elevator back down and then crouched beside Crimson. "Al's here. We're going to him, okay? He's gonna fix you up."

It was harder this time to gather Crimson in his arms and stand. He managed, trying not to hurt him as he held him. Crimson couldn't help him; he was dead weight. His head fell back heavily; his eyes closed once more. "God, Crimson. Don't you dare…"

The doors slid open and Max was standing ready on the other side. Behind him sat his yellow hatchback, the door to the back seat open, the seats folded away so that there was a flat space. A white sheet had been put down, and Alcander kneeled at one corner, a medical cooler beside him and several medical instruments within easy reach. "Put him in the back and get in the front," Al ordered.

Jasper climbed into the back, setting Crimson down in front of the doctor. After a moment's hesitation, Max closed the door behind him and got in behind the wheel. Alcander pulled open Crimson's jacket and cut open his shirt with a pair of scissors. The wounds in his chest were black and gaping, lazily pumping out black blood. They hadn't tried to heal at all.

"I got the bullets out," Jasper explained as Al started to examine the wounds. Using a pair of long metal forceps, he dug around in the one in the werespider's sternum, dropping two smaller pieces of gold on the sheet. Crimson reacted with a twitch of his eyelids and nothing more. "Let me help. Please."

Alcander started to flush the bullet holes with some sort of solution. They practically steamed. Crimson didn't move.

"Al, *please.*"

"You can help," Alcander said, not looking up as he worked, "by being quiet." He didn't seem bothered by the movement of the vehicle, which was a little strange since normally he couldn't even sit in one without having a panic attack. In fact, he was entirely calm. Jasper didn't understand how he could do it. Grinding his teeth together, he forced down the words that were so desperate to get out, and balled his hands into white-knuckled fists. He was about to speak again, to ask if there was *something* he could do, when Al gestured to the cooler. "Get him a unit of blood. A cold one first, and then the warm one."

Jasper obeyed, opening the cooler and grabbing the first bag of blood he saw. A sticker on the bag read "St. Mary's Hospital" and the date the blood was drawn as well as the type it was.

"You'll have to feed it to him," said the vampire.

Jasper moved so that he was sitting behind Crimson's head, angling him gently so as not to move his body much while Al worked. Drawing a blade from his belt, Jasper cut the corner and carefully poured the thick fluid down his throat. It was gross, but the separation between blood and an actual human person made it bearable. Crimson didn't appear to be swallowing or drinking the blood, but it slowly drained down his throat. Jasper was half scared he would choke.

The first bag was spent, and Jasper set it on the sheet. He grabbed the second bag, nearly dropping it as soon as he touched it. The bag lacked the label that was on the first one and, most jarringly, the blood inside was still warm. The cold blood obviously came from a semi-credible source, donated by willing donors (though probably not for vampire consumption). But where would Al get such fresh blood?

"It is Maxwell's," said Alcander, noticing his hesitation. "Try not to think about it."

Jasper tried and succeeded. He cut open the bag and brought it to Crimson's mouth, trying not to spill any between the motion of the vehicle and his shaking hands. Jasper thought he saw Crimson's throat contract, and the werespider began to drink, just barely at first, but then with more vigor, his pale lips closing around the bag, sucking. Beneath his closed lids, his eyes moved. Hope swelled in Jasper's chest. Was he really going to be fine?

The bag was empty all too soon. Jasper wanted to get him another, but Alcander had only said the two, and Jasper didn't know enough to know what to do. It seemed like Crimson should have more, he was suckling from the empty bag, a small frown line between his brows. The half-blood gently smoothed it out with his thumb, setting the empty bag aside. Alcander plucked another sliver of gold from a wound and flushed it again. The black blood coated his hands, which were covered in plastic gloves. The blood seeping slowly from Crimson's wounds began to take on a redder tint. Jasper hoped that was a good thing.

"We're almost there," came Max's voice from the front seat. Jasper had almost forgotten he was there at all. "Which door should I go to?"

Al threaded a long needle with seasoned ease. "The back, there's a shortcut." He sewed the larger of the two wounds closed, each stitch tiny and perfectly uniform.

They pulled into the parking lot in front of Alcander's, and Max drove around to the back. The human got out of the car first, opened the back door for them, and then disappeared inside to unlock the door.

Alcander snapped off the gloves, putting them on top of the few tiny pieces of gold. "Carry him downstairs and take him to the lab."

"Is he going to be okay?"

The doctor looked to Crimson's face, held carefully in Jasper's lap, and then to Jasper himself. "Yes."

Jasper's eyes made a second attempt at tears, his relief was so intense. He drew in a shuddering breath, then pulled Crimson into his arms once more, and carried him inside.

#

Max was in the living room, already setting up an IV, though Jasper understood intrinsically that it was not for Crimson. At least, not yet. "You should take some of mine instead," he said before the human could put the needle in his arm. In the fluorescent light, he looked almost as pallid as his keeper.

"No," said Max. "It will be okay, just this once."

"But—"

"Jasper, please understand, you are not human, and we do not know what your blood may do to him," explained Alcander. "There is every chance it may do as much harm as good. However…" He leaned around him, his gaze focused sternly on Max, who still seemed focused on attempting to find a vein. The vampire moved over to him and plucked the needle deftly from his hand. "Absolutely not."

"He looks really bad though," said Max.

"So will you if you lose another pint of blood," replied Alcander. "Go eat something."

The human looked pained, but did as he was told, and Alcander led Jasper the rest of the way to the lab, where a table and some plastic tarps stood in place of an operating theater.

Jasper set the werespider on the long table, then pulled up one of the swivel chairs beside it.

"You should eat too," said Alcander. "And rest."

Jasper looked again at Crimson. He had barely moved in the past few minutes and was still hardly breathing. If Jasper hadn't known better, he would have sworn he was dead. The half-blood shook his head and scooted the chair close enough to where he could comfortably hold the demon's cold hand. "I'll wait."

Chapter Twenty-Three

—

Betting Games

Nine days had passed since their run-in with Shane.

He and Crimson, having decided to stay in for the night, were playing Texas Hold 'Em. Since money held no value to the werespider, and since Jasper had none anyway, they transformed it into a drinking game, where antes were upped with shots in place of chips, with a buy-in using cigarettes and spare lighters pilfered from dozens of locations in the attic. The first to empty his bottle lost. "Or won," said Crimson. "Dependin' on how you see it."

By that logic, Jasper was either losing quite badly, or on a fantastic hot streak.

He squinted at Crimson suspiciously over his cards—a mismatched two and seven. He barely ever played poker, yet he knew that was no good.

Crimson's cards still lay facedown on the table, where they had been dealt. He thumbed up the corners, glanced at the number and suit, then let them lie back down, and rapped his knuckles on the wood. With nothing on the line, there was no harm in staying in, so Jasper matched his check and flipped the first card to reveal the seven of hearts. A pair was better than seven high, he supposed, but not by much.

Crimson poured a drizzle of tequila into the shot glass in front of him, the amount small enough that Jasper was left to wonder whether he somehow had been dealt a worse hand, if such a thing were even possible. He decided to risk it and matched.

The last few days felt surreal.

After waking up at Alcander's, Crimson had gone for a "walk." When he came back, he had guzzled down a full bottle of wine "for the pain" and then passed out on the bed in a deep, sound slumber that lasted nearly a day. Whether the pain was physical or emotional, he did not say, and Jasper did not have the nerve to ask.

When he woke, he was surly, and he only kept himself up long enough to walk home with Jasper, where he went immediately to the couch and listed in and out with the television on and a bottle in easy reach.

On the third day, when he seemed to be feeling a little less depressed, Jasper timidly asked him what all he remembered. Crimson claimed to have lost track of the situation back in the alley, when he had been shot, and that most of what came before and after was a little fuzzy. Jasper didn't know if he bought that, but he also didn't know if he was ready to deal with whatever feelings the werespider was hiding. He had been keeping them secret all this time, after all, and things between them were good. He didn't want to risk messing that up.

After a few more days of rest, Crimson's recovery seemed fuller, enough so that he was awake more than he was asleep, though his energy was still low and he resisted any course of action that involved leaving the house for more than an hour or two. This had happened in Florida too, and Jasper decided perhaps it was just part of the way he was. As the saying went, things that went up, always eventually came down. Crimson simply went up higher than most, so he had further to fall, and the resulting impact left him no less pained than if he had actually struck the ground.

With his days and nights suddenly free, Jasper entertained himself by wandering the city alone, visiting the local libraries and parks, grocery shopping, and reading voraciously. All the while, he kept his senses strained for Shane, even going so far as to inquire about him at some of the demonic haunts where he was seen as a friendly face. Either no one had seen him, or the ones who had were too scared to talk. In any case, he didn't sense him, and before long his concern over the matter began to fade. If the guy had any sense, he had hopped the first plane to Mexico and wouldn't come back.

As for Jasper, he had the credit card Alcander had given him, the cash from the Hunting Agency a distant memory. The card adequately covered all his needs, but he felt bad always using Alcander's money. If he wasn't going to be a Hunter anymore, there seemed no choice but to start looking for a civilian job. Alcander still had to help him with his credentials (and his résumé—he'd never written one and had no clue where to start), but he had put in applications at all the surrounding bars, apart from Rascal's, which felt slightly too personal a place to work. He had gotten a call for an interview next weekend, and the game was their way of celebrating.

Now that he had bought in, Crimson raised the bet substantially. The clear tequila bubbled over the lip of the shot glass. Jasper shook his head, folded, and took his quarter shot with a grimace, while Crimson scooped the cards back together and shuffled them to redeal.

"So if you get the job, what'll you be doing?" asked Crimson conversationally. "Like, bartending or something?"

"Probably just washing dishes or sweeping floors, shit like that," said Jasper, though bartending did sound kind of cool.

"I don't even like to wash my own dishes," said Crimson.

"I noticed," said Jasper.

His hand this go-around was decidedly better than the last. Two kings. But it must have showed in his face because Crimson folded right off the bat. Jasper threw the cards on top of the pile. "I've never had a job before. Not a normal one anyhow." He shuffled the deck, feeling along the edges for dog-ears or indentations. It would be just like Crimson to cheat, even in a game meant purely for fun.

"I used to run liquor for Tommy Rascal, scare away cops, shoot mobsters. It was fun."

"I don't think that counts as a job, Crims." But the mental image of Prohibition-era Crimson made him smile.

Crimson opened his mouth to say something, and Jasper held out a hand to stop him. "Neither does any sort of robbery, piracy, larceny, arson, assassination, or espionage."

Crimson closed his mouth. Jasper dealt him two fresh cards. Crimson peeked at them and poured two fingers of tequila into his glass. "Bet."

"Raise," replied Jasper.

Crimson matched. "I played piano over at Moonlight."

"I thought that was a strip club." Jasper had never been inside, but

St. James was well aware of the place. The only reason they had never done away with it was because the only humans who ended up there were the sort that wanted to, and the demons who ran the place knew better than to have it any other way.

"Strippers gotta dance to something." Crimson laughed as Jasper revealed the first three cards. "We didn't always have your fancy, newfangled radios." The werespider scooted a second glass in front of him and filled it halfway. "Raise."

Jasper was sitting on three of a kind and aces no less. "Match," he agreed. "I guess that counts as a job. How was it?"

"Didn't like it. It's all schedules and routines. Go here at this time, go home at that time, play that same song. Play it again. Time I quit, I hated being there so much I didn't go back for months."

"How long'd you make it?"

Crimson squinted an eye halfway shut. "'Bout three weeks, I'd say. Wouldn't recommend it."

Jasper laughed. "Well, I *like* schedules. And I *like* routines."

"Bizarre."

They went back and forth with the bets until each had three full shot glasses in front of him. The quarter bottle of whiskey (Jasper couldn't stomach the tequila) he'd drank prior was already fizzing in his senses, impairing his judgment, which was probably why he thought it would be okay to bet such an extravagant amount. He had him this time for sure.

They revealed their cards. Jasper swore. A full fucking house.

He took his three shots. By the third, the whiskey went down easy.

Like most drinking games, once you started losing, it was hard to do much else. They played for another hour, Jasper getting foggier all the while. They were technically supposed to play until one bottle was entirely empty, but Crimson called the game while Jasper's was still a fifth of the way full.

"You drink any more and we'll have to finish the game on the floor with a bucket." Crimson laughed.

"Yer jus' scared Imma make a comeback an' beat'choo," accused Jasper in a slur that did nothing but prove Crimson's point.

"Yeah, sure. That's it, kid. Whatever you wanna tell yourself."

Jasper glared at him. He glared so hard, in fact, that he just closed his eyes. Once closed, he saw very little reason to open them again.

He went to prop his chin in his palm, missed, and set it on the table instead.

Crimson made a soft clicking sound with his tongue. "Looks like it's time for bed."

Jasper's eyes snapped open. "Not tired," he announced, sitting up again.

"You can sleep at the table if ya really wanna," said Crimson, "but don't bitch to me when your neck is sore."

"Not tired," Jasper repeated, reaching for the cards to shuffle them. They flew out of his hands and across the table, many fluttering to the floor.

"C'mon, kid." Crimson hauled him up from his chair, arm tight around his waist. They hobbled gracelessly across the room to the beds. Crimson let him drop onto the mattress. Jasper lay back and looked up at the spinning ceiling. Oh, that wasn't good. He sat up again.

Crimson was still standing beside his bed, giving him a look he couldn't quite read. Jasper gave him a look back, squeezing one eye shut while studying him with the other. *Had* he always looked at him this way? Maybe he only imagined it.

The surplus of alcohol made him feel bolder. "It true—what Shane said?"

Jasper didn't have any trouble reading the disgust that quickly crossed the demon's face at the mention of the incubus and just as quickly disappeared. His face transformed into a look of cool indifference.

"Yeah, I *can* speak Atlantean." He said something in a language that sounded like bubbling water and crashing waves. Jasper didn't know enough about it to tell if he was bullshitting or not.

"Nah, not 'bout that. The other thing."

"Don't know what you're talkin' 'bout, kid."

"Quit callin' me kid. And quit playin' dumb. I'm talkin' 'bout the thing about you 'n me." Crimson was unreadable once more. It was extremely frustrating. "You... like me?" That wasn't exactly what Shane had said, but Jazz couldn't bring himself to use the same words.

At first Jasper didn't think Crimson would answer, he was silent for so long.

Finally: "Would it matter if I did?"

"Course it would."

"How so?" asked Crimson. He hesitated a beat, then took a seat on the edge of the bed, some distance from where Jasper sat. "Let's say I was in love with you. Hypothetically. No matter how much I loved you, it ain't gonna change the fact that you don't feel the same way. So what's it matter?"

Crimson's voice was soft and rhythmic, and Jasper's alcohol-sodden mind was having trouble understanding him through the gentle melody, but one word rang clearer than the rest. He sat up a little straighter. "Love?"

"Hypothetically," repeated Crimson, firm. "It's like with you and your friend Adam. You felt one way. He felt another. Sometimes them's the breaks."

"Wha—*you told me you didn't remember that!*"

Crimson smiled weakly. "Yeah, I was sort of bluffing. I mean, it's kinda vague. What I remember. But it, uh… just seemed easier."

"Shouldn't've lied about it." Especially since he was the only one who knew the truth.

Crimson shrugged. "Me knowing doesn't change anything… Does it?"

In general, the whole social-interaction thing was not Jasper's forte. He knew how little seven-year-old him had felt when Adam turned him down. And he had been only a child then, without any real concept of love and only a vague understanding of rejection, but even then, he knew enough to understand he was well and truly hurt. He didn't want Crimson to feel that way, but he didn't want to lie to him, nor risk leading him on either. It wasn't fair.

"I, uhh… guess not," he said. His chest ached. "I'm sorry." He leaned closer to wrap him in what would have undoubtedly been a very clumsy hug, but Crimson caught him gently by the forearms and pushed them down in front of him, not cruelly, just firmly.

"Nothin' to be sorry for." He raised an eyebrow, a sparkle of mischief in his eyes. "Kid." He stood up quite suddenly. "You're really drunk. You probably ought to sleep."

"I'm not tired," Jasper insisted, his voice small.

Crimson surveyed him a moment longer and shrugged. "Alright. Do whatever you want. I'm not your father." Stretching, he dropped down on his own bed and sprawled out with a yawn. "*I'm* gonna sleep though."

Jasper watched the werespider turn away from him, staring at his back for a long moment before lying down himself. Pulling a pillow over his face, he tried to sleep.

#

The next day they didn't talk about it again. Jasper wanted to, but he never could figure out what to say, and Crimson was right, it was easier to pretend.

Alcander was supposed to call him and invite him over to work on his résumé. His interview was coming up, and he was nervous. Drop him in an angry coven of vampires and he was fine, he knew what to do to get out of that situation, but the idea of having to sit down and convince someone to let him wash dishes had him anxious enough to consider not going at all. He couldn't wait any longer for Al to contact him; he'd be chewing his fingers off at this rate.

He called Al's cell and it went straight to voicemail. He must have been working on something. The last time they'd talked, after he and Crimson came back home, he had thought he'd made a breakthrough with his synthetic blood formula. Jasper didn't understand half the things he said about it, but he hadn't wanted to disturb him while he was working. Al must have been so involved in what he was doing that he had forgotten to charge his phone or something. He tried calling Max instead.

Max didn't answer either.

Jasper called him back. It went to voicemail again, and he stood up from the table, sliding his phone shut as he went over to the couch, where Crimson was watching a movie, half dozing.

"Hey." Jasper tapped his arm to get his attention. "I can't get a hold of Al or Max."

"Did you call his numbers?"

"I called his cell and Max's."

"Al's got a thousand phones." Crimson took his phone from his pocket and dialed a number from memory. After a few seconds of waiting for an answer, he hung up and dialed a different number. He did this two more times before the languidly irritated expression on his face began to change into something else.

Snapping his cell shut, Crimson was on his feet. "Get your gun. We're going over there."

#

The entrance to the basement was hanging wide open, the stairwell below a dark spiral. Crimson and Jasper almost stuck themselves in the doorway trying to run for it at the same time. "Al!" screamed Jasper. The overhead lights popped on as they descended, one after another. At the foot of the steps, in the entryway, a large black rat blinked its red eyes and then scampered quickly towards the living room to avoid their tromping boots. With a sinking stomach, he watched it dash across the white carpet, towards the kitchen.

He felt very cold.

"Alcander!" He yelled his name again. Crimson was pacing circles in the living room, sniffing the air with a disgusted-looking expression on his face.

He knew that look.

"It was Shane, wasn't it?"

Crimson closed his eyes and lowered his head. "Yeah."

Drawing his gun, Jasper tore through the kitchen, screaming the vampire's name again and again. His bedroom was empty, the comforter crumpled, corners untucked, the indent where his head had lain still wadded in the pillow. He ripped back the sheets, looking for tears or bloodstains or (God help him) a pile of vampire dust.

Finding nothing, he ran for the lab instead.

Apart from the glow of the many screens, it was dark. Three long glass vials of congealing synthetic blood still sat on the workbench. A readout beside them was flashing red with a warning and a scrolling text of data that Jasper couldn't understand. He circled the lab twice.

Still nothing.

Shakily, he turned and ran back the way he had come. Crimson was still standing in the living room.

"What are you doing?" asked Jasper. "Help me look for him."

"The trail is old," said Crimson. "Four days at least, but maybe as long as a week."

"Then we have to follow it," said Jasper urgently. "Which way did they go?"

Crimson hesitated. "I think—" Somewhere, there was an urgent BANG, BANG, BANG, a fist on a door or countertop or wall. He and the werespider exchanged a wide-eyed glance and then bolted towards the source.

The bathroom door had been bolted shut with two steel rods, a folding chair wedged beneath the handle.

Jasper grabbed the chair aside, and Crimson slammed a sizable hole in the wooden panel, then gripped the broken pieces of timber, shredding them into chunks like they were made of Styrofoam. Jasper looked through the gap as the splinters fell away.

Max was huddled on the other side, arms hugged around his chest, one eye black and swollen shut. A heavy-looking chain ran from his ankle to the radiator.

Jasper swore and climbed through. "Max?"

At first, the human cringed away, an elbow raised weakly over his face with his head turned, but when Jasper got closer, he finally seemed to recognize him. His eyes welled. He grabbed Jasper's hand with both of his. "I'm so sorry. I couldn't stop him. It's all my fault. I-I—"

Jasper looked hopefully to Crimson. He stooped to get underneath the upper rod and stepped to get over the lower. Jasper stood aside to let the demon take a knee by the shaking human.

"Shhh, hush now," cooed Crimson. He pressed a finger to the other's lips.

The tears ran suddenly dry, and apart from the odd tremor, Maxwell stilled. He stared back at the werespider with an expression that was nearly bliss. He sniffed once.

"Tell us what happened," said Crimson.

Now that he wasn't all huddled up, it was easy to see his suffering hadn't ended with the black eye. Several other bruises were visible, and there were probably several more that weren't. "There was a man," said Max, in a small voice.

"Medium height, kinda scrawny, with a big hokey cobra tattoo and a goatee that sort of makes him look like the godsdamned devil?" asked Crimson.

"Yes," said Max in that same small voice, barely above a whisper.

The werespider's brows knit in a heavy scowl. "How did he get in the house?"

Max's eyes were still wide and staring, expressionless, but the tears welled in the bottoms of them, filled his gaze like a pitcher, and then overspilled down his cheeks. "I had to buy groceries," he whispered. "It was daylight. I took a cab. I was on my way back and he was waiting outside the building, around the bay doors. He wanted me to let him in. I told him no." He paused. Jasper went to the sink and wet a cloth with ice-cold water. "He grabbed me and I—" He stopped again.

Jasper knelt on the other side of him and pressed the cool cloth gently to his swollen eye. Poor Max had never done any harm to anyone. Jasper bit his tongue to stifle the rage burning inside him.

"I didn't want to," Max said. "He was like you."

Crimson shrank a little at the comparison and suddenly became very focused on retrieving a pin from the collar of his jacket.

"What happened to Alcander?" asked Jasper.

"It was daytime," repeated Max. "He was asleep. The alarms go off any time someone enters the building. They woke him. He could have overridden the controls, made it so I couldn't open the door no matter how many codes I put in. I don't know why he didn't."

"I do," said Crimson. He jimmied open the lock around the human's ankle. Where the shackle had been, the flesh was swollen and angry looking with thin gashes against the shinbone. "There's cameras in the warehouse too. He probably saw the two of you together, thought you were in trouble."

Max swallowed hard. "Yes, maybe." He rolled up the sleeve of his shirt, revealing a string of numbers in black marker. At the tail end was a little cartoon heart with a feathered arrow dashed through the middle of it. "I'm supposed to give you his phone number. I'm supposed to tell you to call him."

Jasper whipped out his phone and dialed the number into his keypad, but Crimson put a hand on his wrist before he could hit "send."

"How long ago?" asked Crimson.

Max looked confused. "I don't know. There are no clocks. It was... Monday? I think."

"It's Saturday," Jasper told Crimson, knowing that he would not know. He looked around the threadbare bathroom. He'd been stuck in here for five days, without food, without social interaction or any sort of external stimulation. That was bad enough, but Alcander had it worse. Alcander was stuck with Shane, wherever he was, and Jasper tried not to think about what he might have done to him or what he might be doing to him right now.

"Hey, Max, listen to me, okay? This isn't your fault. Shane's... Shane's a fucking asshole, okay?" Jasper should have shot him in the head instead. He had never wanted to kill anyone or anything so badly in his life.

Max nodded miserably to show that he heard, and Jasper helped him up. He knew the human needed looking after and quickly, but he was anxious to call Shane and figure out what was going on. He found him fresh clothes and put him to bed with a bowl of canned soup, plenty of fresh water, an ice pack for his eye, and as many extra pillows as he could find. It wasn't ideal, but it would have to do for now.

While he did this, Crimson sat in the living room, staring down at the screen of his phone, thinking.

"What are you waiting for?" asked Jasper, coming back into the main room. "Call him."

"I was hopin' to think of some way around it," replied Crimson. "Or to figure out what he's playing at." He paused. "Guess there's nothing to do but exactly what he wants."

Jasper didn't like the grave sound of this, but there seemed to be no other way. He went and sat beside Crimson on the couch. The werespider dialed the number, then switched it to speakerphone while it rang.

"Howdy, sugar!" The cheerful voice was like nails on a chalkboard. Jasper pressed his tongue to the roof of his mouth and clenched his teeth. "See y'got my message. If I'da known how long it was gonna take for you to find, I'da sent it direct."

"You shouldn't have involved Al in this, Shane," replied Crimson. "I'll go rob a bank with you if that's what it takes to bring him back safe. But eternity's a long time and I'm not gonna let this go."

"Well, if ya cared about the little Dracula so much, why'd it take ya so long to realize he was gone? Poor thing's been whimperin' like a lost dog for ya for days. He *really* doesn't like it when ya pet him though."

"You fucking piece of shit!" burst Jasper.

"Hey! Eye candy!" Shane sounded positively delighted. "Just the guy I wanted to talk to."

Crimson frowned. He looked curiously at Jasper, then back at the phone as Shane's bubbly voice tittered away.

"You an' me got a date. You can bring Crimson along. I don't want him workin' himself into a tiff while I'm not there to take care of him."

"What do you want with Jasper?" rumbled Crimson.

"I'm just a man takin' a gamble, hopin' it pays off," said Shane. "And there ain't no decent gambler in history who won by showin' his cards too soon. You know that."

"When I find you, I'm going to make your *skin* into a deck of playing cards," hissed Crimson. The distinctive difference in his demeanor came in a flash of red. His voice was so different when he was like this, not just in its low, rumbling tone, but in its cadence and enunciation. It could almost have been another person, yet, somehow, it could not possibly have been anyone else. "You have no idea who the fuck you are messing with."

"Ooo, very scary." Shane laughed. "Loses a li'l bit of the bite after ya heard it a couple of times though."

The lower half of Crimson's face grew into a wide, stretching smile that seemed to show an impossible number of teeth. "Oh, Shaney boy, you don't understand. All these years, I've given you a pass because some small portion of me was still a little bit in love with you." Crimson's eyes flickered to Jasper. Away. "I've been cured of that unfortunate addiction, and that means no more free passes. You will stop this. Now."

"Boy, you sure love the sound of your own voice. Y'know, some things never change." The levity was still there, but a little less certain of itself than before. "Y'know what else hasn't changed? The fact that I got your favorite pet danglin' above a vat'a holy water. Or the fact that Al's gonna be takin' himself a nice little swim if you don't do what you're told."

"If you hurt Alcander—" began Jasper.

"C'mon, eye candy. You think you're gonna say something scarier than turning me into playing cards? Cut it out with that."

"Tell us where you want to meet," said Crimson.

"The Crystal Ballroom. Ten o'clock. Let's say... two days from now. Me, you, an' the hybrid. An' don't go thinkin' yer gonna get the drop on me, Crim. The vamp's in real good hands, and they know what to do if they don't get a sign."

"It's a date," said Crimson. "We'll see you there."

"Bet on it," replied Shane, and ended the call.

"Al can't wait two days." Jasper was on his feet as soon as the call ended. "We gotta go find this creep right now and kick his fucking ass."

Still on the couch, Crimson shook his head. "Shane won't be found until he's good and ready."

"Bullshit." They couldn't just sit back and do nothing. Already Al had been with him too long. Jasper felt so guilty it was making him sick. He had been gone for five days, and they hadn't noticed. Al deserved better. "We can track him. You know his scent; I know his—" Jasper's hand fluttered over his stomach. It was hard to explain his talent to sense demons on the best of days, and now, with his mind a flurry of anger and fear, he couldn't even try. "We can find him."

"The trail is five days old. We're in New York fuckin' City. I'm really fuckin' good, but not that good."

"We gotta *try*."

Crimson sighed. "Alan does a lot of work at The Crystal Ballroom and Moonlight. He might be able to lead us to him or lead us to somebody who can, but I'm tellin' you, Jazz, it's a long shot. He might not even be in the city right now. Or he could be in a safe house where we'll get gunned down at the front desk just for asking his name." His throat clicked. "Can you think of any reason he'd want you there?"

"Other than the fact I shot him like six times and spoiled his plans to rob a mermaid bank?"

"The Atlanteans aren't mermaids. They're water folk. Good guess though." He always said stupid shit like this when he was hiding something. If Jasper hadn't known that before, he knew it now.

"You don't think that's reason enough to want me dead?" asked Jasper.

"Revenge isn't Shane's game," replied Crimson. He tapped a cigarette out of the pack, put it between his lips, then glanced at their surroundings, and put it behind his ear instead of lighting it. "No profit in it."

"Then he still wants you to help him rob the bank," Jasper surmised.

Crimson ran two fingers across his jawline. "Nah. Well, maybe, but that doesn't explain *you*. Maybe he just wants to keep you in his sights, I don't know, but it seems like a pretty risky plan. It was me doing it, I'd wanna keep you outta the picture. And he could have done that. If he had wanted to."

"What he wants me for doesn't matter if we find him first and put an end to this before it can begin," said Jasper.

"If," agreed Crimson. He stood up. "We'll try. Don't get your hopes up though."

#

The Silverado was not where they had left it. Crimson lamented that crime in this city was really out of control.

The Crystal Ballroom was only six blocks away, so they went on foot, but Alan and Abby were not there. Nor were they anywhere to be found in the dark, sleazy back rooms of Moonlight. Crimson suggested it was probably a little early in the day for them, then added grimly that if Alan knew anything worth knowing, Shane probably would have shut him up permanently. Leaving loose ends was, apparently, also something that did not fit into Shane's game.

Jasper followed Crimson through haunt after haunt. When he had worked at St. James, Brooklyn was his regular beat, and he believed the Hunters could account for *most* of the demonic safe houses and recreational areas in the borough.

He was wrong.

There were far more than he had anticipated. Some of them were so heavily warded that passing through the charms that protected them gave him motion sickness. One of them (he believed it was called The House of the Setting Sun) could only be entered by jumping up *into* a mural of graffiti. At another, Crimson had to get down on one knee and call into a storm drain until a pair of beady eyes appeared in the slat below the sidewalk, and a large ratlike paw unlocked a hinge to let them descend via ladder.

Whatever Crimson said about Alan, he still managed to stop by his apartment when the whole of Brooklyn came up a dead end and they made their way to Queens. Crimson had earlier called the place a "shithole," and Jasper saw immediately that he hadn't been kidding. The two-bedroom apartment was on the top floor of an old brick building. A surly-looking werewolf in a fast-food uniform informed them Alan was still asleep. The view over his shoulder was grim— piles of scattered trash on a dirty, stained rug, broken-down furniture strung with passed-out demons, barely dressed. It smelled like stale beer, cigarettes, marijuana, and sweltering heat.

The werewolf told them they could come in, and Jasper reluctantly followed Crimson. Thankfully the furniture in the front room was already too full for anyone to invite them to sit. The werewolf who answered the door disappeared down an adjoining hallway that cut straight away from the main room, presumably so he could go find Alan.

After a few moments, some of the sleeping demons stirred at the sounds of two people arguing down the hall, then woke, one by one, as a female voice began to shout and snarl angrily. From the square of laminate that served as an entryway, they could see the dark hallway, lights burned out, bags of trash and junk collected along the sides, unwashed clothes supplementing the carpet. Presently, they could also see Alan, who was propelled out from the second door to the end, as if violently thrown. His shoulders struck the drywall and bounced him back to his feet. He stumbled awkwardly on his long legs and caught himself in time to throw the pair of them a smile.

"Hey, guys!"

There was another roaring snarl from the room he had just exited. He quickly pulled the door shut and made a shushing gesture towards them, though neither had said a word, and he had been practically yelling just a moment ago.

Alan was not dressed for guests. Which was a nice way of saying he wasn't dressed at all. Jasper saw in a hot glance exactly why Crimson put up with him, and quickly looked away.

The werewolf, unabashed, crept closer. "If you're looking for company, we'll have to go back to yours," he whispered, to the warning rumbles of his other packmates. He inched up beside them so he could speak more softly. "Beth'll kill me if I take you back there while she's trying to sleep."

"I was just wonderin' if you'd seen Shane," said Crimson, unperturbed.

"Sorry," said Alan. He said it *soar-ree* rather than *sarr-ee,* a distinction in his voice Jasper had never noticed because he'd never heard him apologize for anything.

Jasper's eyes were still firmly on the linoleum. It was separated from the thin, tattered carpet by a narrow slat of metal that was crusted all the way around with a brownish gray something, impossible to identify. When he shifted his feet uncomfortably, the soles of his shoes made soft suctioning noises.

"He hasn't come to me since you've been back in town," continued Alan. "I thought you off'd him."

"If only." Crimson sighed. "Well… Alright. I just thought I'd ask. I'll catch ya later. Jazz?"

Jasper started to follow him back out the door, but Alan's whispered voice stopped him. "You sure you don't want some company?" To Jasper, it sounded almost like a plea. He sensed more than saw the werespider's gaze on him.

"Sorry," echoed Crimson, and they both dipped out the door.

Then they were off again, this time to a place called the Voodoo Club. It was a fair bit nicer there than at the other dives, more a restaurant than an actual club, and a legitimate business besides, but it was as much a dead end as the other twenty-odd places had been, and Jasper was getting tired and frustrated.

It was very late (or early) when they let out of the Voodoo Club, and if Jasper were tired and frustrated, there were no words for what Crimson was. Perpetually red-eyed and progressively more predatory in his body language, smoking one cigarette after another in an endless chain that made Jasper's lungs hurt just watching. He reached for another, found the pack empty, crumpled it, and winged it under the tires of a passing cab with a hiss.

"Where's left?" asked Jasper.

Crimson laughed in a way that sounded pained and shook his head. "That's what I'm tryin' to tell you, man. *Everywhere.* He could be at the fucking Onyx Eclipse for all we know."

"You know that doesn't mean anything to me," said Jasper.

"It's this big hotel in Manhattan."

"You said we checked everywhere in Manhattan."

"Yeah, everywhere we *could* check," said Crimson. "The Onyx isn't a playground. You don't get to just come and go as you please. You go in there askin' the wrong name, and you don't come out. Ever." He paused. "Do you have a cigarette?"

"You smoked all mine."

Crimson heaved a sigh. "I know the owner of the Onyx. In fact, *you* know her too. She split a joint with us in the Summerlands." A hazy memory tried weakly to surface, of Crimson wrapping an arm around his shoulders then turning him away from a laughing, grinning circle of faces, none of which he could distinctly recall. "She *does* owe me a favor, but it's tricky. If we go in there and say, 'Hey, Morgaine, I'm lookin' for this guy who might be staying here, can you tell us his room number?' she *might* tell us. But that's the only favor she owes me. So then we're square, and she boils all the blood in both of our bodies because we're sniffin' around where we don't belong. I mean, fuck, Morg's a godsdamned gambling addict. She might owe *him* a favor too."

"What if you just ask her to kill him?" suggested Jasper.

"Yeah, that might work, except we're back to square one. Alcander in a vat of boiling water. Wherever they are, they might not be *together*. Alcander might not even be *alive*. So even if we *do* find Shane…"

"It might not matter." Jasper understood.

Crimson pondered a moment longer, then, mostly to himself, said, "'Sides, the Onyx ain't like these other joints. There's demons and mages in there that know a thing or two, and an aura or a scent like yours… I just think…"

"It's alright," said Jasper. With the memory of the Summerlands freshened in his mind, he agreed. Besides, the werespider was tired, and so was Jasper, and with daybreak on the horizon, there seemed little and less to do than to just go back home and try their luck tomorrow. They stopped by Alcander's to check on Max. He was still in bad enough shape that they decided to stay there instead of going back to the house.

Jasper slept uneasily, his dreams plagued by nightmares. When he woke, Crimson was already awake and appeared to have been for some time. Today, he had showered and changed his clothes, which Jasper thought he hadn't done for something like three days. He was sitting slung in the easy chair, using a thread and needle to repair the holes in his jacket while a movie played, muted with the captions on.

Jasper checked his phone. It was only ten a.m. His head ached at the thought of the earliness, but he knew as soon as he opened his eyes that he would not fall back asleep. It would be better if he could. The waiting was the worst.

#

"You're up early," said Jasper.

"I had a nightmare that it was 1955," said Crimson. Only it hadn't been a nightmare. In fact, he couldn't remember the last time he had a *real* dream—nightmare or otherwise. Perhaps it was something to do with his age, or his heritage, or maybe he was just crazy (he didn't know anymore), but his dreamscape was nothing more than a patchwork quilt of half-remembered things sewn and held jaggedly together with gossamer threads of emotion. When the memories were good, it was a blessing. The thing of it was, they usually weren't.

Shane, in that time still more man than monster, was there. Face clean-shaven, flight jacket slung over one shoulder, he smiled and seemed an angel. They were laughing about something, but that was, unfortunately, the other half of the memory, the one he could not recall. Then the dream suddenly became 1961, and they were screaming at each other at the top of their voices from the steel belly of a carrier plane, while an odd assortment of people watched in awkward, wide-eyed silence. Just as the screaming built to a crescendo of ringing white noise, it was 1955 again, and Shane was reaching out from the covers, whispering his name, drawing him closer. In 1997, a glass bottle whizzed by his head, missing only by the grace of Crimson's reflexes, shattering on the wall in a spray of deep amber bourbon and tinkling glass. It was not the first time Shane had lashed out at him—if memory served, it wasn't even the first time *that night*—but for the first time in all the years they had been together and apart and together again, Crimson lashed back.

Strength wise, they were no match. Crimson broke his nose in a single swing.

Shane, looking disgusted with blood pouring from his nostrils and split lip, had called him a "fucking egomaniac" and "controlling psychopath." That was what had finally woken him up.

He tied off the knot he was working on and broke the thread with a tug. There were no more repairs to be made on the jacket. Nor were there any more guns to be cleaned, nor knives to be sharpened. "I'm gonna make some more coffee. You want coffee?"

Jasper's expression was written in concern. About Alcander, he figured.

"Sure," he agreed after a long moment. "I'm going to check on Max, see if he needs anything."

"Alright." Crimson went to the kitchen. A few moments later, Jasper joined him. He got a clean bowl out of the cabinet. As he was checking the labels on the varied cans of soup from overhead, Crimson asked, "How'd you sleep?" though he already knew. He'd listened to him toss and turn and mumble for most of the night.

Jasper's brow crinkled. "I had a *weird* fuckin' dream, man."

"Weird how?"

"Well… It's hard to remember." Jasper popped the lid on the soup can and poured the slimy contents into the bowl. It was made of limpid-looking chunks of soppy wet vegetables, wriggly noodles, and some sort of whitish meat, all floating in a greasy yellow fluid that reeked of salt. Jasper stirred all the hunks around a bit, added a dash of pepper (his sinuses stung), and put it in the microwave. "I think…" He punched some numbers on the keypad and then hit the "start" button. As the table inside started to turn, the room was filled with the scent of dead, reheated flesh. He wondered how he used to stomach the stuff. Honestly, it was so disgusting. "I think at one point I was a ham."

"Like in Looney Tunes?" asked Crimson.

Jasper shrugged. "Maybe." He sat down at the table, his knee bouncing impatiently. "Should we be making some sort of plan?"

"Like what?" asked Crimson.

"Well," said Jasper, "we could…" His voice trailed off. "Like, I don't know…"

"The only thing to do is wait," said Crimson. He took a seat beside the half-blood, hesitated, then put a hand on the other's knee. The bouncing stopped, and Jasper's gaze cut to his. He withdrew his touch immediately, putting his fisted hand firmly on his own knee, where it could do no further harm. "Trust me, I don't like it either."

#

The Crystal Ballroom didn't open until nine, and Jasper and Crimson were the first customers there. The place looked especially sad with the lights flashing over the empty dance floor, which seemed to be permanently sticky from a thousand spilled drinks. The music bounced like an echo around the open room. They grabbed a booth where they could see the door and watched as people began to show up. A server stopped by their table, dropping off a trio of shots for Crimson and a dark red Manhattan for Jasper. Jasper was too anxious to drink his and just spun it idly between his hands; Crimson didn't have the same problem.

Ten o'clock rolled around. Jasper drank half his drink. He kept checking his phone for the time, wondering with every painfully passed minute where the fuck Shane was. At 10:21 he finally sauntered in with one of his vampires and another demon he didn't recognize. Jasper moved to leave the table, to confront the incubus at the door, but Crimson stopped him with a touch on the wrist and a minute shake of the head. They waited for Shane to come to them.

"You're late," Jasper snapped.

"Sorry, bright eyes. I was settin' something up."

"Where's Al?"

"Safe as houses," said Shane. The vampire slid into the booth across from them, and Shane sat beside him on the outside. The other demon pulled a chair up to the end of the table and dropped into it, between Crimson and Shane.

"Then you won't mind if I speak to him," said Crimson.

Shane pouted extravagantly. "What's the matter? You don't trust me?"

"Right," said Crimson. He stood up, looking at Jasper. "Let's go." The demon at the end of the table rose, facing him, and the werespider snatched at the same moment, twisting the arm holding the drawn gun with one hand and grabbing his revolver with the other.

"Jesus, Mary, and Joseph!" hissed Shane. "Don't go makin' a scene, either of you."

"Then let us talk to Alcander," said Jasper. The idea that he would actually just walk away was absurd, but Crimson had decided to bluff, and he obviously knew better what to do in a hostage situation (well, he hoped he did anyway), so Jasper followed his lead. "We just want to know he's safe."

"Don't be so dramatic. A'course I'm gonna let you talk to him." Shane gestured to the recently disarmed demon, who was currently holding his wrist and scowling openly at Crimson, who already looked at the razor's edge of turning the whole place into a shooting gallery. Jasper tugged on the werespider's sleeve, and he dropped back into the booth beside him and stretched his long fingers out for Shane's phone. He was wearing the leather gloves. The incubus put it on speaker and handed it to him as the ringtone began to sound.

Eventually there was a click, and a gruff voice asked, "Yeah, boss?"

"Put the vampire on the phone," said Shane, raising his voice to be heard across the table.

There was the sound of a key rattling in a lock, the squeak of an unoiled door hinge, and the rough rumble of the voice again, now far enough away from the receiver that no words could be discerned.

"Hello?"

Jasper knew Alcander's voice at a word. He spoke before Crimson could. "Al! Are you okay?"

"Jasper?" The vampire's voice went up in pitch, very nearly becoming a squeak.

"It's us," said Jasper, and at very nearly the same time, Crimson said, "Be calm, Al."

"Crimson, you get Jasper the hell away from him." Jasper's ears rang. He had never heard Alcander swear. *"Do you understand? Don't let him—"* A loud CRACK was followed by the sound of something striking steel, punctuated by a mewl of pain.

"Gimme that," growled the unfamiliar voice. Jasper numbly listened to the sound of a very brief struggle, snarled words, thudding punches and kicks. He made it all of five seconds before he cracked. "Tell him to stop!"

Shane narrowed his eyes at him slightly, the corner of his lip curled.

Then it was Jasper's turn to stand, though what he actually tried to do was lunge across the table, his eyes flaring white with fury. Crimson's fingers closed on the strap of his belt and pulled him firmly back into his seat.

"See? Now that's the sorta show I was hopin' you'd put on," said Shane. He made a "give me" gesture with his hand, and Crimson, still holding Jasper back, slapped the phone into his palm with a surly, red-eyed scowl. "Let up on the vampire, Rick. I seen all I need t'see."

"Yeah, boss," replied the voice, as if that were all it could ever say. Then the line went silent.

"Shane," rumbled Crimson, "this is between you an' me. It's got nothing to do with either of them."

"Actually," said Shane, "*you're* the one it's got nothin' to do with. I mainly just invited ya here so I could see yer head explode when you realize yer not the center'a the fuckin' universe."

Crimson barked sarcastic laughter. "I'd tell you to go *fuck yourself* if I thought you'd actually be able to feel it, you little shit."

Shane held his fisted hands on either side of his own head, then splayed his fingers while imitating a muted "BOOM" with his mouth. Then giggled. "Right on schedule." He dropped his hands to his sides and looked at Jasper. "It's like a dog barkin', y'know? They only do it when they feel threatened or want attention."

Jasper did not reply. He was still having trouble processing what was going on. Shane had kidnapped Alcander, beat the living hell out of Max, and was currently playing poke-the-bear with Crimson, all because of… him? That didn't make any sense.

"Jasper couldn't even help you rob a liquor store," snapped Crimson. "Much less a *bank*. You're barking so far up the wrong tree the racoons are laughin' at you, dipshit."

"Oh *yeah*, the *bank*." Shane laughed, delighted. "Well, I might still let you help me do that. If you behave. But like I said, this ain't got nothin' to do with you. It's all about bright eyes over here."

"I don't understand," said Jasper finally.

"Y'know, neither did I," said Shane. "I been around for a minute, not as long as Mr. Tall, Dark, and Dramatic over here, but long enough. Used to freelance as a mercenary afore my demon genes kicked in. Seen all sortsa stuff. And it's the damnedest thing, I never seen nor heard of a demon with eyes what glow white. And Ralphy over here—" he gestured to the demon sitting between him and Crimson "—never Seen one with an aura like that neither. And Jim—" he gestured to the vampire, who had sat silent and stony-eyed for the entire conversation "—never smelt one with a scent like yours *either*. What about you, sugar? You ever met one like him?"

"Sure," said Crimson. "Off world. In Necropolis. White wraiths are a dime a dozen out there. And he's really only a measly half-blood. Barely any demon in him."

Jasper looked at him with a mingling of shock and anger, that he could have known this all along and never once said.

Then Shane leaned across the table. "You ever hear the phrase 'you're so full of shit, your eyes are brown'?" He swiveled his gaze back to Jasper. "I had a hunch, so I decided to do some diggin'. Consulted lots of brains, includin' your vampire pal. Turns out you're pretty rare. One of a kind, even. Unique." He grinned. "People pay big money for unique."

For a moment that seemed to last an eternity, Jasper only stared at Shane, though he wasn't *seeing* Shane, as it were. The incubus just happened to be in his eyeline.

What he was seeing was his life in rewind. Crimson telling him he could not come inside the Onyx Eclipse because he would draw attention. The hooded figure in the Summerlands gargling something at him, then the urgency to find some way of masking his aura. Ivory purring with curiosity. A three-thousand-year-old, extremely elusive, exceptionally paranoid werespider dropping out of the sky just to talk to him, then agreeing with little or no convincing that he should come live with him.

Some dozen-odd vampires flaring their nostrils, the snap-to of Seers' and psychics' eyes as he walked through the agency day after day. Charlie telling him he was different. Charlie telling him to be careful. The jagged toothed thing in an alley in Seattle, screaming about white light as it ran screeching and pouring blood. A mother and father he had never known, and a question that loomed over his entire life, unanswered.

"Do you know what I am?" Jasper heard himself ask.

"Valuable," said Shane.

Jasper swallowed the rebuttal. The incubus didn't know any more than Crimson did.

"Now," said Shane. "Here's how this is gonna work. You two are both gonna come with me. You're not gonna make a fuss. There's not gonna be any threatening or yelling or fist throwin'. We're gonna get in the car, and we're gonna go somewhere, and when we're there, *you*—" he pointed at Jasper "—will come with me. And *you*—" he pointed at Crimson "—will get an address for where you will find Alcander."

"How about instead of all that, I just blow your brains across the room?"

Shane shrugged. "Alright, well, that's on the table a'course. You can if you wanna, but I bet you won't."

Jasper put his hand on the werespider's wrist, shook his head once, then looked at Shane. "If I do this, Alcander goes free, right?"

"That's right," said Shane. "And if you don't... bye-bye bloodsucker. I don't mean to press ya or anything, but I'm kinda on a timetable right now. So decide real quick-like."

"No." The word growled out of Crimson, low and dangerous. It was not so much heard over the club's music as felt. "No fuckin' way."

"Crimson." Jasper spoke quietly too, but without the demon's viciousness. "It's not up to you. This is the only way to help Al." He looked across the table. Shane smiled smugly back. Jasper hated him with all his heart. "Fine. Let's go."

"I knew you'd see it my way, bright eyes."

Chapter Twenty-Four

—

On the Block

They left the club and got into the Range Rover waiting for them outside. Crimson was red-eyed beside him, his grip on Jasper's wrist so tight it was almost painful. The half-blood found it grounding.

Once in the car, Shane told them to give over their weapons. Crimson had a whole new slew of curses for him at that request, some of them in languages Jasper didn't understand.

"Temper, temper," tsked Shane, and Crimson grudgingly handed over his gun, as did Jasper. The incubus twisted around in his seat. "*All* of them," insisted Shane. "Less you're lookin' to get frisked."

Jasper dug the knives out of his pockets and off his belt and handed over the small-caliber pistol holstered on his leg. Crimson bundled up his jacket and winged it at the half-demon's head. "I expect that back. The gun too."

"Only if you play nice with the other monsters," said Shane dryly, and shoved the jacket underneath the dashboard. The vampire was on Jasper's other side. He gave them both a quick once-over with only his eyes, then flashed Shane a thumbs-up. Shane nodded towards Ralphy, and Ralphy pulled away from the curb.

Jasper wondered where they were going and what exactly would happen when they got there. He had a rough idea. Shane said he was valuable. In some ways, he wondered why no one else had ever tried to use him this way before. It had never been a problem at the agency, but he had had his father and the power of the other Hunters behind him. It had never fully occurred to him how important that connection was. But then, it had also never occurred to him that he

276

didn't really want to be a Hunter. It had already been decided.

The car felt like it was moving too quickly through the streets, making him dizzy. He tried to focus on coming up with a plan, but without knowing where he was going and what would happen, he didn't have much to work with. Crimson would get Al back safe, that was the most important thing. Jasper would figure something out.

He focused instead on Crimson's hand on his wrist. He could feel his own heart pounding in his chest and knew the werespider would be able to feel it in his pulse. Jasper turned his wrist so that they were holding hands, gripping his fingers with what was supposed to be assurance, but felt more like desperation.

Jasper was surprised to see they were heading towards Manhattan and, it appeared to him, directly for St. James. He couldn't make sense of this information and was on the cusp of asking where they were going when Crimson turned his head and spoke in a soft whisper just for him: "We're going to the Onyx Eclipse."

He nodded to show he understood.

"No secrets, lovebirds," said the vampire.

Jasper ground his teeth together, sure that his eyes were showing white, and carefully removed his hand from Crimson's, feeling colder without the touch. He balled his hands into fists on his knees instead.

They pulled up to what looked like a high-rise office building, not unlike many of the buildings around here. Jasper's stomach twisted as they got out of the car, the vampire so close behind him that he imagined he could hear his breathing, though that wasn't true. Jasper's mind was too loud for that, filled with his own breath and heartbeat and worry. He looked at the building, feeling the aggressive pushback of the glamor. Even with all his training, he found it difficult to pull back the layers of illusion to reveal the tall, dark building underneath. It was black, which fit its name, and outfitted in a pseudo art deco style he associated with the novel *The Great Gatsby*. It was at least fifty stories high, and without the wards, it was pulsing with enough energy to make him feel sick. Jasper took his cigarettes out of his jacket pocket and lit one, but only began to draw back on it before it was plucked from his mouth.

"No smokin' in the Onyx, bright eyes," said Shane, sucking back on the smoke. Jasper would have punched him were it not for Alcander.

They went inside.

The lobby was wide and open, with lavishly high ceilings and a swirled black-and-white tiled floor. At first Jasper thought it was just because he was feeling so disoriented from the night's events and pushing through the glamor, but he realized, no, the floor really *was* moving, the black-and-white swirls twisting together and coming apart like a living Rorschach test. Why anyone would find that at all appealing was beyond him. Focusing on a point on the wall ahead of them, he tried his best to ignore it.

They walked past the large black and gold reception desk, behind which stood several demons who were varying stages of passing, some looking perfectly human, some looking anything but, and went to the elevator. Crimson, looking just about ready to burst into legs, said nothing, but Jasper was sure Shane knew of his distaste for small spaces and was simply being cruel.

The lower lobby was populated with all manner of monsters, many of them holding or carrying objects. The door to the theater beyond was slightly cracked. Presently a voice called out, "Next on the block, lot 115, the Scroll of Renewal." The usher opened the door, and a skinny man slung a long canister not much smaller than he over his shoulder and went trotting through with an equally skinny Siamese cat bouncing along at his heel.

Jasper could feel the demons on the other side of the door, more powerfully now than he had when they pulled up beside the building. He felt like he would be sick. "Okay," he said. "We're here. Tell Crimson where Alcander is."

"Not 'til they call our lot," said Shane.

"That wasn't the deal," said Jasper.

"Awfully eager t'part ways," said Shane. "Go on an' say your goodbyes. I love a good drama."

If Shane had not said it the way he had, Jasper was sure he would have hugged the werespider as tightly as he could have, but he found himself not wanting to give the incubus the satisfaction. Jasper held out his hand to shake instead. "Take good care of Alcander and Max, alright?"

Crimson stared down at his hand for a long moment then took it in his. "I'm going to find you."

Jasper was doubtful, though he believed the other would certainly try. "Just don't do anything stupid, Crims."

Something sparked behind Crimson's eyes. "No promises." He brought Jasper's hand to his lips and laid a quick kiss on his knuckles. "Good luck."

"Bye," breathed Jasper, and Crimson let go. His hand tingled where he'd touched him.

Through the open door, an auctioneer cried, "SOLD!"

Crimson stalked over to Shane. "Give me my shit."

Shane had his jacket draped over his arm. He held it out to him and Crimson snatched it away with a growl. Shane barely seemed to notice. He took out his wallet and removed a small business card. "Go to this address; take the elevator down to the basement. I'll let Rick know you're on yer way. And don't be loiterin' around here tryin' t'cause trouble. You don't make it there in the next twenty minutes, he'll let the vampire drop anyhow."

"It's on the other side of the city," said Crimson.

"Guess ya better run fast, huh?"

Crimson looked fleetingly at Jasper.

"Go," said Jasper. This whole situation was bad enough without the risk of it having all been for naught. Of course, if Crimson made it in time or if he didn't, Jasper supposed he would never know. Ripping the card out of Shane's hand, Crimson threw the jacket on and spun away, gone from the room almost more quickly than the eye could follow at close range.

When he was gone, Shane took out his cell phone and sent a quick text message. As he was putting the phone back in his pocket, the voice of the auctioneer called for lot 116. "That's us," said Shane. He twirled a pair of handcuffs out of his pocket and, keeping Crimson's gun aimed carefully at Jasper, used the barrel to make a little "turn around" gesture. "Hands behind your back."

Jasper was liking his odds less and less, but with the vampire and the empath on either side of him, and with Shane pointing a gun right at his head, he didn't really see a whole lot of other options. He hesitated, still.

"You'll be worth a lot less with a couple'a bullets in you, but I reckon I could still make a mint."

That decided him. He put his hands behind his back, and Shane tossed the cuffs to Ralphy. He snapped one to his wrist, strung the chain and cuff through his belt, and then snapped the other into place. He gave him one last quick pat down, then nodded to Shane, who looped an arm through Jasper's and grinned.

"Showtime."

Jasper thought about running but didn't think he'd get very far surrounded by so many demons and being unarmed and in cuffs on top of that. He had to hope for another, better opportunity later. If he didn't have hope, he wouldn't be able to walk through the theater doors and onto the block. If he didn't hope, he would only despair, and he would not let the incubus see him scared.

He wasn't prepared to see the theater. He was sure that under much different circumstances he might have thought the place to be beautiful. The high golden dome of the ceiling did not give away in any way the fact that the theater was underground, nor did the balconies draped in red and gold fixtures. All the seats looked toward a wide stage of highly polished dark wood, dressed on either side with lush curtains in a red so deep and dark they looked black. It was a place more than suited for *Macbeth* or *Hamlet*, but that was not its purpose this evening.

Most of the dark-upholstered chairs were filled, especially those nearer to the stage, with many manner of demons. The twisting in his stomach was almost unbearable, and he had to fight hard to keep himself from doubling over in pain or throwing up. Bodies turned to watch them come down the aisle, and Jasper fixed his eyes on one particular fold in the dark red curtains, willing his features into a look of what he hoped was passive indifference, or at least an expression that did not betray the terror he tasted in the back of his throat. He'd think of some way out of this. Crimson said he would find him.

Curious chittering followed them as he climbed the short set of stairs to the stage with numb legs. Shane steered him to the middle, turning him to face the crowd, and Jasper jerked his arm out of his grip. Now facing the crowd, it was harder to ignore. Jasper let himself look at them for a moment, his hands balled into tight fists behind his back, nails digging into his palms. They were a mix of human looking and demonic, some dressed smartly in expensive business wear, others looking ratty in aged robes. He caught the eye of a tall man in white snakeskin, a baby dragon cradled in his arms like a cat, and looked immediately away, up towards the domed ceiling.

"Ladies and gentlemen," Shane's voice rang out from beside him, his twang more polished than usual, "people of varying degrees of gender or lack thereof, my name is Shane Robinson, and I have a treat for you. This gorgeous specimen beside me is one of a kind. A half white wraith, from off world. He is immune to most, if not all, demon persuasions, from vampire hypnosis to werespider pheromones to incubus venom."

Shane's voice carried on, announcing his superior strength and speed. Jasper tried not to listen to him. His eyes had found, in the high hidden corners of the room, golden statues of child-sized cherubs. And then he noticed the fangs and the wings that he had at first thought were feathered but were actually leathery and sharp at the points. Fucking demons.

Shane smacked his arm, drawing his attention. "Show 'em the eyes."

Jasper glanced back at the crowd and then away again. "I can't just make it happen," he explained tightly. "I can't control it."

"Alright," Shane said and then stepped in front of Jasper and slapped him hard across his face. He hadn't been expecting it, and the force jerked his head to one side. At first all he felt was the burning sting Shane's hand had left behind, but after his brain caught up to what had happened, he felt something else: pissed. His arms strained against the cuffs and he all but growled at him as Shane took several steps backwards, out of range. Any satisfaction of seeing the incubus scared quickly evaporated when he turned back to the audience with a gesture. "See? It happens whenever he gets upset, and good news for his new master, he's very *sensitive*. I open the bidding at five million."

Jasper wanted to laugh at the number, but the reality of the truth in front of him kept him sober and queasy. Several of the demons and spellcasters began throwing out bids, the numbers steadily growing higher. Beside him, Shane smiled to himself, pleased as punch, and rolled his hand in a "hurry-up" motion. Magical items popped up beside the numbers. Persian flying carpets. Cloaks of invisibility. Magical gemstones and ancient amulets of protection. How on earth Shane could keep track of them was impossible to imagine.

Jasper became increasingly unsure whether or not his legs would keep holding him up. His gaze cast around again, looking for an escape route. The aisle was too long and narrow, the audience too numerous to be realistic. Off to the left side of the stage stood auctioneers and hotel staff, and on the other, Shane's hangers-on. There were only two of them, the vampire and the empath. Jasper wondered wildly if he'd be able to get by them, handcuffed and unarmed. He strained his arms again, feeling the cuffs dig into his wrists.

A deep, booming voice cut through his panic. Up until this point he was sure its owner hadn't spoken, and now that they had, the crowd grew quiet, some of them turning in their seats to look at the man it belonged to while others kept their gaze pointedly away.

Jasper found him easily enough, sitting in the middle distance and off to one side. He was a large man, fitted for his thunderous voice; though Jasper could not tell how tall he was sitting down, he thought he would be taller even than Crimson. His shoulders seemed impossibly wide, his arms as thick as tree trunks, wrapped in a dark silk suit just a few shades darker than his deep brown skin. His yellow eyes stood out, cutting easily to Jasper. They were slitted like a cat's, predatory and hungry. Other men with similar complexions and eyes sat around him, but even at a glance they were small and unimportant next to him. He radiated power.

Shane waited a short moment, perhaps hoping someone would outbid the cat-eyed demon, and then clapped his hands together once when it became obvious no one would. The ringing in Jasper's ears prevented him from hearing what Shane said (everything sounded and felt very far away), but it was obvious the auction was over. Shane grabbed his arm and pulled him off to the side of the stage where his lackeys were hanging about. The man who had bought him stood up, straightened his suit, and started towards them.

"Look alive, bright eyes," said Shane, tapping the same cheek he had slapped. "We just made a helluva deal." Laughter was bubbling within his voice, and his eyes sparkled with a joyous light.

"Touch me again and I'll rip your throat out." Jasper tried to sound as vicious as Crimson could but didn't quite get there. The laughter that had been growing in Shane burst out. Jasper pulled so hard against his cuffs that he felt blood begin to drip down his wrist.

"Let us get this out of the way." The voice was even deeper when it rang out directly behind Jasper, shaking in his chest. He jumped at the sound, turning quickly so that his back wasn't facing him. Up close, the demon was even larger than anticipated. If he wanted to, he could crush Jasper's head between his massive hands with ease. His yellow eyes looked over Jasper quickly and with satisfaction, and then went to Shane.

He snapped his fingers, and one of the other men, this one with golden-green cat eyes, stepped forward with a large briefcase and handed it to Shane's vampire companion. The vampire opened it and flipped through the bundles of cash before nodding to Shane and snapping it shut. A different cat-eyed demon and a second case, this one larger and boxier, made of light brown leather worn around the edges. Shane was impatient as the demon dug around inside it and began removing items: a necklace made of delicate gold chain link, several canisters covered in intricate runes, a small silver-backed hand mirror. There was more in the case, much more than its size would suggest.

After all the items were bundled and in Shane's empath's arms, the incubus took the tiny handcuff key and tried to hand it to the large demon. One of his lackeys took it instead, careful not to touch his skin to Shane's.

"Pleasure doin' business with you, Mr. Folami." Neither offered their hands to shake. He nodded to the vampire, who passed over another small box. "Personal effects come with the purchase. Think that makes us about square. Hate to take the money and run, but we gotta jet." He turned his attention to Jasper, and although Jazz would like nothing more than to slam Shane's head onto the floor until it was nothing but a puddle of shattered bone and brain matter, he found he didn't want him to go, didn't want him to leave him with the cat demon Folami and his crew. "Jazzy," said Shane, almost tenderly. He grinned, slapping his shoulder. "Good luck."

Jasper wasn't gifted at reading magic levels, but he still felt the wave of power come off Folami, hot and dry like burning electricity. "Do not touch my property, Mr. Robinson."

Shane flinched. "Right. Sorry." Without any more quips, Shane nodded to his companions and then to Folami and then was gone, taking his winnings with him.

A warm hand wrapped around his upper arm, enveloping most of his arm between the elbow and shoulder. Despite his size, Folami moved quickly and quietly. Jasper tried to step back and jerk his arm out of his grasp, but the demon held him firmly. "Do not be afraid," said the demon. "I will not harm you."

A bright surge of energy flowed through him, and Jasper managed to break from his hold. "Stay away from me."

Folami smiled like one might smile at a disobedient puppy. He clicked his tongue and two of his goons stepped forward to grapple Jasper's shoulders. It was hard to fight back with his hands behind his back. Jasper strained his arms and felt, along with the blood falling fresh from the wounds, a slight give in the chain. If he could just get his hands free…

Folami covered the short distance between them effortlessly and raised his massive hand to Jasper's face, brushing his temple. His pointed black nails tickled his face, and he felt a wave of magic flow through him. "Rest," purred Folami, and Jasper couldn't fight it. His body slumped, suddenly heavy. Darkness rushed up to meet him and there was no more.

Chapter Twenty-Five

—

Here's Lookin' at You, Kid

The office building Shane directed him to was all the way in the East Village. Crimson could not run as fast as a car at top speed, but in Manhattan he would have considered himself lucky to get a car up over forty miles per hour, and even at that he'd risk killing a pedestrian or two. It would be more expedient to cut out the roads entirely and go on foot. There was no time for him to consider other options. He scaled the nearest building in leaps and bounds and then ran over the rooftops at a dead sprint.

He had known this city for hundreds of years, watched as it had grown from a tiny little settlement on the banks of the Hudson River to a gargantuan urban sprawl. The buildings just kept getting taller and taller, and the population just kept swelling, like a balloon about to burst. There were so many people, in fact, that any one person amongst them became invisible—a nondescript tree in a forest, a stone amid a pile of rocks, a blade of grass in a pasture. There were probably thousands of eyes staring out windows, looking right at him, but at such a height and distance, and in the dark, he appeared no more conspicuous than a small spider crawling along at the top of a shelf.

He tried not to think of Jasper, his entire focus on hitting the marks at the end of his jumps, on getting to the East Village, on finding Alcander. One disaster at a time, as his sire, Apocalypse, would have said.

When he passed the Empire State Building, he realized Alcander would not be capable of making the mad dash back alongside him.

That was no good. He needed him. Maybe not *with* him, but certainly in range of easy contact.

Not breaking stride, he juggled out his cell phone. Then he realized he did not know Max's number from memory, nor did it appear to be in his contacts. Swearing, he tried one of Alcander's phones, then another, then another. *Finally*, Max's voice, sounding groggy and a bit timid, came on the line.

"Crimson?"

"Took you long enough," snapped Crimson. The building in front of him was much too tall for him to leap to the peak of it, so he jumped for the ledge instead. Wedging the phone between his shoulder and his ear so that he could use both hands to scale the facade of the skyscraper, he said, "I need you to go to the Estate center in the East Village. Quick as you can."

"I don't know where that is," said Max, and Crimson had to bite his tongue to keep from blowing up on him. The vampire's familiar was less than useless, but it wasn't his fault, and it was difficult to be angry with someone so eager to please.

"I'll give you directions. Write them down." The climb took him to the top of the skyline. The wind was stronger here, ice cold even in the early autumn, and tearing at the hem of his jacket as if it would like nothing better than to send him catapulting down to the blinking lights of traffic below.

"It's kinda hard to hear you. Are you in a tunnel or…?"

"Shut the fuck up and *focus*!"

"Sorry," said Max, his voice small.

Crimson heard him rummaging around, looking for paper and a pen. He kept moving. The gaps between buildings were fairly narrow, and where they were not, he took running leaps towards rooftops situated lower than the peaks. In his youth, he had dropped himself from great distances in failed suicide attempt after failed suicide attempt, and he knew a fall from such a distance might not kill him, but it would shatter every bone in his body, burst blood through his insulated skin, and damage his brain badly enough that, even after healing, he'd probably lose a few memories. It would certainly spell the end for both Jasper and Alcander.

"Alright, where's the East Village?"

Crimson recited the street names as he climbed down the building, pausing only to take the last five stories at a jump. He landed in an alley just across the way from the building in question. Crossing the street at a run, he chanced a glance at the clock on his phone screen. He had less than a minute, though he hoped Shane was exaggerating. Surely, he wouldn't put him through all of this just to kill Alcander. If not out of any sense of decency, out of an instinct for survival.

Several faces turned towards him when he came bursting in through the double doors. He had never been in this building and he had no idea what the purpose of it was. Modern humans seemed to spend a vast amount of their time standing in lines, and the ones inside the building were no different. When they saw he wasn't brandishing a gun or wildly screaming threats about shooting the place up, they all returned their attention to whatever it was they were doing: their cell phones, crosswords, playlists, whatever. Crimson veered past them.

The vents overhead pumped out an oversweet "Hawaiian Breeze" scent, reminding him of every single one of the hundreds of hotels he'd been in, in this century. Here, as there, the smell of industrial-strength cleaner underneath burned his sinuses and stung his eyes.

"What's the address?" asked Max.

Jabbing the DOWN button on the elevator, Crimson took the small white card from his lapel and read the shiny golden print out loud. The doors opened to reveal a smattering of people, most of whom exited immediately, but one of whom took her dear, sweet time, texting on her cell phone as she lingered in the door. Crimson shouldered into her pointedly, and she turned to say something to him, an angry expression on her face. Then she saw his eyes, and her face changed. She took a step back. The doors closed.

"I'm on my way," said Max.

Crimson, his chest too tight to make words, said nothing.

The lift stopped, and for a hysterical moment of absolute panic, he thought it was stuck. But that was nothing new. He always thought that.

Then the doors whooshed open (just as they always did) with a soft ping. The basement was dimly lit, with exposed piping on the ceiling and a lane of hot water heaters along the wall. Alcander's scent was here, soft and clean, surprisingly warm for a vampire.

Snapping the cell phone shut, he followed the trail through the darkness. On his way he picked up a stray hammer but set it down in favor of a rusty crowbar resting alongside the wall, like it was waiting just for him.

He found Alcander in the next room.

He was not, as Shane promised, suspended over a vat of holy water. He was locked in a small steel cage that probably once functioned as a cash office or vault. A burly man in a pin-striped suit was standing beside him, smoking a cigarette as he taunted the vampire with the muzzle of his gun.

Shane had not given him the revolver back, and the majority of his knives were also missing. The revolver, a vintage Peacemaker, one of only a handful still in working order, had been a gift from Nightwind. Sentimentality aside, the cheap pistol in the large vampire's hand would work just as well. Holding the crowbar low at his side, he started towards him.

Crimson was almost on top of the other before he noticed him. It was not his soft steps that gave him away, but the slight flickering and widening of Alcander's eyes.

"You're late," said the vampire. He saw the crowbar a split second later and flashed his fangs with hints of amusement. "I hope you're not planning on trying any—" In a single, hard upswing, the crowbar caught his jaw. The steel cage rattled as his back struck it. He started to raise the gun, and Crimson brought the bar back down across his knuckles with a crack almost as loud as a gunshot.

The pistol hit the cement with a definitive clatter.

"Holy shit, man." The flesh on his split knuckles stitched itself back together as if under the needle of an invisible thread. "Take it easy. I'm gonna give you the vampire, just—"

Crimson struck him with the crowbar again, shearing away his words mid-sentence. The curved tip tore away a sizable chunk of his face, as well as the better half of his nose. The vampire (Rick, he thought Shane called him, but it hardly mattered now) grabbed the bar with both hands and a strangled cry as the werespider came in for another swing, and Crimson took the opening to kick him squarely in the groin. He went down to his knees with a wheezed swear.

Crimson took two quick but steady steps to the side of him, lined up the bent end with the back of his head, then cocked the bar up over his shoulder like a batter up to swing. He swept the crowbar in an arc, throwing all of his weight and supernatural strength behind it. There was a sickly, wet-sounding CRUNCH and a brief jarring halt as the prongs stuck at the base of the vampire's skull. It only lasted for the split second it took for the brainstem to break and the vertebrae to fracture. Stepping through the cloud of ash as it settled to the floor, he picked up the pistol and holstered it where the Peacemaker should have been, then wedged the tooth of the crowbar into the steel door seam and wrenched.

The lock burst away. The hinges screamed. The uppermost one popped loose and dropped the door crookedly to its side as it yawned open.

On the other side, Alcander stood with his hands fisted at his sides, fangs bared. "What are you doing here? Where's Jasper?"

"You're welcome," said Crimson, dropping the crowbar on the floor, turning right around, and stalking back the way he had come. The vampire scurried to catch up with him, bitching the entire way.

"You didn't *actually* let him go with Shane, did you? Are you *insane?*"

"Well, maybe if *somebody*—" he threw a withering look over his shoulder "—could stay out of trouble for five fucking seconds, it wouldn't have been an issue." He jammed at the UP button several times, as if this would somehow make the elevator move faster. It didn't, of course, but dumb luck brought it down quicker than it had when he was waiting for it to come up.

"He was going to kill Max," said Alcander.

"Great, so you sacrifice yourself for Max. Jasper sacrifices himself for you. And now I get to be the one who *actually dies* trying to clean up the *massive mess* created by *your* bleeding hearts."

This put a stop to the bitching. They both stepped into the lift.

Alcander looked like a puppy whose owner had just dumped him at the pound. Crimson wished he hadn't been so mean about it. It wasn't Alcander's fault any more than it was Max's fault or Jasper's. *He* was the one who kept letting Shane back into his life and, of all of them, *he* was the one who should have known better.

Yet it was Alcander who apologized. "Crimson, I'm sorry. I did not know he was after Jasper. I thought he was just trying to con me out of money or get me to help him with some idiotic scheme. If I had known his plan would bring harm to either of you—"

"Yeah," interrupted Crimson. "I know. Me too." The doors opened, and Crimson swept through the lobby, straight out the door, with Alcander following him, having to take two hurried steps for his every one stride. "It's already done. Forget about it. All that matters now is getting him back." That scenario posed its own problems, the sheer multitude of which might have been enough to sway a less single-minded man towards despair, but with the two halves of his whole united to the purpose, quitting never crossed his mind.

"Max is gonna pick you up. You got some way of tracing Jazz?" He could try to follow his trail. Even in a city as large as this one, Jasper's scent was unique enough that he could probably do so for many miles if he stayed on foot, or even if the window of whatever transport he was in was left open, but failing those two scenarios, he needed a backup plan.

"I can trace both of your cell phones," said Alcander. "But if it is not on him—"

"Is that the best idea you have?" Crimson interrupted.

"In this moment? Yes."

"Okay," said Crimson. "Do that. Unless you think of something better. Then do *that* instead." He didn't wait around for the vampire to argue with him. If he could make it back to the hotel before Jasper's buyer left the property, he could follow them that way. And if he made it back to the hotel, only to find that the half-blood's buyer had butchered him up for pieces, and all hope of rescue was already long gone?

Well...

It still ended one of two ways: (a) with a pile of their bodies, or (b) with a pile of *most* of their bodies, plus his own.

With the tips of his fangs pressing through the roof of his mouth, and the bitter taste of venom on his tongue, he ran back in the direction he had come. From there on, he didn't think about Alcander or Max or about the danger that lay ahead of him. His entire focus was on hitting the marks at the end of his jumps, on getting to the Onyx Eclipse, on finding Jasper.

One disaster at a time.

#

Crimson made it back to the hotel in good time. After a brief, mostly verbal, altercation with the doorman, he told the guy he knew Morgaine Onyx and was let in.

Morgaine, resplendent in a long flowing purple gown patterned and enchanted to look like a starry view of the night sky, was in the lower lobby. The polished ivory of her skull mask looked sharp against her dark skin. Even all the way over at the elevator, he smelled the blood mixed into her lipstick and nail polish.

"Where were you thirty minutes ago when I actually needed you?" hissed Crimson as he cut across the room, heedless of the two zombified bodyguards who came galloping after him like a pair of clumsy puppets. Morgaine shooed them away as they grabbed for his arms.

"Crimson darling, did you come for the auction? If so, I'm afraid you're rather late. We're at the tail end now."

"No, Morg. I didn't come here to join your rich asshole club. Have you seen Jasper?"

"Jasper?" repeated the woman, as if tasting the name for the first time. "Which one is he?"

"He was in the Summerlands with me," explained Crimson, some of the venom going out of his voice. She was a very busy lady, and he should not have expected her to remember. "He was there when you introduced me to your husband." If you could call him that. The patchwork man was not so much a husband as a vessel, and the thing inside him, Crimson was certain, was not in this plane of existence by choice. "Little shorter than me. Curly hair, beautiful green eyes, lips that practically beg ya to—" He cut himself off. "He looks around the age I look."

Morgaine's eyes lit up. "Oh yes. I remember. He thought the hallucinistem was a cigarette."

"Yes. Him." It seemed so long ago now, in that strange, uneasy time before the Hunter burrowed fully into his heart. Three months was too short a time to give a name to the feeling, yet he had felt it so many times before, in so many ways, all the same, all different. He knew exactly what it was. "Did you see him?"

Morgaine's expression changed from one of curious delight to leery uncertainty. "But... if that was him, then..." Her voice trailed off. "Oh, you poor thing, if I had known that was him... or if you had come a little earlier..."

He bristled. "Don't play games, Morg. Didja see him or not?"

"Yes," said Morgaine. "Now that you mention it, I did. He was up on the block thirty, maybe forty minutes ago. He went for a very high price. I didn't know he had been stolen from you or I would have stopped the whole affair... Or at the very least offered you a cut."

Crimson had to focus to control every muscle in his face just to keep from cringing. "Who bought him?"

Morgaine held a finger against her lips in a shushing gesture, her heavily makeuped blue eyes sparkling from the hollows of the skull's gaze. "You know we have rules about such things."

"I also know that you owe me a favor." He had won it in a poker game of all things. The blood mage had also tossed her firstborn child into the pot, but the joke was on everyone else at the table, seeing as she hated children and never had any. That was more a relief than anything—he couldn't take care of himself, let alone a child. "I think I'll be collecting that now."

Morgaine scoffed. "You've been dangling that over my head for two hundred years. I would be relieved to have it gone. So go ahead, ask away."

Crimson paused.

Knowing the name of the demon who had taken Jasper would do him no good. He needed to buy more time for Alcander to get to a computer, and for him to close the gap between them and him. The only good thing about Max was that he didn't drive with the caution his age would suggest. He was probably already to Alcander by now; hopefully he'd had enough common sense to bring the vampire's laptop with him. "I need a traffic jam."

"That's easy enough," said Morgaine loftily. "Where at?"

Crimson turned the question over in his head, then said grimly, "Everywhere."

#

When Crimson left the Onyx, Alcander still had not called him. The auction had come to a close, and several of the bidders were letting out at the same time as he. Most of them headed for the hotel's parking garage, so Crimson went along with them, sniffing and tasting the air.

Jasper had been here. The scent of his blood was very faint, but there was enough of it to let him know that he *had* bled; whether because he had been harmed intentionally, or because he had left it as a deliberate lead, Crimson couldn't guess and didn't try.

The trail ended practically before it had begun, on the first level of the parking garage, near the front. There were no indicators as to where he had gone from there. He tried to inquire amongst the dissipating flow of demons and spellcasters, but most of them shied away or outright ignored him when they found out which of the evening's collectibles he was after.

That did not bode well.

The only one who told him anything useful was a friendly, fox-faced anthromorph, whose growly-yipping dialect was so thick Crimson could barely understand him. In bits and pieces, he gathered that the demon's name was Folami, that he was a very wealthy collector of rare specimens, and that he had left well before the end of the auction, in a big black car. He also kept howling a word that might have been translated as "magic" but could have also been "elephant." Crimson decided it was probably "magic," said his thanks, went back outside, and climbed as high as he could to get a better sense of the air.

His cell phone rang.

"Gods! You took forever!" Below, there was a series of squalling brakes and clashing metal. Still holding the cell phone, he jogged to the edge of the rooftop. The horns intermixed with the shouts of angry motorists, soon joined by the wail of sirens, both of the police and ambulatory variety.

He could barely hear himself think over the racket. He looked along the road. Green lights twinkled as far as even his eyes could see. The windows of the Onyx were likewise glowing green, though outside the glamor, he supposed they didn't appear so. He couldn't imagine the sort of energy it would take to cast even a small illusion over every streetlight in New York. Morgaine must have had the entire staff of the hotel helping her, their blood aiding her magic. She would not be able to maintain it for long.

"Where is he?"

"They are on their way to the Washington Bridge."

Crimson looked out across the sea of stalled traffic. It was not so far as a demon ran. "Got it," said Crimson. "Stay on the line. Tell me when I'm getting close."

#

Alcander kept him up to date on the car's slow progress. If it were not for the stalled traffic, Crimson knew he would have lost it by now. Leaping across buildings and over streets, he raced towards them, closing the distance between them with ease. They would not get away. Crimson wouldn't let them.

He saw the car, a large black tank of a vehicle, working its laborious way through the traffic as it began to diverge around the scene of the fender bender currently in the middle of the intersection. The police had not yet arrived at this location, not that it would have mattered to Crimson if they had.

The only reason he didn't blow out the windows of the car right away was because they were of the blackout variety, and his vantage point did not allow him to see which part of the car Jasper was in. He could have been in the front seat or the back, or unconscious in the trunk for all he knew, and he didn't want to risk hitting him.

So he watched.

And waited.

The car made it through the intersection and took a left-hand turn onto a less congested road. He cut across the corner of the building and stopped. Now he saw that there were two cars, identical to one another in every way, excusing the license plates. The second was catching up to the first, which slowed down to let it.

He jumped down to a lower building, following along at the side of the vehicles, then sprang out onto a fire escape that hung almost directly over their path. It would be safer for him to follow them out of the city, where an altercation could be had without any prying eyes, but he didn't know what sort of magic this Folami guy was packing, and he did not want to run to a location where the spellcaster would feel bold enough to start uprooting trees and hurling them at his head.

He waited until the first car passed near his perch, then jackknifed over the railing, and dropped feet first towards the roof.

The impact rattled up through the soles of his boots, but his bones held strong. The body of the vehicle was less fortunate, compacting below him with a crackling CRUNCH. The driver threw on the brakes. Crimson braced himself to keep from rolling down onto the hood.

The door on the passenger's side flung open, and a lanky man with surprised, catlike eyes poked his head out. Crimson, already standing, slammed the toe of his boot into his nose, sending him sprawling back into the gutter. He hopped down and turned to point the gun through the open door. The driver (a human from the look and scent of him) half-raised his hands. Crimson's gaze darted over him to the back seat, where he found the other three passengers already clamoring to get out of the car. None of them were Jasper.

He heard a squeal of tires, and from the corner of his eye saw the second car go tearing past them, shearing off the side mirrors of both vehicles, and taking the paint off more than one of the cars in the other lane.

Bad guess.

He lowered the gun and started to run after the second car, but the whizz of a bullet drew his attention back to the first. He hit the ground to the screams of several pedestrians and rose to them scattering away as he sprang back up and returned fire.

The one who had fired at him never stood a chance. The bullet struck him between the eyes. He staggered with his hand clapped stupidly to his bleeding forehead, but this was only reflex. The better portion of his brains had splattered out the back of his skull, all over the pavement behind him. His two comrades sensibly dove behind the rear of the vehicle, and the fatally wounded demon crumpled to the ground. As this happened, the driver lunged out of his seat and went running into the throng of fleeing pedestrians, and the two remaining demons opened fire.

Familiars, thought the Spider gratingly as he danced around the flying bullets, avoiding them by small margins. At least he wouldn't have to waste a shot on him.

He dipped low, aimed underneath the car, and squeezed the trigger. One of the demons, now shy a shin, dropped with a yowl. His face appeared underneath the car, twisted in agony. Crimson's next shot silenced him completely. The other tried to creep around to the side and catch him from behind, but Crimson went straight after him, weaving to draw his fire, then feinting to race up right beside him.

He slammed into him hard enough to throw him from his feet, pinned his chest under his foot, and in a fit of bloodthirsty rage, unloaded what was left in the gun into his face.

The humans were in sheer panic now, the cars ahead of him vacant of their passengers, the street quickly clear. Crimson picked up the fallen guns, holstered the two that still had ammunition, and scavenged two extra clips and a long curved blade from the bodies. He could smell Jasper's scent on them, lingering in their oily odor like a ray of sunshine in the dark.

Behind him, he heard the rumble of an engine.

For a moment, he simply stood, watching curiously as the motorcyclist, obviously unaware of the danger, wove his way through the stopped lines of traffic. With his visor down and with Crimson standing in the way, it was probably safe to say that he did not see the three bodies sprawled out on the pavement. Or, if he did, he likely thought it some manner of accident, the likes of which needed observing. Humans, Crimson knew, loved to come and gawk at accidents. He quickly holstered both guns, adjusting the jacket to cover them, and forced himself to be still.

When the man drew close, he swerved to a stop and popped open his visor. He did, indeed, have the face of a man who was here to gawk. "Holy shit, what happened?"

Crimson seized the front of his shirt and jerked him off the bike. He hit the asphalt with a grunt. "Sorry, man," said the werespider, swinging a leg over the seat. "I gotta run." Lining the tire up with the yellow line, he twisted the throttle. The front end rose slightly at the sudden influx of speed, but he threw his weight forward, and the bike settled back onto the yellow line, the rumble of the engine underneath him.

Tracking a vehicle by scent was largely unreliable, but his sense of smell was better than a canine's, and at close range, the drip from the car's air-conditioning unit (carrying with it all the air molecules, skin cells, and other assorted particles collected from the cabin) was enough to give him a pretty good idea. The scratched paint and damaged sidewalks where the vehicle had forced its way around stopped traffic sufficed as a trail where the scent did not.

He saw the taillights of the black car but didn't slow or turn aside. Rather, he got the motorcycle going as fast as it possibly could, and drove it straight into the back. As the handlebars crunched into the taillights, he let go of the grips and sprang from the footrests. This vaulted him over the vehicle. He drew both guns, turned into his fall, and fired at the only place where he was sure Jasper would not be— through the windshield, into the driver's seat.

He hit the hood, bouncing once, and rolled quickly aside, out of the way of the tires as the vehicle fishtailed. The front end slammed into a lamppost, sending it careening over to smash through the window of a closed coffee shop. Crimson pushed himself up off the asphalt and, still gripping a pistol in either hand, marched towards the car.

He was over halfway there when a sudden force blew outwards from the vehicle, like the heat of an explosion without the boom. He was thrown back to the ground, more in surprise than anything, and was back on his feet before he knew it. A large figure was climbing out of the back seat of the car. Crimson, who was taller than most, wasn't used to having to look *up* at anyone, but this creature was a giant of a man. He was most of the way to eight feet and very wide at the shoulders, all muscle. As he strode towards him, his eyes shone with reflected yellow light, the pupils thin slits. Elongated fangs showed in his snarling mouth, and black claws grew from the tips of his hands, which turned, twisting all the way around until they were backwards.

Crimson, who had seen nearly everything there was to see in his long life, had known creatures like this before, though only in the East. The name swam around in a sea of half-remembered information.

Rakshasa.

"*Spider*," Folami roared. The word was a curse and a spell all in one. Crimson felt the hairs on his arms and on the back of his neck stand on end, and moved out of the way of the concentrated blast just in time, firing half a dozen shots from his pistols. The bullets bounced off the rakshasa's chest like flicked pebbles.

Crimson swore.

For the most part, the rakshasa were a fairly harmless species, different from mortals of the human variety in ways that were mainly cosmetic. But every once in a great while, just like humans, they were born with inherent magical capabilities.

A second burst came in his direction. A manhole cover an inch to his right burst from the ground, flung away by the blast. It crashed into a taxi; the rounded edge sank through the metal like a blade. Crimson took cover behind a car whose engine was still running, though its owner was long gone.

"Look, man, I'll cut you a deal." The magically afflicted were rare. Amongst their own people, they were often viewed as religious figures—demigods of sorts. And for good reason, they were very difficult to kill. He couldn't even remember how one went about doing so. Was it iron? Did you have to have a pure heart or something (that would put him out of the running)? Or was that just folklore?

It would be better if he could avoid the situation entirely.

"You give me back my hybrid, I'll forget this ever happened!"

The car trembled and began to slide. It struck another car with the sound of crumpling metal, then threw itself in reverse, the tail end targeted in his direction. Crimson jumped onto the trunk, then the roof, but that posed its own problems, as now he was an open target, and Folami took another shot of magical energy. This one struck him in the chest, cracking two ribs, lifting him from his feet, and throwing him back through the storefront behind him.

Burglar alarms wailed as glass shattered. He slammed into a showcase filled with silver and gold chains and rings. The leather jacket protected him from the worst of it, though he felt the sizzle on the back of his hand and surged quickly free with a hiss of pain. "Alright, asshole! You wanna do this the hard way? I'm game."

He tore out of the shop, running and jumping and weaving between and over blasts as they came. Folami might have been a powerful magician, but the werespider's reflexes were slightly sharper, and the flourishes of the rakshasa's casting gave him away.

He slammed into the other demon the same way he had slammed into his minion up the road, trying to throw him from his feet, but Folami only staggered a step back, then seized his throat with a hand that felt more like a shackle. Sharp, hard claws bit through the skin on the nape of the werespider's neck. Blood trickled down his back.

Folami hoisted him up to eye level, fangs bared. "I will turn you inside out, spider." He lifted his other hand, fingers curled, his wrist spinning slowly.

Crimson spit venom in his face, hitting him in the eyes, the nose, the corner of his mouth. The feline spit out a hiss, maybe of pain, definitely of disgust, and pawed at the viscous fluid. Gripping his wrist in both hands, the werespider swung his legs up, planted his heels firmly on his chest, and pushed as hard as he could. The claws tore through the back of his neck and the sides of his throat, but the fingers lost their hold, and he fell backward, catching himself on the palm of one hand and flipping himself back onto his feet.

The venom did not have the desired effect. Even a small dose could usually cause temporary paralysis. A large dose was often fatal. But Folami did not fall inert, as Crimson had hoped he might. It seemed to have only affected the area of contact, for no matter how Folami wiped his eyes, the lids would not open entirely. He brought his other hand over his head in an overarching swing, and Crimson, who had just regained his feet, did not have the opportunity to evade. The energy came down in a slash that cut through his jacket, his shirt, and the flesh underneath, tearing a gash from the inside of his shoulder, all the way down his torso, to his hip. Bone showed through muscle. Another rib cracked. This one splintered up into his lung, and he choked on the flavor of his own blood.

The pain was excruciating, but ephemeral.

The blood loss was another matter.

He could hold the spider no longer. Throwing his jacket off, the spider's legs tore out of his spine, ripping through the ruined remains of his shirt. His skin hardened and blacked to the spider's exoskeleton. The fangs pushed themselves through the roof of his mouth and pressed forward, bisecting his lips as his second set of eyes blinked into existence.

Screeching, he sprang at Folami.

\#

Jasper's eyes snapped open, already aglow with white light. He was lying down in the spacious back seat of a very expensive town car. Small lights ran along the ceiling and across the doors, the one opposite him hanging wide open, showing the bizarre dreamscape of the inside of a coffee shop. His ears were ringing—wait, no, that wasn't right, it was a chorus of far-off sirens and alarms rising together into a mess of noise. Jasper sat up and ran a hand over his face. A metal cuff jingled at his wrist, the broken chain rattling. He stared at it, confused, but then the sound of an explosion commanded his attention. He scrambled out of the car and into the coffee shop.

Broken glass and rubble crunched under his feet. The entire front wall was collapsed, which was not unusual when you drove a car through it. Live wires sparked and crackled, hanging from the ceiling like deadly vines.

Through a gap between the crumbled wall and the car, he saw two shapes doing battle out in the street. A titan of a man, very nearly a giant, and a red and black spider, not much smaller than a lion. At first, his mind was too sick and groggy to understand what was happening, then the spider screeched, broken, almost human words mingled in the cry, and everything came rushing back.

"Crimson?" Jasper knew he should not have assumed his demonic form in the middle of the street, right where any and everyone could see him. Ducking under the sparking wires, the broken links around his wrists still rattling, he stepped out onto the sidewalk.

Rows of crookedly stopped cars surrounded the pair of demons. Neither seemed to hear the wail of the sirens, both of them fully consumed in the task of killing one another. Presently, Folami wrenched his arm free of the werespider's grasping appendages and fired a blast of magic that sent the spider cartwheeling back. He slammed into the side of a taxi, breaking the windows and crumpling the metal, then slid down, legs wilting around him. He was back in his human form by the time he hit the street.

Shit.

Jasper reached for his gun, but found the holster hanging empty.

Folami started in the werespider's direction, his steps slow and heavy. His eyes were nearly swollen shut, steps a little unsteady, but he seemed otherwise unharmed. Across from him, Crimson stirred and slowly lifted his chin from his breastbone.

Shit, Jasper thought again. He didn't have a gun or any of his knives. He picked up a sharp, heavy chunk of the broken wall, the closest thing he could find to a weapon, and lobbed it at the back of Folami's head. "Hey!"

It struck him on the crown, the plaster breaking and dusting over his shoulders. It left no mark, but the demon wheeled around with a hiss. "You will return to the vehicle and wait!"

"Jasper, run!" shouted Crimson.

Jasper ignored both of them, selecting another chunk of concrete and pitching it straight at Folami's face. "Why don't you come and make me?" Whatever this thing was, Crimson was obviously having a hell of a time killing it. "Unless you're scared of a half-blood, you—you—" This taunting thing really wasn't his racket.

Crimson cupped his hands to his mouth. "Call him a *pussy*. Get it? Cuz he's a—"

Folami gestured curtly, and the werespider's voice cut out as he was propelled straight upward. He twisted in the air, grasping for something to catch onto, then dropped like a brick, thudding down on the other side of the cab, out of view. Folami pointed back at Jasper. "I am losing patience with you. Do as you are told."

"No," Jasper said stubbornly. He did not see Crimson rise from behind the yellow taxi. If he was hurt, or worse…

Folami strode towards him, giant strides making short work of the distance. Jasper tried not to be frightened, but he was. He just prayed it didn't show. Bending to retrieve another chunk of rubble, he saw the curved metal leg of a table, half-buried, and grabbed that instead, wielding it like a sword. "Leave us the fuck alone," he warned. Folami waved his hand as if shooing away a fly, and the piece of metal started to pull from his hand. Gritting his teeth, eyes burning white, he held tight. "Pussy," he added for good measure.

"You insolent little cur," cursed Folami.

Jasper swung the table leg at him, aiming for his face. Folami caught it, the muscles in his arm straining underneath the silk. He seized the front of Jasper's shirt, claws tearing through the fabric, grazing his skin. His breath was hot, sharpened fangs an inch from his nose.

Jasper slammed his balled fist into Folami's face. The impact rattled through his knuckles; pain exploded in his hand. Folami shoved him, and he went skidding across the tile floor, stopping only when he impacted the counter at the back of the shop.

"Return to the vehicle before you damage yourself further." Jasper was still gripping the table leg. The ears on the sides of Folami's head had grown long and pointed, and they swiveled like radio disks, homing in on the sound of Jasper's breathing. "You are too valuable to be wasted like this."

Jasper pulled himself up using the counter, grabbed hold of the cash register, ripped it free, and winged it at Folami. The demon swatted it right out of the air and advanced on him as Jasper vaulted over the counter and grabbed whatever he could lay a hand on. Various objects—mugs and bottles, shakers and parts of coffee machines—bounced off Folami, clattering to the floor, but he just kept coming. He snatched for his throat, but Jasper took advantage of his impaired eyesight and stepped aside, his fingers only closing on empty air.

"Little hybrid," growled the demon, "you are playing a very dangerous—"

CLANG!

Folami stumbled. He caught himself on the counter, then spun towards what had struck him. There was a second loud *CLANG*, and Folami's spin went further than anticipated, blood bursting from his lips as he cantered several feet to the left and collapsed a table. As he went down, Jasper saw a very surprised-looking Crimson dressed only in his jacket and holding a manhole cover in both hands. "Huh, I didn't know they still made these things outta iron."

Folami surged back up, toweling the blood from his lips. "Spider, I have had about enough of you."

"Oh yeah, I've never heard that before."

The caster flourished towards him, the distance between them too narrow to be avoided, but Crimson planted the circuit of iron on the floor and curled behind it like a shield, and Jasper threw himself to the floor behind the counter.

What few windows remained burst outward in a shower of glass. The mirror above him shattered, raining glittering shards. Rows of ceramic mugs on the shelves exploded. Jasper crawled to the end of the counter, thankful for the leather of his own coat, and peered around it.

Crimson was stubbornly back on his feet, and the blast appeared not to have hit him, though the town car had been repelled back out into the street and the tables and chairs were blown against the walls.

Folami was gone.

Jasper scrambled out from behind the counter and grabbed Crimson's hand, dragging him towards the crumbled wall and snatching up the fallen table leg as he went. "C'mon, we gotta go."

Crimson stumbled after him. "Jazz, wait, you don't understand. It didn't—"

A massive clawed hand seized Jasper's other arm and ripped him away from the werespider, nearly tearing his arm from its socket. He struck the asphalt. Glass tore through his clothes, pierced his skin, and he screamed before he could stop himself. Folami loomed above him, his face a mask of blatant insanity.

"It just knocked him out the window," Crimson murmured.

Thanks for the heads-up, thought Jasper dazedly. He tried to rise, but Folami's booted foot struck him under the ribs, knocking the wind out of him. Coughing, lungs burning, he fell back into the glass and rubble, blinking the dark spots out of his vision.

Overhead was the *whipper whap* of helicopter blades. A bright light burst down on the three of them.

Folami grinned savagely and stomped down between his shoulders, pinning him to the ground, as Crimson stopped short.

"I really should thank you, spider. My amassed wealth has made expanding my collection such a mundane task. The pair of you have made it much more interesting." Overhead, a man was leaning out through the open door of the helicopter, screaming through a megaphone for all of them to remain still. "But now, I am afraid, it is time for us to go." He stepped off Jasper's back, grabbed him by the hair, and raised his open palm towards the helicopter.

"You crazy bastard, don't you dare!" shouted Crimson.

A surge of energy erupted from Folami's palm. Two of the chopper's blades split away. A plume of flame ignited in the cockpit. The helicopter listed then swerved, then spun out and plummeted towards the ground. Folami readjusted his grip around Jasper as he struggled, locked an arm around his throat, and then moved with sudden, deceptive speed.

The helicopter struck the ground behind them, erupting in a burst of fire. Jasper felt the heat even a dozen meters away. His feet tried to find purchase against the ground, but it was too far away, and with

304 JAY WRIGHT & E.M. JEANMOUGIN

the crushing arm latched around his throat, his vision was growing dark.

"Hands in the air!" A row of armed police officers emerged, over the hoods of parked cars, from the alcoves of nearby buildings, wearing riot gear and carrying useless shields. Jasper tried to scream at them to run, but it only choked out as a rasp. The sounds of their gunfire split the air.

Folami made a sweeping gesture, and Jasper watched in horror as the bullets twisted around in midair and flew back in their direction, striking half a dozen of the humans dead in a single gesture.

Folami moved, taking a step up onto the back of a Ford; then his feet suddenly went out from under him. They both slammed down on the roof of the car; Jasper twisted out of the headlock and threw himself to the cement.

Crimson barely looked like a person anymore, flesh charcoaled and oozing with lesions, eyes two fiery pinpricks in a mask of blackened skin and pouring blood. He strained back with Folami's ankle gripped in his hands, only to take a hard kick right in the chin.

Jasper, white eyed and furious, looked around. The tailpipe of the Ford was old and loose in its mount. He seized it with both hands and twisted it free. A rusted section cracked into a splintered tip. He forced himself to his feet, turned the sharp end of the tailpipe between him and the caster, and threw all his weight forward.

There was a sickening, wet squelch. His arms jarred. The metal sank through the demon's torso and struck the carriage of the car behind him. Jasper wrenched it back and forth, skewering his innards as the demon shrieked and flailed wildly at him with both hands, catching him with his claws, gargling and screaming for him to stop. He ripped the pipe out of Folami, cocked it back, and slammed it across his lips instead.

The demon fell aside and started to crawl away. Jasper sent the broken sharp end spiking down into the back of his neck, pressing until the unyielding resistance of the pavement below stopped him.

For a moment, Folami's toes drummed on the ground, muscles twitching. Then he lay still in a widening pool of his own blood. Jasper felt no surge of victory, nor any sense of joy. Then Crimson's fingers were on his wrist, and what he felt was impossible to describe.

Crimson stumbled, and Jasper caught the bulk of his weight, but his own legs felt weak and shaky, and they both ended up going down, almost in slow motion.

"Both of you stay where you are!" a nearby voice warned. Jasper followed the sound of it and saw an officer creeping slowly out from behind a car, gun raised.

"Possums," muttered Crimson, and slumped suddenly lifeless beside him. Jasper had seen this trick enough to recognize it, but not emulate it. Going to his knees, he half-raised his hands as the cop shouted into his radio for backup.

"What the fuck is going on here?" he shouted at Jasper.

"He was trying to kill us," explained Jasper as calmly as he could. "I, uh… don't think you should get any closer."

"Don't threaten me," said the officer. "You say any more creepy shit like that, and I'm gonna put a bullet in you. Can you walk?"

"Yeah," said Jasper, and he was pretty sure that was the truth.

"Then keep your hands up and get over here. Slowly."

Keeping his hands raised, suddenly and painfully aware of every cut and bruise on his body, Jasper got to his feet and walked slowly towards the cop. Their eyes were focused on one another, so the other man didn't see the spider until it surged past Jasper in a blur of black and red. His gun went off twice, directly up into the air. Jasper lowered his hands and walked past the crouching eight-legged horror, trying not to look at the massive fangs as they injected venom into the man's throat, or at the man himself as his innards began to melt, and his body started to deflate inside his uniform, eyes bulging in disbelief.

He just kept on walking until he made it into an alley, where he stood, resting against the wall and breathing deeply to try to clear the panicked sickness in his mind.

Chapter Twenty-Six

—

Gimme Shelter

Jasper was in the alley no more than five minutes when he felt Crimson's fingers on his shoulder. Shakily, he turned to face him. The lesions were gone. The copper color of his skin was now returning, chasing away the charcoaled black like a ripple in a still pond, but many of his wounds were still open, some of them still bleeding. His coat was torn at the shoulder, folded closed over his otherwise bare body. He was basically naked and still a mess of blood and burn and wear, but Jasper hugged him anyway, though quickly and not too tightly.

"I told you not to do anything stupid," Jasper whispered. The relief was enough to catch his breath again.

"I told'ja to run," replied Crimson, squeezing him closer. The cuts on his arms and chest ached, but in that moment, Jasper would not have traded the pain for ecstasy. "Good thing we're both bad listeners, huh?"

"I guess," replied Jasper. He knew he should have been angry at him for having killed the cop, but he couldn't imagine what other choice he had. Just lay there, pretending to be dead while the police arrested Jasper and then hauled him away to the morgue? He would still have had to hunt. The hunting was part of who and what he was, just as it was part of who and what Jasper was. He let go, looking nervously up towards the sky. The police officers would send more helicopters, more men. "We need to hide. Did you find Alcander? Is he—"

"Al traced your cell phone. That's how I found you."

He remembered Shane handing one of Folami's men a box of Jasper's "personal effects." His phone must have been among them, probably as well as his gun, and Crimson's. He wondered if the incubus had done it on purpose. Surely, now he'd had ample time to get as far away as possible, ensuring that Crimson couldn't hunt him down and skin him alive.

"So he's okay?"

"Yeah."

Jasper heaved a relieved sigh. He wanted to say something else, to thank him or... something, but he didn't really know how. He would try later, when time was not so short and words were not so hard. "Alright. Let's get outta here."

#

The city was swarming with police. There were accidents (mostly small ones) on nearly every corner, and Jasper and Crimson, dressed mainly in their own blood, were extremely conspicuous.

They took shelter in a church, which was closed due to the late hour and thankfully did not seem to have a security system. There, they found spare clothing and blankets in a donation bin, as well as water and wine to wash the cuts on Jasper's arms, and an emergency medical kit containing gauze to dress them.

Halfway through this process, Alcander called. They took turns assuring him they were okay, promising him they would find their way home in the morning, swearing they weren't in any sort of danger. By now, Shane would be a thousand miles away, and Folami and every single one of his men were dead. Jasper was a little worried about the incident in the street, but he was sure the Hunters at St. James would already be rushing to cover it up, and Crimson told him the demons had their own division for cover-ups, as did the spellcasters. Since the scuffle between them and Folami touched all three factions, he was sure it would be handled with due haste on all fronts.

Jasper tried to let this comfort him... though he thought of the way Hunters "handled" such things, usually involving the lethal disposal of the parties involved, and was a little worried something more dangerous than human law enforcement officers might soon be out looking for them if they weren't already. He couldn't handle any more fighting tonight, nor any more running. His arms and legs felt like they had been injected with liquid lead, and his emotions were so raw from the extreme roller coaster of fear and panic, rage and horror, heartache and relief, that they seemed to have whittled away into nothingness, leaving him numb and hollow.

Crimson led him up a flight of stairs to a balcony overlooking the pews. The space seemed rarely used, probably reserved for special occasions when the congregation was larger than usual—Christmas and Easter sermons, the occasional End of Times scare. Crimson used spare blankets and clothing to build a makeshift bed in the corner, where the carpet was softest, and the draftiness was minimal. Jasper, exhausted beyond exhaustion, nestled in with him.

All he wanted was sleep, but now that the opportunity was here, he felt like he could hear every siren in New York. The church itself was dead silent apart from the whistle of crisp fall wind through its lofty eaves. Overspill light broke in through the long stained-glass windows. Mostly white. Occasionally red and blue. Pulling a blanket over his head, he rolled to face Crimson. "Are you asleep?"

A sliver of red glinted. "Not now."

"It's too loud in here," whispered Jasper. "Or too quiet. I can't tell which. I don't understand how you can sleep, with your ears and everything."

"Same way I always sleep," said Crimson, both eyes opening now. "Pick a sound; focus on that. It's easier when there's another person. The sound of your heartbeat just sorta blots everything else out."

"Oh," said Jasper. This was new information and connected some of the dots as to why demons probably kept familiars in the first place, but it didn't help him now. "I can't do that."

"I can keep talking," said Crimson, "'til you fall asleep."

"You don't mind?"

"My sire used to say it was all I was good for."

Three months earlier, Jasper would have said that this wasn't far off the mark, but now he disagreed. It occurred to him that Crimson never mentioned his sire. Jasper had never thought to ask. "What was he like?"

"Jazz, we can talk about anything," said Crimson. He sat up a little, propping himself against the wall. "Except him."

Jasper edged into the space he had left, almost but not quite against his hip. "You brought it up."

"Yeah," said Crimson. "I guess I did." His fingers stole down to Jasper's hair, stroking gently through the curls.

Jasper tensed at the touch, suddenly nervous of the werespider's intentions, but when it went no further, he relaxed. When he put the anxiety from his mind, he actually found it quite soothing, the light graze prickling delicately, easing the buildup of tension. He hadn't known the space between his shoulders was so tight until it wasn't.

"But if we talk about Apocalypse, then *I'll* be the one who can't sleep."

"That's your last name," commented Jasper, not a question.

"Yeah, that's sorta how it works. My human name was Zahir. When we're reborn, we change. Not just... physically. Our minds, usually our personalities. So our sires give us new names and we take their first name as our last. Mine wasn't all that creative. Red marks. Red name." He was silent for a long moment, then, "I don't even like red."

Jasper laughed at that, though he didn't mean to. "Sorry," he said quickly. "I, uh... couldn't you just change it?"

Crimson shrugged. "I did, sort of. I mean, it's in English now. But it's, y'know, *my name*. I guess I'm kinda attached to it. Besides, I like the way this one sounds."

"It sounds kind of ridiculous," replied Jasper, breaking this to him as gently as he could.

"Yeah, I know. That's kind of why I like it."

"I like it too," Jasper admitted. The name suited him, and Jasper could no better think of him with a different one than he could imagine him as a human. He looked up at Crimson, just able to make him out in the low lighting, the curve of his high cheekbones, the faint glisten of his burgundy eyes, a shade almost like velvet. His dark hair was still damp, shiny as a raven's feathers, and tousled in the sort of carelessly deliberate way that a human would have needed full hours and plenty of product to achieve.

Jasper thought about how he wanted to run his fingers through the damp ends of Crimson's hair, and about how tired he was, tired physically but also tired of not doing the things he wanted to do. He was tired of being scared, so Jasper touched the werespider's hair, smoothing it gently behind one perfect ear. It left his fingers wet and cold in the cool air of the church and left the rest of him shockingly warm.

Crimson's fingers paused in their own stroking, then moved to trace the curve of Jasper's jaw, sending creeping warmth through his veins. He tilted back Jasper's chin, thumb grazing his lower lip, and leaned closer. Jasper took a short breath in but did not draw away. He looked into Crimson's eyes, trying to tell him what he wanted without words, and Crimson closed the small gap between them, pressing their lips together in a soft, slow kiss.

His lips were even softer than Jasper imagined they would be, and sent a shiver of arousal racing through him, lighting him up from inside. It was like coming alive. Before he knew what he was doing, Jasper wrapped his arms around the back of the werespider's neck, pulling him closer and kissing him back with wild, desperate need.

He'd kissed people before—girls—but it had never been like this. He'd never liked it so much. Dizzy and breathless, Jasper broke their lips apart, panting. Shaking his head lightly, he looked into Crimson's eyes. "Please don't stop."

Crimson's long fingers dug deeper into his curls, pulling him closer, though not, Jasper thought, close enough. "I'm just gettin' started." His hands left his hair, running down his back to wrap around his waist. He hoisted Jasper up and into his lap, the half-blood's legs straddling his, their chests pressed together. Jasper was rock hard, his erection pressing against Crimson's stomach through the borrowed sweatpants, Crimson's own cock against his backside. The werespider brought their mouths back together, more forcefully than before, kissing him until his lungs burned for breath, then rocked Jasper onto his back, his lips going to his throat.

Jasper's knees squeezed around his waist, a little groan escaping him. Crimson gave a small growl, letting his teeth brush against the thin skin above his collarbone. "Gods, Jazz," the demon breathed. The tips of his fingers traced across Jasper's hips, going under his shirt and up his stomach, igniting nerves he never knew he had. "You're so fucking gorgeous."

Jasper was thankful for the dark. Though he knew the other could see as well as he could in the light, he could at least pretend that the high flush of color in his cheeks wasn't visible. Crimson's words seemed to help him find words of his own though, and that was clearly what the other wanted. "Your lips feel amazing," he murmured huskily.

Crimson nipped softly at the lobe of his ear, his fingers easily working the buttons of his shirt open as he rumbled, "Wait until you feel them on your cock."

Jasper's breath caught. He didn't know if he was ready for that. Or for what inevitably came after it, but Crimson was already moving down from his throat, over his pec. His tongue teased his nipple until it was almost as hard as his dick, and Jasper let his head loll back, eyes rolling closed. Relief ached through him, almost like pain, but as pleasure instead. He wanted to give himself to him, wanted to let the demon touch him and kiss him and suck on him and, yes, maybe even fuck him until they were both satisfied, but there was still this feeling of *shouldn't* deep in his stomach. Of *too much* and *too fast*.

Pushing himself up on his elbow, he looked down at the werespider as he trailed kisses over his abs, tongue tracing his navel, fingers slipping between his legs and up his length, massaging him through the fabric, urging him to let go. God, he looked amazing. He felt amazing. Jasper heard himself make a small sound, the like of which he'd never heard himself make—a whimper of lust and, yes, maybe of submission.

Then, as if he could feel Jasper's hesitation, Crimson stopped and looked up at him, eyebrow raised, almost as if to ask permission.

"I, umm…" He was sweaty and shivering, his mind foggy. "I've never really… If maybe we could just…"

"You know it's okay if you don't wanna do it all at once, don't you?" asked Crimson. "You can tell me no. I won't be mad."

"It's just a little fast," said Jasper. "It's not that I don't wanna. I *do*." This fact surprised him, all by itself. He looked away, focusing instead on the rumpled blankets. He nervously smoothed a crease, waiting for the blood to come back to his brain. "I've kind of been through a lot today, and you're, y'know, really important to me, and I don't wanna mess it all up, or, like, go too fast, or—"

Crimson turned his face gently but firmly back in his direction and silenced the explanation with a quick kiss. "Jazz, it's okay. Okay?"

In the barely there light, Jasper saw Crimson looking at him, his eyes so warm and tender that Jasper felt something swell in his chest.

He smiled, feeling almost shy. "Okay." His hands found their way back to Crimson's hair. It really was fantastic hair. "I really like kissing you, though."

Crimson brought their lips together again, soft and slow, like the first. "I've wanted to do it for a while."

"Yeah," agreed Jasper.

They kissed again, and again, the heat returning. Crimson's hands roamed, though they stayed for the most part above the belt, caressing his chest and stomach, running down his arms and shoulders, sending delicious shivers all through his body. Jasper couldn't stop touching him, all the places he'd wanted to before: his hair, his neck, the curve of his collarbone, the hard muscle of his arms. Their hips moved together, the friction driving him so crazy he almost reconsidered his earlier sentiment. But there would be time for all of that later. They were safe and together and they had time.

When the heat between them had tempered a little, Crimson coaxed him down on his stomach to rest. Jasper didn't want to at first, but the werespider rubbed his neck, his shoulders, his back, massaging out the kinks and knots, taking care not to press where he'd been bruised.

He spoke of his cousin Nightwind and the adventures the two of them had shared together—in the blistering hot deserts of Egypt, out on the high seas, in the East and in the West, and everywhere and when in between.

Jasper lay with a winter jacket bundled under his chin, the fever cooling in his flesh as he listened to the soft melodic sound of the demon's voice and let the talented stroke of his fingers carry him away.

Eventually, he slept.

He dreamed of the Summerlands. Of a lilac twilight sky, of an orange tent filled by smoke, of Crimson dancing by a bonfire, and when he held his hand out to Jasper, this time he took it.

Chapter Twenty-Seven

—

Crazy Little Thing Called Love

Jasper woke to a gentle shaking, Crimson's hand on his chest. He didn't know how long they had slept, but he could tell it wasn't nearly long enough. He pried his eyes open, though they were very reluctant to do so. Dim yellow light filled the church, almost hazy with slow dust; through the bars of the balcony he saw the stained-glass mural of the Virgin Mary lit by daylight, and though it was still very quiet, Jasper could tell they were no longer alone.

"What's up?" Jasper asked in a whisper. Crimson didn't look worried, so Jasper wasn't exactly worried either.

Well, for the most part.

"The priest is in," Crimson explained. "We should go."

"Okay." Jasper grabbed the flannel he'd taken from the donation bin from where it had been discarded the night before and pulled it back on, casting Crimson a quick, shy smile before hiding his eyes behind his curls.

They got up and set the blankets on the back pew. Jasper was sure they were quiet as church mice as they crept down the stairs and towards the side door, but when he glanced back at the altar where the priest was sweeping the floor, he was paused, watching them. He saw Jasper seeing him, and nodded, not angry, and Jasper timidly raised a hand in reply before following Crimson out onto the street.

Crimson offered him his hand, and Jasper took it. For the first time he noticed how smooth it was, no fingerprints, the lifelines on his palm barely a shadow. He squeezed it tightly, his smile a little surer of itself, and then, together, they worked their way back towards Alcander's.

The door was open when they got to it, Alcander waiting within the light of the stairs. Jasper was so happy to see him looking unharmed that he did not consider the vampire's aversion to physical contact and wrapped him in a tight hug. He remembered quickly and went to step away, an apology already on his lips, when Al hugged him briefly back.

"I'm really glad you're okay, Al." They'd said as much on the phone the night before, but it felt important to say it again.

"Thanks to you and Crimson."

Jasper thought it was also *because* of him that Al and Max were in danger at all but didn't say so.

"I wish you hadn't been so reckless."

Here Jasper began to protest, but Al cut him off, insisting they come downstairs so he could examine and redress his wounds.

"The official story is that it was an act of terrorism," explained Alcander as he laid a neat, precise row of stitches up a particularly nasty cut on Jasper's forearm.

Jasper had to look away for this. He could handle being cut or stabbed or even shot, but when it came to repairing the damage, the sight of a needle digging under his skin freaked him out.

"You two were all over the news last night." Alcander snipped the end of the thread and wrapped the cut in fresh gauze. "They have been running the clip from right before the helicopter went down nonstop. Somebody—the Hunters I expect, maybe the spellcasters—managed to pull the footage from the street cams before the media could get ahold of it. I got the footage from the jewelry store." He turned Jasper's wrist, examining his hands. They hadn't landed in the glass when he fell, thank God, and the damage there was minimal. Using a cotton swab, Alcander cleaned the small cuts and scratches.

"So they think we're terrorists?" translated Jasper.

"Hmm… No, not exactly. Crimson, please do not touch that." Alcander interrupted himself, and Jasper followed his gaze to the other side of the lab, where Crimson was half an inch away from picking up a beaker of brightly colored fluid. Crimson muttered something under his breath but left it alone.

Alcander's eyes followed him until he was a safe distance away;

then he shook his head and returned to his nitpicking. "Where was I? Oh. To all appearances, Folami was the one who brought down the helicopter. The video makes it look as if he threw something... or perhaps gave some manner of signal to another source. Prior to that, the two of you are seen to be fighting with him. After that, there are no recorded accounts of the incident, only eyewitness testimony."

"Guessin' alotta very forgetful people in that neighborhood," said Crimson. "Can't remember a thing."

Alcander shrugged. "The stories vary a bit, but most of them are somewhat the same. *Suspiciously* the same, in my opinion. The Magicians Guild is really losing their touch."

"Memory alterations?" guessed Jasper. "That must have taken a lot of magic."

"Yes," agreed Alcander. "So must have changing every stoplight in the city. The police were hours sorting out the traffic situation. And, of course, that led to other, smaller incidents. Honestly, so much was going on all at once the media does not really know which story to latch onto."

"Do you think they'll come after us? Not the human police..." Jasper knew he should be concerned about that, but he wasn't. He was trained to hide in plain sight, and he could get away from mortal officers easily enough. "The spellcasters or the Hunters or, uh... other demons?"

"The other werespiders won't be happy if word reaches them," answered Crimson, though he was not the one Jasper had been asking. "But if the spellcasters are keeping word from the humans, and the Hunters are keeping word from everyone else, I dunno how it would. Least not in a way that they could be bothered to drag their lazy asses all the way across the ocean to try to find me." He had run out of small curiosities to stare at in the lab, and since he wasn't allowed to touch any of them (at least not without having Alcander scream at him), he looped around and hopped up on the table behind Jasper, leaning against his back. "The casters'll definitely talk to Morgaine first, and as far as *she* knows, *you* were stolen from *me*. It's a little iffy, on account of the way the laws work—there's different rules, depending which group you're with. And Folami was a demon and a magic user, so that muddles it up worse, but *basically* Folami's the one who fucked up. You fuck with someone else's familiar, they're allowed to fuck you up. That's basic. By the book. Traditional, even."

Jasper bristled a little. Among Hunters "familiar" was a dirty, filthy word. It was almost worse than being called a "demon," and he certainly hoped Crimson didn't think of him that way. At its best, it could be translated to mean "pet," but usually it meant "slave" or sometimes something worse. He had to work to keep his voice even as he pointed out, "I'm not really your familiar though."

Crimson waved it away. "Details. People see what they wanna see, and wanna see what they expect to see. I don't think it'll matter big-picture wise."

"You probably should not have transformed into a spider," said Alcander sternly.

"Hey, he started it. With his stupid, weird twisty hands. Magicking around cars 'n shit."

"A man they had on early this morning said he had his motorcycle stolen by a gothic Arab," continued Alcander. Crimson looked at him, and the vampire shrugged. "His words, not mine. There was a homeless woman too, ranting and raving about tigers and spiders and flying men. Luckily, she went on to claim that an angel had descended from heaven on big fluffy white wings to end the whole affair. She also sees Jesus about once a week and has a close, personal relationship with a talking rock. Dementia probably. I do not think anyone took her seriously."

"So that just leaves the Hunters," said Crimson.

"The video quality on the street cameras was not pristine. I doubt anyone could identify you if they were not already looking for you. The camera in the helicopter fared better... but it was taken from overhead, and the chief focus *was* on Folami. It is not like in the movies. There is pixelization, a great deal of shadow, plus the blood and dirt and grime. *If* someone already knew your face, *if* someone knew they should be looking, yes, you could be identified, but if you are concerned that you will not be able to go to your favorite coffee shop any longer, I would say you should not be. As to the Hunters, if they saw you as a spider, *if* they were the ones who pulled the footage and it *was not* the spellcasters, yes, I suppose they could be a problem. You may want to consider lying low just in case."

Jasper managed not to sigh aloud. Crimson didn't. He couldn't blame him. He wanted to go home. He liked Alcander's for the most part, but he could only handle being cooped up for so long and knew Crimson felt even more strongly. Besides, he thought they would like to be alone for some time. Things between them had changed, and Jasper was excited (and, truthfully, a little anxious) to learn how. It wasn't that he wanted to hide it from Al and Max, just that he wanted to keep it as their own for a while. But it was hard to argue. Even with the warding charm and all the traps in the old house, Alcander's was still safer.

Alcander finished with his hands, and Jasper slid off the table. "Thanks, Al."

"You are most welcome," replied Alcander. "I would recommend you eat something before you rest. This time of day, Max is probably already making lunch. I am sure he will not mind. Then you need to rest for a good, long while. The echoes of a traumatic experience can often linger, as I am sure you well know. Give yourself time to heal, physically *and* mentally."

"I think I'll be fine," said Jasper. The truth was that the last twenty-four hours felt more like a hazy dream than reality. He was still digesting it. "But I'll try to get some sleep." He looked towards Crimson, who hopped down from the table. It must have been nice to spring back from a confrontation so quickly. Jasper had not suffered much in the way of physical harm, but even if he had woken up with no memories, he would have been able to tell he had been in a fight almost as soon as he opened his eyes. Folami had broken a quarter of the bones in Crimson's body and singed off a good portion of his skin, but here he stood, bouncing on his heels and smiling at Jasper like he'd already forgotten that he'd had a helicopter dropped on him the night before.

They went into the other room, leaving Alcander to his work.

Jasper wanted coffee, but Max was using the coffee machine to heat water for tea, and caffeine would only keep him up anyway, so he drank a mug of herbal tea and read the newspaper over Crimson's shoulder while Max cooked. Under the table, the werespider's fingers crept onto his knee. Jasper laid his fingers over his, smiled slightly, and kept reading.

An hour later, freshly showered and dressed, he crawled into bed with Crimson and kissed him the way he'd wanted to kiss him since he woke up.

#

The stay at Alcander's was not so bad this time around. The vampire was busy, as always, and though Jasper had not said a word to Max about his and the werespider's relationship, the human gave them their space.

Crimson was the same yet different. It was in the little things mostly, the way he laid his arm around his shoulder instead of over the back of the couch, the little excuses he found to let their fingers brush, how he held him when he slept. He promised to take things slow between them, and he kept his word, pushing him only to the edge of his comfort, then receding.

At the end of a week, when the worst of the media frenzy began to die down, they ventured out to the old movie theater to watch the black and whites that ran late into the night, and to share drinks and (in Jasper's case) dinner at the restaurant just around the corner.

The fight with Folami had damaged Crimson's jacket beyond repair, but he did not seem overly distressed by this fact. "It might be a good idea to change my look for a little while anyhow. Keep off the radar. You too."

"What do you think?" asked the werespider in a small clothing store four blocks from Alcander's. "Glasses? No glasses?"

"You look like you're gearing for a promotion at Google," said Jasper with a grin to let him know he was only teasing. The werespider had the sort of face that could change greatly depending on the way he chose to wear his hair. Half of it was tied loosely back, the rest free.

Jasper stepped beside him, looking at the pair of them in the dressing room's full-length mirror. The werespider's overcoat was dark, navy blue, left open to show the deep plum dress shirt below. Crimson turned back the cuffs and pinned them with silver links that matched the chain of his pocket watch, which was snapped to the belt loop of his slacks. The small studs he'd driven through his earlobes completed the ensemble, though the holes would go away just as soon as the piercings were removed.

"The glasses make you look smarter," Jasper allowed after a

moment. "You might have to drop your dumb-guy routine."

"No idea what you're talking about," replied Crimson. He took the glasses off and put them on Jasper instead. "What's a Google?"

"It's an internet thing. You use it to search for information." Jasper knew next to nothing about computers, but even he knew that. "Should I cut my hair or something?"

"I'll cut it for you if you want. The glasses look cute with the curls though." Only he didn't really *say* "curls." It sounded closer to "coils" with his accent. Jasper didn't have the heart to tell him no one (not even in New York) had said it that way in something like fifty years.

"I'm not *trying* to look *cute*," said Jasper instead, but looked in the mirror again despite himself.

The frames were made of thick black plastic, the sort popularized by television and movies, and they did seem to suit his face. Crimson draped a light scarf around the back of his neck, wrapping it once around his throat, and then put his arms around his waist as he laid his chin on the half-blood's shoulder. "You don't have to *try*, Jazz. You'd look cute in a garbage bag."

"Well, let's hope it doesn't come to that," said Jasper, relaxing his weight onto the inside of the demon's shoulder. He was wearing the body-regulated sweater Crimson had bought for him in the Summerlands, his shirt, robin's egg blue, untucked underneath. He grabbed a knit beanie from the pile of odds and ends that Crimson had dragged into the dressing room in spite of the six-item limit sign, and put it on. The curls still found a way to peek out along his brow and at the nape of his neck, but with the scarf, hat, and glasses, he hardly recognized himself. "How's that?"

"Sexy."

Jasper nudged his shoulder. "Be serious."

"Fine," said Crimson. He wrapped his fingers around the ends of the scarf and pulled him into a hard, passionate kiss that tapered reluctantly at the end. "*Very* sexy."

He was still getting used to the way the werespider looked at him, as well as the indiscreet way he chose to voice and display his affections. Jasper smiled at him and gently tugged the ends of the scarf out of his hand, smoothing it down and looking away. "I guess it'll have to do," he said. "You giving up the leather for good?"

Crimson raised an eyebrow at him. "Why? Are you into it?"

"*Crimson.*"

"What? I'm just askin'." He snapped a heavy silver chain around his neck and undid the first two buttons of the undershirt so that it wouldn't hide the necklace. Then he rolled back the cuffs and pinned them higher, just above his elbows. "I gotta know stuff like that, y'know?" He popped on a pair of sunglasses with small square lenses, tinted slightly purple, untucked the undershirt, and spread his arms slightly. "Now?"

"Now you look like a James Bond villain." Jasper laughed, but drew a step closer, touching the chain. His dark skin made the silver look sharper, shinier than it really was, and the color of the lenses reminded him of the hue Crimson's eyes sometimes took right after he kissed him. "I like it."

#

They returned to their own home three days later. The temperature outside had gone down dramatically, an early cold front in late September; he hated to think what the winter was going to be like. Crimson said he could turn the thermostat up if he didn't mind the likelihood of the whole place going up in flames; he hadn't cleaned the air ducts in thirty years.

"Just use the fireplace." The cold, empty grate in the attic room looked like it hadn't been dusted since before the vents. He barely ever even noticed it before, situated in the corner, the mantel covered in old trinkets and framed photos, the piano shoved practically in front of it. There was no firewood, but Michael had apparently rigged it up with magical flames, because it burst on at the flip of a switch. Like the bonfire in the Summerlands, the flames changed colors, going from blue to green, green to violet. The heavy black curtains kept the heat from escaping through the poorly insulated windows, and the flames kept the attic warm despite the lofty ceiling.

One afternoon, Jasper woke to the rhythmic sound of a hammer and found Crimson downstairs, repairing the broken windows on the lower level. He had torn up the majority of the damaged carpet, revealing the hardwood floors underneath, and seemed set on fixing the lower floors into something halfway livable, though Jasper told him probably twenty times that he really didn't mind the space in the attic.

Crimson, visibly on the upper end of one of his moods, cheerfully told him it was really no problem, he needed something to do anyway. "Besides, you shouldn't have to live in an attic. Especially not when there's a whole house just sittin' empty." It was impossible to reason with him when he was like this. Besides, it would be nice to have a little extra space. Jasper helped in what ways he could.

During the days, Crimson kept on the project. During the evenings, he ran all over the town with Jasper—to movie theaters and concert halls, to restaurants and museums. He was always in the bed when Jasper fell asleep, but always up well before him, and if Jasper had considered him amorous before, there was no word for it now. He hung on him whenever there was opportunity, and even convinced him to dance with him in the clubs once or twice.

It passed, of course, not all at once as it sometimes did, but gradually, less noticeably. One night, he would want to go home early. Another, he wouldn't want to leave the house. The pace of the renovations slowed from a hyperactive whirlwind to a resentful plod, and then were abandoned altogether. Some days, after waking, Jasper would stay in bed with Crimson all the way to nightfall, talking to him, or reading with him, or simply holding him while he dozed. Others, he gave him his space.

He painted the walls that were already stripped of rotting paper, put throw rugs in the two finished front rooms, and hung curtains over the new windows.

One morning, two weeks to the day since they had been home, just as he was about to fall asleep, Crimson murmured that he loved him, his voice barely audible over the crackle and snap of the fireplace.

He slipped into slumber before Jasper could find the courage to say it back.

Chapter Twenty-Eight

—

Nothing Gold Can Stay

It was late afternoon when Jasper left the house. The first real hint of autumn was in the air, a light crispness that tickled his nose and had him zipping up his hoodie. He was glad for the gray beanie pulled down over his ears. He knew Crimson preferred cooler temperatures and hoped it would cheer him up some, thinking maybe he'd be able to convince him to come out later. He knew Crimson couldn't help his moods, and knew it had nothing to do with himself, but Jasper didn't like seeing him so down and wished there was more he could do to help him out of his funk.

Many of the restaurants and bars around the house were still closed, and the ones that weren't didn't appeal to him. He didn't think he'd ever tire of Brooklyn-style pizza, yet here he was. Max had been teaching him a few cooking techniques, but he still wasn't confident enough to cook more than eggs and toast and hadn't wanted to bother Crimson with his bumbling and banging around. There was a nice diner several blocks away that wasn't too expensive, and that was where Jasper headed. He took his time, cutting through a park and enjoying a cigarette on his way.

The diner was half full when he arrived, and he grabbed a seat at the counter, smiling at the waitress who came over to him and poured him a cup of coffee while he looked over the menu. He ordered a chicken Caesar wrap then took the paperback he was reading out of his back pocket while he waited.

The bell over the door jingled, and someone sat down next to him. He glanced up from his book mindlessly, the movement

322

drawing his attention, and started looking back at the page before his mind caught up with his eyes. A middle-aged man with neatly parted dark brown hair that was gracefully fading to gray, wearing a dark suit paired with a bright blue tie, sat next to him, calm gray eyes looking into his startled green ones. It took his mind another long moment to communicate with his mouth, and when he spoke, he almost didn't recognize his own voice, it was so thin.

"Dad?"

"Hello, Jasper," said Charlie evenly. "Happy hunting?"

"What are you doing here?" Jasper looked over his shoulder to the glass door as if he expected to see a whole squad of agents accompanying his father. In the small parking lot he saw a single black company car. The windows were too dark to see inside, but Charlie seemed to be alone. "How did you find me?" He'd given his old phone to Al when he'd gotten a new one and could think of no other way to track his location.

"It wasn't very hard. I know the werespider's address and the vampire's." Of course he did, Jasper had told him himself, hadn't he? A cold knot of guilt formed in his stomach. In the early days he'd told Charlie everything. It hadn't seemed like such a bad thing when it looked like Charlie wanted to forget he'd ever existed, but now...

"What do you want?"

"I know what happened the other weekend," he said.

Jasper instantly thought of the dark church, of Crimson's mouth crashing against his, and felt the blood drain from his face.

"With the auction," Charlie clarified, and Jasper felt mildly relieved, though the sick feeling stayed with him. "I'm impressed you were able to take care of the rakshasa on your own. I've never faced one myself."

"I wasn't on my own. Crimson helped me. He saved me."

Charlie looked unhappy at that. "Yes, well, when I learned about what had happened, I began to reconsider my earlier decision."

The waitress returned and set down a plate with the wrap and a mountain of hot french fries beside it. A few minutes prior Jasper would have dug in immediately but now found he was no longer hungry.

"Anything for you, sir?" the waitress asked Charlie, and he shook his head politely.

"No, thank you, I was just meeting my son. Actually, could we get that to go?"

Jasper said nothing as the plate was taken away, a cardboard box arriving in its place.

"Let's talk in the car."

Jasper bristled. "I'm not going anywhere with you."

"I just want to talk to you, Jasper," Charlie said reasonably. He was always so reasonable. "I'm sorry for how things happened."

"You mean for banishing me and deleting my entire existence?" It was easier to be angry with him.

"How did you—ah, yes. The vampire, right?"

Jasper said nothing.

Charlie touched his elbow gently. Jasper did not pull away. "Can't we talk? You can pick the place."

For another moment Jasper still said nothing. Then, "Okay." He didn't want to talk here, where anyone could hear them, but he certainly didn't want to get in that car. He didn't want to go back to St. James.

Grabbing his book and his sandwich, Jasper stood up. "Come on," he said and then went out the door, Charlie a few steps behind him. He went back the way he'd come, bringing Charlie to the small park several blocks away from the house. It was close enough that Jasper was afraid Crimson would find them, while another part of him hoped he would. They sat on a bench in front of a drained fountain, and Jazz took out a cigarette. Charlie clucked his tongue softly. "You're not actually going to smoke that, are you?"

Jasper gave him a look and lit the cigarette, breathing the smoke pointedly away from Charlie. "What did you wanna talk about?"

"I told you I heard about the auction. Truthfully, I've always been afraid something like that would happen. I promised your parents a long time ago that I'd protect you from this sort of thing." This piqued Jasper's interest. He and Charlie had talked about his parents countless times before, but Charlie had never once mentioned any sort of promise. "I'm sorry for my reaction before. I was angry and disappointed, and I acted rashly. What you needed was help, and instead I pushed you away. This whole situation, it's my fault for sending you on that stupid job. It's not worth it. Nothing is worth losing you. I'm sorry."

Jasper's throat felt tight. Although they disagreed, Jasper still missed his father and had been hurt when it seemed as if he wasn't missed at all. Charlie's words cut through his anger, to his heart, and he tried to tell himself that the stinging in his eyes was from smoke, not tears. "I'm sorry too."

"Won't you come home? You'll be safer there. I'll make sure nothing bad happens to you."

Jasper was already shaking his head. "I can't."

"We can take care of the werespider. He won't be a problem." Charlie found himself on the receiving end of the half-blood's white-eyed glare.

"Crimson is not the problem," he said, sucking back on the cigarette until it was just a nub between his fingers. He dropped it on the ground in front of him, crushed it under his boot, and then pulled out another though he was too agitated to light it right away. "The problem is that I don't want to go back. I don't want to kill innocent people anymore."

"And what do you think *they* do?" Charlie's jaw clenched.

Jasper shook his head again. "I'm not going to argue with you about this." Charlie wouldn't get it. It wasn't as simple as Charlie believed it was, the line between good and evil not so definite. His father was strong and smart and stubborn, but so was he. "And I'm not going back there. I'm done."

Jasper got up to walk away, and Charlie stood as well, grabbing the sleeve of his hoodie, his fingers pressing into his skin. Folami's face jumped to the forefront of his mind, his cold yellow eyes staring at him, appraising. He jerked his arm back. "Don't." His voice was quiet but firm.

"You don't understand how dangerous it is for you."

"I can take care of myself. And I have Crimson."

"No matter how impressive you think he is, he is not enough to keep you safe. How many demons and spellcasters were at the auction? Was Folami the only bidder?"

Part of him whispered that Charlie was not wrong. He tried not to listen to it. "Why are you trying to scare me?"

"You know you're safe at St. James. I've never let anything bad happen to you."

Jasper thought of Adam, of the dozens of demons his father had sent him to kill without trial or even thought, and almost argued with him. "I'm going *home*," he said instead. "Don't follow me. I'm not fucking around. I'm not interested."

"If you will not come back on your own," Charlie called after him, pausing his exit, "then I will take you there, and I have no qualms about going through that werespider to do so."

They looked at each other across the path, neither one of them recognizing the man they saw.

Charlie continued, "We will dispose of Crimson"—he said his name like a curse, filled with more venom than Jasper could ever remember hearing in his voice—"and we will kill Alcander *and* his familiar, Maxwell, and then I will drag you back."

On his own, Jasper knew Charlie wasn't that much of a threat. He was one human, edging closer to fifty than forty, and though he was in good shape, that would hardly matter against someone as strong as Crimson or even himself. But even if Jasper could entertain the idea of actually hurting him (he couldn't), he knew Charlie was not speaking just of himself. The Hunters were a force that should not be reckoned with. If they had their minds set on a target, they would get them. Even Crimson would be no match for the entire agency.

They'd have to run. Already Jasper's mind was forming a plan. They could go to the west coast, or to Canada, where there were still Hunters but not the same ones. He hated to uproot everyone, but what other choice did they have? He couldn't go back.

"How far do you think you'd get?" Charlie asked, like he was reading his mind. "It wouldn't be like Miami. The Hunters here are the best in the world."

Jasper knew he was right. His mouth felt dry, his mind dizzy. He took the cigarette from his mouth, spinning it between his fingers until the paper broke. "If you hurt them," he said, the words shaking out of him, "I'll never forgive you. I'll run away and never come back. I'll fight so hard you'll have to kill me."

"I won't have to hurt them if you come back."

Jasper was quiet for a moment. "How do I know you won't hurt them anyway?"

"I'll promise you no one will touch them. I'll wipe their files, and as long as they don't do anything stupid, they'll be safe."

Given that Crimson was extremely prone to doing stupid things, he didn't think it was a particularly good offer, but it was the best he was going to get. "You promise?"

"Our people won't bother him."

Jasper took out his cigarettes and tapped one out. The pack was nearly empty. He'd have to stop by the corner store before he went home. His fingers were numb, though it wasn't really all that cold, and he struggled with his lighter before the spark caught. "How much time do I have?" He couldn't leave right now. He'd told Crimson he was just going out for a bite. If he woke up and Jasper wasn't there...

The smoke wasn't helping; he only felt sicker.

"Come with me now."

"I *can't*." He hated the whine in his voice but couldn't stop it. He felt like crying. "I have to—I have to say goodbye. I need time."

He chanced a glance at Charlie. His father was looking at him with barely concealed distaste. It wasn't hard to imagine what he was thinking; the word *familiar* was active in his own mind. "A day," Charlie said.

Jasper felt like throwing up. "A week," he countered. A week was nothing.

"Three days."

"Six."

Charlie's eyes all but flashed. His hands were rolled into thick fists, though his shoulders were deliberately relaxed. "Five."

Jasper tried to swallow the lump in his throat. "Okay." Five days was no time at all. He needed five times that amount. Ten times. A hundred. "I'll be there." Unless he came up with a better plan. There had to be something...

"Good. I'll be watching."

Jasper's stomach shifted uneasily. Were there cameras on the property? Inside it? Had his father actually *seen* him sprawled out on the couch night after night, letting himself get felt up by a demon, and enjoying it? Did he know they now shared a bed? That the consummation of their relationship was now only a formality—a "when" rather than an "if," a "soon" rather than a "later"? That, for maybe the first time since Adam had died, he was happy? That he was loved? That he...

But no, if Charlie knew everything, if he knew the true nature of their relationship, he wouldn't have asked Jasper to come home. He would have put a bullet in his brain.

Of course Charlie *would* be watching and listening and waiting. He was a good Hunter, not the sort to let a target out of his sights. Jasper wondered who was on his case, and then told himself not to think about it—any of it. He gave a stiff nod, not meeting the Hunter's gaze, and started quickly away. Charlie did not follow him.

He felt like he was in a daze or caught in a dream, like his body was far away and he was somewhere else. He was through the park and walking into the corner store near their house without his realizing it, the bell above the door jarring him back to himself. He was having trouble breathing, trouble focusing. He started to leave the store before he remembered he was almost out of cigarettes and went to the counter to buy two cartons of Marlboros. Crimson would want some when he got home.

He floated down the street and through the metal gate, up the front path and into the front room. That felt like a dream too, his eyes still unused to the changes. It looked much better than it had when he had first seen it—the walls freshly painted in a warm yellow, rotted floorboards replaced and polished, covered by a soft area rug, the years of grime swept or scrubbed away. The rest of the house still had a bit longer to go along before it was entirely livable, but if the werespider hit another spurt, it would easily be done before the year was out. They were going to get a new couch, and Crimson said they'd get a reading chair to put by the nonmagical fireplace. The upstairs closets were packed with boxes and boxes of old vinyls, and just yesterday he had suggested they could maybe frame some of them and hang them on the walls, since most of them weren't doing anything other than collecting dust. He already had a few in mind: *Damn the Torpedos* by Tom Petty and the Heartbreakers, *Jumping Jack Flash* by the Stones, Queen's *Night at the Opera*.

Jasper pulled himself up the stairs to the attic room.

Crimson was still in bed, though he was sitting up, one of Jasper's books open in front of him. His deep brown eyes turned towards him as he came up the short flight of stairs. A small smile curled at his lips and just as quickly was gone. "What's wrong, love? You look pale."

"I'm not feeling very well," Jasper admitted. He knew he should tell Crimson what had happened. Together they could come up with a solution.

The words failed to come to him, and instead he went over to the bed, dropping the bag of smokes on the floor beside it before crawling in beside Crimson. The werespider pulled the comforter over his shoulders and wrapped his arm around his waist, pressing a kiss to the nape of his neck. "Do you need anything?"

Jasper closed his eyes, shutting away his tears. "This. Just this."

Chapter Twenty-Nine

—

Don't Wanna Miss a Thing

Jasper wanted to believe his meeting with Charlie was nothing more than a bad dream, but even as his eyes opened that evening, he knew it wasn't. Crimson was awake before him for the first time in a while, smiling almost cautiously at him, his head propped up in his palm. "Good morning," he said, placing his hand on his chest, rubbing slow circles on it.

"Hey," Jasper said. He cursed himself for wasting so much time asleep. Almost a day gone, all that time lost for good. He hoped Crimson didn't notice the way the panic seized his heart.

"Are you feeling better?"

"Yeah." Jasper took Crimson's hand in his own and moved it to his mouth, pressing a kiss to his palm. Truthfully, he didn't feel better at all, but he didn't know what he should say, so he said nothing. He could barely even think about it. Turning on his side facing Crimson, he kissed him again, this time on his lips. They were deliciously soft, moving in response to his own in a way they hadn't in days. "How about you? Feeling better?"

"Yeah, I think so. A bit." He paused. "Sorry I've been so... y'know. I don't want you feeling like it's on account of you or anything like that." Crimson misread the situation. He didn't know if he should be disappointed or relieved.

"It's okay. You didn't do anything wrong." It would have been easier if he had. "Do you wanna go out later? We could go dancing."

Crimson brightened a little at that, showing him a brief flash of his trademark movie-star smile. It dug deep down into Jasper's heart and

330

ripped a gash in its walls. "I love dancing."

"I know, that's why I suggested it."

"But you *hate* dancing."

"Only with everyone but you," replied Jasper, surprising himself. Crimson raised an eyebrow, and Jasper grinned. "Alright, you're right. I hate it no matter what. But it's growing on me. Slowly."

When they arrived at The Crystal Ballroom, they found it packed almost to capacity. It really was a horribly tacky and trashy bar, but standing in it now, Jasper found that he would miss it and its graffitied, mirrored walls and the way the bartenders always knew what he wanted to drink even when he didn't.

They ran into Alan over near the bar.

"*He-ey!* I saw you on the news." The werewolf laughed when he spotted them. Jasper's arm was around Crimson's and they were standing close together, but either Alan did not notice or did not care because he grabbed Crimson's free hand, drawing in close. "My famous boyfriend."

If Crimson hadn't been there to stop him, he probably would have broken the werewolf's nose, but Crimson tightened his arm around Jasper's, holding him subtly back, and pulled his hand out of Alan's of his own accord. "Sorry, man. I'm involved."

Alan must have actually been *that* oblivious (and not just intentionally rude) because he followed the werespider's gesture down to their linked arms, then grinned, and then positively beamed back at Crimson like he had just realized the greatest thing in the whole wide world. "You owe me ten bucks."

Jasper shot a glare up at Crimson, who smiled nervously. "Don't look at me like that. It was months ago."

"A bet's a bet," chirruped Alan happily. He held out his hand and made a gimme gesture. "C'mon. Pay up."

Crimson shrugged. "I don't carry money on me. You know that."

Jasper sighed. "*Here.*" He dug out his wallet, removed a ten-dollar bill, and placed it in Alan's hand.

"Thanks, Jazzy," said Alan. He took a step closer, this time in Jasper's direction. "You know, if you've got a few more of those in there, I'd *love* to give the happy couple a discount. Maybe we could–"

Crimson pushed him towards the dance floor, not aggressively, but not exactly in a friendly way either. "Beat it."

"Yessir." Alan gave one of his patented werewolf barks of laughter at their combined scowls. "Alright, alright." He tugged the rumpled mesh of his shirt straight, still smiling. "I know when I'm not wanted. You crazy kids have fun." He started away but turned, walking backwards and pointing towards Crimson as he disappeared into the crowd. "Hit me up after he ages himself to death, yeah?"

Crimson didn't respond, pretending very convincingly not to have heard. "Thanks," he said to Jasper. Alan was already gone anyway. Jasper wondered jealously if Crimson would be right back with him the moment he returned to the Hunting Agency. Then he felt bad for even thinking that the werespider should think twice about doing so. If they couldn't be together, Jasper couldn't expect him to be alone. He was already lonely enough without Jasper wishing it on him.

God, he hated this.

Crimson nudged him. "You ready?"

"Yes." Then, thinking that if it worked for Alan, it would probably work for him too, he added in a half-teasing way, "Sir?"

The look on Crimson's face was truly priceless. Jasper wished he could have saved it in a snapshot.

"Are you not into that?" asked Jasper, dropping the round off his vowels to imitate Crimson's voice. "I really ought to know these things, y'know?"

"You're a riot," said Crimson. He put his hand on the back of Jasper's neck, drawing him as close as he could, and spoke into his ear. "You can call me whatever you like, but when you beg me to fuck you, I want you to use my name."

The club around them seemed to momentarily fall away, Jasper's blood pulsing with the idea. He squeezed Crimson's shoulders, wishing he still had his jacket, then drew away with a shy laugh. "I'm not gonna *beg.*"

"Mm-hm," teased Crimson. "We'll see."

"Shut up," said Jasper lightly. "Let's dance."

They made their way out into the sea of bodies. Dancing really wouldn't be so bad, thought Jasper, if it weren't for all the other people. "I don't know why you're so freaked out!" called Crimson over the music. "You're doing fine!"

"That's what people say when someone's doing really bad!" Jasper yelled back, and Crimson laughed.

"Here, I gotta idea." Crimson's arm suddenly tightened around his waist, and he pulled him through the crowd, to the smoking patio. Though it wasn't exactly cold, it was cool enough to keep people from lingering longer than it took to smoke a cigarette. The music could still be heard here, muffled by the door.

Crimson didn't stop on the patio, but dragged him on, through the side gate and around the building.

"Where are we going?" Jasper laughed, but even as he spoke, they drew to a halt. Crimson lifted him suddenly from the ground.

"Hang on." The werespider took five running steps, and Jasper realized what he was doing just in time to throw his arms around his neck. Crimson caught the sill of a window on the second story and then jumped the rest of the way up to the third, putting them on the flat top of the roof. The music thrummed underneath their feet, the light-stained night sky overhead, buildings towering all around them like a forest of concrete, metal, and glass.

"Is this better?" asked Crimson. He set him down, but they were still standing together, swaying slightly, not quite to the beat of the music below.

"Yes," said Jasper, resting his head on the inside of Crimson's shoulder and closing his eyes.

He didn't know how long they were up on the roof, only that it was not long enough.

#

When they climbed down and walked back around the building, on their way home, they found Abby standing alone on the sidewalk just outside the entrance, watching the cars as they passed by. Jasper tried to walk on past, but Crimson slowed. "Whatcha doin' out here, Abs?" He glanced around, expecting to see Alan, but the other werewolf was obviously still inside. "You okay?" he added when she didn't answer.

Abby's big empty eyes moved slowly, first to Crimson, then to Jasper, then back to Crimson.

Crimson felt a slow, sinking sensation. The werewolves weren't his responsibility by a long shot, but they hung in or around his territory so often that he sometimes felt like they were. He stooped down to get a better look at her and spoke a little more slowly. "Did you get lost?"

"No," answered Abby. Her gaze finally stopped tick-tocking, focusing now directly on his. "I came to say I'm sorry."

Beside him, Jasper stiffened slightly. Crimson, one ear turned ever in the direction of his heart, heard it quicken.

"Sorry for what?"

She dreamily reached for his face, pressing two fingers lightly to his brow and trailing them down his cheek to his chin. "Don't cry, Crimson." He felt a chill, not on his skin, but underneath it. "It will be okay."

"Abby, stop being so weird," huffed Jasper. He took hold of her wrist and pushed it gently back to her side.

Abby let him stop her, but she did not look away or even acknowledge him. She was staring at Crimson, fixed as a cat staring at a mouse. "It will be okay," she repeated. "Just remember that you…" But what she wanted him to remember, they would never know. Her gaze lost its focus. Just like that, she was looking at neither of them, looking at nothing. She craned her gaze around, moving in slow motion, as if she had been suspended in water, then turned and wafted back into the bar without another word.

Frowning, Crimson straightened up. "That little pup gives me the creeps," he told Jasper. Half the time she seemed barely present, but every once in a while, he felt like she saw through him like he was made of glass. She made his skin crawl, and for a guy like Crimson, that was quite a feat indeed.

"She's really weird," agreed Jasper. His voice sounded strange. Bitter. "Let's go back to the house."

"I can't think of anything I'd rather do," said Crimson, and meant it. It was finally all starting to come together and, despite the reservations both his battle-scarred heart and his common sense told him to hold, he was optimistic. He loved this stage of a relationship—actually, he loved *all* the stages of a relationship, the way they were all different, the way they were all the same, the way love could sprout and bloom and grow.

He knew it would end in heartbreak; it always did with the mortals.

But Jasper was young, his life only just beginning to unfold, and though death would take him eventually, as it always did, it wouldn't do so for some time. He was excited to be along for the ride. Excited to make the minutes count. Excited to be in love.

Crimson slapped him playfully on the shoulder. "Race ya," he said and then shot ahead of Jasper before he had time to understand what had been spoken. Jasper came sprinting in pursuit, yelling that he was a cheater through laughing breaths. He was smiling, his eyes misted with the barest veil of white light, and for a moment Crimson imagined he could almost see the glowing aura the others were always talking about—shining, faceted, like a diamond.

He didn't think he had ever seen anything so beautiful.

Not in this life.

Nor in any of the others that came before.

Chapter Thirty

—

The Collector's Daughter

Time passed too quickly. Jasper tried to make every moment count, proposing dates and activities he thought Crimson would enjoy, trying to keep the dark clouds of the future at bay. There would be time to be sad later. Crimson deserved happiness.

They went to movies and museums, bars and bookshops. Jasper couldn't help but notice how much bigger his world was with Crimson in it. He had lived in New York City for almost three years before meeting him and had nothing but blood and vampire dust to show for it.

One night, after they returned home and were curled up together on the couch watching a movie, a musical, Jasper commented on how he had never seen one in person, had never been to an actual theater. Crimson announced that this was "unacceptable." The next day they went to a fancy clothing boutique and spent what felt like hours picking out suits. Jasper did not complain about trying on a dozen jackets that all looked the same to him, nor about spending Alcander's money. The spark in Crimson's eyes as he picked out a deep wine-purple tie for him, the easy way he joked and teased, the honey-sweet kisses he gave Jasper were too rewarding.

Alcander got them tickets to a show on Broadway for that night. Jasper was surprised the vampire was able to secure them such good seats on such short notice. They were just a few rows back from the front, dead center. The lights dimmed, and Jasper grinned at Crimson, who grinned right back and placed his hand on Jasper's thigh. Music grew in the darkness, and the half-blood laced their fingers together, eyes on the stage.

#

They left the playhouse, spirits high. Jasper had drank more champagne than was strictly necessary. It was the evening of the fourth day, and tomorrow he would be back at St. James. He still hadn't told Crimson. It never felt like the right time.

With clasped hands, they walked down the street towards the subway entrance that would bring them back to Gravesend. Crimson was chattering on about the musical they had just seen. It was new, just out this year, so neither of them had seen it before, but still Crimson had a lot to say about the actors and the setting and the music. Jasper hung on his every word. He looked beautiful in the streetlights, dressed in dark finery, his hair slicked smartly back. He looked at Jasper, with sparkling eyes and smile, and Jasper felt like his heart was breaking.

"What?" He realized Crimson had asked him a question he hadn't heard.

"I asked what your favorite part was."

"Honestly? This part." They were passing by a narrow street, much less popular than the one they were currently on, which was congested with their fellow theatergoers and other people out on the town. Jasper tugged Crimson down it, the werespider following easily behind him until everyone else was a mere rumble behind them. He looked behind them, checking that they weren't being followed. Crimson let Jasper push his back against the dark window of a closed storefront, eagerly accepting the kiss he gave him. To hell with the Hunters—if they were watching, then let them watch.

"Has anyone ever told you how hot you look in a suit?" Jasper asked, feeling bold on champagne and lack of time.

"A few times," admitted Crimson, his hands pushing through Jasper's curls, knocking the knitted hat off his head, "but I'd love to hear it from you."

"I cannot remember one single part of that play," he said, pressing their bodies together.

Crimson wrapped an arm around his waist and pulled him even closer.

"I couldn't stop thinking about you in that suit and gettin' you home and gettin' you out of it."

They shared a kiss, open and hungry. Jasper forgot about the street around them, nearly forgot about the fact that he was leaving. Crimson broke the kiss first, just barely. Jasper could feel his smile, felt his lips move as he spoke in a whisper against his mouth. "Very nice, Jazz. You're getting pretty respectable at flirting."

"It's the champagne," he assured him. He couldn't imagine being so brave otherwise. Bringing their mouths back together, Jasper kissed him until he was dizzy. It was their last night together, and Jasper wanted it to count. He wanted to say the words that had been growing in his chest, wanted to finally take that final step and *be* with him.

He just didn't really want to do it in the street.

"Let's go home," he said. "Please, Crimson, take me home."

Crimson's eyes were that beautiful shade of burgundy that Jasper liked so much. He took Jasper's hand and began to lead him back the way they'd come.

They both stopped at the same time, sensing the danger in their different ways. Jasper's stomach twisted in a way that had nothing to do with champagne. Crimson's attention had already snapped towards the rooftops, nostrils flaring. In the seconds it took Jasper to pinpoint the location of the demon, the werespider swept him behind his back, standing between him and what was on the roof.

From over Crimson's shoulder he saw a dark shape untouched by the streetlights. He made out the outline of a long coat, of tall heeled boots, and the glimmer of coiled gold. Jasper drew a silver knife from under his jacket. Crimson already had a gun in his hand. "Could you maybe just... not... do whatever you're about to do?" Crimson said. "We're sorta on a date."

"I believe you 'ave something of mine," the demon replied. The voice was female and accented. French, Jasper thought. She stepped forward, off the roof, and landed with feline ease on a small patio on the second floor. Jasper now saw her blue eyes, slit like a cat's, and the way her hand turned, snapping the golden whip to the side. Fear coursed through him. "I 'ave come to retrieve it."

"Yeah," called Crimson, as if she had not spoken. "Like I said—not right now." He waved her away with his free hand. "Go on! Shoo!"

The woman's lips curled in a disgusted-looking sneer. One long canine showed. The rakshasa hissed softly. "Are you ze creature who slew my father?"

"Don't make me get the spray bottle!"

"Spider—"

"*Lady, take a fucking hint!*" The mocking tone ruptured around a snarl, then sank to a low, dangerous rumble. "Leave. Now."

The demon narrowed her eyes at him, sizing him up. She sniffed once, cleared her throat, and began again. "Spider—"

The revolver kicked in Crimson's hand with a *BOOM*.

The rakshasa spun to avoid it, too fast to not have magical aid. The window behind her exploded inward. In the same spin the whip came down towards Crimson.

White-eyed, Jasper pushed him out of the way, and the whip coiled instead around his forearm, cutting through the sleeve of his coat and suit to bite into his flesh. It hurt like hell, and Jasper couldn't stop the cry that burst through his lips.

"Look what you made me do, *araignée*," the rakshasa hissed.

Crimson grabbed hold of the whip and gave it a hard yank. It ripped free of her grasp, the coil leaving scorch marks on the palm of his hand as he cast it aside. "*Encule toi salope.*"

Jasper, who knew just enough French to ask where the bathroom was, didn't know what that meant, but judging by the look on the rakshasa's face, it wasn't anything nice. She spoke in quick French that Jasper couldn't hope to follow, practically spitting the words. Crimson sneered and shot back a string of retorts, punctuating them with another boom of his revolver and a very rude hand gesture that translated just fine.

The rakshasa sprang higher, now back to the third story. "Stop with your nonsense," said the woman. "My father paid a small fortune for this shiny little trinket. By right, he belongs to me."

Crimson fired again. "What's left of your daddy is buried in an unmarked landfill behind St. James Academy, you stupid bitch." And again. "Learn from his mistakes." And again. "And keep your filthy fucking paws off *my* hybrid."

The rakshasa danced around every shot, but the last grazed her cheek and puffed back a lock of her hair. She had retreated all the way to the sixth floor and was crouched there on the corner of the balcony. "I'm asking nicely now. Next time—"

Crimson raised the gun again, as if to fire, but his other hand went under his jacket. As he squeezed the trigger, the rakshasa moved again. The bullet missed, but the throwing dagger was still leaving his hand and, as she alighted again, it struck her inside the shoulder.

She yowled and ripped it away, flinging it back to the ground, only to have Jasper's dagger sting her arm. Jasper reached for his next knife, and Crimson snapped open the cylinder of the gun to reload, but the rakshasa chose to make her exit and went scampering up the building, just like a cat up a tree. High up, just above the light, she called back to them, "I will *not* be so nice next time."

Crimson glared up after her for a long moment, perhaps following her progress beyond Jasper's line of sight. Then, shrugging away the stiff, poised stance, he turned back to Jasper. "Do you wanna go after her?"

Yes, thought Jasper, because some primal part of him deep down *did* want to go after her. But he said, "No," because all the other parts of him just wanted to go home and try to salvage what remained of their perfect evening. The long gash on his arm was a brutal dose of reality in what seemed like a dream too near its end.

Crimson agreed without argument, then asked if Jasper wanted to go to Alcander's. The half-blood shook his head. The wound on his arm hurt, but it wasn't so bad, thin and shallow enough that it was already clotting as they waved down a taxi and got it to bring them back to Gravesend. Jasper knew if he let himself go down into the security of Al's, he would not come out, and he knew if he wasn't back at the agency tomorrow, they would come looking for him.

He wouldn't be able to live with himself if the others were hurt because of him.

Chapter Thirty-One

—

Mockingbird

Crimson helped Jasper up the stairs to the attic room and sat him down at the kitchen table while he fetched water and clean cloths and a roll of bandages. "You know," he said, dropping down in the chair beside him and holding out a hand for Jasper's arm, "I always liked cats. Think I might be starting to lose my taste for 'em though."

Jasper didn't respond. He watched Crimson clean the cut, then dress it. Aside from being a little put out by the interruption, the werespider didn't seem all that concerned about the rakshasa or the fact that she would certainly come back. Crimson had been so happy these last few days; it was contagious. Jasper thought about moving closer and picking up where they had left off in the alley. Then he thought of the smile falling from Crimson's face when Alan told him, no, he would not be staying after all. He imagined him waking up to an empty bed, to panic and heartache and betrayal.

"Shame about the suit," continued Crimson. "You sure you're okay?"

"I'm fine," said Jasper. He had to tell him. He had to tell him *right now*. "It's just a little cut."

"Wasn't talking 'bout the cut," said Crimson.

"I..." Jasper must have rehearsed in his head how he was going to break it to him a hundred times. None of it was ever good enough. In fact, it was so not good enough that he wanted not to tell him at all. "I think..." His lips struggled against the words they didn't want to say. "That maybe... me and you..."

Crimson's eyes widened just a little. He spared him one last pain. "Are you about to break up with me?"

Jasper swallowed hard and started in a rush. "It's not that I don't care about you. It's just that... I don't think this is gonna work. That demon is gonna keep coming back."

"So we'll kill her," said Crimson. "*I'll* kill her."

Jasper shook his head. "You can't protect me."

"Jazz, c'mon." There was still a little levity in his voice, a feeble attempt to smile. "I'm tellin' ya, that bitch isn't gonna be a problem. I got her scent, and she ain't as strong as her old man. We can take care of her. Easy. I'll go right now if it'll make you feel better."

"It's not that *easy*, Crimson." Jasper thought of what Charlie had said in the park, about how others like Folami would come looking for him. The thought was frightening, but he knew he would not face them alone with Crimson. The werespider would die trying to save him before he'd let someone take him away. That thought frightened him even more. "There'll be more. Lots more. You can't stop them; you're just one person."

"So then we'll go somewhere else," reasoned Crimson. He still didn't understand the full extent of the problem, and now Jasper knew for sure he couldn't risk telling him. "We don't have to stay here. We can go anywhere you want. Anywhere in the world."

Jasper wished that were true. "I wanna go home."

Crimson glanced quickly around the attic apartment and then back to Jasper, who looked down before their eyes could meet. "What do you mean?"

"I mean—" Jasper let out a shaky sigh "—that I think I should go back to St. James."

Crimson's shocked silence was everything he dreaded and more. "You're deciding this... just now? You don't wanna think about it... or...?"

"I've kind of been thinking about it for a while," admitted Jasper.

"Oh." The shock and disbelief in his expression was replaced in a thunderclap. "Thanks for letting me know." The sharp sarcasm in his voice cut more deeply than the whip, but Jasper tried to take comfort. Better that he should be angry. Better that he should move on. The werespider stood suddenly from the table, putting some breathing room between them. "I guess that means I probably can't talk you out of it."

"I have to go," repeated Jasper firmly.

Now Crimson did not respond.

"If I don't, we're always gonna be running. We're always gonna be in *danger*. Crimson, if there were any other way—"

"I know, I know," interjected Crimson. He drew in an agitated breath, closed his eyes, and opened them again. "I get it. It's too dangerous." He looked away, using his cigarettes as an excuse. "I guess I can't blame you for doing what's best for you. This ain't no kind of life for a human, half-blood or otherwise. I get it. Really. I do. But, uh..." He found the pack, but couldn't find his lighter. Jasper stood up to offer him his, but Crimson took a step back, out of his reach. "I think I need to... not be in this room right now."

"Please don't say that," whispered Jasper. There was no time to reconcile. This was his last night with him, possibly his last night of freedom, maybe forever. He didn't want to spend it alone. "I'm sorry." His resolve broke before he could stop it. "I didn't want it to be like this. Please don't leave right now." He knew he was being unfair, but he couldn't help it. Tears burned in his eyes. "I'll stay the night. Stay with me? Please. I... I love you."

Crimson took another leery step back. "What do you mean, stay the night? Are you leaving *tomorrow*? Shouldn't you make sure they're even willing to take you back? Unless..." The werespider's dumb-guy routine was, indeed, just a routine. "You already did."

The thing about lying was, once you were caught in one, the rest unraveled easily. None of this was going right. "I spoke to my father," explained Jasper.

The look Crimson gave him was worse than if he hit him. "That's weird, cuz it seems like I remember you swearing on your mother's fuckin' grave that you were done with that shit. How long have you been lying to me?"

"I haven't!" Jasper insisted. "It was *just* my dad. And it was only once."

Crimson shook his head. "I wanna believe you, Jazz. I've *always* wanted to believe you. But I don't think I will. Not this time."

"It's the *truth*," said Jasper, but it wasn't, not really.

"It doesn't *matter*," replied Crimson. "If you wanna be with me, *be* with me. If that's what you really want, *we can figure it out*. But if that's not really what you want—if what you want is to—" his laugh was weak, completely removed from anything resembling humor "—convince me that you love me, that way I'll just let everything go, and stand here, and pretend like I'm okay right now—" His voice cracked, and for one terrible moment Jasper thought he was going to cry. But he didn't. "Then I guess you're just gonna have to be disappointed. You can't have it both ways."

Jasper almost relented. He *did* want to be with Crimson, more than anything else in the world. He just couldn't see a future where trying didn't end with one or both of them dead. He swallowed his regret. "I'm sorry," he said again.

"Me too." Putting his unlit cigarette between his lips, Crimson turned and made for the stairs. "I'll sleep in the other room." He stopped on the first step, his eyes turned down. "You can wake me up if you change your mind."

"And if I don't?" whispered Jasper.

"Then make sure not to leave any of your shit behind." With that, he was gone. He didn't even give him the chance to say goodbye.

Every instinct told him to go running after Crimson, to beg and plead and apologize, to tell him everything about this horrible choice he had to make, to fight for him the way the werespider had fought for him against Folami. He would run away with him and be happy for a while, at least until the Hunters and demons caught up with them. And then everyone he loved would be dead, and he would still have to go back to the agency, probably in chains.

Jasper didn't run after him.

He went to pack his things.

He had started the conversation with the intention of breaking up with Crimson, but now, alone in the attic, it felt strangely like Crimson had broken up with him. He wished bitterly that the other had been crueler about it. That he had shouted and snarled, lashed out at him, thrown him out of the house, told him to get lost, and warned him never to come back. That he had done something, in short, to show Jasper he was all wrong for him anyhow.

Instead, Crimson left him to remove the pieces of himself from the home they had shared, with only his guilt and heartache to keep him company. As he wadded up his clothes and shoved them one after the other into his backpack, rapidly blinking back tears and sniffing back sobs, he changed his mind. *This* was the cruelest thing Crimson could have done, and no less than he deserved.

He got three-quarters of his stuff stowed away before he realized there wasn't enough room. When he had arrived, the backpack had been all he had, and it had held everything he owned with space to spare. Of course, it had also been packed very meticulously by a Hunter preparing for battle, not a heartbroken teenager barely able to see through the tears veiling his vision.

Jasper unpacked everything, folded it more neatly and carefully, bundling it all together as tightly as he could.

Still, it didn't all fit.

The presents from Crimson were the problem—books and CDs, gimmicky trinkets from their road trip, about a dozen Bic lighters, and one Zippo. And clothes. More clothes than he had ever realized he had. He tried to remember if he had ever bought Crimson anything other than cigarettes and the occasional shot at the bar but came up lacking.

It was this realization that finally broke him.

Sobbing wretchedly, Jasper dug back into his backpack, grasping around frantically until he found what he was looking for. He drew out his mother's copy of *To Kill a Mockingbird,* took it over to the counter and shakily dug through the junk drawer until he found a pen. Before he could second-guess or stop himself, he flipped open the book and wrote a short note on the inside of the cover. He paused for a long moment, staring at the words, wishing they were enough, knowing they were not.

He signed it "Love, Jasper."

Holding it cradled against his chest, he carried it over to the bed and set it on Crimson's pillow.

Then he stuffed the backpack full until the seams threatened to burst, threw it up on his shoulder, and left as quickly as he could.

Epilogue

Jasper walked around all night. He couldn't go back to the house, nor could he bring himself to go to Alcander's. He wasn't going to go back to St. James a moment before he had to; he'd rather freeze. The cold bit at his hands, the chill wind drying the tears on his cheeks. It was not yet October. It was going to be a long, long winter.

Part of him hoped Crimson would come looking for him, though he couldn't imagine what either of them would say. Another part of him hoped Folami's daughter would show up just so he could feel the narrow-minded focus a fight demanded, all other senses and emotions dulled, leaving only himself and his opponent and the warm grip of a gun beneath his palm.

Neither came for him.

He spent his night looping through parks and down the same streets over and over until, slowly, the dark sky turned gray and purple, then yellow like a fading bruise. Jasper walked towards his destination, the sun slowly warming his shoulders, though the air still felt cold. The Manhattan skyscrapers were gold in the dawn's early light, and St. James Academy shined brighter than most, a sharp blade in the Heavens.

About the Authors

E.M. and Jay met on a virtual pet site when they were both fourteen and were brought together by their love of awful (awful) movies and supernatural monsters.

They've been writing together ever since.

Find out more about them and their upcoming novels at their website:

hunterandspider.com

Made in the USA
Middletown, DE
30 October 2023

41551119R00210